Praise for the work of Lori L. Lake

"[Lori L. Lake] is a keen observer of the telling detail, be it a bit of clothing, a perfectly named character, a sound, or the expression on a human face, and she can find the words to inspirit them with life. She's a superb seat-of-the-pants linguist and she puts all of her skills to work in the service of her engaging stories."
~ANN BANNON, author of *The Beebo Brinker Chronicles*

"Considered one of the best authors of modern lesbian fiction, her work – part action, part drama, and part romance – gleefully defies categorization."
~LAVENDER MAGAZINE

"Lori is a first rate storyteller. She pulls you in with beautifully crafted tension from the first few sentences, and then keeps you in the story with prose that is as smooth as silk."
~ALAN CHIN, author of *Island Song*, *The Lonely War*, and *Butterfly's Child*

"It is no wonder that Lori Lake's books are best sellers. Her characters are deep-bodied, multidimensional, and convincing. Her plots unfold like petals on a flower, coming to full bloom at just the right moment."
~FOREWORD MAGAZINE

BOOKS BY
Lori L. Lake
====================

Romances
Like Lovers Do
Different Dress
Ricochet in Time

The Gun Series
Gun Shy
Under The Gun
Have Gun We'll Travel
Jump The Gun

The Public Eye Mystery Series
Buyer's Remorse
A Very Public Eye

Historical
Snow Moon Rising

Collections
Shimmer & Other Stories
Stepping Out: Short Stories
Romance for Life
The Milk of Human Kindness:
Lesbian Authors Write
about Mothers & Daughters

Eight Dates

By

Lori L. Lake

Launch Point Press
Portland, Oregon

Eight Dates is a work of fiction. Names, characters, places, and incidents are either the product of the author's imagination or are used fictitiously. Any resemblance to actual persons living or dead, business establishments, events, or locales is entirely coincidental. Internet references contained in this work are current at the time of publication time, but Launch Point Press cannot guarantee that a specific reference will continue or be maintained in any respect.

A Launch Point Press Trade Paperback Original

Copyright © 2014 by Lori L. Lake

All rights reserved. No part of this book may be used or reproduced in any manner whatsoever, including Internet usage, without written permission from Launch Point Press, except in the form of brief quotations embodied in critical reviews and articles.

ISBN 978-1-63304-000-7

FIRST EDITION
First Printing, 2014

Editing: Nann Dunne
Copyediting: Luca Hart and Jessie Chandler
Proofreading: Carol Poynor and Pat Cronin
Book format: Patty Schramm
Cover design: TreeHouse Studio

TreeHouseStudio

Published by:
Launch Point Press
Portland, Oregon
www.LaunchPointPress.com

LAUNCHPOINT PRESS

Printed in the United States of America

This one's for my Sweetheart who knows that:

Love does not consist
in gazing at each other, but
in looking outward together
in the same direction.

~**Antoine de Saint-Exupery**

Acknowledgments

As this book came together, I received invaluable advice and support from Jessie Chandler, Betty Crandall, Pat Cronin, Patricia Downing, Verda Foster, Judy Kerr, and MB Panichi. Thank you once again for always providing open hearts and listening ears.

Thank you to my Chief Editor, Nann Dunne, for yet another just-in-the-nick-of-time critique. Copyeditors Luca Hart and Jessie Chandler did a bang-up job smoothing over many bumps, Pat Cronin stepped in to do a final proofread, and much gratitude to Carol Poynor who, as usual, did an eagle eye proofread with grace and humor.

I am especially grateful to Ann McMan of TreeHouse Studio for advice and wisdom regarding covers and graphics, to Patty Schramm for the overall book design, and to the Story Goddess who gave this one to me in an almost linear fashion. Will wonders never cease!

One of the characters in *Eight Dates* is named after the amazing poet, memoirist, actress, singer, and dancer, Maya Angelou. The day I finished the final edits of this novel, Maya Angelou's soul left this earthly plane in what I'm sure must have a blaze of glory. May she continue to inspire generations to come.

Lori L. Lake
July, 2014

Chapter One

I WAS KNEELING ON a hideously ugly orange shag carpet, unpacking one of three boxes that contained most of my important worldly possessions, when I heard a quiet tapping on the door of my apartment. Since it was October 31st, I wasn't inclined to answer. It's not like I had a big sack of M&Ms or fun-sized Snickers to hand out to a bunch of trick-or-treaters. I didn't have any food at all, not even a single item in the crappy little fridge that sat on the corner counter in the world's dinkiest kitchen. I've never seen a stove with only two burners, and I've seen larger sinks in Barbie dollhouses, but the price was right. Funds were tight, so I would put up with my miniature kitchen until finances improved.

The knock came again, a soft tock-tock-tock. With a sigh I got to my feet and pulled on the rickety knob.

On the walkway outside, Xena Warrior Princess peered up at me. Miniature Xena, that is. A dark-haired little girl with a pale face shivered in the doorway. She wore tan Ugg boots, a black and brown striped skirt, and a tiny leather bustier. For the Xena breastplate, she'd spray-painted a couple of dessert-sized paper plates with gold and connected them with paper clips. More paper clips were hooked together over each of her tiny shoulders. She wore what looked like a pair of black socks on her forearms to simulate Xena's vambraces. A sword handle poked up over her right shoulder, and the outfit was made complete by a gold circular chakram hanging from her hip. The razor-edged weapon that the real Xena carried could slice through metal, but the girl's version was raggedly fashioned.

"Is that a Frisbee?" I asked, pointing at her chakram.

"Yeah, I cut it out with a knife. It didn't come out so great."

"You did a great job painting it gold."

"I guess." She held up a hand, which was stained gold across her palm. "The paint isn't sticking too good. Wish I had a real chakram."

Once upon a time I *did* have some Xena paraphernalia, including a heavy-duty glittery gold chakram. I wondered where it all went—probably lost in the breakup.

I said, "The sword is very realistic."

She reached over her right shoulder, pulled it out, and brandished it for me. "Got it at Target."

"What the heck are you using for a scabbard?" I leaned forward and looked closely at the long gray tube she had duct taped to her shoulder. "Is that a vacuum cleaner attachment?"

"Yeah. I didn't have anything else. I tried to make one of cloth but it wouldn't hold."

"I see. You've been very resourceful. Seems to me that you've put together a pretty decent costume."

She squinted up at me. "If you let your hair grow long, you could get a Gabrielle costume and some red boots and be her."

I ran my hand through my short light-brown hair. I look nothing like the actress who played Gabrielle—except that I do have blue eyes. I ignored the kid's comment and said, "Are you trick-or-treating?"

"Kind of," she said, her voice now soft and shy. She'd been glancing past me into my place during the brief conversation, so she probably already knew that no candy was forthcoming.

"But you don't have a bag or pumpkin head or whatever to put candy in."

"I guessed most people here wouldn't have any treats."

"Sorry, I don't have anything to hand out. I'm just moving in, and I pretty much forgot all about Halloween."

She opened her other hand and showed me an open pack of Lifesavers. "Mr. Allen gave me these. He said they were good."

"Butter rum, huh?"

"Whatever that is." She sighed. "Nobody else has been opening their door. Not a very lucky day."

"So you live here?"

She pointed to her right. "We're next door to you."

I felt sorry for her. This ancient motel-turned-into-apartments didn't seem to be a good place for kids. I'd seen only older residents and some ratty-looking middle-aged guys, most of whom looked like they were no strangers to alcohol.

"Can't your mom or dad take you somewhere else—to a neighborhood?"

"Mom's working."

"And your dad?"

She looked down. "He's not around."

"I see. Well, I wish I had some candy for you, but today I don't."

"The guy who lived in here before had a iguana."

"*An* iguana?"

"Big and gray and green, kinda like a mini-dinosaur. He wore it on his shoulder a lot of the time. He also smoked some weird cigarettes. My mom said he was a dee...dee...degen..."

"A degenerate?"

"I think that's it."

That explained the funky odor. Iguana plus marijuana equals apartment stench. I'd already cleaned extensively, and I'd vacuumed so much that the canister filled up twice, and I was well on the way to packing it full a third time. The two rooms weren't filthy anymore, but in some ways it was good that I had so few possessions to get in the way. In the next few days I planned to look for a cheapo special at some carpet cleaning company so they could come in and do a thorough once-over.

"What's your name, kid?"

She peered up at me, her dark eyes serious. "Maya. What's yours?"

"Skylar. Or you can call me Sky."

"Is that your real name?"

"Yup."

"It would be cool if you had a sister named Moon."

"I once had a cousin nicknamed Sunny."

"Once had? What happened to him?"

Astute kid. My cousin was ten years older than me and got his nickname because of the movie, *Butch Cassidy and the Sundance Kid*. Our family name is Cassidy, and my uncle's nickname is Butch, so naturally his namesake, Matthew, Jr., ended up being called the Sundance Kid, which got shortened up along the way. Sunny wasn't a bank robber like Butch and Sundance, but he did like drugs a little too much. He died of an overdose when I was still in high school, and my uncle never got over it.

I ignored her question. She didn't need to know that Sunny offed himself. "How old are you, Maya?"

"Eight."

"Does your mom know you're out and about?"

She looked away, her expression conflicted. Before she could answer, I heard footsteps on the cement stairs that led up from the courtyard below. A dark head bobbed above the rail, and the rest of the person's physique was gradually revealed as well. A woman in loafers, jeans, and a vest over a dark purple blouse reached the head of the stairs and hastened toward us along the outdoor walkway.

"Maya, you're not supposed to be—what in the world are you wearing?"

The kid let out a sigh. Frowning, she turned to face her mother.

And the woman was clearly her mother. With their brunette hair and dark eyes, her kid was the spitting image of her, with "spitting" being the operative term here. The mother looked mad enough to spit nails. Despite the restrained anger, she was attractive. Very pretty, in fact. In contrast to her daughter's short, near-black hair, hers was shoulder length.

"You are *not* supposed to be out of the apartment, young lady." The woman came to a stop near the rail across from my apartment door and folded her arms over her chest. "You just got off restriction for your last foray out without permission. Do you want that again?"

"But, Mom—"

"Don't you 'But, Mom,' me. I told you I would take you out trick or treating, and now I'm not so sure we ought to go after all." She glanced at me. "Has she been causing any trouble?"

"No, not at all," I told her. "She's a very nice kid." What I wanted to ask was why an eight-year-old was being left to her own devices. Instead I said, "You work nearby?"

"In the office downstairs."

"Here, you mean? For the complex?"

"Right." She reached out a hand. "I'm Rebecca Talarico, and you've obviously met my naughty daughter, Maya."

"Skylar Cassidy." I shook her hand briefly, not knowing what to say to about her naughty daughter, especially since Little Miss Xena was looking so incredibly miserable. I felt sorry for the kid. "When do you get off work?"

"Obviously not soon enough for Maya." She glanced at her watch. "Sorry if she bothered you."

"Oh, no. Not a problem at all."

Rebecca put her hand on the small of Maya's back and guided her away. "You need to get inside right now. I'll return by six, and we can go out then. What's wrong with the costume I got for you?"

Even with her back to me, as Maya scuffled away, I heard her whine, "No way. I'm too old to be a bumblebee."

"But it's cute. You look darling." She unlocked their door and pushed the kid inside. Last thing I heard was Maya saying, "I'm not wearing..." and then the door shut sharply. I was left standing in my doorway alone.

I gazed toward the units on the other side of this crazy little motel and met the eyes of an elderly woman sitting in a window. If I had a tightrope, I could have strung it from my railing to hers and crossed it in ten steps. Maybe that would have caught her attention. The woman didn't blink or look away. I blinked, though. She looked pretty intense. I gave a half-hearted wave, but she didn't respond, so I ducked back into my place and shut the door.

I WAS THANKFUL THAT the apartment manager let me in a day before the first of the month, even if it did mean that I was dragging things up the stairs from the parking lot on Halloween. Someone—I assume the management or perhaps Maya's mom—had scattered a bunch of pumpkins and a bale of hay near the bottom of the stairs that led up to the second floor. The damn pumpkins were inconveniently placed, and I still had a couple of mattresses to bring up. I wasn't sure why they'd bothered with the autumn theme. No amount of gourds or decorative items would ever cover up the fact that The Miracle Motel was seedy. A beat-up relic from days past.

When the place was built—back in the Forties, I'd guess—it would have been called a motor court or maybe a motor inn. Travelers who needed to stay in Portland for business or pleasure would have had space to stay for a few days and make meals right in their room. Back then—seems like a century ago—people's needs were simpler, and I suppose they were less likely to eat in restaurants or go out on the town, and TV wasn't all the rage. Instead, they might sit on the back balcony and watch the sun set. They might have taken a walk around the tree-lined avenues. Back in the early days, the scarred cement courtyard below might have been a pretty garden. It was long and narrow, too small to have had room for cars. All of the parking spaces were around the outside perimeter of the building, and there weren't too many. I had parked on the street today.

Out front, an old-fashioned metal sign rose up out of a big lump of concrete. A faded yellow arrow along the top pointed toward the motel. Once upon a time, the arrow had sported a line of lights along the edge, but there were no bulbs in there now, and the holes left behind looked like they had wept rusted tears. The oblong sign below proclaimed the place "The Miracle Motel." Each letter of Miracle was once painted bright, flashy colors, but now the background was brownish, and all the blue and green and gold and red lettering was washed out.

Underneath the big, bold lettering I could just barely make out some other white letters. After a bit of study, I realized the words were "It's Magical!"

The Miracle Motel's two-story layout was a narrow U-shape. The manager's office and reception area were located downstairs at the bottom of the U, with a laundry room on the second floor above. The sides of the two "arms" of the U formed outside corridors. The upper apartments faced each other and overlooked the courtyard. Stairwells at each end and near the bottom of the U allowed access to the upper story.

The arms of the U had eight doors upstairs and eight doors downstairs on both sides. I'm such a math wizard that I counted 32 units, but no. Somewhere along the way, somebody decided to turn the motel into apartments. One of the two adjoining doors inside pairs of apartments was removed which explained why my 600-square-foot unit had two balconies on the back side of the apartments, two bathrooms, two exterior doors, and two kitchenettes. Lucky me, if I got hungry in the middle of the night, I could whip up a snack from the side of my bed.

In the past, putting a bathroom in the back corner of a motel room might have seemed like a good idea, but what idiotic designer thought it was a good idea to put the door next to the kitchenette? The right-side room, which was where the entrance was, had a breakfast bar—a floating island with two creaky stools—on the living room side. In order to access the bathroom door, you had to go around the bar, walk through the galley kitchen, and enter the restroom. Nowadays there were rules about how close a bathroom could be to the kitchen where you cooked, but back in the Forties, maybe not.

The left-side room didn't have a breakfast bar at all, and the fridge in there was about seven hundred years old. To keep the electric bill down, I figured I'd never turn it on, and I planned to use the cupboards in that area for overflow kitchen stuff.

The two rooms weren't huge, but they seemed a lot more spacious than modern day hotel rooms. With only one bay window at the front, and a porthole of a window in the back balcony door, it was dim inside. I didn't plan to spend any significant amount of time on either of my rickety balconies. They were surrounded by rusted wrought iron railing and looked shabby as hell. Then again, it was bigger than the footprint of my bathroom and kitchenette combined, so maybe I'd figure out how to use it as extra space for storage.

I went to the front window, opened the mud-colored curtains, and looked out. Not much light leaked into my quarters, but what did I care? I could buy a lot of lamps and keep my crap acquisition low.

The courtyard below featured chipped and cracked cement punctuated by weeds shooting up here and there. Someone had obviously weed-whacked in the recent past, and dead stalks lay here and there, drying in the afternoon sun. Four circular concrete flower beds, placed in a row and knotted with thistles and dandelions, were a real eyesore. The Oregon summer sun had done a number on the plants, and weeds choked out whatever flowers might have once been there.

I backed away from the window. I was focusing too much on my surroundings, but since I would be living here for God knows how long, I couldn't help it. A twinge of pain tightened in my chest. Once upon a time, I co-owned a house, a car, a truck, and an entire household of "stuff." How far had I fallen? I had next to nothing now and no immediate plan for restoring all that I'd lost.

All I could tell myself was that things mean nothing and money wasn't everything.

I was not comforted by the thought.

BY SIX P.M. I had everything up from the car except for my mattresses. I was puzzling about who to call to help me when a knock came to the door. More Halloween visitors?

"Yoo hoo, baby doll. Open up."

Oh, brother. My friend and business partner, Mitchell Hightower, posed in the doorway, one hand on his hip and the other holding a paper-clad bottle in the air as if he thought he was the Statue of Liberty. He wasn't wearing a long green dress, but his shirt was bright emerald green and tucked into tight black pants. As usual he also wore shiny black boots.

"Baby doll?" I asked. "Do you have to call me that in such a loud voice that now my neighbors think I'm some sort of weirdo?"

"Would honey-pie work better?"

I rolled my eyes and stood aside so he could enter.

"Love what you've done to the place."

"Don't be critical."

"Sweetheart, if I wanted to be critical, I'd be using words like dive, hole, and hovel."

"You exaggerate."

"When you said number 204, I should have known you were up a flight of fifty stairs."

"It's not that bad."

"If you say so." He held up the bag. "I've brought us a nice pinot."

"I'll have to find something to put it in."

"Maybe you could also turn up something for us to put our asses on."

"Very funny." I had a flash of brilliance. "Hey, I bet you could help me with something."

He grumbled the whole time, but he helped me cart my twin bed mattresses up and assemble the bed. Now I had one item of furniture in the bedroom and none in the living room.

As I dug around in a box, Mitchell said, "If I'd known you were going to make me labor like this, I wouldn't have worn my best shirt."

"You off to a party tonight?" I pulled a couple of coffee mugs out of a box and set them on the little counter in the galley kitchen.

"Of course there's a party, and you're coming with me."

"Oh, no. I've got a lot to do here."

"Yes, I can see that. For one thing, you need to look harder for your wineglasses."

"Sorry, pal. I don't believe I got them in the breakup."

"That's unacceptable!"

"Don't get me started on all the unacceptable losses." I pointed at the mugs. "Best I can do on short notice."

Mitchell gave a dramatic sigh, but his blue eyes were merry. He was the prettiest man I'd seen in ages. His blond hair was artfully styled. And I should know. For the first eight months after the breakup, I lived with him in his two-bedroom bungalow that only had one bathroom, and he certainly had spent a lot of time on his hair. Now that I had two bathrooms, he could spend as many hours as he wanted and I wouldn't be stuck waiting.

He poured me a glass—correction, mug—of wine, and handed it to me. "Try this."

"Aren't you supposed to let it air or something like that?"

"Why bother. I got it for five bucks at Trader Joe's."

"I feel so important."

"You are."

Mitchell was like a brother to me. We met at work six years ago and learned quickly that we made a great team. He was good with software and programming, and I could assemble hardware and repair and refurbish computers like nobody's business. Working with someone and living with him, too, got old after a while. Once he started dating a guy seriously I knew it was time to find my own place.

Mitchell held up a mug. "Cheers to you for bravely going where no man has gone before." He looked around the room. "No gay man anyway. Just what will you make in that appalling little oven? Cornish game hens? One at a time?"

I laughed. The oven below the two-burner stove was indeed miniscule. I wasn't sure if even the smallest pan I owned would fit in there.

The wine was crisp, and I sipped it with appreciation. "Not bad for a five buck bottle, Mitch."

"I should have brought a bottle of spray cleaner instead."

"Ouch. I'm going to get a complex if you keep bitching about my bachelor pad."

"You have a lot of work to do, sweetie, to get this place up to bachelor pad status. It's so small. And what's with the twin bed? I've been telling you for weeks now that you've got to get back on the market. Find a new squeeze. Have a few one-night stands to build your confidence. You'll need a bigger bed for that."

"Pulllease. You know I don't operate that way."

"You haven't been operating in any way since Britney dumped you."

"Yeah, yeah, I know. I haven't got any desire to get involved with anyone. I'm perfectly fine on my own."

"Oh, really? You need some companionship, little miss, at the very least. It's not like you can have a dog here."

I wouldn't be able to have a dog at all, even if I wanted one. I've committed the Lesbian Cardinal Sin of being deathly allergic to pets.

"Sky, honey, you've got needs. Get out and find some women to fill them."

I finished the last of the wine and felt it warm its way down to my stomach. I hadn't eaten for far too long. "You want to order a pizza?"

"Hell, no. Andrew and Brian are having a gourmet potluck tonight for Halloween."

"Not a costume party?"

"Of course it is. I have my outfit all laid out and ready to go.

That's why I'm here so early—to get you. You simply must come along."

"I've got too much to do here. I want to get settled and be ready tomorrow morning when Eddie brings over the first load for me to work on."

Mitchell did that little tsk-tsk thing with his teeth that I hated. "You can't hide away forever, Sky. You're missing out on a whole lot of fun and excitement. You've got to go out and find someone. And I'm going to help you."

"No, no, trust me, that's not necessary."

"You'd do the same for me."

"Actually, no, I don't think so."

"Don't disappoint me with timidity."

Oh, God. I had no idea what he had in mind, but I was pretty sure I wouldn't like it.

Smiling widely he said, "You leave it all to me. I'll get you a woman post haste."

"I don't want one, not post haste, not pre haste, not any kind of haste."

"That's what you say now. You'll thank me later." He set down his mug and came over to put his arms around me. "It'll get better, doll. It will, trust me."

"Thanks, Mitchell. Go have fun and report in later."

He stepped back and gave me his version of a salute. "Sure you don't want to go to the party?"

I shook my head. An evening of conversation with three or four dozen guys dressed like Liza Minnelli and Barbara Streisand and Katy Perry didn't appeal to me at all. "What's your costume this year?"

"Don't you remember? I told you weeks ago." He batted his baby blue eyes at me. "Marilyn Monroe, remember?"

"Oh, sure. Yeah. Marilyn."

"I've even got a fan to blow my dress up."

"Of course you do."

Chapter Two

AFTER MITCHELL'S APPEARANCE THE night before, I should have known I was in for it. I didn't realize how bad it could be until I opened my email. But that didn't happen right away because I had to get up early and prepare for my work delivery.

In addition to going out in the field to help people set up their computer systems, I diagnose and repair computers. Mitchell and I opened our own business a year ago, but the downturn in the economy has taken a toll. Our premium office space in the Lloyd Center mall is small and costly, so we do our repair work offsite. While I lived at Mitchell's apartment, I worked out of his garage. Now I'd work out of my living room.

I'd stayed up late in the night to set up tables and assemble a heavy-duty four-shelf unit, which I put along the wall near the front door. I also configured an air-card so I'd get Internet service. Now I plugged in surge protectors and strung extension cords. I was going to have to get a computer desk of some sort. For now, I put my laptop on a fold-up table, fired it up, and opened email.

I didn't get much email ordinarily, so the one from GirlsGaylore caught my eye right away. Heart sinking, I opened it.

Welcome to GirlsGaylore.com
where sexy, creative, and
fun-loving women are found

With increasing alarm, I scanned the message. When I came to a line that urged me to click on the link to see my profile, I wanted to scream. Damn Mitchell anyway. He knew my passwords, so I didn't even have the opportunity to reject the registration he'd done for me. I was going to kill him. No doubt about it.

I let my finger hover over the mouse, reluctant to click on it but also curious. As I agonized, I heard a pinging sound and the symbol popped up indicating I had a new email. Instead of clicking the profile link, I went to my email inbox.

Three emails from GirlsGaylore? What the hell? I opened one.

> Dear GeekGrrl,
> OMG—u sound like u r the kind of person i m looking for. Am a 26-year-old femme who's sensitive and caring and likes cuddling. Would u like to get together 2 see if any sparks fly?
> FemmeFatale249

There were 249 femme fatales? The lesbian dating world should be very afraid.

Even scarier, Mitchell gave me a screen name of GeekGrrl? What was he thinking? It brought to mind dweeby emotionless dorks with giant, black plastic, pop-bottle-thick eyeglasses. If I saw a screen name like that, I'd run screaming.

I was already prepared to run screaming from Ms. FemmeFatale. Even if she was Number 1 instead of 249, why would I be interested?

But OMG was right. All of this was so alarming that I felt speechless. If Mitchell walked in the room right now, I wouldn't know what to say. I'd just have to kill him.

What other lies and misinformation had he put in the profile?

I went back to the original email, clicked the link, and read, soon glad that I'd not yet eaten or I'm sure I would have puked.

He'd filled in the general details to say I was five-seven, 150 pounds, medium build, light brown hair, blue eyes, and a non-smoker. Accuracy went right out the window after that. I don't have a "master's degree in the sciences." I haven't gotten my undergraduate degree completed. I'm 32, not in my "tantalizing twenties," and my profession would never be described as "software magnate." I'm not a social drinker, don't own a Ferrari, and would never say I was "sophisticated."

He'd also written that I was buff and physically fit, that I liked risks (but wasn't overly risky), enjoyed adventures, and loved kayaking, whitewater rafting, and competitive swimming.

I'm a *terrible* swimmer. I wouldn't even swim in Vancouver Lake—and it's only six or eight feet deep. My ex and I used to canoe every once in a while with me in a massive life jacket, but that was it. The rest of the description was pure and utter crap, but the part that infuriated me the most was this:

I'm told I'm generous, reliable, and a good conversationalist. My friends describe me as a sexy butch with great legs. I love affectionate women who like to cuddle. I'm sensitive, caring, and looking for a hot lover who will also be my best friend. I'm interested in a committed relationship with a sensitive, thoughtful woman who's a great cook and even better with her hands. <vbeg> I'm completely ready for a life-long romance of intimacy and friendship. Are you?

Where did he crib this bullshit from? No doubt, I was going to have to kill him.

Someone beat on the door with a heavy thunk-thunk-thunk, and I knew it'd be Eddie, the driver we paid to bring the morning load of computers and return at the end of the day and take the repaired ones back. To save money, Mitchell and I had talked about doing the delivery and pickup ourselves, but I didn't want to waste ninety minutes a day in traffic.

Still feeling sick to my stomach, I got up to open the door and let Eddie in. He's a foot taller than me and resembles an NFL football player. He wheeled in a stack of boxes and parked them near the shelving.

"Great idea to rent an apartment for this, Sky." He looked around with admiration on his face. "And it even comes with a kitchenette so you can make your lunch. Cool."

Such a different response than what I'd heard from Mitchell last night. Of course Eddie probably had no clue that I lived here, and he didn't need to be enlightened.

"This it?" I asked.

"Oh, no. I've got another stack."

"Sorry there's no elevator."

"No biggie. Be right back." He picked up the dolly with one giant mitt and carried it out.

I stood in the cool morning breeze. The temperature was surprisingly comfortable for the first of November, and the sky was clear.

The door to 204 smacked open. Mini Xena, minus the Xena costume, stepped out onto the walkway, and I could tell she was in a huff. Her little face was all scrunched up and red, like she was about to cry but was holding back.

She said, "I don't see why I can't."

Her mother stepped out of the apartment, pulled the door shut, and stuck in the key to lock it. "You don't need Halloween candy as part of your lunch."

"But I want it. I worked for it."

I laughed. What kid called trick or treating work?

Surprised, Rebecca Talarico looked toward me. "Oh, good morning."

Her dark eyes met mine and my stomach did a tiny flip-flop. She was very attractive. Too bad she was also straight. "And to you as well," I said. "Sounds like somebody's not yet enjoying the day."

Maya looked up at me, eyes slitted and face closed. Whoa, she was monumentally pissed.

Rebecca said, "She didn't get enough sleep. Excess chocolate and sugar do not agree with young people." She looked pointedly at her daughter.

Maya stomped down the walkway. Eddie was at the far end wheeling a stack of boxes my way. As Maya got closer, Eddie cracked a smile. "You having a bad day, little lady?"

"What do you care?" I heard Maya say.

Eddie said, "See if I ever give you a dolly ride." He passed the child, and I stepped aside to let him into my apartment.

Rebecca said, "She's a very strong-willed little girl. Thanks for being kind to her yesterday."

"She was perfectly polite. She's a smart kid for only eight."

"Eight going on twenty. Looks like you're getting all settled in."

She had no way of knowing that I was as settled in as I could be for now, so I just nodded.

She said, "I better get to the car or she'll decide to walk to school."

Behind me, Eddie called out, "Sky?"

I gave a wave to Rebecca and said, "Have a great day at work."

"You, too."

I went back into the apartment and signed for the delivery.

"Same timeline?" Eddie asked. "Back at four?"

"That'd be great."

I fussed and fumed all day while taking apart computers and diagnosing why they weren't functioning properly. Four out of eight were all jammed up with malware and viruses. They didn't take long to cleanse. The others were more challenging, but I was able to repair all of them by noon. Time to go to the office and have a little chat with my sneaky business partner.

I CHARGED INTO THE office of Sky High Computer Experts so fast that Mitchell didn't see me coming until I was halfway around the counter with my blood boiling.

He rose from the desk, hands up and palms facing me. "Now wait a minute, Sky—"

"I will not. What the hell were you thinking?"

"Come on, you need—"

"You can't tell me what I need." I wanted to stick my finger in his face, but I restrained myself.

"Please. I just want to help. You know that."

"I told you last night I don't need help."

"A little female attention wouldn't be a—"

"Shut up." I was mad, but I wanted him to understand my point, so I spoke slowly with the hope that his pea-brain would hear me. "I know you're trying to look out for me, but I need some space now. I don't need a bunch of people emailing me and trying to hook up with me. When I'm ready I'll let you know."

"Okay, okay."

"You're going to lay off all this pressure now." I glared at him until he let out a breath and seemed to deflate.

"Yeah, whatever. Sheesh, I thought you were going to hit me."

"Don't make me," I said in a mock serious voice.

He looked at his watch. "Shop closes up in ten. You want to grab some tacos?" This was always Mitchell's offer. He's gluten intolerant but he can eat beans and rice and corn tortillas, so when he wanted comfort food with me—or for me—that's what he offered.

"Just make me one promise," he said. "When you do decide to go out on a date, will you please let me cut and style that mop you're wearing? God forbid that you should be seen in public with some woman when your hair looks like that."

"Has anyone ever told you that you really know how to hurt a girl?"

"Just looking out for your best interests, baby doll."

I resisted rolling my eyes, but I still wanted to smack him.

Chapter Three

A FEW DAYS PASSED, and mostly all I did was sleep and work on computer repairs. I didn't quite have the heart to do much more with my new living quarters, though I did get some groceries. Stress and big changes are hard. But after some time passed, I gathered up enough energy to start turning my new crib into a nest I could live with.

I found a small table and two chairs on Craigslist along with a sturdy TV stand, the latter going into my bedroom. I wanted to get a folding screen to block the sleeping area off from the space I designated for my TV room, but I didn't have a couch or easy chair yet. For a while I'd be watching TV lying on the bed.

Occasionally I felt sorry for myself. When I moved out, Britney let everyone know that I'd left her, and all of our friends had sided with her. How unfair was that! Melissa and Mindy, Dee and Beth, our neighbor Selena, even the loose-knit group of women who went camping and hiking with us. Everyone was mad at me because I was the one who moved out. Dear sweet Britney hadn't informed any of them that Rita was more than a friend. I felt so ashamed that Britney had basically thrown me over for Rita that I didn't even mount a defense. Maybe that was wrong, but if "our" friends didn't think enough of me to ask for my side of the story, why bother? The loss of everyone familiar had been like a cold plunge into a mountain stream. I still hadn't begun to recover. Instead, I was turtling—hiding in my shell and waiting for the pain to pass.

The morning of the 11th, I awakened, realizing it was Veteran's Day. I thought of my dad. He was a career military man, often away from home during my early life, and when he and my mother divorced, I didn't see him again for a long time. He remarried when I was nine and moved across the country to Wisconsin. I didn't see him much while I was growing up, and a couple of years had passed since I'd seen him or my now-grown half-brothers. Funny how people float away, even if they're your own father.

One of my favorite memories was of being in kindergarten and having the day off for the annual Veteran's Day Parade. Dad dressed in his uniform, and we went down to Sandy Boulevard, by the Ross Funeral Home, and watched the parade go by. I loved the high school marching bands and jugglers. The bagpipers scared me, and I held my father's hand tight and pressed my face into his wool coat. Families, local politicians, and a whole lot of military people in smart-looking uniforms went by. Members of a motorcycle club came by in formation, waving and smiling. The parade paused in front of us at one point, and a huge motorcyclist decked out in black leather put a giant foot down on the ground to wait. To my eyes, his boot looked big enough for me to step into with both feet. He wore his gray beard so long that it reached his motorcycle saddle. He saw me staring and reached into a canvas bag, pulled something out, and offered it to me. I looked up at my dad. He met the man's eyes, and they both nodded. Dad pushed me forward so I could accept the item.

I squeaked out a thank you, and scurried back next to my father. The man snapped off a salute, and my dad returned it. The guy revved his engine and rolled forward.

I didn't know what he'd given me at first. I pulled apart clear plastic to remove a black cloth beret with white writing and a picture of a man bowing his head.

My dad squatted down. "You know what that is, kiddo?"

"Nuh-uh."

"Some soldiers went to war and didn't come back. They were captured by the enemy. See these letters? P-O-W. That means Prisoner of War. What are those letters?"

I wasn't reading too well yet, but I knew my letters. "M-I-A."

"That's right. That stands for Missing in Action. Do you know what that means?"

His question sounded very serious, and I didn't want to get my answer wrong. "Like, the soldier is lost?"

"Yes, that's exactly it. He might have died or he could be a prisoner somewhere, but we don't know for sure."

"Why did that man give this to me?"

"He probably has a friend who's lost."

"Why don't you go find him, Daddy? If he's a prisoner, someone needs to find him and bring him home, right?"

"We try. Sometimes the enemy hides our soldiers very well, and we can't track them down."

I was struck by a pang of fear. "That can't ever happen to you, can it?"

"No. I work stateside. This happens far, far away, and only when there's a war going on."

"What is this other writing?" I recognized the first word, You, and said it aloud. I was trying to sound out the next word when my father said, "You are not forgotten."

"The soldiers?"

"Yes, we will never forget them. We'll keep looking for them until they're found."

I opened up the beret and put it on my head, comforted by the thought that my father's job was to find lost soldiers and return them to their families. The beret was too big, but I adjusted it so I could see.

I still have the beret in a memorabilia box along with my mother's wedding ring, my baby shoes and baby book, a sheaf of report cards, and my high school diploma.

I decided to go to the morning parade and got ready. Eddie dropped off the day's computer work, and after he left, I stepped out into a cold, clear day. Portland rain was no fun at a parade, so I was thankful for a reprieve.

I cut down a side street to Sandy and walked several blocks. The boulevard was blocked off from 40th to 48th Avenue as usual. Kids ran along the sidewalk waving miniature American flags. Scads of people had set up lawn chairs along the curbs of either side of the street. A street vendor rolled a cart by. I hadn't eaten breakfast, and whatever he was selling smelled delicious.

I threaded my way through a pack of teenagers all wearing earbuds connected to their iPods and talking loudly and laughing. A kid on a tiny red bike with training wheels cut in front of me and I stopped abruptly.

From behind, someone bumped into my legs. The collision didn't hurt, but I turned to see who the clod was. "Maya?"

She smiled up at me. She wore red jeans, a blue t-shirt, and a black nylon jacket. A red corduroy cap adorned with a zillion shiny silver sparkles sat on her head.

"Are you following me?"

"Not really. I just saw you."

"Where's your mom?"

"Back home."

"She let you come out alone?"

Maya squinched up her little face. "I'm not a baby."

"Does your mom know you're here?"

She put her hands in her jacket pockets and looked away. "Hey, look." She pulled a hand out of her pocket and pointed. Three Army utility vehicles chugged by.

"You sure you shouldn't let your mom know where you are?"

"I can take care of myself." Her tone told me she was irritated I'd asked the question.

"All right then. Don't get me involved if you get in trouble for being here."

"I wouldn't."

"Have you seen the parade before?"

"Last year. With my mom."

"Is she working today?"

Reluctantly, she said, "Yeah."

"Since we don't have chairs, why don't we go over there where we'll have a good view."

We found a good spot in front of Killer Burgers behind some folks sitting in lawn chairs.

Maya said, "Don't you wish we had chairs?"

"I don't have one to bring, so it doesn't help me to wish."

"We have four or five. I could have brought us two."

"I'm sure your mom would have noticed that. How did you get past the office, anyway? Doesn't she have a good view out the window?"

Maya gave me a sneaky smile. "Not if you hunch down when you sneak by."

"I bet you get in big trouble."

"Only if you tell on me. You won't, will you?"

"You put me in a difficult situation. I won't lie to your mom if she asks."

She let out an exasperated sigh.

"I won't go out of my way to rat you out, but still…"

The sound of horns wafted on the breeze. Maya gave an excited squeal. "I love the bands! I want to play trumpet in the school band."

The thought of an eight-year-old practicing any kind of horn next to my apartment wall wasn't pleasant. Why couldn't she pick the guitar? Or maybe the triangle?

"My teacher said that the mayor was going to be in the parade."

"Is that so?" I asked.

"How come you don't you know that?" She seemed seriously puzzled.

"Just because I'm an adult doesn't mean I know everything. I've been busy getting settled."

"They said so on TV. Don't you watch TV?"

She didn't need to know that I wasn't certain of who the current mayor was or that I'd spent most of the night before binge-watching DVDs of the first season of "The Walking Dead," so I changed the subject.

Someone blew a loud whistle three times, and the heavy beat of multiple drums pounded in the distance. A horn section joined in, and Maya again squealed with delight. I looked down at the kid. Her face lit up with excitement, and her eyes shone with happiness. Oh, to be a young person again. I remembered being little and how much simpler things were. Then again, she had no power. At least as an adult I can make a lot of choices. Maya is entirely dependent upon the actions of adults.

The crowd along Sandy Boulevard took in a collective breath, and people in seats along the curb leaned forward. The first marching band came into view. Over a hundred students made up the Grant Senior High School's marching band. They were playing Chicago's "25 or 6 to 4." I remembered it from my own band days.

We listened to the music and watched National Guard and ROTC contingents pass. Military vehicles, veterans' units, and honor guards and more went by. A lot of men from the American Legion marched along in colorful t-shirts. One of them grabbed Tootsie Rolls out of a big bucket and tossed them into the crowd. Maya scrambled forward and snagged three or four of them and came back jubilant. The next group, the VFW, threw little boxes of Nerds. Maya might not have gotten a lot of Halloween candy around the complex, but it looked like maybe today would make up for it.

Another band approached, this one from Madison High. Right behind them came the Paralyzed Veterans of America, all in wheelchairs. Some of them rolled forward under their own steam while others were being pushed or used chairs operated by battery.

Maya said, "How come those guys are in wheelchairs? Can they really not walk?"

"Nope."

"What happened to them?"

"I don't know. They must have been injured in battle."

"Like how?" She looked up at me with sorrow in her eyes.

"I don't know."

"It's very sad if they can't walk."

"Yes, it is."

"Look," she said, "there's the mayor. I told you he would be here. My teacher was right."

She was only eight but already a little know-it-all. I let the comment pass and watched the Royal Rosarians approach. I wasn't sure what Rosarians were. I knew a rosary was a religious thing for the Catholics but not what it would be if it were royal. Maya solved the problem of me not knowing by asking in a loud voice, and a woman in a lawn chair in front of us turned and said, "The Royal Rosarians are, like, ambassadors for our city who the mayor appoints to march with the bands and floats. Haven't you seen them in the Rose Parade?"

Maya shook her head, and I said, "I don't believe I've ever seen that parade."

"You should," the woman said. "You and your daughter would enjoy it." She turned back to the action, leaving me a little stunned by her assumption. Why would she think we were related? Did I look like somebody's mother? I snuck a look at Maya. She was frowning up at me with, I assume, the same expression on her face that was on mine. We didn't look a bit alike. Her hair and eyes were dark, and I've got light brown hair and blue eyes. Complete opposites.

Another marching band whizzed by, and soon the last stragglers at the end of the parade arrived. Rather than walk up to the ceremony on 48th and Sandy, I decided to head home.

"See you, kid."

"Where ya going?" Maya asked.

"Home."

"Okay, I'll come with you. Do you think we'll have a war here?"

"What—no. We're safe here."

"How do you know that?"

"I just do."

"You didn't even know who's the mayor, so how can you be so sure?"

"Listen, kid, I've been alive long enough to know that we're not going to have a war here."

"My teacher said that in the last war, people from Japan shot at Oregon."

"She said Japanese fired guns here?"

Maya shrugged. "I guess."

Either her teacher was a nutcase or Maya heard her wrong. The last war the U.S. was involved in was in the Middle East. I searched my memory. The only times the Japanese were at war that I could recall were World War I and II. "I think you heard your teacher wrong. Japan hasn't had a war since the 1940s. That's a long time ago."

"She said they shot at us from the sea."

"Maybe that's possible. Why don't you ask your teacher about that tomorrow?"

I turned down the side street and saw the beat-up sign for the apartments. I also saw a wiry, dark-haired woman moving toward us at a rapid pace.

Rebecca Talarico broke into a run, and as she got closer, she shouted, "What are you doing with my daughter?"

I stopped. "What?"

She grabbed her kid and faced me. "I should call the police."

"What for?"

"You can't take my child without my permission."

"I didn't take your kid. She followed *me*. Maya, you tell your mother you snuck out on your own."

Rebecca turned to her. "Is that true?" Her mother still held her arm and leaned down, protecting her child from me with her body. Maya stared up, dumbstruck.

"Oh, great. I can tell by the look on your face..." Rebecca seemed to deflate then. After a deep breath, she met my gaze. "I'm sorry. I shouldn't have assumed—"

"No, please, don't worry. She's your kid. I'd be scared, too."

"You," Rebecca said, tugging on Maya's arm. "You are in such big trouble."

"Mo-o-m!" The word came out of Maya's mouth as a three syllable whine.

"Don't you 'Mom' me. You are so grounded." She grabbed hold of the back of Maya's jacket and hustled her toward the apartment.

I stood and watched them. When I was eight, was I that brash? I know I wasn't toward my father. Maybe I was a little sassier with my mother, but I never would have left the house without my parents knowing where I was. Then again, when I was eight, I was never left alone. I didn't become a latchkey kid until after my dad left.

Hands in my pockets, I strolled along behind Maya and her

mother, not in any hurry to reach my apartment door since theirs was so close to mine. I yawned. The parade had sapped me of energy, and the confrontation with Rebecca had scared me. I wanted nothing to do with their messed-up lives. The thought of being accused of kidnapping some stupid kid made me shudder.

THE NEXT AFTERNOON I sat working on a crappy old Compaq computer and cursed the burden placed on me by many of our repeat customers. Luddites. That's what they were. Totally opposed to technology and progress. I'd worked on this computer before and had to replace much of it. Instead of allowing us to provide a different refurbished machine, the owner was adamant that he wanted to keep this model. So I was stuck trying to cram a new motherboard into inadequate space inside the tower. Ha. You could hardly call it a "tower." Try a shoe box.

From the corner of my eye, I saw a flash of movement and turned toward the kitchenette to look at the dirty little window in the door there. Must have been a bird.

How could I talk the elderly owner of this ancient machine into upgrading? He'd already spent more on retrofitting the tiny interior fan than it would have cost to get a whole new hard drive. But he only used the machine to write emails to his adult children and play Mahjongg. It's not like he needed a top-of-the-line unit. Still, what a waste of his money and the time it took to get repaired.

I saw motion in my peripheral vision again. I rose and went to the kitchenette door to look out the porthole. The glass was so old that it was rippled and cracked. Isinglass? Wasn't that what people used before clear glass was invented? I had a vague recollection that isinglass was made from fish bladders. Could that be right? I'm staring out at the world through a freaking fish bladder?

I saw motion outside again but couldn't see anything clearly, so I turned the bolt and opened the door.

Maya crouched there, holding some sort of leather-clad doll. She stared up at me with an expression of embarrassment.

"Maya?"
"Yeah?"
"What are you doing?"
"Nothing."
"Why is all this nothing taking place on my balcony?"
"'Cause mine is boring."

I stepped out into a brisk breeze, looked over toward the balcony next door, and did a double-take. The eight crappy cement balconies, each enclosed with the same rusted wrought-iron fencing, didn't appear any too sturdy. But the real kicker was that they were each only about three feet apart.

"Maya, you climbed over here from your apartment, didn't you?"

"No, actually, I flew."

I wanted to yell at Little Miss Smart-Mouth, but I kept my voice calm. "You've done something very dangerous. That's a big gap. You could have fallen."

"I'm like a monkey. I wouldn't fall."

Oh, boy. Rebecca wasn't going to be happy to hear about this. And there was no way in hell I would keep it from her, not even if Maya begged.

The kid rose to her feet, still clutching the doll.

"What is that?" I asked.

She held out an Indian figure not quite a foot tall. He wore tiny blue moccasins, tan leather pants, and a long-sleeved leather war shirt cleverly decorated with the kind of beads you could only string with the smallest of needles. Somebody had done a lot of fine work on the clothing. One of his two braids was tangled in the bow and arrow looped over his shoulder. An oversized sword, medieval, I was sure, was tucked into a piece of twine tied around his waist. He wore an expression of surprise on his plastic face.

"Where did you get this figurine?"

Maya said, "My grandma sent it to me. She made the clothes and shoes."

"Wow, your grandma is talented."

She smiled proudly. "I love those blue moccasins. Blue is my favorite color. I made the belt so he could also have a sword. Cool, huh? His name is Minco. That means Chief."

A gust of wind blew and I shivered. "I think you better come inside."

"Nah...I'll go home."

She tried to step around me, but I blocked her. "No way in hell. That's way too dangerous for you to climb over." I grabbed the wrought iron and shook it to find more than an inch of play. "You've got something in your hands, and the railing is rickety."

"No big deal." She leaned around me to toss the doll over to her balcony, but it caught in the wind. For a moment Minco paused in midair, then he plummeted between the two sets of railings and fell all the way to the ground floor.

I felt sick to my stomach. "That could've been you." I grabbed her wrist and jerked her into the apartment.

"Hey, what about Minco?"

"You can get him later. What's your mom's cell number?"

Her eyes narrowed. "I don't know."

Right. She was lying through her teeth. I shut the door, threw the bolt, and got my cell phone out of my pocket. I had the apartment office number programmed in, so I dialed it, hoping Rebecca would be there.

YOU COULDN'T PAY ME to be a parent, that's for sure. For one thing, it would be a lot of work, but the bigger problem is that I'm pretty sure I wouldn't be a very good example. I'd end up laughing my ass off half the time.

When Rebecca read Maya the riot act, the kid's reply was classic: "You said I couldn't step foot out the front door. You never said anything about the *other* door!"

I wouldn't be able to argue with that reasoning, and in addition, I'd fall on the floor laughing. The kid was so comical. I had to turn away from Rebecca for fear that she'd see my snickering and think me disrespectful.

Tight-lipped and furious, Rebecca took Maya over to their apartment. Despite the thick cement walls, I heard a lot of hollering.

I forgot about them for a while when Eddie came to take away the latest load of computers, but once my work table was cleared off, I went to the back door and looked through the mangled glass. What possessed that stupid kid to crawl over from one balcony to the other? And if this was how rebellious she was at age eight, how would she be when she hit the teen years?

I was on Day 13 of my tenure at The Miracle Motel, and already I was mired in neighborly problems. Oh, boy.

LATER THAT NIGHT, I was streaming the fourth episode of *Breaking Bad*'s first season when a knock came on my front door. An apologetic Rebecca Talarico stood exactly where I ought to have a Welcome mat. I made a mental note to find a mat, and then she was inviting me to come over for a cup of tea. I had never been much of a tea drinker, unless it was of the Long Island Iced variety, but since the breakup, I'd found tea to be rather comforting. I stepped out and pulled my door closed. She'd left her door open, and we hustled in, shutting out the chill of the night.

"Where's Mini You?"

I saw a ghost of a smile on her face. "Her regular bedtime is eight p.m. I sent her to her room after dinner, and I'm hoping she's asleep now."

But of course she wasn't. I saw her little face—actually just one eye—peeking through a slit in the doorframe.

Rebecca saw my glance and spun around. "Young lady, you get back in bed."

The door opened. Maya's flannel pajamas were dotted with black blobs and something red, green, and yellow. I squinted as she ventured into the living room until I made out Batman and Robin on the PJs. This kid reminded me of me. "Hey, Maya, I had Batman pajamas when I was about your age." I didn't admit that I was wearing Batman boxer briefs right now. Or that I owned Tweety-Bird briefs. And Shrek. Oh, and how about the Incredible Hulk. Those were my favorites because they fit so well.

"I want some Thor jammies. And a hammer to go with 'em. Mom says maybe Santa will bring me some."

"You don't need a hammer," Rebecca said, "but I need a coil of rope to tie you to your bed."

"Aw, Mom, can't I be out of the doghouse yet?"

She asked so plaintively that I would have instantly given in.

Rebecca was made of stronger stuff than I am. "Nope. Come with me." She patted her daughter on the back and led her away.

"G'night, Sky," Maya called out over her shoulder.

"Good night, kiddo. Sleep well."

"Grab a chair wherever you like, Skylar," Rebecca said from the doorway. "I'll be right back.

Maya must have been particularly cooperative because her mother was gone less than a minute.

"Okay, she's crashed now."

"She's a handful, isn't she?"

"Yes, but I have to cut her a lot of slack. She's had a hard year for such a little squirt."

"Oh?"

Rebecca went to her galley kitchen and grabbed two mugs off a rack on the wall. I'm not sure why, but her little kitchenette seemed so much larger—and more useful—than mine. She had a microwave cart off to the side, and she'd put two stools up to the tiny counter to make it into a sort of breakfast bar. There was a vertical dish drainer to the side of the sink that made clever use of the lack of space, and she had a pot and pan rack hanging in the corner up and out of the way. I ought to do that with my pans. As it was, they took up a whole cupboard, leaving room for little else.

"Tea then?" she asked. "The water's already hot."

"Sure. What have you got?"

"Name your poison, I probably have something that comes close."

"A lemony blend?"

"Will Lemon Zinger do?"

"Perfect. With a bit of honey or sugar if you have it."

Rebecca whipped together two cups in less time than I had to consider the rest of her space. I did note that she had a comfy-looking couch, an end table with a funky-looking mood lamp on it, and a large circular rug in front of the couch and lamp, which was covered with Legos and other little toys. The crowning glory of her place was that the shag carpet was a mixture of dark blue and dark green, much more attractive than the hideous two-tone orange in my unit.

"Here you go." She set the steaming white mug in front of me.

"Thanks." I turned the mug and saw Garfield the Cat on the side. Her mug was dark blue with a snow scene and advertisement for a bank. She must have got it from some other area of the country because I couldn't imagine any banks around Portland using snow as a draw. We almost never get any snow, and when we do, everyone goes crazy. The government practically shuts down, and people hole up in their houses with canned goods and flame throwers and act like they're trapped in The Great Blizzard of 1888.

She sat in the chair across from me. I saw that her hands looked strong with long fingers and tapered fingernails. Beautiful hands, like the ones I tried to draw in Senior Art all those years ago. What was that girl's name who modeled her hands? I didn't remember. High school seemed half a life ago.

I said, "It's nice and warm in here. Are your heat bills reasonable?"

"Not too terrible. Next to nothing in late spring and into September, but it gets a little too damp for my liking in the winter. The baseboard heat tends to dry things out somewhat."

"I've never had electric heat anywhere I've lived."

"Me neither. These rooms aren't too big, so that's helpful since you aren't heating the Taj Mahal. Of course, it starts feeling extremely cramped during the long, dark days of winter. Keep the lights up, and you won't get such bad cabin fever. I even have one of those special lamps that give the extra spectrum of light and help avoid depression."

"That's cool. I'm looking into computer screens all day. I wonder what kind of light spectrum that provides. Maya was surprised to see how many monitors I have today."

"I have to tell you how much I appreciate your kindness toward Maya. She's really taken to you."

I thought I'd better come out with it now, before she and her kid got too attached. I sipped a bit of the tea. It was too hot to take as big a slug as I wanted, but trying to slurp up a little gave me time to gather up my courage. I set the mug down. "I have to mention this. I hope you don't mind, but—you know I'm gay, right?"

"I don't make assumptions—at least not ones that I don't eventually check out." She smiled. "I had a hunch though."

"So you're okay with that, with your kid being around me and all?"

"You don't seem like the type to do anything to a child."

"You're right. I never would."

"I figured as much. I'm a pretty good judge of character."

I had a momentary image flash, the one where she came flying down the street on Veteran's Day ready to clobber me and snatch her child away. I guess I'd managed to reclaim some level of trustworthiness.

"How old were you when you realized you were gay?" she asked.

"Maybe Maya's age, although I couldn't have defined it as such. I liked playing football in the street with the boys and building tree houses and model airplanes and that kind of thing. To tell the truth, I pretty much thought I was an honorary boy. I was perfectly happy until sixth grade. Everything changed then."

"How so?"

"The boys started shunning me, and I didn't know how to deal with the girls. They seemed so mean. I was lonely for a very long time until I got into high school and joined sports teams. Then I made some friends, but by then, most of the girls had been friends all the way back to grade school. They accepted me to a certain degree but not entirely."

"Sounds kind of lonely."

"Definitely."

"Do you keep in touch with any high school pals?"

"Nope. Haven't been to any of my reunions either. You?"

"Oh, hell, no. I never fit in very well either. I was a math egghead and no good at team sports. I was a mathlete and participated in those kinds of competitions. The entire competitive realm was ninety-five percent boys. By the time I was sixteen, I quit. The boys weren't welcoming."

"That sucks," I said. "High school sucked a lot. I was glad to be done with it."

"Do you mind telling me how old you are?"

"Thirty-two. Turnabout is fair play. How old are you?"

"I'll be thirty pretty quick here."

"You're a rare person to admit that. Most people would say they're 'twenty-nine and holding' and not admit the upcoming birthday."

"Age isn't all that relevant to me. Neither is sexuality or race or politics or whatever. I'm just trying to accept people for who they are."

I liked her for that. I blew on the tea in my mug and took a couple of sips. The lemon tasted sharp and the honey was sweet, a good combination. "Maya mentioned her father but said he hasn't been around. What happened to him?"

"He definitely made himself scarce. I'm not sure where he is. That's why we're stuck here in this dinky little place. When he left us, I had to make some real quick adjustments. I'd been working part-time in a dentist's office. They couldn't give me more hours, so I got the position working here full-time, and this apartment is an additional benefit. We're making ends meet, though Maya's father isn't paying any child support."

"How long have you been here?"

"Since mid-summer last year."

"Not so long, then. What did you do with Maya before school started?"

"After her dad split, Maya was a little bit traumatized. She'd come down to the office with me and put Legos together under the desk. But once she got into the school routine, she snapped out of that quiet mode and turned into quite the chatterbox. The office, Legos, drawing, everything quiet was boring to her, and Pete Trestle, the owner and manager, felt she interrupted us too much. It's not like Pete is in the office all that much, but you've seen how gabby Maya can be."

"And curious. She wants to know about everything. I don't think I've been around a kid who asked so many questions."

"She's definitely like that. Pete's such an introvert, though, and he's got zero parental instincts. He tries to treat her like she's a miniature adult, but that doesn't work at all. Maya dislikes him."

"He did seem shy to me when he showed me around. All he must do is deal with cranky people who have leaky faucets and stopped up toilets. He doesn't strike me as the kind of guy with much fortitude for that. Why's he in apartment management then?"

"Inheritance. His dad operated the place until he died two years ago. Pete tried to handle it himself for several months before finally giving it up and hiring me. I end up being the one handling the leaky toilets and stopped up faucets."

I laughed. "Not a fun prospect. What did Pete do for a living before?"

"Something computer related. Not sure of what. He still works for that employer on swing shift. That's why he's here in the mornings and I handle the afternoons and early evenings. You work with computers. Do you like that?"

"Most of the time."

"What brought you to the opulent Miracle Motel?"

"You mean, is this apartment a step up from my previous urine-soaked fleabag hovel? Or are you asking if I have fallen from the lap of luxury where I used to have servants and a Mercedes?"

Rebecca reached over and smacked my hand playfully. "Yeah, one of those."

How did I explain the events of my recent life? I was still reeling from a lot of it. "I was in a relationship for a long time, then she decided I wasn't enough."

"Sounds like it was very painful."

"It was."

"So she broke up with you?"

"Oh, no. She said she still loved me and wanted me in her life. She just wanted to have a second lover as well."

She set her mug down with a thunk. "Are you saying your ex cheated on you?"

"I wish that was it. But no. She came to me and said she wanted us to find a third person to get involved with. When I said I wasn't interested in any kind of *ménage à trois*, she said that was okay, but she was going to look for a second lover.

Maybe you've heard the term lesbian bed death?"

"Uh, no..."

My face flamed, and I was sure I must have looked exactly like a red Christmas bulb, but I forged on. "I don't know what happened to us. I thought we were getting along all right, though we'd had a dry spell of, er, you know, intimacy. I didn't understand what had come between us. I thought it would resolve because I cared about her deeply. So for her to want to take a second lover was a huge shock to me. We argued. Well, I guess I was the one arguing. She had an answer for every comment. She told me she'd come to understand she was polyamorous."

Rebecca wrapped both hands around her mug. "What did she mean by that?"

"Polyamory—you know, the opposite of being monogamous?"

"Oh." She had a bewildered look on her face.

"Yeah, I keep thinking the opposite of monogamy should be polygamy, but that's not it. You look as befuddled as I was. I had to go search out information on the Internet, and wow, did I feel stupid. I guess there's a whole world of people out there in open relationships with multiple romantic partners. I tried to be open-minded, especially when it was all a theoretical thing, but then she found someone."

"What was her name?"

"My ex?"

"Yes, and the home-wrecking interloper as well."

"I like that—interloper. She definitely loped right into my territory and stole my peace of mind. Her name was Rita. My ex's name is Britney."

"You must have been so confused and hurt."

"What could I do? I gave her an ultimatum—Rita or me—but she patiently fed me a bunch of rationalizations. She didn't want me to leave. She said she still loved me, but it was clear to me that we didn't have a good connection at all anymore. I honestly don't know how that happened. Maybe it was my fault. I should have said something, done something. Instead, she spent a great deal of time with Rita. She wanted all three of us to hang together, to be friends, besties in all ways. Good Lord, I didn't have it in me. Rita didn't seem to be a bad person, but after a while, I couldn't stand being around her."

"You actually tried?"

"What could I do?"

Rebecca raised both hands and wiggled her fingers. "Maybe scratch her eyes out?"

I was starting to really like this woman. Smiling, I said, "I might have pulled my own hair out, but that's about it. I finally gave in, threw in the towel."

"I don't blame you. I'd've done the same, though I must admit that I've always wondered what throwing in the towel means."

"Boxing reference. Do you watch the fights?"

"Never."

"You look a little horrified."

"I don't like blood or violence at all."

"Didn't you just offer to scratch my ex's lover's eyes out?'

"C'mon, I was kidding."

"I know. I am, too. Have you ever watched *any* boxing?"

"Not really."

"If a boxer is getting the stuffing beat out of him and there's no hope of victory, his corner crew throws a towel into the ring to let the referee know to stop the fight."

"Ah, I see. I always wondered about that. I never use that phrase or comparison or whatever it is." Rebecca rose, got the teapot, and poured more water in both of our mugs. "I guess Steve threw in the towel, then."

"Your ex?"

"Not yet, but soon. Have to find him to serve the divorce papers." She put the teapot back on the stove and re-seated herself.

"Were you beating the stuffing out of him?"

"No."

"Then it seems like he's not the one who threw in the towel. Sounds like you and Maya are the ones who took the figurative whupping and had to toss the towel."

"I guess that's more accurate. I have to admit that even though your breakup isn't quite the same as mine, it does have some passing familiarity for me."

"How so?"

"Steve had an affair. When I look back, I'm pretty sure when it started, but I didn't let it into my consciousness for a long time. He kept on with me, acting like all was well. I should have known because we also had the—what did you call it?—het bed death."

I sucked in a gasp and almost breathed in tea. Coughing, I choked out, "Sorry, sorry. I shouldn't laugh. You caught me by surprise."

She plucked a napkin from the dispenser and handed it to me. "I meant it to be a little humorous, Sky. Don't worry about it. Steve was perfectly capable of carrying on with two women at once, that's what I was getting at. When I finally let myself realize what his late nights and the smell of someone else's cologne meant, I was probably as heartbroken as you were. Your ex was more up-front, but when I confronted Steve, he copped to it without batting an eye and wanted to carry on as usual. That so did not work for me. Not one bit."

"Seems like we've both gotten the shaft. Now there's a phrase that I have no idea of the actual origin."

"I happen to know that one," Rebecca said.

"I'm sure many straight women can comment on that."

She looked at me blankly for a moment before bursting out in hysterical laughter. "No, no, no, you've got a dirty mind. That's not it at all. It goes back to something like the Middle Ages. Digging holes for burial was hard work, and space was limited. Lots of times the dead got buried standing on end, more than one in a shaft. Horizontal burial was for the rich and getting the shaft was for the poor and disrespected."

"Come on, that can't be true."

"You're the computer and Internet expert. Look it up."

"Where did you hear that?"

"Took a class on the Middle Ages."

"I thought you were a math major."

"I loved history, too. If I'd graduated I might have had a double major."

"Why didn't you graduate?"

"Got pregnant with Maya."

"Were you disappointed to leave college before you graduated?"

"Always meant to go back but haven't yet."

"Maybe you can sometime when Maya is a little more independent."

"I guess I hope to. Do you have a degree in computer science?"

"I have a degree via the School of Internet Searching." She looked at me funny. "Yes, that's right. I'm a hundred percent self-taught. Everything I've learned has been from the Internet. I did take one year of college when I left high school, and another couple of quarters a few years later, but I studied history back then. I worked full-time all through my twenties. Britney worked off and on, and she's the one who got a degree in business. When it was my turn to focus on a degree, she bailed emotionally, so everything I've learned about business I've learned the hard way."

"That sounds unfair."

"At least she's stuck with her own student loan bills. That's one debt I didn't walk away with." I didn't mention how many other bills got dumped on me. We didn't have joint credit cards, and over time, it seemed like I ended up charging the lion's share of items whether it was for clothes or travel or household things. Britney was now cheerfully enjoying the washer and dryer that I'm still paying off. Thinking of that made me angry.

"What's the matter?" Rebecca asked.

"Nothing. Just a bad memory."

"Seems like we've both got a number of those."

We sat silent for a few moments. I felt a wave of fatigue wash over me. The tea was obviously herbal because it wasn't giving me one bit of a caffeinated rush. Instead, I could have laid my head on the table and gone to sleep. "I had better get out of here and let you hit the hay."

Rebecca picked up our mugs and stuck them in the mini sink. When she turned back to face me, she looked as tired as I felt.

I said, "I'm sorry if I overstayed tonight."

"But you didn't. Not at all. I didn't sleep well last night. Hell, I haven't slept well for a very long time. So it's not you. Sometimes it just hits me, especially since that was chamomile. Always makes me tired."

"Thanks for the tea. It was good."

"Next time I might even offer you some cookies."

"Whoa—you'd really do that?" I meandered toward the door, and she followed me.

"Good night, Skylar."

"Hope you actually get some sleep," I said, "and that your kid doesn't decide to sneak out and take a boat down the Willamette in search of adventure.

"Me, too."

I opened the door and stepped out onto the landing. I hadn't worn a coat, so it felt particularly chilly. I dug my keys out of my pants pocket and stuck the key in the lock. She shut the door and I heard her work the bolt. Though our apartments were mirror images of each other, mine looked and felt an awful lot less welcoming.

Chapter Four

IN THE TARGET STORE, I searched high and low for a decent portable external hard drive, finally concluding that they were out. It was so late on a Friday evening, I wasn't sure where else I could go to buy a backup drive for an elderly customer I'd be returning a computer to the next day. Disappointed, I cut around the corner in Electronics, wandered down a few aisles, cut past a display, and WHAM. I ran into a large immovable object. Correction: a person, not an object. I looked up at a kind face with smiling eyes and recognized the woman but couldn't for the life of me place her.

"Skylar? Sky Cassidy?" she said.

"Uh..." I gazed up into amused brown eyes. She had a nose ring, an eyebrow piercing, about a hundred earrings, and curly black hair cropped tight against her scalp. She was familiar, but I couldn't recall where from.

"It's Tamra. Tamra Jaworski. From Grant High?"

"Oh, yeah." Now I remembered. "You're the actress."

Tamra had been in all kinds of musicals and choir events. I remembered a skinny tough girl with a soaring contralto voice. "Didn't you go off to California after graduation?"

"I got a scholarship to Cal Poly in Pomona. I went for two years but didn't finish."

"Why not?"

"My mom got sick. Breast cancer. I came home and took care of her 'til she died."

"I'm so sorry. You were young then."

"Only twenty."

"Are you still singing?"

"Yes, lately in the Portland Lesbian Choir. Mostly I manage the registrar's office over at PSU."

"Ah, I see."

"What do you do for a living, Sky?"

"A partner and I run Sky High Computer Experts. It's geek work to fix people's computers. Sometimes we go out and do training in small businesses or with individuals." I was struck by a memory of sitting next to her in the science lab. "In high school, didn't we dissect a mink or something like that?"

She laughed. "Sure did. It was disgusting. I would've passed out if not for you."

"Really? I must be so traumatized that I can hardly remember it."

"Not half as traumatized as the poor little critter we dismantled. Oooh, ick. I probably should still be going to counseling."

Still? So she went to counseling? I wondered what for, but knew it'd be impolite to ask.

My neck was starting to hurt so I tipped it down and turned from side to side to stretch it. Had she been so freakishly tall all those years ago? I looked at her feet and saw black spike boots that gave her at least five or six inches of extra height. She wore black leather pants that were filled to capacity, and under a fleece jacket, the lacings of a dusty blue bustier were strained by what I can only describe as an amazing bustline. My mother taught me to use the term "bustline" whenever a woman's breasts were as big as my head. My cousin Sunny had called a large bustline "bodacious ta-tas." Either way, Tamra was such an imposing, dominating presence that it was now difficult for me to meet her eyes—and I didn't even consider myself a breast woman. I met her gaze and realized she'd caught me staring.

I felt my face flush and I stammered, "So, what are you doing here?" then almost kicked myself for sounding so dopey. Obviously she was hunting for leftover Halloween candy to take to the costume party she had to be going to.

She pointed to a display of multicolored duct tape. I noted she held a roll in one hand. "I'm off to a very special get-together, and you ought to come with me."

I wanted to say there was no way I was going anywhere with anyone I hadn't seen in the better part of fourteen years, but there was something so compelling in her gaze that I felt drawn to her. I don't know how to explain the effect she had on me. It was like she glittered. I was a moth attracted to the light, and I couldn't resist.

"Where are you going?" I asked.

"It's an amazing social event, a fun play party."

"Ah." I remembered going to a couple of gatherings of actors and directors and theater tech folks back in high school. I'd always been a little too shy to get involved with the theater department, but a couple of my friends got bit parts in the productions, and I remember going along and enjoying all the fun they had at cast parties.

Tamra asked, "Do you still live in the area?"

"I do. Down near the Pepsi bottling plant."

"Great. That's not too far. Why don't you come with me tonight? I'd be happy to have you be my guest. It's three blocks away, but parking over there is horrible. I suggest you leave your car in the lot here and ride over with me. I won't be drinking at all tonight. I promise. In fact, this isn't a party with any drugs or alcohol at all."

I didn't feel the need to get drunk anyway. I'd be glad to hang out with some people. If the party was only three blocks away, I could always hoof it back to my car if I wanted to leave before she was ready to go. "All right. I'll go."

She held up the duct tape. "One quick transaction, and we're on our way."

IMAGINE MY SURPRISE WHEN we arrived at a giant house, and upon entering the party, Tamra was greeted as though she were the Second Coming of Christo. She handed over the roll of duct tape, and I wondered if some special artist types would take it and start wrapping trees or whatever like the famous Christo artists did. I never found out where that duct tape went, but it could easily have been used to seal up drafty spots or perhaps to block the light.

We passed through a dimly lit series of rooms to stairs that led to the basement. Tamra led me down a long flight to what I can only describe as a dungeon. I was reminded of the Black Box at the Ashland Theater where I saw "Hamlet" in high school, though this space wasn't nearly as big. Cement walls, weird strobe lighting, people jammed everywhere...and then there were the two half-naked men chained to a wall. What the hell kind of play was this going to be?

A crowd of people sat to the side on folding chairs. One of them was snacking on chips and cheese. Suddenly I was hungry, and I felt a strange sense that I wasn't in Kansas anymore. A bunch of clattering behind me signaled the arrival of more people, and suddenly the room was so full, it was downright claustrophobic.

Tamra removed her fleece jacket. Someone let out a low whistle. I was glad it wasn't me being so impolite, but clearly it wasn't just me who couldn't help noticing her generous endowments. She went to a side table, picked through an assortment of items, and came up with a three-foot-long thing that looked like a riding crop with a lot of leather strips hanging from it. Tamra moved to the center of the room, raised the mini whip overhead, and brought it down against a wooden bench with a resounding CRACK! The noise echoed through the space, and everyone fell silent.

"Ladies and gentlemen, doms and subs," Tamra said, "and all you voyeurs who get off on the watching, welcome. I am Mistress Mephisto, your guide for the first part of the evening, and all present will obey me. Two major rules, nobody touches anybody on display here unless I expressly demand it, and don't even come near my toys and equipment."

Holy crap. I was pretty sure this wasn't "Hamlet." I could hardly take my eyes off of Tamra, but I did keep sneaking glances at the guys squirming up against the wall, shirts off, muscles bulging. One of them wore tight jeans, and the other was incased in leather pants that looked like they'd been melted onto his very shapely legs and ass.

Tamra had continued speaking, but it seemed that my heart was pounding so loudly that I missed everything but her final comment. "Let the pleasure and pain commence!"

I felt like a sardine. There wasn't a single chair left to be had, and the air was thick with expectation. It was like we were all holding our breath.

And then Tamra laid the first stroke on Contestant Number One, then on Number Two. I watched the strands of leather attached to the handle as they sliced through the air. I didn't find out until later that she was wielding a flogger. It was like watching the strangest ballet I'd ever seen. I wasn't sure how she managed such a perfect rhythm to alternately whip the two guys with such style and grace. My shoulders got tired just watching.

I felt like I shouldn't be seeing this, that it was private, but I couldn't tear myself away. The worry that there would be blood came to mind as their backs reddened, but that didn't happen. How long would this last? How long could she keep up that pace? And how long could they stand it?

I drew a deep breath and looked around at the crowd. Seemed like about equal parts men and women, some dressed in leather, some scantily clad in lingerie items, and a couple people dressed casually like me. A contingent of men along the far wall was dressed in denim and black leather chaps. They stood, backs against the wall and hips thrust forward. I wasn't the slightest bit interested in guys, but I couldn't avoid seeing the prominent "packages" they possessed.

I noticed the seated guy had stopped shoveling in the chips and cheese. He held a chip aloft, frozen near his mouth, with a string of gobby cheese dripping from it. That was almost freakier than what Tamra was so energetically accomplishing.

The crowd settled in, and the expectant hush turned to murmurs of appreciation and quite a bit of heavy breathing. Someone tapped me on the shoulder. I turned to see a woman with a pixie face. She was dressed in a green felt-like costume and wore a matching green Robin Hood cap complete with a red feather. Who was this—Maid Marian?

"Hey," she whispered, "wanna come upstairs and play? Or are you totally engrossed in the flogging?"

I blinked. I opened my mouth to reply and no words would come out. Maid Marian gestured to my hand. I reached out to shake with her, but she grasped it and tugged. She dragged me through the crowd, and I let her pull me upstairs. We came upon the kitchen where a whole raft of people stood around snacking, drinking sodas, laughing. I'm pretty sure I hadn't been able to close my mouth for about the last ten minutes, and I was feeling parched. A bottle of root beer on a tray seemed to call my name, so I snagged it in my free hand and continued down the passageway where Miss Pixie was leading me.

We passed two rooms, one on either side of the hall. I caught a glimpse of unclad people moving about in dark, partitioned areas in the room on the left, and in the room on the right, I heard a lot of nervous laughter, but it was so dim in there, I couldn't see a thing.

We passed another open door, and I saw a platform suspended from the ceiling in the middle of the spacious room. The interior walls were lined with people observing two men on the platform. A bare-chested man—correction: nude man—knelt behind a bucknaked guy on his hands and knees. To avoid having my eyes bug out, I hastened past.

"Where are we going?" I asked my new pal.

She stopped. "You looked uncomfortable. So I'm taking you to the cuddle room."

"Cuddle room?"

"Yes. You seemed a little freaked out. My job is to flit about watching for people who might benefit from a little different scene. I'm also available to answer questions—if you have any?"

I had a few dozen questions but felt embarrassed to ask. "What's your name?"

"I'm Ariel, Woodland Sprite of the Cascades. And you?"

"Call me Sky."

"Oooh, I like that." She smiled at me and touched my arm. "Come with me, Sky."

I popped the screw cap off the root beer, took a slug, and let her lead me into the next room. Of the dozen or so people dressed like Ariel, I counted three men and the rest women. I've never seen so many pillows flung everywhere in my life. They were colorful and all sizes, much like the people lounging on them. The fairies were circulating from one person to another stopping to rub shoulders and stroke cheeks and whisper in people's ears.

But the oddest thing of all was that I noticed some of the sprites were kneeling behind regularly dressed folks combing their hair. For a minute, I wasn't sure if it was for relaxation or looking for lice. That thought made me stifle a laugh.

Ariel beamed up at me as she led me to a space in a corner. I gulped down some more root beer and sat on the fluffy red pillow she indicated.

Ariel said, "May I comb your hair?"

I shrugged and said, "Okay, why not."

Next thing I knew she was running her fingers through my hair. I looked around and had this bizarre memory of being eight years old and going to a party at Sandra Horton's house where the major activity was combing out the hair on a herd of My Little Pony dolls. I hadn't enjoyed that party, especially when combing the birthday girl's hair went on for what seemed like hours. By the time they wanted to work on my hair, I decided to call my mother and go home.

Too bad my mom is dead now, and I can't call her to come get me.

I wasn't sure how to extricate myself from this situation, but I didn't feel threatened. The house was huge, and I suspected there might be worse places to be—such as next door—and I did have a tasty root beer to drink, so for the moment I'd be all right. A few minutes later, when I set aside the empty bottle, someone came by and handed me a paper cup full of pink lemonade. It wasn't even spiked. And then a basket of something I could only describe as crumpets was passed around.

I looked at the other Little Ponies. They were busy chewing, most appearing stoned out of their minds. I wasn't sure if it was from the cozy experience or if they'd arrived inebriated. I accepted one of the biscuity things, bit off one corner, and the roof of my mouth went numb. The taste of jalapeños flooded my mouth. I spat out the bite and hoped I wasn't going to die. Or go on some LSD-laced trip that would induce me to show up in the dungeon and offer my back for Tamra's ministrations. I didn't think they'd accept me, though, since my pants weren't leather nor were they spray-painted on.

Twenty minutes later, I stumbled out the front door, pretty sure my hair was standing on end but that I was mostly intact. Did I feel all right to drive? I stood in the cool air on the sidewalk wondering, but there were three blocks to march to the car, and by the time I got there, I felt clear-headed and totally normal, with the exception of the roof of my mouth.

I wasn't sure how to contact Tamra again. I was almost certain that I wasn't going to want to, even if she did have bodacious boobies.

As I started the car's engine, the biggest question I had was whether I could tell Mitchell what had happened and do it justice. I felt like a big boobie myself.

I AWAKENED THE NEXT morning feeling strangely hung over. At least I had the feeling back in the roof of my mouth. Not sure what had been in those pixie treats, but I guessed there must have been some really potent jalapeños.

I barely had time to get out of bed before Eddie was beating on my door to drop off a load of work. Did I want to sit in the apartment and repair computers today? Not much.

I looked around the front room of my place. Industrial shelves near the front door, a messy kitchenette, two big tables along that south wall adjoining the bedroom, and a couple of office chairs. In the middle, and along the north wall, was a great gulf. I had room for a tiny bit of furniture there. Why not do something productive and fix up my hovel? Rebecca and Maya's place was just as shabby as mine, but somehow their front room at least looked inviting.

I drove over to the nearest thrift store, wishing I'd gotten the late model Toyota Tundra truck in the divorce, but oh no, I'm stuck driving a sixteen-year-old Honda Civic. If I bought any furniture bigger than a rocking chair or table, I'd have to figure out a way to get it delivered.

I wheeled up to the front of the store on Sandy Boulevard and did a double-take. When did this place go out of business? Irritated, I pulled away and searched my mind for the location of another store. I headed for MLK Boulevard and traveled south where I knew a bunch of thrift stores were located.

Today life felt meaningless. Yes, I had my own crappy apartment, and I was making an adequate enough income, but I was alone. When Britney and I first got together seven years earlier, I took it for granted that I'd never be alone again—or at least not until we were about ninety and one of us shuffled off to kingdom come.

But the plan was what shuffled off.

I spent a lot of time trying not to think about all I'd lost, but every once in a while I couldn't help but feel a little depressed. My mom used to call it being down in the dumps. I knew retail therapy wasn't going to help me, but perhaps if I bought a couch I'd have somewhere to lie around and wallow.

I cut down to Third Avenue and found my way to City Liquidators. I love that place because they have everything from armoires to zippers, not to mention the fact that they have an entire 1930s-style warehouse showroom crammed full of sofas displayed on racks at three or four levels. Last time I'd been there, I actually managed to crawl up to the fourth level to try out a leather monstrosity before the sales guy screamed at me and made me get down.

Just like before, they had the couches stacked high to the ceiling. They tended to be organized by color, one end of the warehouse dull black and brown all the way to the other end full of neon yellows, oranges, and pink. It was like going to a giant couch junkyard.

I headed for the blue section. After all, I HAD the blues—I might as well get a blue couch. I found one that seemed comfortable, and there was a matching loveseat. I loved the electric neon blue color, so out came the old charge card, and I made arrangements to have both delivered later in the day.

On the way home, I stopped at the Goodwill in Southeast and bought a low coffee table for eleven bucks. I didn't care if it had a couple of light scrapes. I planned to use it as a footstool anyway. I also found a tall stool for the breakfast bar and a couple of mismatched wood TV trays that I thought would come in handy. I crammed all that in the car and drove back to The Miracle Motel. All was quiet, no one in the courtyard, nobody out and about. The sky was dark, cloud-filled with rain threatening to fall anytime. I hustled to take the table and trays up before the storm began, wondering if my furniture would get all wet when the delivery came.

The rain started to fall as I closed the door to my apartment. I stood looking out the window for a few moments. Was it possible that the sky got even darker than it had been? Very depressing. If my couch had been delivered, I could have wallowed on it. Instead, I went back to bed.

Chapter Five

MONDAY OF THANKSGIVING WEEK dawned partly cloudy with more than a chance of depression. I wasn't proud of it, but lately I hadn't been able to pull myself out of the doldrums. All day long, I hardly had the energy to work on computers. In the late afternoon, when Eddie came to take away my finished units, I'd only finished two. Hard drives from the end of last week were still stacked up on my shelving. I needed to focus and power through a few more, but all I'd been finding the energy to do was click the TV remote and watch whole seasons of TV shows like "Breaking Bad" and "Dexter" and "Nurse Jackie." I had the very first episode of "CSI" cued up next, and the thought of it scared me. I think there are about fifteen seasons of "CSI." If I didn't pull out of these low spirits soon, I could end up a real couch potato.

The new loveseat in the living room was so bright and fluffy it looked like an electric blue Easter Peep marshmallow. It clashed in a spectacular manner with the orange shag carpet. All I needed now were some multicolored Sesame Street characters to complete the look. What was I thinking when I bought that thing? Might as well have a big bundle of nuclear waste in my living room. The full-size couch here in the TV room was even scarier, so glaringly large and colorfully intense it could practically be used as a night light.

Someone thumped on the door. I set down the remote and rose reluctantly. More pounding. "Cut it out," I said quietly as I passed through the doorway into the main room, dragging my ass to the door. As I swung it open, I heard more banging and realized the knocking wasn't on *my* door, but at my neighbors' place.

An agitated man dressed in an ill-fitting tan suit stood on Rebecca and Maya's welcome mat. His hair was dark brown and sprinkled with gray and a bit of rain water. His suit looked odd because it appeared too tight across the shoulders and around the middle, as if he'd gained weight. I suspected that he wouldn't be able to button it up if he tried.

His angry face turned to me. "What do you want?"

I stammered, "Uh, can I help you?"

"Only if you know where my daughter and her bitch mother are."

"Oh." No way was I willing to tell this badly dressed screw-loose moron how to find either of them. I knew Rebecca was downstairs in the office, and Maya was supposed to be locked in the apartment. If the kid was hearing all the beating on the door, I wondered if she was scared. "I think they're out of town right now."

He stepped toward me and raised his hand to point a finger close in my face. "You tell that bitch I'm looking for her."

I backed away, hand on the doorknob and ready to duck inside and slam the door shut if he moved any closer. He wasn't a bad-looking guy, but his face was so red and twisted with anger that he seemed genuinely scary. I asked, "Who exactly are you?"

"Her worst nightmare." He spun on his heel and stomped toward the far stairwell.

I shivered. How in the hell could that be Rebecca's husband? How could she have gotten involved with someone so frightening?

I watched his back as he reached the top of the stairs farthest away from the manager's office. A noise came from the opposite end of the walkway, and Rebecca skipped up the last couple of steps of the stairwell to my right. Before stepping down, the man hesitated, one hand on the railing.

Don't look back, I thought. Just go down the—

He glanced over his shoulder.

Oh, crap. He saw Rebecca and reversed course.

Shaking rain off her windbreaker, Rebecca didn't notice him at first. He called her name, though. Her head jerked up and she stopped, squinting at him, then met my gaze. I saw momentary panic, then her face went blank and she strode forward, passed me, and stood in front of her door with her arms folded over her chest.

"You stupid bitch!" he said as he approached.

"A happy hello to you, too. Long time, no see."

Was he going to pop an artery? His face was so red I could see a vein pulsing in his forehead.

He poked her in the chest with an index finger.

"Hey, watch it, buddy," I said.

He roared, "You butt out. Shut your door and go back inside."

I couldn't retreat now. I was worried about what he might do to her. But I also felt awkward standing there in my doorway.

Rebecca maintained her composure. "Why are you here, Steve?"

He whirled back to her. "You know why, you greedy bitch. I got your legal bullshit served on me, and it ain't gonna fly."

Rebecca said, "You need to talk to my attorney. I can't—"

"You want to suck me dry? You want money for yourself? I can see paying for the kid, but I'm here to say you won't get a penny for yourself. And five hundred bucks a month for Maya? That's bullshit!" His voice rose until he was screaming. "Anything besides food and clothing will go toward your selfish needs, and I'm telling you I won't pay."

"It's been months and months, and you haven't paid a cent toward Maya's needs. We lost the house because of you. You have a legal responsibility, Steve."

"Bullshit. More selfish bullshit."

I heard the creak of a door opening. A tiny voice said, "Daddy?"

He literally stepped back. "Go back inside, Maya."

"Daddy?" The voice was plaintive. She sounded like she was going to cry.

He pushed Rebecca with one flat hand to her chest. "Tell her to get in the house. I'm not kidding, Becca. Do it or—"

"Or what," Rebecca said. "You'll smack her around? Threaten her like you always do to me?"

He grabbed the front of her windbreaker and started shouting. I wasn't sure what he was saying. I saw motion from my right. Maya stepped out of the apartment and shrieked, "Stop, Daddy. No!"

I heard a metallic sound. *Cha-chunk*. In my peripheral vision, a tiny, gray-haired woman in white tennis shoes and a pale pink velour tracksuit materialized like someone had beamed her down from the Starship Enterprise. Where the hell did she come from? I noticed she held a shotgun about the same time I recognized her from the apartment window across the courtyard.

"Buzz off, bucko," she said. "Leave the lady alone, or you'll be picking birdshot out of your eyeballs."

Steve backed away, hands out to his side and stuttering like an idiot. I took the opportunity to step out, grab the back of Maya's collar, and jerk her into my apartment. I shut the door as fast as I could and locked it.

If Maya's head could have spun around, I think it would have. She was clearly befuddled and could only mumble, "Mommy...Mommy..."

"Shhh, it's okay. Stay with me for a few minutes."

The kid kept whispering, "Mommy, Mommy..." She was crying so hard that she was hiccupping.

"She'll be okay." I had no idea if that was true. I might be lying through my teeth. "It's okay. Don't cry. Sit down right there. Please, Maya. Sit down and wait until the adults sort this out."

She sank down against the wall behind the door, weeping, still saying, "Mommy..."

I dug into my pocket and fished out my cell phone. Before I could input 9-1-1, there was a tap on the door.

I moved to the window, peeped out, and saw Rebecca and the little old lady from across the way.

I moved back to the door. "Yes?" I called out.

"The coast is clear." Rebecca's voice sounded calm.

I cracked the door open, still nervous, and said, "Come in. Quick!" I ushered them in and smacked the door shut as fast as I could. The woman still held the shotgun cradled in her arms. It was very nearly as long as she was tall. Rebecca wasn't a big woman, but she loomed over her, and I felt like an Amazon giant.

"Could you set that down, ma'am?" I asked.

"It isn't loaded." She cracked it opened and showed me, then smiled like a tiny, mischievous elf. Rebecca disregarded everything to squat down and take Maya into her arms.

I held a hand out to the neighbor and told her my name. She gave my hand a squeeze. "I'm Norma. Norma Whitehawk. Don't worry. That fool won't be coming back any time soon. I told him I'd shoot his balls off." She made a heh-heh-heh sound that made me like her.

"What possessed you to come over and get involved, Norma?"

"I saw him threatening you first, then he came back to pick on her." She pointed at Rebecca with her thumb. "I don't take too kindly to men inflicting harm on women and children."

Rebecca rose, pulling Maya up with her. "I'm sorry, Skylar. And you, too, Norma. Sorry you had to see all that."

"I'm concerned for Maya," I said. "Why don't you all sit down, and I'll make something hot to drink. Would you like some hot chocolate, Maya?"

The kid was a wreck. She pressed her face into her mother's midsection, and her little shoulders shook.

"I should take her home," Rebecca said.

"Hey, Maya," I said, "check out my new loveseat. You're

going to like it because it's your favorite color."

That got through somehow. Maya sneaked a peek past her mother.

"I've only sat on it once," I said. "Go give it a try." The kid didn't budge, though.

Norma said, "I believe I'd like to check it out." She plopped down and held her velour-covered sleeve next to the loveseat arm. "Hmm...this clashes in a big way."

She was right. Her pink tracksuit looked like barf next to the electric blue. She rose and sat in one of the office chairs. "I'll let Rebecca and the child sit together. Did I hear something about a warm drink? I could go for some hot cocoa."

I went to the kitchenette and pulled out the cocoa can to mix up some fresh stuff. I wanted Rebecca and Maya to stay. I felt such sympathy for Maya. I was reminded of the loss of my own dad. Granted, my father wasn't an abusive ass like Maya's apparently was, but he'd deserted my mother and me all the same.

Rebecca led Maya over to the loveseat.

"Why is Daddy so mad at us?"

Rebecca shook her head. "He's not mad at you, honey. Just me."

"But he was mean to me, too."

"Your father was angry and he *was* mean. I'm sorry he scared you. I'll talk to him another time when he's better behaved."

"Yeah, he needs to be put in timeout."

Rebecca smiled. "Isn't that the truth." She turned her attention to Norma. They already knew one another, it was clear. "Thank you for coming to our defense. I totally didn't expect that. I'll have to remember to call you if I'm rounding up a posse."

Norma said, "Once upon a time, I could've brought a horse along and made it an actual posse."

Maya brightened up. "You have a horse?"

"I don't anymore, young lady, but when I was your age, I lived on a ranch with dozens of horses."

"Can we go there?"

For the first time, the tiny woman's expression clouded over. "The ranch is long gone. It was a lovely place, but it no longer exists."

Sounded like there was a story behind that admission, but I didn't ask, preferring instead to pour the cocoa into mugs. "Anybody want marshmallows?"

"I do, I do!" Maya said.

The adults weren't interested. I sprinkled a liberal number of mini-marshmallows into Maya's cup and beckoned to her. "Why don't you come sit at the bar here so you don't have any spill problems. You want some Oreos?"

Maya looked at her mother.

Rebecca nodded. "Go ahead, sweetheart. Have a snack."

Maya clambered up onto the stool, tucked one leg under her, and put both elbows on the counter. Probably only two minutes had passed since she'd been sobbing, and already the waterworks were clearing. Though her face was still pink, she looked almost back to normal. If I'd been as upset as Maya, my eyes would be red and swollen and my face blotchy for at least an hour.

I put three Oreos on a napkin and slid them over to her along with my biggest mug which held a 50/50 mix: half cocoa and half marshmallows. I handed her a spoon. "Sounded like you like marshmallows a lot, so you may want to stir them and make them all melty."

The kid's face lit up, as if I'd just given her ten pounds of Halloween candy. I left her spooning up globs of marshmallow and carried the other two mugs over to Norma and Rebecca who had been talking about security for the complex.

"...and that's when I got myself the shotgun. That dingbat Pete didn't put in decent doors until a year later."

"What happened?" I asked as I gave them their mugs. I got my two TV trays and set them up beside them as Rebecca said, "Norma was just saying that the doors here used to be no better than cheap plywood."

"That's right. The little girl over there could've kicked them in. And it's not like the old man would put in screen doors that could be locked. That would've helped, but oh no, he'd have had to lay out some cash. Pete's a cheapskate, but his father was the worst kind of skinflint. After the old man died, we talked Pete into getting new doors. It helped that the government offered some energy efficiency rebates."

I got my own mug from the breakfast bar and noted that Maya had dismantled the Oreos. Four halves lay on the napkin, and she had one half of a cookie in hand, her little tongue busily removing the white crème filling.

"How long have you been here?" I asked Norma. I leaned against the end of the breakfast bar.

"Seventeen years."

"Wow, you must have seen a lot of changes over the years."

"I've mostly seen the place go to pot. It's been better since Rebecca got here. The sewer pipes to the street need to be replaced. Every time there was a toilet backup in the past, the old man would let it go for weeks because we all have two bathrooms in our units. At least Rebecca fixes them right away."

"That's my job." Rebecca laughed. "Have snake, will travel."

"It makes a big difference," Norma said. "Now, if only you were the owner instead of that dingbat Pete."

"Why do you say he's a dingbat?" I asked. Pete had been the one who showed me around, and he'd seemed harmless enough.

"He's not lazy like his father," Norma said, "but he doesn't stick around to do any work here either. There he is—a perfectly able middle-aged man—and he can't even figure out how to change a light bulb."

Rebecca said, "It's not quite *that* bad."

"Really? He couldn't get the cover off the overhead light in my apartment. How embarrassing. He sits around the office shuffling papers while you do all the work around the place."

"What kind of work?" I asked.

Norma said, "She paints and cleans gutters and gets up on high ladders. She came into my place and replaced the overhead fluorescent light, which completely baffled Pete. I think he might be scared of heights. Now who's scared of going two or three steps up a ladder?" She pointed at Rebecca. "My dear, you could be making a lot of money as a handyman."

"I'm not all that handy, actually, but I've sure learned a lot from the Internet. When in doubt I look it up on the computer."

Norma glanced around my front room. "Skylar, either you're some sort of computer hacker, or else you do a computer job yourself."

"I do. Repairs, mostly, and a little computer installation."

"From across the way," Norma said, "I see that giant guy come with computers every day. Is his name Gulliver?"

I blanked. "Gulliver?"

"Don't you young pups ever read *Gulliver's Travels* these days? Gulliver was gigantic."

Maya spun on her stool. "Sky, I have the movie if you want to see it. Jack Black is really, really, really funny as the big guy. All the island people he visits are teensy."

I chuckled. "Pretty scary that an eight-year-old knows more than I do."

Rebecca said, "No kidding. She notices things I don't see and remembers lots of details. And then she's totally oblivious to all the Legos and dirty clothes she leaves all over the place.

"I can't be perfect, Mom." Maya twirled back to face the counter.

I stifled a laugh. Probably not a good idea to encourage the kid to have a smart mouth.

Rebecca said, "Now that the altercation is over, I feel exhausted."

"It's the adrenaline," Norma said. "I hope your fella is having plenty of anxiety himself."

"Don't call him *my* fellow." Rebecca lowered her voice. "I ceased to like the guy a long time ago."

If he wasn't Maya's other parent and if I were Rebecca, I wouldn't want to see him ever again. I felt concern for her about having to share Maya with such an angry, reactive person. "Do you think we ought to make a report and get this—what did you call it, altercation?—into a police report?"

"Oh, no," Rebecca said. "I would prefer to keep a low profile."

"I understand that," Norma said. "I remember moving here under similar circumstances."

"Husband?" Rebecca asked.

"Nope. Girlfriend. A very possessive girlfriend. Or maybe I should say *possessed*."

I was doing the math in my head. Norma had to be pushing seventy. Her face was lined, and her hair was silver and gray. I didn't want to be ageist, but she was way up there in Grandma Land. If she was, say, sixty-seven, then she'd have been fifty when she moved to The Miracle Motel. I was too curious to keep my mouth shut. "Long-term girlfriend?"

"Nah, she was a rebound thing. I'd broken up with a gal I'd lived with for almost a decade, and I met this other hyena woman on the rebound."

I stifled a laugh. "A howler? A whiner?"

"No, no, she was a sneaky vicious little thing, more like a jackal. She'd get an idea in her head about money or possessions or whatever, and she insisted on having her way. The most high-maintenance woman I ever dated."

I glanced over at Maya. She was humming as she dipped a spoon into the sticky marshmallows, and I didn't think she was listening.

Rebecca said, "Sounds like you've had some difficult times in your life, Norma."

"Ten-four on that. Had a lot of tough times, but I had a lot of fun, too."

"So you've been single here," Rebecca asked, "since you came to this place?"

"Not at all. I was in a partnership for over twelve years. She died two years ago, before you got here. Stroke."

I felt sad for Norma but didn't quite know what to say. Rebecca is such a nice person, though. You couldn't ask for a more sympathetic response from her.

"I'm so sorry to hear that," Rebecca said. "Seems like that would have been terribly difficult."

"It was the worst thing that ever happened to me. We found each other very late, but we were the most compatible couple I ever knew. I miss her every single day."

"What was her name?" Rebecca asked.

"Helaine."

"Pretty name."

Rebecca continued to empathize with Norma while I tuned out their words. Norma was calm and centered, even philosophical. My ex hadn't died, and I was nowhere near her level of balance. If I were Norma, I'm not sure I could talk about those kinds of experiences without crying. I still had a hard time going into any details about Britney and her heartless two-timing desertion of me before we'd ever actually split up. I wasn't over that, and I wondered how long it would take before I stopped feeling so broken. But at the same time, I didn't want to go on the way I had been lately. Watching TV, avoiding the stacks of computers, and feeling sorry for myself only served to increase my loneliness.

The couch and loveseat had been here for a day and I'd hardly had a chance to wallow on either of them before admitting that *maybe* Mitchell was right. I felt strongly that I didn't need a serious girlfriend, but a friend to go out with could come in handy. Maybe trying out the dating world in the future wasn't such a bad idea after all.

I was amazed that this conclusion was hitting me upside the head. Very unexpected.

I took my half-full mug to the sink and poured out the now-cool liquid. "Does anyone want to go out for a pizza?"

I'd interrupted the two women. They both looked up, smiling, and said "yes" at the same time.

Maya let out a quiet burp. "I wanna go, but I'm not very hungry right now."

I peeked into the giant mug and could see why. She'd consumed every last bit of cocoa and gobbled up all the marshmallows. All that was left of the Oreos were a few dark crumbs on the napkin.

Chapter Six

MY MOM USED TO say that I did a lot of things by sheer dint of will. I didn't get what "dint" meant for a lot of years, but today I was doing my best to force myself to stay disciplined and get my backlog of computer repairs done. Sheer dint of will was what was keeping me going. I had five hard drives plugged in on the long tables and was running anti-virus and malware detection programs on three of them and defragging the other two. A sixth unit needed the memory replaced, so I was unscrewing the back of the hard drive when I heard a soft knock at my door. Ever since the fiasco with Steve Talarico, I'd been a lot more careful with opening up automatically. I went to the window and looked through the curtains.

Maya. She held a sheaf of papers in one hand and a pencil in the other.

I opened the door. "Are you supposed to be outside?"

"I called my mom, and she said it was okay if I checked in with you."

That was a funny way to put it. I waited to hear more.

"But she said I have to leave the minute I get in your way. Mostly I wanted to ask you about some computer stuff."

"Okay, come in."

As I shut the door, Maya said, "Wow, you sure got a lot of computers today."

"That's my job, kiddo. So, tell me what your question is?"

She went to the breakfast bar, got up on the stool, and set down the papers. I stood next to her. The title on the top page of the paper stapled together was "Internet Searches."

"It's my homework, and it's due tomorrow before we get to have vacation for Thanksgiving. But it's kinda hard to do because I don't have a computer, so I figured you could tell me some of these answers."

I wasn't at all interested in doing the kid's homework for her. Did she expect me to rattle off answers like a trained pup? "What grade are you in—third?"

"Yup."

"How many third graders have computers?"

Maya let out a sigh. "Pretty much all of them. Two of my friends have tablets they bring to school every day. When you don't have a device, you can use the library computers."

"So why aren't you doing that?"

"I don't have time. I have to take the bus home right away after school because I'm not in any after-school activities."

"Why doesn't your mom have you stay for that?"

"I think it's 'cause everything ends before my mom can come and get me, so I can't miss the bus."

"I see." She could be doing something athletic or taking arts classes or whatever else the school offered, and she was missing out. The kid needed an outlet for all her energy, but I understood why her mother couldn't allow the extra activities. It was too bad about their situation.

I looked at her handout. Each of the four pages had instructions to search out information about a subject by using Google, Bing, Lycos, Ask.com, Dogpile, DuckDuckGo, Lycos, or Excite.com. She could select one of three topics to research on page one, and they were The Oregon Spotted Owl, Netarts Bay Oysters, and Acid Rain in Oregon. The second page had three sports teams, the third listed Oregon's main industries, and the last page covered Mount Hood, the Willamette River, and the Pacific Ocean.

"So you have to use the search engines and write a little report about what you find out on these topics."

"Yeah, I know. Half a page minimum, Mrs. Randall said. Minimum means that's the least you can write. Everyone says if you write in big letters, you get to write less."

"You might get interested in what you find out and *want* to write more, you know."

"Uh-huh. Maybe." She didn't sound convinced.

"What search engines do you like best?"

"Dogpile and DuckDuckGo and...probably Yahoo."

"Why—because they sound cool?"

She shrugged.

Maya hadn't picked the most widely used search engines by a long shot, but who was I to say anything. Then again, she'd asked for my help. "If I were you, I would try out all eight of those search engines and see what you get."

"Why?"

"Because you may find you like the layouts of some of them better than others. Just because it has a cool name doesn't mean it'll work for you."

"Oh."

I went to my shelving unit and fished around in a cardboard box until I found one of the many Netbooks I'd collected over time. I was pretty sure this one worked. I hunted up a power cord and took it to the breakfast bar, plugged it in, and fired up the unit. Sure enough, it was still operational.

"This is awesome, Sky. I can use it, for real?"

"Uh-huh."

I set up the password to be MAYAT8, connected it to my wireless system, and spun the Netbook to face her. The expression on her face was nothing short of delighted. She put her fingers on the small keyboard and caressed the keys.

"This is the perfect size for my hands. The one in the library has got an ugly, dirty huge keyboard. I like this better. Where do I attach to the Internet?"

"It's wi-fi."

"So I could take this in your other room and watch TV while I do my homework?"

"I'm not sure that'd be a good idea."

"Sky! We're supposed to multitask. My teacher says we'll all have jobs that require us to get lots of information and know how to work on a bunch of projects at once."

"There's no such thing as multitasking. Your brain switches from one thing at a time to another, and it's not all that efficient. Just because you have several projects doesn't mean you can work on them simultaneously."

"At home, I work during the commercials and watch the cartoons." She paused. "But I work *some* during the cartoons, too."

"Okay, let's do a test. You do page one right here, right now, and I'll time you."

If I were her, I'd've done a verrry slow completion of the first page of research, but she put her head down and gave every indication that she was racing right through, not hesitating or stalling.

I surveyed the computers I was working on. One of them still had hours of defragging to do while the other had completed its review. I sat in an office chair and finished cleaning up the defragged one so it'd be ready to return with Eddie when he arrived.

"Sky. You're right. Some of these search engines are icky, and I like some of the others a lot better."

"Why?"

"Colors. And...where the box is that I put the words in I'm looking for. Also, the printing size."

"Font?"

"Yeah, I forgot that's what it's called."

"Did you like Dogpile?"

"It was okay. The comics were stupid looking."

"What's your favorite search engine?"

She didn't answer right away. "I guess I like Google because it's only a search page. Some of the others have a lot of ads and blinking stuff and I don't like that."

"Good observations."

She rose and unplugged the Netbook and looped the cord around her arm.

"Where are you going?" I asked.

"Into your TV room so I can show you I can do the work fast while I'm watching TV."

"Let me see your first page."

She handed over the packet. In a cramped style of printing, she'd written a lot of notes and thoroughly covered the topic of the Spotted Owl. She even knew to use quotation marks properly. I remembered learning how to use the dictionary and encyclopedia and reading Little House on the Prairie books when I was in third grade. Nowadays eight years olds were expected to use the Internet to research topics. Were children these days smarter? It was hard to tell. Seemed like technology was making the world very different for kids compared to my childhood.

I handed her the packet and beckoned her to follow me.

In my TV/bedroom, she found the outlet and plugged in the Netbook. I pulled my new folding screen behind the couch to block off the back half of the room. "If you need to use the bathroom," I said, "come around to the front room. I don't want you in my bedroom."

"Don't worry." She sprawled onto the crappy carpet in front of my TV. "I know how to expect boundaries."

"You mean respect boundaries?"

"Whatever."

She pointed the remote at the TV and found her station.

"You can start timing me now. I'm going to work on the Oregon Ducks Football team."

"Alrighty then." I looked at my watch. The first section had taken her about fifteen minutes. Would "Phineas & Ferb" help her concentration or not? I had my doubts.

I went into the living room and set to work on another computer. After a while, Eddie came by and took away a stack of repaired and cleansed units, but I kept on working. I was determined to clear as much of the work as I could.

I glanced at my watch and realized how much time had passed. In the TV room, Maya lay stretched out on the floor, asleep, her cheek pressed against her right arm. The Netbook was cradled in the sweep of her left arm. "SpongeBob SquarePants" was playing, the volume down low. At least she wasn't one of those kids who required blaring sound.

I didn't know if Maya's mom would want her to sleep now. Would that mean the kid wouldn't sleep later? Seemed like growing kids should get all the sleep they could, so I left her there and went back to work.

Time flowed, and suddenly it must have been six p.m. because Rebecca knocked on the door. It was raining outside, and her jacket had beads of water on it.

I noted the worried expression on her face. She said, "You've still got Maya here?"

"Yes. She's in the TV room."

"I'm so sorry—very sorry. She wasn't supposed to stay more than a few minutes. All she said was that she had a computer question."

"She did. But what she needed was Internet access."

"And you let her use a computer?"

"Yeah, that was easy. I've got stacks of them here."

"It looks like you do." She smiled. "Let me get her out of your hair."

I stepped aside. She called out her daughter's name as she moved to the doorway of the adjoining room.

The kid sat up, rubbing her eyes. "Hi, Mom."

"Time to go home now, Punkin. Please thank Skylar for all her help."

Maya popped up off the floor like a little marionette. I wished I could still rise from the floor like that. Of course, she was less than four feet tall—much easier to get up when you didn't have to go so far.

"Did you finish the homework?" I asked.

"Not quite."

She showed me page three which was only half done.

"So multitasking isn't all it's cracked up to be, huh?"

In a slightly huffy voice, she said, "It's hard to multitask in my sleep."

I was starting to like this kid's spirit. Nothing got her down for long. "Take the Netbook and use it so you can finish your homework."

Rebecca said, "Sky, we don't have Internet."

"Actually, you do, if you know the password. My wi-fi probably reaches the whole complex. It'll be powerful enough for next door, and the Netbook she's using is already signed on." I grabbed a Post-it note and wrote down the network password and the new password for the little computer and handed it to Maya. "Here's what you need to get access if you get booted off."

She looked at the Post-it, then gazed up at me, puzzled. "Why did you pick that password?"

"For the Netbook?"

She nodded.

"Maya T is your name, and you're eight years old. I thought you would be able to remember it easier."

"What happens when I turn nine?"

"You change it."

Rebecca said, "You won't have the Netbook when you turn nine, Little Miss Talarico. You can give that back to Sky right now."

Maya's face took on that expression of stubborn determination that I was getting used to seeing. I realized that the kid was getting through her life by sheer dint of will. She reminded me of me.

"I don't need it, Rebecca. Really." I gestured toward the box of Netbooks I'd left on the floor. "I've got old computers and parts coming out of my ears. It's spare equipment worth nothing much. I'm not using it, and someone should. It'll help her get her homework done."

"Are you sure?"

"Yes, absolutely."

She looked doubtful, but Maya cut in, hopeful and face shining. "I'll take excellent care of it, Sky. I promise."

"Of course you will. Once the battery charges fully, you can use it without the cord. But you ought to recharge it regularly and not let it get below half." I showed her where the indicator for battery charge was located and saw them out.

At the door Rebecca said, "I owe you a dinner for that."

"It's no big deal. Don't worry about it."

Chapter Seven

THANKSGIVING MORNING AROUND TEN a.m. someone knocked on the door. I figured it would be Rebecca or Maya, but when I looked out the window I was surprised to see Tamra Jaworski. All clad in black, she sported knee-high boots that laced up the front, leotards tucked into the top of the boots, and she wore a voluminous velvety cape that swirled in the wind. Her neck was wrapped multiple times in a wool scarf, and the whole outfit was topped off by a black beret.

Surprised, I opened the door. "How did you figure out where I live?"

"I stopped by your office yesterday afternoon, and your business partner, Mitchell, gave me directions. He's a flaming fool—very funny guy."

"He sure is. Very amusing." I wasn't amused though. So much for security. What if it'd been someone else, someone who I didn't want to know where I lived? I was going to have to smack some sense into Mitchell.

"Aren't you going to invite me in? It's windy out here." I stepped aside and she went immediately to the loveseat. "Brrr, it's really cold." She sat, unwound the scarf, and dropped it on the cushion next to her with her beret. "How are you doing?"

"Good, real good." I faced her in one of the office chairs and put my hands on my knees. I didn't know what to think. The last time I'd seen her, she'd been dressed up like Cruella de Vil and whipping the snot out of two guys.

"I didn't get to say goodbye that night we went to the play party."

"Uh-huh." That's not all she hadn't said.

"Ariel said you didn't stay too long. I was concerned. She seemed to have gotten the impression that you left feeling uncomfortable."

Oh, boy. How was I supposed to respond to that? Instead of answering, I said, "How did you get involved in BDSM?"

"Through acting, actually. A lot of the scenes I participate in are all about plain and simple acting. I get a cut of the gate, and every little bit of income helps."

"I didn't realize it cost to get in."

"You got a pass because you came in with me, but usually it's fifteen or twenty bucks. Sometimes more if there's something truly unusual happening. They have to use some of the funds to pay for snacks and libations."

"So you're not actually a dominatrix bound for world domination?"

She laughed. "I am a bit of a top, but not all that much of a dominatrix."

"You were very effective, Tamra. You held a lot of people spellbound."

She blushed and thanked me. "Are you doing anything tonight?"

"You mean for Thanksgiving?"

"Not exactly—but are you going to a turkey celebration or something like that?"

"I'll go by my business partner's place and hang out for a while this afternoon. You?"

"My sister and her family have a big meal in the early afternoon, but later tonight I'm in a play over at Fascination, The Playhouse for Enchantment."

"I've never heard of that."

"It's new. Used to be a completely different repertory theater over in Sellwood that went belly-up. Some people in the arts community formed a collective to buy and restore it. It's a very cool place, sort of cave-like, and it's got great acoustics. I've made one appearance there so far."

"In what?"

"It was a performance of songs from *Forbidden Broadway*."

"I've never heard of that."

"Do you like show tunes?"

Over the years, I'd seen a Broadway musical every year or so. Britney and I had seen four plays in a week while in New York for our fifth anniversary. "Yeah. I've seen *Rent* and *Les Misérables* and *Wicked,* you know, popular shows that come through town. *The Book of Mormon* was hilarious."

"Exactly. That's the kind of music we sing, only *Forbidden Broadway* parodies it. I sang a bunch of stuff like 'Madonna's Brain' instead of 'The Rain in Spain' and 'The Ladies Who

Screech' instead of 'The Ladies Who Lunch.' Totally a hoot."

"You're doing that again tonight?"

"No. We're doing a bunch of songs about the downside of American experience. Ennui, displacement, loneliness, bigotry. Sort of a fair and balanced look at the way Thanksgiving gives thanks for an incursion into another culture's world. You know, a happy, cheerful kind of play." She laughed.

Sounded grim and awful. Before I could make a comment in response, she said, "I know it sounds kind of bleak and harsh, and it is, but we have some amazing vocalists performing, and I get to do a song from the Broadway musical *Working* which James Taylor wrote. 'Millworker' is the song. I've got comp tickets, so will you come?"

I didn't know anything about that play, but I didn't have any plans for the evening. "Yeah, sure. I'll come check it out."

"The pianist is picking me up for an early call time, so you'll have to find your way there." She told me the address and pulled out her phone. "Let's exchange phone numbers. You text, right?"

I nodded, and we input data in our phones.

Tamra rose, rewrapped her scarf, and planted the beret on her head. I felt so short next to her. She was like a tall black tarantula, all limbs and velvet. I wasn't sure what I thought of her. Or what she thought of me. I felt awkward and unsure. Was this a date? Did I want it to be a date? Before I could ask, she moved to the front door, grabbed the knob and stepped out. "See you tonight," she said gleefully. "I think you'll like the show. Hope you have some good food today."

"Oh, I will. It's always a gourmet Thanksgiving at Mitchell's house." I moved to the door, shivering in the cool wind.

"He said he brined the turkey and has four different kinds of cranberry sauces."

"Sounds like Mitchell."

"Bye, Sky."

I stood for a moment in the doorway listening to the clacking sound of Tamra's boots as she moved toward the distant stairs. A man in a suit passed her and came my way. He was a handsome young guy, perhaps in his late twenties. His shaggy blond hair whipped in the wind as he looked at a sheet of paper in his hand, then examined the numbers on the apartments he passed. He stopped at the Talarico's door.

I figured Rebecca had a date coming for dinner. None of my

business, but I didn't shut the door entirely. The man knocked, and I heard Rebecca's voice.

"Hello, ma'am," he said as he pulled an envelope out of his breast pocket. "This is for you."

"What?" she said.

"You've been served. Have a good day, ma'am." He marched off a lot faster than he'd arrived.

I poked my head out the door. "You okay?"

Rebecca stood in her doorway in a light blue housecoat, her hair tangled, and wearing the oddest expression on her face. "Who serves legal papers on Thanksgiving?" she asked. She ripped the envelope open.

"Mom?" Maya's voice sounded whiny. "You're letting all the cold air in."

"Oh, my God," Rebecca said. "He's suing for custody."

"What?" Maya asked. "What did you say?"

"Never mind." Rebecca met my gaze and mouthed the word, "Later," and gave me a nod, then ducked back into her apartment and closed the door.

I felt sorry again for Maya and Rebecca. Seemed like they were on a rough road right now. I felt kind of numb at the same time. I closed the door and looked around my place. I was either going to have to do something to make it look more inviting or else get used to this feeling of low-level depression. I didn't want to feel this way anymore. I needed to get out of the apartment and find some holiday cheer.

ARRIVING AT MITCHELL'S HOUSE at noon cheered me up. Until my breakup, I hadn't ever spent a major holiday with him. In the past, I'd always gone with Britney to her wild and crazy family celebration. She had older and younger brothers and sisters, most of whom had at least a couple of kids, and they all ran in a pack, excited and exuberant. I didn't miss Britney so much anymore, but I'd gotten to know all those little kids and loved some of them like they were actually blood relatives.

I got out of the car, grabbed a bag, and stood on the sidewalk gawking at the front of Mitchell's house. The man was an inveterate decorator, but nothing like your typical tasteful gay man. For starters, an eight-foot-tall blow-up turkey stood near his front door, kept inflated by a noisy generator. Strung around the door frame and the front bay window were illuminated plastic pinecones. The front window glass sported one of those clingy plastic pictures of a cheesy-looking cornucopia, this one at least three-feet square. On the porch I counted seven pumpkins of various sizes, but they'd all been spray-painted a shiny gold. I was tempted to go back to the car and find a black marker and draw garish faces on some of them.

Inside it wasn't any better. Gourds, dried cobs of corn in wicker baskets, and candles of gold and brown and orange were scattered everywhere. A life-size brown owl sat nestled in a bundle of corn husks. Shiny plastic leaves hung in strands from the chandelier over the dining room table. And that wasn't all. I could go on and on. It looked like the home of an insane pilgrim. I expected Mitchell to show up in a black and white tunic, matching black calf-high knickers, a colonial shirt with a rounded collar, and a faux-gold belt. He'd look pretty funny in those old-fashioned buckled pilgrim shoes and white socks, too. Puritan maidens could flock around him while he frolicked in front of the fireplace.

Instead, he came out of the kitchen wearing a red apron over a plain black polo and blue jeans. Maybe he'd change into his pilgrim costume after the food was all in the oven.

"Sweet-ums," he said, "what have you got there?"

On the table, I set down a bag filled with liters of soda pop.

He put a hand on my shoulder and kissed me on the cheek. "You look pale. And unhappy."

I gave him a fakey smile.

"You need to come in to the office more often and go to lunch with me. Please start thinking about getting out and being with people."

"I've been with people."

"Oh, please. Who?"

"I'll have you know I have a date tonight."

His jaw dropped, literally.

"Flies will get in there if you don't close your mouth."

"I'm just surprised, that's all. Who're you seeing? Someone from the online dating site?"

"Hell, no. A woman I ran into who I used to know back in the day."

"Old flame?"

"Not at all."

"Well, Sugarplum, you should have invited her to our fabulous repast this afternoon."

"She had other plans."

Eyes gleaming, he said, "I hope to meet her soon. I'll be sure to contribute, you know, say a few good words about you."

Just what I needed. "You've already had a sneak peek. Without even asking me, you gave her my address."

He did a quick intake of breath. "Her? That woman? Oh, no, honey. She's going to be bad, bad news."

"If you're so concerned, why the hell did you tell her how to find me?"

"She went to high school with you, she said. I had no idea she was trying to *date* you. I figured she needed some computer repair done. She was like Olive Oyl, all tall and gangly and gawky-looking. Not someone who would look good on your arm."

"You're the one who wants a date to look good on your arm, not me. Where is Philippe anyway?"

"He's at his house preparing pies."

"French Silk?"

"Don't be silly. Pumpkin and apple."

Mitchell came across a little queenie at times, but Philippe was a whole different story. There was something about him that didn't ring true. Perhaps it was the romance novel last name, Devereaux. Or maybe it was the halting, fakey-sounding French accent. He seemed nice enough, and Mitchell was quite taken with him, but he didn't seem to know a thing about France. I wondered where he got the accent—from Pepe Le Pew cartoons?

"Doll, I could use your help peeling potatoes. The second turkey's in the oven."

"I can tell. It smells amazingly good." I reached up and smoothed a lock of his hair. "This curliness is unusual for you."

"Good Lord, I know. The moisture in the kitchen has simply ruined my delicate coif. I'll be employing a generous amount of gel later on to make sure I don't have a seriously bad hair day."

I bet he would. Little was more important in Mitchell's world than how he looked.

LATER, TWO DOZEN GAY men, two straight ladies and their husbands, and three self-confessed "fag hags" arrived loaded down with side dishes and more autumn centerpieces and knickknacks. I pondered why I was the only lesbian on hand. Mitchell was missing his perfect opportunity to set me up with someone.

The array of foods was staggering. Mitchell had, indeed, brined one turkey and simply baked the other. He'd made four kinds of cranberry sauce, two kinds of dressing, and more gravy than he could have come up with from the drippings of two turkeys. I'd have to ask him how he managed to create that huge vat of gravy.

Despite his questionable decorating taste, Mitchell's cooking abilities had never been lacking. He'd made two kinds of winter squash, sweet potatoes, and a boatload of mashed potatoes that had taken me the better part of an hour to peel.

By the time Philippe arrived with pies, we had set up tables in the dining room and all around the living room. With so many people on hand, there was no possibility for a sit-down meal. If you couldn't hold your plate and eat on your feet, you were stuck. Some dumbass brought a Crock-Pot of noodles and dumplings. I saw the look on Mitchell's face when that came in the door. He got out some bowls, but I knew he was hoping nobody would spill.

I went around the tables and helped myself to turkey and gravy, a bit of hominy, a deviled egg, and a scoop of roasted turnips, Brussels sprouts, and parsnips. I skipped the green bean casserole topped with corn flakes. Who brought that? Certainly no self-respecting gay guy would be caught dead sharing that sad little dish.

I skipped the sauerkraut and peas and carrots but helped myself to a flaky croissant dripping in butter. I would have loved the cornbread and biscuits, too, but I couldn't fit everything on the plate. I followed the noisy crowd around to several cold salads and huge veggie and dip trays but just scooped up some olives. My plate was full, so I found a spot along the wall and tucked into the turkey, which was salty and succulent.

A slim man dressed in jeans, tennis shoes, and a red turtleneck sidled up next to me. Vegan guy, probably. His plate was full of vegetables, no meats, no sweets. He should have gotten some green bean casserole for color.

"Hey," he said softly. "My name's Trey. Trey Newton."

"I'm Skylar. Glad to meet you. How do you know Mitchell?"

"My sister's husband met him through Philippe. My brother-in-law works at the restaurant."

"Ah." I hadn't yet been to the fancy French bistro where Philippe worked. He called himself a chef—but he wasn't *the* chef. My understanding was that he served as one of many sous chefs. I didn't bring that up though. "What do you do?"

"Sell shoes at Nordstrom."

"No kidding?" Trey frowned as if I was mocking him, so I hastened to say, "That seems like such a hard job. Lots of work trying to help people find boots and shoes." Worst job on the planet in my book. Smelly feet. Sweaty toes. Ick. Every time I'd ever gone into Nordstrom, the shoe department was under siege. I never bought shoes there, partly because they didn't tend to carry the kind of athletic shoes I'd want, but also due to how busy it was.

He said, "It's very busy, particularly this time of year, and I'm on the floor periodically. But usually I do the ordering and general managing, so it breaks up the job quite a bit. What do you do?"

Around a bite of croissant, I said, "I'm Mitchell's business partner."

"Ohhh...Skylar. Sky. Mitchell has talked about you." Suddenly he seemed much more engaged. "You're the computer expert."

"You get hacked, I'll get you back on track."

He smiled. "That ought to be your tagline."

"It pretty much is." We both finished our plates at the same time and discussed having seconds but I felt nearly full and Trey said he was satisfied. I said, "Do you do desserts?"

"Some. It's my weakness."

He didn't look like he had a weakness for any kind of food—unless it was watercress and broth. He was scarily thin. "Let's hit the pie table and try a few bits. I don't need a huge piece of any pie, but it's nice to taste the variety."

"Okay."

I knew which were Philippe's pumpkin and apple pies, but I also saw mincemeat, pecan, cherry, sweet potato, and chocolate cream pies along with three kinds of cookies and enough boxes of fine chocolates to give us all diabetes.

Mitchell came through the room carrying a steaming bowl of something he proclaimed a "figgy pudding." Wasn't figgy pudding a Christmas thing? Who knew with him. Next thing, he'd probably dish up Valentine's Day hearts.

People called out comments and somebody called for a "hurray" for Mitchell.

"Thanks for hosting, Mitchell," someone said.

He set the bowl on the table and turned to face his guests. His face was red and mottled, and he was sweating, as if he'd run a long distance. He affected a pained smile. Something was wrong. I stepped forward, but before I could get to him, he let out a groan and clutched at his chest. He crumpled to the floor without another word.

Panic broke out. Too many people crowded forward while not enough others backed away.

"Give him some room to breathe," a man's voice cried out.

Another man said, "I'm calling 9-1-1."

I went to my knees next to another guy, and we turned Mitchell over. Someone else knelt behind me, near my shoulder. "I'm a doctor," she said. "Let me."

I scooted out of her way, my heart beating into my throat. What was wrong with him?

"He's breathing," she said.

He was gasping, actually. His eyes opened and he seemed to be gazing sightlessly all around.

"Mitchell," the woman said, "it's Susan. Just relax. Keep trying to breathe. Help is on the way."

And it was. I heard the thin, thready sound of a siren and felt thankful that we were so close to the fire station. Less than three breathless minutes later the medics were inside the house, stabilizing Mitchell, packing him onto a stretcher, and carting him away. It happened so fast that once the screen door slapped shut, everyone in the house stood around holding their plates in shock.

"Philippe," I said, "what do you want to do?"

"What do you mean?"

"I want to go to the hospital. You want to come with me?"

Philippe's face turned a shade of blue-green. "I don't do hospitals."

It figured. "I'll follow and see what's happening. Will you stay here and clean up?"

The whole room was full of people saying they'd help. "I'm going." I headed to Mitchell's bedroom to find my coat, and Philippe followed.

"Will you call me, Sky?"

"Yes. Give me your cell number. I'll call you right away, as soon as I know something." I took a moment, impatiently, to input his number into my phone, then headed for the door.

Trey followed me. "I'll stay and take care of things here. Don't worry."

"Thanks," I called over my shoulder.

ALL THE WAY TO the hospital I had bad memories of the same trip when my mom collapsed. Philippe wasn't the only one who hated hospitals. Spending days on end at your loved one's bedside, hoping they'd live, but then waiting for them to die wasn't a pleasant prospect. I tried not to let myself think of that in regards to Mitchell. But what would happen if he croaked? He wasn't even fifty yet. He couldn't die. Maybe he had a panic attack. He was definitely the anxious type.

I made it into the ER and was surprised to see a couple of men from the party already there. I pulled their names out of my memory, Kevin Liggett and Oliver Randall, two of our business clients who I hadn't talked to in ages. "Do we know anything yet?" I asked.

They shook their heads, and Kevin said. "They're examining him."

I called Mitchell's sister Violet in Seattle and discussed the situation. She was in the middle of her own Thanksgiving meal. I told her I'd keep her posted, then I paced while Oliver and Kevin sat holding hands in a double seat.

Over time, more people arrived, and pretty soon gay men ringed the room, talking quietly. Seemed like it took forever, but a doctor finally came out. I presented myself as Mitchell's "partner," which I am—technically—and the doctor didn't ask questions. Everyone crowded around, but the doctor focused on me.

He said, "First thing is that we've administered painkillers and Mitchell is resting more comfortably. He's not in pain now, so please don't be concerned about that. We've done blood tests and an EKG to test his heart. A vasodilator drug was administered to expand his blood vessels, and we've given him beta-adrenergic blockers to calm the heart."

"What's wrong with his heart?" I asked.

"We think he has a clot that's blocking a vessel, and we need to get that opened up. We may be able to do that with a clot-buster drug. Or we may need to do a form of catheterization where we squirt dye in and examine the blockage, then break it up."

I wondered how invasive that would be. "Does he need bypass surgery?"

"Not sure about that yet. I'm hoping not. The clot might be soft enough that we can break it up by inserting the catheter. He's young. He's strong. Once we get him past this first phase, we'll know more. He'll be in the CCU—Coronary Care Unit—through the night."

"But he's going to be all right?"

"We certainly hope so. He got in here very quickly. We began treatment within a few minutes of his symptoms. That's promising." The doctor looked around the waiting room at the pack of men. "You're all welcome to stay, but Mitchell is going to be under my care for the rest of my shift, and then the nighttime cardiologist will monitor him. I don't expect any changes tonight, so if you like, you can go home and rest, then come back tomorrow. We'll know a lot more then."

"Can I see him?"

The doctor shook his head. "Not at the moment. They're getting ready to move him to CCU. We have him partially sedated, so he's not with it at all. Once he lands in the CCU, a nurse will come out and take you to him."

"I'm staying until I can talk to him."

"That's fine. We'll get you in there as soon as possible."

He encouraged me to see the intake people to help fill in the blanks for Mitchell's health facts and insurance, then instructed me to make sure reception had my phone number. With that, he was gone.

I thought about all the days when gay people were denied the right to be with their girlfriends and boyfriends, and now it seemed like doctors were a lot less picky.

I called Mitchell's sister to update her. I knew he and she had some strain in their relationship, but Violet sounded very worried. She didn't mention any plans to rush down from Seattle, though, so maybe she wasn't as concerned as she made it sound. She asked me to keep her in the loop, but not to call after ten p.m. unless he took a turn for the worse. What a coded message that was. If he died, I could call. Otherwise, no. I felt unaccountably sad about that.

I went to reception and caught sight of the clock on the wall. 7:22. Hours had passed, and I'd had no sense of it.

I was able to answer about a third of all the questions the clerk asked me. Seemed like it took forever to get through the paperwork. I didn't know a lot of stuff about Mitchell's health, but the hospital had access to his records, which showed that he hadn't had a physical recently, though he'd seen the doctor earlier in the year for bronchitis. They had a fair amount of data in the computer from then, including the fact that he'd designated me as a proxy and a person who had access to his medical records. Weird that he'd never mentioned that to me. I'd never put him down as an emergency contact for myself. I might have thought of it if I'd seen a doctor in the recent past, but I hadn't needed any medical treatment in ages. If I didn't feel sick, why waste the money? Then again, look where that got Mitchell.

I went back to the waiting room and found four guys still there: Trey, Kevin and Oliver, and Philippe, who had finally shown up looking very rattled. I updated Philippe with all I knew, and we settled back to wait. The chair wasn't very comfortable, but I put my head back against the wall and closed my eyes. I was just starting to drift off when my phone rang.

"Sky?" a woman's voice said. "Where are you?"

"Uh..."

"It's intermission, and I didn't see you in the audience. I thought you were coming."

Tamra. I'd completely forgotten about her. "I'm at the hospital."

"A likely story." Her voice was calm, but it didn't sound like she believed me.

"My business partner had a heart attack."

"Oh, no. Where are you?"

"Providence. Coronary Care Unit."

"I'll check on you after the show. Gotta go now." She hung up.

"Who was that?" Trey asked.

"Somebody I was going to meet up with tonight."

The next couple of hours crept by. A new cardiologist came on duty and came out to talk to me, but nothing had changed significantly. I couldn't stop worrying. Finally a nurse sought me out and opened up the locked bay so I could see Mitchell. I followed her with trepidation. She made me apply hand sanitizer, then cautioned me about his condition, telling me that he had a lot of wires and tubes attached, but that it was all normal stuff to monitor him.

I stepped into the bay where he lay on his back, the bed inclined enough so that I could see his gray face quite well. His arms and shoulders were bare with a sheet pulled halfway up, and there were wires taped to his upper chest. He had a nasal cannula delivering oxygen. The nurse hadn't been kidding about all the equipment surrounding and attached to him. I'd seen some crazy computer wiring that was less complex. I went to the side of the bed and touched his hand, which was warm.

His eyes fluttered open. It seemed to take a moment for him to focus, but once he did, his eyes widened in alarm.

"What?" I asked. "Are you in pain?"

His voice was raspy, but I heard him clearly. "What have

you done to your hair? You look like hell."

I ran my hand across the top of my head. My hair felt like a mess, but I didn't care. "I've been sleeping out in the waiting room marking time 'til you came to. You think I've got a problem? Wait'll you see what they did to your chest hair."

"I know," he rasped out. "It'll probably grow back."

"If not, you can always get a rug."

He winced. "Don't make me laugh. Can I get some water?'

I pressed the call button and a pretty blonde nurse scurried in. I requested water for him, but she said all he could have at the moment was ice chips. He groused, but once he had some melting chips in his mouth, he settled down.

"When am I getting out of here?"

"You may have had a heart attack, dumbass."

"I know. They told me. Did I ever tell you my dad died at 62 of a heart attack?"

"No, I believe you left that out. I called your sister."

"Dear old Vi. She wasn't too concerned, I bet."

"Actually she was. But she didn't rush down to fawn over you. If I was her, I'd've driven down. What's wrong with her?"

"She's got that sweet gay boy son. Still a teenager and she thinks he's impressionable. I haven't been welcome up at their house for years. She's thinks the kid will get into my sphere and suddenly turn gay. Hello. Her kid is who he is, with or without me."

So that was why he wasn't close to Violet. Interesting. I changed the subject. "You really know how to wreck a good party."

He yawned. "Please tell me someone made sure the house was locked up and the food taken care of."

"Oh, yeah. I put Philippe in charge of that."

"Where is my knight in shining armor?"

"Fretting out in the family room."

"Can you send him in next?'

"If he'll come. I get the impression he's scared shitless that you'll die. He's yet another one of us who hasn't had the best of experiences at the hospital."

"Baby doll, please tell him I won't die. I may be heartless, but I'm not going to kick the bucket any time soon."

I resisted complaining about the way he kept addressing me. Here he is in the hospital, and I have to be all kind and patient, but I sure wish he'd quit with the cheesy endearments. "You better not die. I'd be left schmoozing customers and you know how well I accomplish that little task."

"I'm aware of that deficiency." He closed his eyes.

"You're tired. We can all go home and let you sleep."

"I'll sleep when I'm dead. Send my boyfriend in. I want to kiss somebody, and you know it isn't you."

"Meow. I just have to say that he'll run screaming when your dragon breath comes floating out."

A wisp of a smile crossed his lips. "He'll forgive me, I think."

I had no idea what to say to him for encouragement, and I surely hadn't been anything but cranky with him. My heart kept kicking up, and I felt a little sick to my stomach. I realized that if I didn't get out of there pretty quick, I might start crying. I squeezed his hand. "I'll be back in the morning. Don't do anything stupid while I'm gone."

"Send my boyfriend in, and we can get it on here on this comfortable bed."

"Ha ha."

I cut out of there in a hurry and let myself have a little weep in the hallway on the way back to the family waiting room.

Chapter Eight

RUNNING THE SKY HIGH office all day and repairing computers at night and on weekends kept me more than busy. Starting the day after Thanksgiving, I made arrangements with Rebecca to let Eddie in each morning after I left for the office so he could pick up the repairs and drop off new units. After eleven business days of that wretched schedule, I was wiped out and couldn't wait for our usual end-of-year holiday break.

Tamra left a voicemail message for me two days after Mitchell's collapse, but she sounded pissed that I missed her show, and I didn't call back to suggest a date or anything.

Mitchell got out of the hospital after a week, once they managed to break up the clot. He'd be on home rest for a while—possibly through the end of the year—and I was going to have to maintain a distressing pace for a while.

Mitchell's situation made me think. Did I want to keep trudging along for the next decade and a half, then finally find someone special and have an attack like he had? Granted, who knew what would happen with Philippe, but still, Mitchell had finally found someone after many years of loneliness, and all of that was threatened by his health. He kept urging me to "get back out on the market" and to "find someone who deserved me."

I didn't feel healed from Britney's desertion, but I had to admit I had the sense of time tick-tick-ticking, of life passing me by. Maybe I wasn't ready, but I didn't know if I'd ever be ready, so who cares?

When there were dead times at the office, I went to the Girls-Gaylore online dating website and studied profiles that women had posted. Most had at least one picture, but I was puzzled by the photos people selected. Seemed like there were either fakey-looking glamour shots or grainy old outdoor/sports pictures where you couldn't make out people's faces. In other words, they seemed intent on showing something unrealistic or not showing anything at all. I was more interested in the profiles where there were candid, normal-looking shots.

On the first Saturday in December, when I took a break at home, I redid my own profile on the dating website and took out all the bullshit Mitchell had submitted. I also did an Internet search for suggestions and ideas about how to best utilize an Internet dating site. Assertiveness and confidence were important. And intelligence. How was I supposed to show stuff like that in 1,000 words or less?

What level of flirting or cruising did I find acceptable, given that ninety percent of women supposedly also had a high value for respect and proper manners? What was my stance on public affection, sexuality, and sharing one's level of desire? Oh, brother. How could I put that out for everyone to know?

Did I want to reveal information about tattoos? Interesting scars? Wittiness? Charm? Did I like to tease or be teased? What kind of surprises was I prepared to share with my date? Seemed like a Catch-22. How could I know any of that until I met the woman and got to know her?

My favorite question had to do with uniforms. Did I wear any? Was I attracted to any uniform types? Oh, please! Sure I admired a handsome woman in a uniform, but the femmes seemed more likely to be interested, and I didn't classify myself as a girly-girl.

I basically had no idea whatsoever how to write anything that would attract a nice, kind, fun-loving person who would want to sit around on my Blue Slurpee-colored couch and talk to me while I worked fifteen hours a day. Then again, I needed to get the hell out of the apartment and do something to divert me from worry and depression, so I did the best I could to sound witty, charming, and entertaining. Then I went looking through profiles until I found someone who sounded halfway normal, sent off a tentative inquiry, and put on a warm jacket and a knit cap to go out for a walk.

Outside it was cold and cloudy. I went down the stairs past the bale of hay that was starting to disintegrate. All the pumpkins that had been there had been stolen, according to Maya. Just as well. By now they'd have been rotting.

I passed an old man shuffling toward his apartment, a thin bag in hand that no doubt contained a bottle of liquor. As I went by the window to the office, I saw Rebecca inside, talking on the phone. Across the desk from her, Maya gripped a crayon and scribbled furiously. She glanced up, caught sight of me, and her face brightened. She catapulted up out of the chair and ran to throw open the door.

"Hi, Sky! Hi! What are you doing? Where are you going?"

I paused outside the doorway. "Just taking a walk."

"Can I go with you?"

Rebecca hung up the phone, rose, and came to the doorway. "Maya. That's not polite."

The kid let out a disgusted sound, as if her mother was the biggest pain in the ass on the planet. I said, "It's okay with me. Your call of course, Rebecca. Is she grounded or anything?"

"Nuh-uh. I'm not. Is it okay, Mom?" Maya didn't wait for an answer before grabbing her coat and putting it on.

"Only if it's not too much trouble, Skylar."

"I don't mind if Maya comes along. I need to stretch my legs. Been working too many hours."

"I know the feeling. Pete is sick. Again."

"What's his malfunction?"

"I don't know. I think he's depressed about losing his dad. He's never actually worked that much here, and I can see he doesn't like it. The good thing is that I'm getting lots of hours. That ought to help the Christmas budget."

Maya had no more patience for the adults' small talk. She stepped out and grabbed my forearm. "You ready now, Sky?"

"I have my cell phone with me if you need to call us for any reason." I smiled at Rebecca, and she smiled back, a little nervously.

"Bring her back the moment she wears you out or annoys you."

"She probably won't annoy me."

Maya pulled me away. With a little wave, Rebecca swung the door shut. Maya strode quickly past The Miracle Motel sign, her hands in her coat pockets. She had such a serious look on her face that I could only wonder what was going on in her head.

We walked a full block before she turned her face up to me, her brown eyes serious. "Sky, do you have a dad?"

"Are you asking if I was hatched or born?"

"No, silly. Where's your dad? If you have one, I mean."

"He lives in the Midwest."

"Is that nearby?"

I forget that kids have no sense of time and space and place. "No, it's a long drive. Takes about three days in the car."

"Three days! That's crazy. Do you ever see him?"

"Sometimes."

"Was he mean to you when you were growing up?"

Duh...now I followed her train of thought. Sometimes I wasn't too quick on the uptake. "My father wasn't mean. He just went away. When I was a little older than you, my mom and dad got a divorce, and I didn't live with him anymore."

"So you lived with your mom?"

"Yup."

"Were you an only child like me?"

"Yes, mostly. My dad remarried and moved far away. With his new wife he had some more kids. I have two younger brothers, but I never lived with them, so I guess you could say I was an only child."

"Was your dad mean to your mom?"

"What are you getting at?"

"You know, like, did he yell at her and scare her?"

"Not that I remember. Are you worried about how your mom and dad are fighting?"

"Yeah. Mom is crying, and Dad keeps coming over, and now I can't watch TV after school anymore."

I wasn't tracking on where this was going. I wasn't sure I should be discussing things that Rebecca might want to keep private, but I was curious about the TV comment and asked Maya what she meant.

"After school I have to stay in the office with Mom or else Dad is going to take me away from her. If Pete's not there, I can sit at the desk. If he is, I have to sit on the floor next to the wall by Mom's desk and read or color. It's really boring."

The poor kid. She was caught in a bad war between her parents. I wasn't sure which was worse—your dad leaving you, or using you as a child support reduction bargaining chip.

I cut over to Sandy Boulevard, and we walked silently. We came upon Voodoo Doughnuts down the way on Davis. I asked, "Do you ever go to that doughnut shop?"

"Sometimes Mom and I do. She buys a boring doughnut."

"What's your favorite?"

"I like the one with Captain Crunch on it. Or else M&Ms. Or else purple sprinkles."

"Should we go get one now?"

She looked up at me as if she didn't quite believe me. "I don't have any money."

"I do. Come on." I put a hand on her upper back and steered her down the side street.

The prevailing colors inside the dim shop were brown and Pepto-Bismol pink. Some teenagers sat on a couple of shabby mismatched diner-style benches, while others played on old-fashioned pinball machines. The line snaked around the inside of the shop and to the door, but we managed to squeeze into the warmth to wait.

My phone rang. The low hum of conversation in the shop was actually quiet enough that I could hear. "Hi, Tamra." I was surprised she was calling.

"Sky, are you busy tonight?"

I was hesitant. If I said no, I could end up at another hair combing party. I wanted to swing by Mitchell's and check on him, but other than that, I was footloose and fancy free. "I have some stuff going on in a while. Why?"

"I scored two tickets to the Blarney Meisters. You wanna go?"

I had no freaking clue who the Blarney Meisters were. Jugglers? Singers? Comedians? Irish BDSM masters? The only safe question I could think of asking was "Where are they appearing?"

"The Alberta Rose."

"I'm in a shop. Let me call you right back."

Maya and I were fifth in line now, and that gave me enough time to bring up the Internet on my phone and do a search on the Blarney Meisters. The entry portal to their website was black gauzy crap and blinking silver surrounding a giant green-tinted mouth, which looked a lot like the Incredible Hulk's jaw. When I clicked on the tongue, the next page took me to a photo of three women and two guys holding guitars, mandolin, banjo, and drum sticks. Hailing from County Cork, they were billed as the best thing since Mumford and Sons. I played a sample song and they sounded okay.

We got to the front of the line, and I ordered a chocolate sprinkled doughnut. After changing her mind three times, Maya settled on a monstrosity of multiple frosting colors on a six-inch-wide glazed doughnut topped with clods of Captain Crunch cereal. It looked disgusting, but the kid took a big bite and grinned happily with frosting and bits of cereal clinging to her upper lip.

I grabbed a mitt-full of napkins and led us over to a bench, the one seat in the place without padding, so it was not comfortable. I took a bite of my chocolate doughnut, which was excessively sweet. I'd never been able to eat an entire Voodoo treat in one sitting, and I was pretty sure today would be no different. Maya, though, was chowing down like there was no tomorrow. She had frosting on her hands and sleeve and even the tip of her nose. As my grandfather used to say, she looked happy as a pig in shit.

I one-handed my phone and redialed Tamra. "What time is the show, and how spendy is it?"

"I got the tix comped, and it starts at seven. Doors open at six for general seating."

"Okay, I'd be happy to go."

"Great," Tamra said. "Pick me up at about half past five?"

"Sure." We made arrangements and I hung up, still wondering about her intentions. I supposed I ought to have asked her, but how did I do that? Um, excuse me, are we going on a date? Or do you have no other friends on the planet so you thought you'd hang out with me?

How did I feel about Tamra? If I was honest, I had to admit that she was more than a little intimidating. I'd never dated anyone that much taller than me. Now that I thought about it, it occurred to me that everyone I'd ever kissed had always been my height or shorter. Did I want to kiss Tamra? Would I have to get a stepstool?

Maya let out a little burp. She was half-done with the Crunch Bomb and seemed to be losing steam. "Do you want a bag to take the rest of that home in?" I asked.

"Okay."

I rose and got a couple of wax paper bags and also dipped the napkins in some water from the cooler to clean off the kid's face. Unfortunately, some green and pink and blue remained on her face like dye from hell. I hoped Rebecca wouldn't be upset if her child showed up looking like a semi-disguised clown.

We headed out, bags in hand, toward the apartments. Maya said, "Thank you for that, Sky. It was good."

"Glad you enjoyed it."

"If you don't tell Mom, I could put it in my lunch tomorrow."

"If we tell your mom, why wouldn't she let you have it?"

She didn't answer right away as though she was deciding if she should make up a story or tell the truth. I think she chose the latter.

"She says I eat too much sugar and it makes me crazy."

"You have bad behavior when you eat sugar?"

"*I* don't think so."

"So what's the problem?"

"She says sugar makes me forget to listen."

"Is that true?"

"Aren't I listening to you?"

She had a point. Then again, perhaps it took a while for the sugar to hit her system. Maybe I should make her jog home, and we'd burn off some extra energy. But I had a half a lump of chocolate goo roiling in my stomach, so I sure didn't feel like jogging anywhere.

At the office, Maya was excited to tell her mother about our outing. I winced when Rebecca looked with disapproval at the Voodoo take-home bag, but she didn't say anything other than offering to give me some money, which I turned down flat. She thanked me again for watching her kid, and I went back to the apartment to sort through my limited wardrobe and find something both clean and classy. I was bad about spending my precious time in the laundry room, so my dirty clothes basket was stuffed to the gills. Lately I hadn't worn any of my nice clothes, though, so I cobbled together a pair of black jeans, a dark blue shirt, and a black tie with blue and red and yellow Pacman characters on it. The weather was wet and chilly, so I wore a warm jacket and headed for Mitchell's house.

I tapped on his door, then tried the knob. It was unlocked, so I let myself in. "Hellooo..."

"Kitchen," he yelled.

I made my way through the living room and dining room, shrugging off my coat as I moved. I hung it on a chair and went to the kitchen doorway. Standing with his back to me at the sink, Mitchell wore black scuff slippers and a hot pink colored bathrobe. He turned off the water, grabbed a towel from the counter, and turned to me as he dried his hands. His face still appeared a little grayish and his eyes bloodshot. His normally bright and shiny blond hair was dull and disheveled.

"Dude," I said, "you look—"

"I know, I know." He raised a hand. "Don't say it."

"At least you're up and around."

"There is that." He put a teapot on the stove and turned on the burner. "Your usual?"

"Okay. But are you sure you shouldn't be resting? I could make you something."

"No, I'm not hungry at all. And if I rest anymore, I'll scream until my arteries explode."

"We wouldn't want that."

"Besides, I'm supposed to be up and around many times per day. I'd go crazy if I had to stay in bed."

He updated me about all the medical details—and I mean *all* of them—so much so that my eyes nearly glazed over. He went on and on and after a while, he said, "I have so many prescriptions to take that I have to have a chart to keep track of how many and when." He sighed, and then the teapot whistled, and I was spared further medibabble.

When he came back with mugs on a tray along with every

possible condiment you could add to tea, he changed the subject. "How're things going on the dating front?"

"Fine. I have a date tonight."

"I wondered about that, based upon this natty little outfit you're wearing. Who dressed you? The Eighties?"

"Very funny."

"I suppose the little gobbler things on your tie are meant to be playful, but they smack of desperation. Are you looking for someone to play video games with? Wouldn't you rather do the nasty with a real woman?"

"Why are you so concerned about my love life?" I added sugar to the tea and took one hot sip. It'd be a while before it was cool enough to drink.

"Honey, I knew you BB and AB, and believe me, you're a lot happier person when you're in a relationship."

BB? AB? Then it hit me he meant Before Britney and After Britney. He had a point. I had definitely been a lot happier way back then.

"Who are you seeing tonight?"

"Tamra, the gal you gave all my vitals to."

"Oh, my freakin' God! That sinister creepy Olive Oyl woman with the tarantula legs?"

I couldn't help it—I rolled my eyes. Where did he get this stuff? "Tamra's a perfectly normal person. I went to high school with her."

"She looks far too much like a dominatrix I saw at a party last year. Very kinky."

"Hey, since when do you know what's going on in my bedroom?"

"Well..." He made a huffy sound, as if that had never occurred to him. "If you're into that, then great, but I can tell you that if she's not into BDSM and other nefarious pursuits, I'll eat my hat."

"You never wear hats."

He ran his hand over the top of his lifeless hair. "You're right. Because hats muss up my delicate coif. But that doesn't change the fact that your new girlfriend leaves a lot to be desired."

"She's not my girlfriend. She's just a friend so far. And hey, she's a lot nicer person than Britney."

"She's probably slightly better than the Nurse Ratched I had to deal with at the hospital, but that's not saying much. She's still not for you."

"Even with your infinite wisdom, how in the world could you know this?"

He tapped his forehead. "Superior intuition, Dollface. When you discover I'm right, go ahead and come see me so I can say I told you so. Check out the dating website and find some new blood."

"Geez, Mitchell." I guzzled a big swig of tea and smacked the mug down onto the table.

"Don't 'Geez, Mitchell' me. As far as I can tell, there haven't been lesbians falling from the sky into your lap. Date some women. I challenge you to date someone different every week until your birthday. Meet some different kinds of women. Try a variety."

He rose, went to the calendar hanging next to his buffet breakfront, and fingered the top couple of pages. "There are eight weekends between now and your birthday. Eight dates. Go out on a date every weekend for the next eight weeks, and see what happens."

"So let me make a deal with you. If I go on eight dates in December and January, will you stop poking your nose in my love life?"

"But I *care* about you, Little Miss Dreamboat. I want you to be happy."

"You also want me to do this your way. If I do this, I want you to promise you'll lay off ever discussing my dating habits again."

"For three months."

"No way. Forever."

He let out a disgusted snort. "All right. Deal."

We shook hands over our tea. I picked up my tea and downed the last of it. Time to go if I was going to get Tamra on time. I bid my pesky friend farewell and headed for Tamra's house.

THE CONCERT STARTED OUT great. We had good seats, and the stringed instruments sounded cool, especially the harmonic parts the guitar and mandolin players came up with. Three of the singers harmonized on an Irish song. Then another Irish song. Then another Irish song. Same tempo, same lilting harmonies, same strings. After a while I wondered if they weren't rotating "The Road to Mallinmore," "Danny Boy," and "The Last Rose of Summer." Everything sounded the same.

As we clapped at the end of the first set, Tamra eyed me askance. "Are you loving this show?"

Was I supposed to be polite because she'd invited me or should I be honest? I opted for the latter. "Everything's starting to sound like doodly-doodly-doodly-doo to me. Are they playing the same tunes over and over?"

She laughed. "It is a little monotonous, isn't it? Do you want to buzz out of here and get something to eat?"

"Sure." I hadn't eaten much all day and was suddenly starving. She put on a black cape over her deep purple blouse and leggings. Again she was in boots, but this time rather than the six-inch spikes, she wore square-toed black leather boots with a much lower heel. Instead of towering ten inches over me, maybe it was five.

We went to a Thai restaurant. I had Pad Thai and Crispy Soy Chicken while Tamra ordered Spicy Vegetarian Eggplant.

She asked about Mitchell's health, and I filled her in on his progress, then we reminisced about high school days. She asked me about my breakup, and we talked about that for quite a while before I finally said, "So—I can't help but ask—and you can refuse to answer if you like."

She gave me the eye, as though she wasn't quite sure what I'd be querying about.

"How did you get involved in bondage and discipline? You said before that you had a monetary incentive, but that can't be all of it, right?"

Her face flushed pink. Against her dark hair and eyes, the blush was attractive.

"After my mom died, I was very much at a loss. Actually, I was a wreck, totally going under. Then I met a guy at a party, and I spent the next fifteen months serving as his slave."

"Um, did you say slave?"

"Yeah, that wasn't so much about B and D. I was a mess at the time. My whole life was shattered. Out of control. My master gave me order and security. He gave me space to grieve and grow."

"Oh, yeah? So what was this like? I mean, you had a sexual relationship and everything?"

"Sometimes. It wasn't about sex all that much. He was into light play, not anything heavy or difficult for me. A little flogging, a little bondage. Mostly, he wanted to completely control everything, and at the time, I was more than willing to submit. I committed to a year with him, even did the collaring ceremony."

A collar? I looked at Tamra's neck, which was long and graceful and one of her nicest features. Oh, my God...I couldn't quite stomach the idea of her wearing some sort of collar, but I wasn't going to say anything judgmental. "You said you were with him fifteen months—or did you mean a year?"

"After the year went by, I got my shit together, but I stayed with him three more months, mostly because I wanted to understand how to be a master. Well, I mean a mistress, actually. I'm Mistress Mephisto now. I wasn't well-suited to be in the submissive role, not for long anyway. It worked for me during those first long terrible months after Mom died. Then it got a little old, and once I got on track, of course he let me go. He likes variety, and I think he was ready to train someone new anyway."

This was so far outside my realm of experience that I didn't quite know what to say. "Do you still see him?"

"Occasionally. It's funny how he was the center of my life for all that time...and now his focus is on his newest acquisition. I don't need anything from him anymore, but I feel gratitude for all he did for me. Since then, I've totally moved into my own comfort zone."

"And that would be?"

"A top. Not exactly a dominatrix, but definitely the one who wields the power and authority."

"And the slave is a bottom?"

"Exactly. I've trained and kept three subs so far."

"Subs?"

"Submissives. Slaves, I mean, but sub sounds less power hungry. Subs are bottoms, and doms are their dominant masters. My three so far were quite an experience. Pretty amazing."

"Three at once?"

She laughed. "Definitely one at a time. Takes way too much time and energy to train someone to be a good sub to have more than one."

"Men? Women?"

"All three were women."

"Do they sign on for a year like you did?"

"One did. The other two were for much longer terms, three years and six and a half years."

"Wow. That's pretty amazing."

Tamra beamed at me. "I'm glad you haven't run screaming. Some people don't seem to understand or accept this world or these practices. It's all one hundred percent consensual, and there are safe words and agreements and some people sign a contract."

"Did you—when you were with your master?"

"I did. He wanted us to both be very clear about what we'd signed on for. I don't recall ever referring to it in the entire time we were together. Hmm, wonder whatever happened to it?" She took the last bite of eggplant and chewed thoughtfully.

"How did you make the daily transition from being a"—I stumbled a little bit—"a sub to going off to work every day?"

"I didn't work for that whole first year."

"What did you do?"

"Anything my master asked. I took care of his house and yard and made meals. I gave him massages and bathed him. I ran errands and took care of anything that helped him make his life easier. Whatever he wanted or needed, I made it happen."

"And he supported you financially during that time?"

"Yes."

I pushed my half-eaten meal aside and leaned my elbows on the table. "If you don't mind me asking, do you consider yourself bisexual?"

"Not really. I'm queer for sure. If I had to label myself, I guess I'd say lesbian. Mostly, anyway."

"But you had a relationship with the guy."

"It was a different thing than a typical relationship, you know. Not two people making mutual decisions and building a life into the future. In my case, it wasn't meant to go on forever. Not that a master/slave relationship can't be long-lasting and balanced and beneficial to both people. But back then, I didn't want to make any decisions at all. I was content for quite a long time to exist in an orderly universe, serving him, knowing I was appreciated. Still, after a while, I realized that the opposite role would work better for me. If I hadn't had the experiences with him, I wouldn't have known that."

"I see."

"I'm glad you understand, Sky." She reached across the table and put her warm hand on mine. "I'd like you to consider being my sub."

I was dumbfounded. My mouth went dry, and I must have stared at her like a complete dimwit. She waited patiently for my response. First I felt slightly light-headed, then embarrassed, and my face and neck went all hot. I pulled my hand away and made fists under the table. "Why would you ask me that?"

"I thought you might be interested."

"Why would you think that?"

She took a deep breath and gazed at me, her expression troubled. "I can see—and feel—how out of sorts you are, Sky. You remind me of myself back when my mother died. You're wounded and hurting and not happy. I could take a lot of stress off your shoulders and look after you while you heal."

She honestly thought I'd go for this? Now I felt indignant. So what if I was wounded. What business was that of hers? I didn't know whether to share my annoyance or laugh it all off. I didn't think I could joke about it, though.

I chose my words with care. "I hear that you're trying to be generous and helpful."

"Totally."

"I can't even begin to imagine participating in the kind of arrangement you're suggesting."

"You don't have to give me an answer now. Take some time and think about it."

"You're offering to move me into your house, take care of me financially, and have me wait on you hand and foot. You'd be my master, and I'd allow you to take control and make pretty much all my decisions." She nodded. "And there'd be sex involved."

"I'm willing to negotiate whatever works for both of us." She smirked. "I think we could come to terms that would meet your needs."

"You're wrong."

"Why do you say that?"

"You've completely misjudged me. The answer to my problems and the healing of my grief isn't going to take place in a situation where I have no power."

She sat back and folded her arms over her chest. "It's not like that."

"Did I misunderstand? I'd wear a dog collar and accede to your every wish. My life would be focused on *your* life, not on my own."

"Not a dog collar!"

"Some sort of collar."

"It's representative of the commitment to the arrangement by both dom and sub."

"Oh, so you wouldn't actually lead me around on a leash, huh?"

"Of course not. Unless you wanted that."

"You mean unless YOU wanted that. You'd be the boss."

"It's not like that, not exactly."

"Right." I closed my eyes for a moment and took a deep breath to try to center myself. When I opened my eyes, her face was tight and her eyes hard.

I said, "It sounds to me like the arrangement worked for you during a very difficult time. Losing your mom must have been awful. I may be in a tough spot at the moment as I deal with my own losses, but the answer to my issues wouldn't be what you're proposing. I'm sorry, but I want nothing to do with this. It seems like you want to be helpful, but for me, this is not the answer."

"But I like you. I could help you."

"Not like that."

Her tone became accusatory. "You haven't bothered to consider this or to try it out to see how useful I could be to you."

"Don't you mean how useful I would be to *you?*"

"You don't understand." Her voice took on a petulant tone. "You're not listening."

"I've been listening very closely, enough that I know this would never work for me. I've never been in a situation like that and don't intend to start now."

"Everything you've told me about your ex—Britney, wasn't it?— is that she was the dom in your relationship."

Ouch. That smarted. How I wished I hadn't given Tamra so much information about my relationship and the breakup. Oops. Bad judgment on my part. The worst thing was that I couldn't refute her comment, not entirely, but just because Britney rode roughshod over me at the end didn't mean we were in a master/slave arrangement. She had dominated in a lot of ways and done whatever she damn well pleased, but come on. I never submitted to any kind of unilateral power arrangement. The minute Britney and I ceased making mutual decisions was the beginning of the end.

I said, "My previous relationships have nothing to do with this."

"Listen to me." Her voice was demanding, almost commanding. "You're in a state of grief. You're not clear-headed."

"That's bullshit. You're not listening to me. I'm not so overcome with grief that I'm unable to tell you what I think is best for me."

"I disagree, and I insist that you take some time to think about it."

"Tamra, you have no right to insist that I do anything. I'm very clear that there's no way in hell I'd be a sub to anyone's dom." I stood, took my wallet out of my pocket, pulled out some bills, and set them on the table.

"Where do you think you're going?"

"Home."

"No. You need to sit back down and hear me out." The tone of her voice and her angry delivery reminded me of

Rebecca's soon-to-be-ex, Steve. Tamra wasn't shouting, and she lacked the bulging veins in her forehead, but otherwise, her agitation was similar. She rose.

"Thanks for taking me to see the Blarney Meisters. It was nice of you to think of me. I think it'd be best if you not call me anymore."

Her face was very red now. "You're making a big mistake."

The only big mistake I could see would be subjugating myself to another person. I valued my independence and my ability to take care of my own problems. I didn't do it perfectly, but no way was I giving up my autonomy to someone else.

"Sit back down," she said through gritted teeth. "Right now."

"You seem to have me confused with someone you have power over. I'm not your slave and never will be. Goodbye, Tamra." I snagged my jacket from the back of the chair and got the hell out of there. Not until I reached my car out in the parking lot did I realize that I'd picked her up, so she didn't have a ride home. Too bad. I got in the car and wheeled out of there as fast as possible. She could take a taxi.

BACK AT THE APARTMENT, I paced the front room, unable to sit and chill out. I never saw, never predicted, never even had a clue that Tamra had such a power thing going on. I wasn't going to relish the thought of having to tell Mitchell he was right. With any luck he wouldn't bring it up. No, my luck wasn't that good. I hoped that when he did ask, I'd be able to distract him because I sure didn't want to admit how much better he read the situation than I had.

I made myself sit down at my laptop and pull up email. The woman I'd written to earlier hadn't answered but others had written plenty of messages. When I saw all the emails from the GirlsGaylore.com website, I felt a tight pressure in my chest. I counted the messages. Twenty-seven? I opened the oldest one.

> Hey, Geekgrrl,
> You sound like just my type of womyn and your pretty cute. Wanna go hiking this weekend? U like sex in the stix? Warm cuddles in the woods? Lotsa luvven in the wild? I am wanting your wanting. Interested?
> TreeQueen133

Oh, my God, were all the messages from the dating site full of such inane commentary? Who propositions someone before they've even met?

I closed the browser window in disgust, rose, and went to the back window. Through the rippled glass I could just barely make out a half moon up in the sky. If it weren't so damp and cold, I'd go out and gaze at the stars and moon.

I heard a tap on the door and looked at my watch. Not even nine p.m. yet, though somehow it felt much later. I found Rebecca standing on my non-existent Welcome mat, and I made another note to myself to go buy one.

She held out a plate of cookies. "Got any coffee or tea?"

"Both," I said as I ushered her in. "Where's Maya?"

"On an overnight with her dad's parents." She crossed the front room and set the plate on the breakfast bar.

"Are you worried?" I asked.

"Very much."

"Will Steve be there, too?"

"Probably."

"You sure that's safe?"

"I can only hope so. His mom is a sweetie, so I think Maya will be fine. She wanted to go. She loves Grandma and Grandpa T."

"Should I get out the coffeepot or heat water?"

"You have a preference?"

"Not at all."

She paused and looked upward. "I guess I could go for some tea."

"Coming right up."

Rebecca slid a thigh onto the stool and half-leaned, half-stood next to it. "Have you had a good day?"

Should I talk about my crazy evening? Maybe it wasn't a good idea...but she had a sympathetic expression on her face, and good God, I did want to talk about everything. "You wouldn't believe it if I told you."

"Try me."

I filled the teapot and debated how much of the "date" to share with her. With a sigh, I put the water on the burner and leaned back against the counter, arms folded over my chest. I quickly sketched out the basics of what had happened and tried hard to sound more nonchalant than I felt.

When I finished she was shaking her head as if in

puzzlement. "I don't understand why she thought you would be a good fit for her needs."

"Thank you. My sentiments exactly."

"Must have been quite strange and uncomfortable."

"It was. I didn't know what the heck to do."

"And then she got all huffy and pushy on you. Bad tactic on her part. Could you see yourself wearing a collar? You might have ended up leashed under the stairs in her Harry Potter closet."

I laughed, took the teapot off the stove, and filled two mugs. "I don't understand why she thought being menacing would make me give in to her." I set the mugs on the bar and offered Rebecca a basket filled with tea bag packets.

"She totally misjudged you, Sky. Even if you are in the middle of change and transition, I can tell from our short acquaintance that you're not a quitter. From what you said, her mother's death shredded her down to nothing. You're not like that."

I said, "Thanks for the vote of confidence," but I wondered. The first few weeks after I left Britney, I was a blithering mess, so full of pain and anguish. Who knows—maybe if someone like Tamra had come along back in March, I might have made some stupid decisions myself. Still, I'm pretty sure being a submissive to a powerful personality wasn't one of the choices I'd've accepted. I'd submitted far too much to Britney. I didn't intend to ever have a relationship like that again.

Rebecca dunked her teabag, put a little sugar in her tea, and picked up a cookie. "You don't like chocolate chip?"

"Oh, I do. They're my favorite."

"Help yourself. I made a double batch so I could freeze some to eat in coming days."

"Freeze?" I glanced toward the miniature fridge/freezer. "I can't get ice trays in my freezer."

"I've got a small chest unit in the bedroom behind the door. It's about the same size as a washer and fits right next to the window. It's great for leftover soups and stews and goodies like cookies."

"That's a good idea. I should get one." Yeah, right. Instead of homemade, healthy foods, I could just see all the TV dinners and frozen pizzas I'd be stocking up on. And ice cream. With almost no freezer space, I wasn't able to keep anything more than a pint at a time, and sometimes I missed having some variety, but I didn't miss empty calories.

I picked up a cookie, still faintly warm. "Is it my imagination, or did these recently come out of the oven?"

"Yup. To be honest, baking helps me feel less stressed."

"You're stressed about Maya's visit?"

"Oh, yeah."

The cookie was warm and sweet and succulent. I closed my eyes and savored the flavor. I hadn't had an honest-to-goodness homemade chocolate chip cookie in ages. "I pronounce this cookie yummy." I scarfed it down, and then we each ate another one. I counted nine left on the plate and hoped she planned on leaving them. But I wasn't in any hurry for her to go. I asked, "Have you seen Norma lately?"

"I haven't."

"She doesn't come out much."

"She stopped being able to drive a few months back."

"Why?"

"She doesn't talk about it, but she's got a motor neuron disease."

I had no clue what that was and said so.

"It's not too bad yet, but she gets shaky at times, and her hands aren't reliable. She drops things."

I thought about how casually she handled the shotgun and was once again glad it hadn't been loaded. "Maybe we should check in on her—take her a couple of these cookies?" I choked that last part out. I didn't want to give away any of "my" plate of cookies, but it seemed like a polite offer to make.

"That's a great idea. You want to go over now?"

I looked at my watch. "Sure. It's probably not too late." I reached for the plate.

"No," Rebecca said, "you keep those. I've got a huge stash. Let's pop over to my place and get a plate for her."

We went next door, and once inside the front room, Rebecca waved me toward the other room. "Feel free to take a peek at the freezer and how perfectly it fits in the spot."

I went through the adjoining door. A queen-size bed sat at the far end of the room flanked by two bedside tables. An old-fashioned patchwork quilt adorned the bed with a folded-up blanket at the foot. Along the wall was a giant wire closet structure, complete with those foot-square cubes that pull out and can be filled with socks and underwear and stuff like that. Another good idea I ought to put in place.

Maya's bed was unusually small with drawers underneath a wooden platform. I saw an awful lot of Legos strewn about. She hadn't taken Minco, the Indian chief, with her to her grandparents. He reclined on the bed against a pillow. The pillow sham was decorated with Shrek and Fiona in various poses. A red, white, and blue area rug covered the crappy blue and gold shag carpeting.

Behind the door, the freezer did fit perfectly. I lifted up the lid and saw a multitude of sealed plastic containers and cuts of meat.

Rebecca came around the door. "Don't close it quite yet." She put two zipper-lock bags of cookies in, and I shut the lid. "I rounded up some cookies for Norma. Let's go."

WE LOOKED IN THE front window and saw Norma sitting in her customary easy chair, but she had a book in her lap and was asleep. Rebecca and I exchanged glances, and we both shrugged.

"We'll knock quietly," I said. "If she wakes up, great. If not, that's okay."

Rebecca tapped. Quicker than I expected, Norma whipped open the door. "Well, looky here," she said. "What are you two up to?"

Rebecca held out a paper plate. "Cookies for you."

Norma's eyes widened as she accepted the offering. "Raisin? Chocolate?"

"Chocolate chip."

"Mmmm, these are lovely. Thank you. You want to come in?"

"Sure," I said as she opened the door wide.

The walls in her living room were painted pale yellow and covered with framed paintings of seascapes. Two couches faced one another in the center of the room with a coffee table in the middle. Beyond them, in the left corner of the room, a tall stool sat in the corner with a canvas on an easel in front of it. Three other easels leaned against the wall nearby.

"You paint?" I asked.

"I do. Every painting in the room."

Rebecca pointed at a stormy seascape framed in gold hanging over the couch. "So you got that one finished and framed."

Grinning, Norma nodded. "Cost me a pretty penny, but it looks good, doesn't it?"

Two rock formations thrust up out of the churning ocean. Gray clouds swirled above the waves, which smashed into the beach with unchecked fury. I saw ridges and swirls and all kinds of indentations in the paint, particularly in the waves. I said, "That reminds me of Cannon Beach."

"Good eye," Norma said. "I took a photo of Haystack Rock and the Needles and worked from that. Haystack Rock is nifty, but I was drawn to the other sea-stacks that surround it, so I left the big rock out of the painting and focused on the smaller rocks."

"What are you working on now?" Rebecca asked.

"See for yourself."

We sidled around the furniture and stood on either side of the artist's stool to peer at the canvas. Another view of an expanse of the sea, this time with a brightness in the sky that led me to believe it'd be a sunny rendering. The main areas of light and shadow in the lower half of the work were blocked in, but it wasn't easy to figure out exactly how the painting would look when it all came together.

"Norma," I said, "how many layers of paint do you end up doing?"

"Several. It's all about layering and texturing. Sometimes I don't like what it's shaping up to look like, so I use a palette knife to scrape some of it away. That's one of the benefits of working with oil. It takes days—even weeks—to dry, and I can re-work anything I need to."

"I'm impressed. You're majorly talented."

Rebecca said, "She is. I can't believe she can do one of these in just a couple of months."

Norma said, "I used to be able to create one in a month or less, but I've slowed down in my old age."

"Do you sell your work?" I asked.

"Sometimes," Norma said. "I used to go to half a dozen arts and craft shows every year, but lately, my health has kept me from it."

Rebecca shot a warning look at me. I raised an eyebrow to indicate that I knew not to say a word about the health issues unless Norma brought it up and said, "Have you considered putting them up on Craigslist or eBay?"

Norma's face took on a confused expression. "Put them up?"

Rebecca stepped closer and patted my back. "Sky's a computer whiz. I'm sure she knows exactly how to use the Internet to list and advertise products."

Norma said, "Huh, I wonder...I've had a tough time lately because I grew to depend upon the extra income from selling a couple of paintings at every show. I don't think I've sold one since, well, must be since the end of last year."

"I'd be happy to help you," I said. "I could take a digital photo, post it to an online account with details about your painting, and list a price. When people buy the painting, it would have to be shipped, but the customer usually pays for most of that. I could make a website for you, if you want. How many paintings do you have?"

Norma glanced at Rebecca. "How many was it at last count?"

Rebecca said, "You've got three storage units full. Didn't we count about thirty in each?"

She had something like a hundred paintings on hand? Wow. I thought I could make her some dough. "How expensive is one of these paintings? What do you charge?"

"Oh," Norma said, fingers on her chin, "for just the canvas, a hundred to two hundred dollars. More if I paid for framing."

Incredulous, I said, "What? That's all? These look like thousand-dollar creations."

Norma blushed. "Thanks for your vote of confidence."

"Do you do only seascapes?" I came away from the canvas and examined the nearest hanging picture.

Norma gestured at her walls. "These are all my recent paintings. I get on a kick and do a lot of variations on a theme for a while. When I run out of places to hang new ones, I take a few down to storage and make room for the new stuff. Everything up now I've painted in the last year."

Rebecca said, "Didn't you do several barn scenes before the ocean ones?"

"Yes. And mountains before that."

The art was great, textured and colorful, and I loved it. "Have you considered having prints made and selling those?" Norma shrugged. "Or you could easily do greeting cards and get a lot of yardage out of each image. You could sell whole sets of cards with a variety of scenes on them and see some significant income."

Norma looked doubtful. I still wasn't sure how old she was, but I didn't see a computer anywhere in her living room, so she might not be well-versed in how she might use technology to her advantage.

"I could pull some possibilities together for you and show you how to make some money without leaving the comfort of your home."

"Really?" Norma sounded doubtful. "I don't want to put you to any trouble."

"I could do some quick research. Don't worry. It won't be hard to get information."

Norma looked thoughtful but said, "Let's think about it in the new year and not bother with it now. Let me give it some thought."

She changed the subject. "What are you two up to?" She gestured toward the couch nearest the easel. "Make yourselves comfortable." She sat on the other sofa.

Rebecca sat, slipped out of her loafers, and tucked her feet up under her. I joined her on the tuxedo style sofa. From my recent visit to City Liquidators, I recognized the style. Tuxedo sofas have slightly flared arms that are as high as the back with clean, square lines. I like a couch with a lower arm because it's a lot more cozy for lying down to watch TV, but just for sitting, Norma's sofa was fine.

Rebecca gave me a sidelong look, a smirk on her face. "You want to talk about your evening, Sky?"

My face flamed, but I didn't mind giving Norma a shortened version of my crazy date. I left out some of the BDSM details, but it turned out Norma was a lot more with it than I am. She said, "So this gal is part of the leather community?"

"I guess. I don't know much about it."

"I dated a leather gal briefly after Helaine died. I don't know what the hell I was thinking. I met her in a grief support group. Her girlfriend had left her. Didn't take too long for me to figure out why that happened. She was a biker babe and seemed so nice at first. I went to some leather parties with her and met lots of very nice women, but Scottie ended up liking the drink more than the leather. And she was one seriously mean drunk."

Here I was, in my early thirties and living in a more open and enlightened time, and good old Norma had been out and about experiencing a lot more variety than I ever had. I'd had a high school fling my senior year, and I'd dated a couple of women in my mid-twenties, and then I met Britney and that was all she wrote. I never got involved with anyone after we met, and even now, the times spent with Tamra only qualified tangentially as dates. I felt a low level of shame due to my lack of experience and looked at Norma with new respect.

Rebecca said, "I feel like a real novice when it comes to dating, Norma. I dated a little in high school, then met Steve, got pregnant, and that was the end of my dating."

"You're a sweet young thing. You'll find someone new, you just wait and see."

"What an optimistic take on the situation, but I'm okay with being single, especially since Maya's so young."

Norma smoothed the wrinkles from her Orange Dreamsicle-colored sweat suit. "I understand your reluctance, believe me. But,

Skylar,"—she turned her dark eyes on me appraisingly—"it's good that you're getting out and about. Sure, this first date was a disappointment, but as they used to say, you have to kiss a lot of toads before you find your prince. Or princess. Whatever."

She let out a bark of laughter, and I couldn't help but laugh a little myself. I told her about Mitchell's challenge, and Norma said, "What a great idea. You should definitely give that a whirl."

Rebecca said, "And then when you get home from those dates, we can all get together and analyze the details. If you want to, that is, Sky."

"A psychological autopsy," Norma said, cackling like a crazed hen.

"Oh, gross," I said. But the idea of getting a little moral support wasn't unwelcome. "I'll look at profiles and answer one of the twenty-seven emails. There's got to be someone who sounds normal."

"We can always hold that hope," Norma said.

THE CONVERSATION THE NIGHT before with Rebecca and Norma was the reason I was giving the dating thing another try. I wasn't a happy camper as I sat waiting for a woman named Barbara to arrive. I'd specifically asked to meet at a café or coffeehouse, and she'd picked a "java shop" in Southeast off Belmont. Bars do serve coffee, so technically, she wasn't entirely wrong. But this was clearly a pub, not a coffeehouse. I'd never heard of or noticed Dragon The Lion, which wasn't as seedy as some bars around but still, it was a bar, and I was irritated that this Barbara hadn't been honest about it. Had she ever been here before? It sounded like she had, so why wouldn't she know that the major products for sale were booze and beer not coffee and tea? It'd been a few years since smoking had been legal in bars and restaurants, but I could still smell the musty aroma of old cigars and cigarettes along with a fainter scent of rancid cooking oil. Ick.

After twenty minutes, when I was about ready to leave, Barbara showed up. I would never have picked her out of a crowd despite the two pictures she'd posted on her profile. What the hell was it with people putting up pictures at the Personals site from a decade ago that were too small to actually see details?

She apologized for being late, saying she worked at a weight-loss diet center and had been kept late by a chatty client. Barbara was about my height but much plumper. She'd written on her profile page that she'd "passed the age of thirty." No kidding. I was pretty sure she'd never see fifty again.

When she shrugged off her bulky suede coat, underneath she wore a scoop-necked pale green blouse over forest green slacks. Her Ugg boots were the same basic color as the coat, and even her hair seemed to match the tan coat and boots. Her nose was large and red, as though she'd been out in weather at twenty-below, but actually it occurred to me that maybe it was a whisky nose. I knew I was right when she summoned the waiter and ordered a Vodka Seven and offered me one. "It's Happy Hour," she said. "Come on, get happy."

I declined. She frowned, clearly disappointed. "Just have a beer. How about a lite beer, Kyla. Almost no calories. Not a high proof at all."

"It's Skylar."

"Oh, yeah, Skylar. I knew that. Sorry. What do you do for a living?"

Did she not read my profile? I was either a computer whiz or software magnate, depending upon when she'd looked at the Girls-Gaylore site. "I fix computers."

"That sounds hard. And actually, maybe a little boring."

Her bluntness wasn't music to my ears.

The waiter brought her the drink and me a glass of ice water. I took a big swig of H2O and she took a bigger gulp of her vodka. Watching her down a third of the drink like it was Kool-Aid, I steeled myself for the rest of the date. I was already not hopeful.

She'd billed herself as a health care official who loved hiking, camping, and sports. She supposedly liked warm cookies, walks in the rain, and trips to the Oregon coast. She'd encountered many challenges in her life and managed to get through them "with all flags flying." I had no clue what kinds of flags she referred to—a freak flag? In her profile, she sounded like someone who had her shit together. What I found out in person was that in her younger days, this gal was a hard-drinking, hard-smoking, tough-ass butch. Now she was a hard-looking, non-smoking, still hard-drinking woman who looked more worn than my mom did when she died.

"I lost my last partner to smoking," she said.

"I'm sorry to hear that. What happened?"

"She died of lung cancer in May. Really set me back. I stopped smoking myself after she died."

What the hell? *After* she died? She smoked through her

partner's cancer treatment? How bizarre. Or should I say disrespectful? I stifled my reaction and said, "Congratulations on conquering cigarettes."

"Thanks." Her blues eyes were watery and bloodshot. She might not smoke anymore, but she made up for it by drinking. How did she function all day at a diet center?

The waiter came to take our order. I'd specifically requested a coffeeshop meeting because I wanted to buy a hot drink at the counter and be able to cut out if the situation wasn't ideal. Now there was a waiter involved, dammit. I already wanted to leave but didn't quite know how to do it without being rude.

"I'll have a blooming onion," she said. Along with the chili sauce and sour cream that it came with, she asked for a side of ranch dressing and also a dish of mayonnaise. I ordered a tea.

"You sure that's all you want?" Barbara said. "Aren't you hungry?"

"No, thanks. A hot tea will be perfect."

"So you're good with computers?" Before I could answer, she said, "I'm terrible with tech stuff. We have a system at work that isn't easy to deal with. I ought to learn to type. That would sure help." She nattered on about how difficult the work situation was until the waiter arrived with her Heart Attack on a Platter. Her eyes lit up upon seeing the plate. I'm not sure how they create a Blooming Onion, but it was practically as big as my head. Greasy moisture floated up from the food, and I was pretty sure I could smell the diabetes wafting off it. She dug in, cutting away big hunks and dipping them in the four bowls of sauces.

"You want some?" She held up a fork on which she'd stabbed a worm-like clump of onion dipped in bloody-looking chili sauce.

"Thanks, but no thanks." I sipped at my tea, contemplating how I could get the hell out of the bar, preferably within the next seconds.

"It's good to be able to order something healthy."

I wondered what her version of unhealthy was. "Didn't you say you work at a weight-loss center?"

"Yup." She shoveled in a big bite coated in sour cream.

"What do you do there?"

Mouth full, she smacked at the food while saying, "Client assistance and support. I weigh people, help them understand what to eat, and keep the records."

I imagined her in a small doctor's office holding up placards that displayed pictures of blooming onions, deep-fried doughnuts, bacon-wrapped meatloaf, cheesecake with nutty caramel chocolate sauce, fried triple-burgers topped with slices of cheese and guacamole.

Then I imagined her sneaking out the side door to scoot down to some purveyor of the above items and downing them like a starved sailor.

She swallowed a bite and guzzled the rest of her drink, then raised the glass. The waiter hastened over to take it and bring another. "What do you do for fun, Skylar?"

"I like to skydive and parasail."

"Wow." She sounded impressed. "Never done that."

"Scuba diving is also fun."

"I tried that once when I was in Hawaii. Back when Sue was still alive. Too expensive now."

I wanted to say it wasn't nearly as expensive as the quadruple bypass she was heading toward. Instead, I said, "Bungee jumping is a real kick. So are zip-lines." I couldn't stop myself. "Ever do any rock climbing?"

"Actually, my favorite sport is bowling."

I managed not to laugh hysterically. "Bowling?"

"Great strategy involved. Also an element of chance." She mopped up the last of the mayonnaise with one final bit of onion, stuffed it in her mouth, and chewed like she needed to get it down before it escaped. I couldn't believe she'd eaten that entire thing and lapped up every bit of the sauces. There must have been two cups of dressing and mayo and dips and a pound of onion and grease. Did I mention Ick? I almost wished that I was drinking after all.

I took the napkin out of my lap and set it on the table. "Gotta run now."

"What? We've just started to get to know each other."

I knew all I wanted to know. And then some. I held up my watch and made a show of looking at it. "Drop me an email if you like. See you later."

I tossed a five-dollar bill on the table and scrammed out of there as fast as my legs could carry me. A light rain was falling. I didn't bother to pull up my hood. I made a beeline for my car. As I reached it, I glanced back and saw her standing under the overhang in front of the restaurant.

"Hey," she called out. "Wait…"

I didn't obey. Before she could come any closer, I had the key in the ignition, turned the engine over, and peeled away with a heavy weight coming off my chest.

Two down, six to go. Surely the third time would be a charm?

LATER THAT NIGHT, I knocked on Rebecca's door. Through the front window, the twinkle of Christmas lights sparkled against a dark evergreen tree. She opened the door and invited me in.

"Nice tree," I said.

"Thanks. It's a Charlie Brown tree more than anything."

She was right. Maya must have had a hand in the decorating the five-foot-tall artificial tree. The string of lights wound around from the bottom and snaked upward in a disorganized manner, and the few bulbs and ornaments tended toward the middle.

"We decorated it tonight, and I'll even it up a little more later. I think we need to pick up a few more ornaments. How was the date?" she asked, her voice cheery and a little excited.

"Awful."

"Really?"

"You have no idea."

"Tea?"

"I'd rather have some water if you don't mind."

"Camp out on the couch then. I'll grab some for both of us."

"Where's Maya?"

"She crashed a while ago. She's had two days of swim lessons, and it's kicking her butt." She brought over a couple of glasses, set them on the coffee table, and angled herself into the corner of the couch with her slippered feet tucked under her.

I leaned against the other couch arm and faced her. "It's great that you got her into some after-school activities."

"This isn't something the school offered, and it's only for this week. My mother-in-law paid for Maya to have a cycle of lessons at the Northeast Community Center."

"So Steve's parents are cool."

"Mostly. But only with Maya. They coddled Steve way too much. They still tend to make excuses for him, but lately they've seen some pretty mean stuff from him, and they don't want Maya to be hurt. They love her very much. No question about that. I just wish they hadn't spoiled their only son rotten. They certainly didn't spare the discipline to his sisters. I thought Steve would grow up when we married. No such luck."

"Is Maya doing well with swimming?"

"Not at all."

"She isn't? She can't swim?"

"Not yet."

"She hasn't had lessons before?"

"Nope. My kid is seriously afraid of the water."

"Oh." I was surprised by that. Maya had an attitude of toughness that I hadn't noted in many kids. Then again, I didn't know many eight-year-olds. I did remember how I felt at eight, and I don't think I was as brave as Maya seemed to be. "She acts like she'd attack the water with a vengeance."

"You'd think that. There are some things that she shows bravado about, but a lot of the time she tries to hide that she's afraid."

I remembered how scared the kid had been when her father threatened her mom. She was terribly young. She was smart, even precocious, but still only eight.

"Doesn't she have a break from school pretty soon?"

"Starting next Monday. Not sure what I'll do with her. I was hoping to set her up with some play dates with classmates, but no dice. I'll guess I'll have a little ghost flitting around here with me."

"You can't take any time off?"

"If I don't work, I don't get paid."

"I know how that goes."

"That's enough about all that," Rebecca said. "Tell me about your date. Wasn't this the hiker?" I rolled my eyes, and she laughed. "That bad, huh?"

"Oh, yeah." I sketched out the circumstances, and she started giggling.

Through laughter she said, "Surely you're going to at least go bowling with your new girl."

"Yeah, that'd be fun, I'm sure. As far as I'm concerned, I'm not interested in being friends with any woman who thinks drinking unlimited beer is being a light drinker, that bowling is an aerobic sport, and that she's a healthy nonsmoker when she recently quit after forty years of it."

"Amen."

"The scary thing is that she works in a diet center."

"Whoa, that's one place I'd never go for weight loss."

"Lucky you don't need to lose weight."

Rebecca blushed. "Of course I do."

I didn't think that was the case at all. I didn't want to look her over and embarrass her, but Rebecca had a great figure. All I could tell her was, "Hey, you look terrific. You don't need to worry about it."

I sipped water from the glass and wondered why she was embarrassed about her weight. Time to change the subject. "Isn't it shocking how fast Christmas is coming on?"

"Yup. I'm for sure not ready."

"Can you believe the miserable traffic everywhere? I had to hook up a bunch of computers yesterday at an insurance office across the street from Clackamas Town Center, and they were having cars towed from their lot. There must have been thousands of people shopping."

"I take it you love to shop."

"Ugh, not a chance. I suppose you do."

Sweeping one arm out in front of her, she did her best imitation of Vanna White. "As you can see from the amazingly gorgeous décor here in this lovely apartment, I'm clearly a big proponent of shopping." Her face lost the humorous cast, and her forehead wrinkled in worry. "To be honest, I couldn't do much shopping if I wanted to. Money is a real problem now, if you don't mind me talking about such a personal subject. I know you saw Maya's dad at what looked like his worst, but apparently he's not done being an absolute ass. A man showed up at the office earlier today—a collections agent."

"Were they looking for your soon-to-be ex?"

"Not exactly."

"Some guy actually came to see you in person? Usually collectors call and harass you on the phone until you want to send a stink bomb through the phone lines."

"Not in this case. He wanted money to repay debts Steve incurred. Or a check, I should say. He said he couldn't accept cash. It's not like I had either to offer."

"Wait a minute. These are Steve's debts?"

"According to Mister Collections, since we're legally married, Steve's debts are my debts, and he's running around buying stuff like there's no tomorrow."

"Like what?"

"A new car he isn't paying on. Expensive dinners. Tons of stuff on charge cards. The collections people said if I don't make a payment plan, they're going to get a garnishment thing going."

"On your paycheck?" I was incredulous. "They can't do that!"

"This guy seems to think they can. I'm barely making ends

meet now with my crappy paycheck. I guess it's lucky that I do the payroll and pay the bills here at The Miracle Motel. I'm certainly not going to dock my own paycheck." She reached for her water glass, and I saw her hand shake a little.

"Have you talked to your attorney to get the garnishment warning taken care of?"

"Every time I have any contact with my attorney, it costs me at least a hundred dollars. I don't have it. I owe so much for legal fees now that I'll be paying until I'm well into retirement. But now I suppose I'll have to call him."

"I don't know that much about divorce proceedings. When will it be granted?"

She shrugged. "Steve is dragging his feet and contesting everything. It could be weeks—or months. I haven't got a clue."

"I'm so sorry. It sounds awful, Rebecca." I thought about my own financial circumstances. "Sounds like we both managed to get hooked up with irresponsible mates. Like you, I'm still paying off debts that aren't mine either. Totally sucks. What are you going to do about Christmas?"

"I can't do what I did last year."

"Which was?"

"I bought a ton of toys and stocking stuffers at the dollar store. We've shopped so much there since then, though, that there's nothing Maya hasn't seen. The cheap stuff that passed last year won't fly this year."

That gave me an idea, but from everything I'd seen about Rebecca, she was far too intuitive, so I hastened to keep the surge of glee from showing on my face. "I hope your luck turns soon."

"Me, too. And maybe your luck will as well."

"My luck?"

"Sure, with the dating game."

"Oh, yeah. I'm not holding my breath. But I've got a couple dozen more emails to go through. Maybe someone there will be halfway normal." I downed the last of the water, set the glass on the coffee table, and rose. "I better get back to work."

"Work?" she said as she stood. "Isn't it kind of late?"

"Mitchell's feeling better, but he's still not back to the office, so I've been pacing myself and pretty much working off and on all day and evenings, too."

"You are sleeping, right?"

"Yes, but my waking hours are mostly claimed."

I moved toward the door, noting on the way past the tree that there weren't gifts under it, and now I knew why.

Chapter Nine

FOR THE NEXT TEN days, I put my nose to the grindstone and worked hard keeping up with all the work, both at the office and stacked up in my apartment. I did squeeze in Date #3 the previous Friday at a Thai restaurant where I met a dainty, fragile-looking girl who was very active. She did like to hike. She ran. She biked. She spent hours in the gym lifting weights and using the sauna and therefore looked like a desiccated squirrel. Her name was Linda, and she worked for a waste management company, and all she could talk about was her ex-partner who had left her for a man and was now five months pregnant.

Can you spell gloomy? It was Friday the Thirteenth, too, and I couldn't get out of there fast enough.

Now with only seven days left until Christmas, I was feeling proud of myself for getting caught up on the repair backlog.

When I looked at all the parts stacked up on my shelves and in buckets and baskets, I found I had several nearly new CPUs, a video card, a stack of hard drives to pick from, three power supplies, and a DVD drive. Every chance I'd had over the last three days I worked on retrofitting a laptop with a fifteen-inch screen.

I sifted through all my cast-off parts, surprised to find dozens of RAM sticks here, there, and everywhere. I gathered up a couple dozen of them and drove over to Cahill's Computer Cave to trade them in for a new motherboard. Even after that trade-in, I had enough credit that I was also able to pick up a mouse pad with a purple dragon on it, a couple of 4GB flash drives, and an unusually small wireless mouse perfect for a kid's hands. It was bright red and looked like a Ferrari. My favorite purchase, though, was a pair of used speakers sporting the colorful faces of Mickey and Minnie Mouse. I took all the goodies home and assembled the parts, turned on the laptop, and was pleased that it fired right up. I loaded the latest PC operating system, anti-virus protection, a word processing program, and a few game apps that I thought would be fun. After running several tests I was satisfied the unit worked fine.

The kid was going to love it. I was thrilled with the whole setup, and I couldn't wait to give it to her.

But there was one little problem: Rebecca.

Where could I get an elf who would deliver the package? And how could I deliver the gift in such a way that Maya had no clue where it came from, but Rebecca couldn't refuse it?

Someone knocked on my door. I looked at my watch: 9:40. Had to be Rebecca. Who else? I leaped out of my chair, looked around in a slight panic, and saw a dish towel over on the breakfast bar. I grabbed it and laid it over the laptop, then looked around at all the gear spread out on my computer tables. How would Rebecca even notice?

At the door, I took a deep breath and composed my face. I still didn't want Rebecca to ask any questions about my glee level.

I swung open the door, a happy hello on my lips, and froze.

"Sky, hello."

I couldn't get my tongue to work. Britney stood there wearing a long red wool jacket over jeans and dark brown cowboy boots. I remembered the boots. I'd spent almost three hundred dollars on them a few months before the breakup. In fact, if I remembered correctly, I was still paying off that credit card bill.

"What do you want?"

"Sky," she said impishly, "no need to be so cold. I haven't seen you for a while, so I thought I'd drop in. I heard through the grapevine that Mitchell had a heart attack, so I decided to come by."

"It wasn't a full attack, and he's okay."

"Good to know. Aren't you going to invite me in?"

Hell, no, I didn't want her to come in. She was used to fine and fancy things, and I feared she'd mock my shabby little motel apartment. But she was stepping forward, and like the wuss I always was around her, I backed up and she breezed by while I rued the day I'd given her my forwarding address.

"Interesting how they re-did this old motel," she said. "I've gone by here often over the years and had no idea it was apartments. Somehow I've always had visions of 1940's movie stars wandering around here—you know, the women using cigarette holders and wearing furs and the men in evening suits and fedoras." She looked around, appraising the place as though she actually approved.

I felt a stinging pain in my heart. One of the things I'd loved about Britney was her colorful imagination. She was fun to listen to, fun to laugh with. I should have asked questions about why lesbian bed death had occurred. Why had she needed another lover? To this day I feel like a lunkhead. Near the end, even after the long absence of sexual intimacy, I remembered lying in bed with her and talking about wild ideas and plans for the future and things that mattered to me. When I moved out, that was the thing I missed the most.

But imagination wasn't always a good thing. I didn't miss obsessively envisioning Britney in Rita's arms, laughing, talking, whooping it up while I was left to keep up our home, work in the yard, and spend hours and hours alone. The thought of all that loneliness made me feel a little sick to my stomach.

"New couch, huh. Or did it come with the place?"

I didn't trust that she wasn't going to make fun of me, and I already felt at too much a loss to respond. "Why are you here, Britney?"

A couple of emotions crossed her face. I knew her well enough to see irritation, then reluctance. For a moment, she hesitated, then said, "I'm moving, and I've been packing."

"You and Rita find a place?"

Her face turned pink. "Not exactly."

I waited to find out what that meant.

"I'm moving back to Dad's house."

"What? You kidding me?" She and her dad got along like two pit bulls in a dog-fighting ring. I couldn't begin to visualize them living together. "Why?"

"Lost my job at the end of the summer."

"Really. Wow." Britney had worked in the office at an auto parts center for over five years. "What happened there?"

"Downsizing. New management. It wasn't pleasant at the end."

"I'm so sorry, Brit. You loved that job."

"Yeah, I did. Haven't found anything half as good since."

"So you've been job hunting all this time?"

"Yup, and it's miserable." She pressed her lips together and put her hands in her coat pockets.

"I'll bet it is." I was nodding and feeling sympathy...then suddenly felt myself falling over the cliff right into empathy and understanding. I heard a firecracker go off in my head—a warning flare, I guess. I shook myself, literally, and took a deep breath. I couldn't afford to lapse into some kind of rapport with Britney. Not now, not ever. She had a way of charming me right into a basket, and next thing I knew, a passel of snakes would emerge and bite me on the neck while she took off with my money and self-assurance. "Why don't you move in with Rita?"

She glanced away, then looked back and met my eyes, her face ravaged with sadness. She hadn't shown any grief when I left. She hadn't believed me when I said I was done for good. She'd kept saying she knew I'd come to my senses and return.

But I hadn't.

"She left you?" I asked.

Eyes brimming with tears, she nodded.

I wanted my heart to harden. I wanted to grab her by the ear and throw her out of my apartment. A mean-spirited part of me wanted to tell her it served her right, but I couldn't muster up enough energy. I wanted to go to her, hold her, soothe away her worries, but I knew for sure that was a trap. I stood feeling completely torn and vulnerable. All my strength flowed from my hands and out my fingers to collect in a pile at my feet.

I was saved by the bell. Or, rather, tapping.

I snapped back to my senses, hastened to the front door, and pulled it open. Rebecca stood there, shivering, a box of tea bags in one hand and a plate of cookies in the other. "I should've worn my coat. Brrrr...it's cold out here." She opened her mouth to say something further then must have seen Britney behind me. "Oh, I'm sorry. I didn't know you had company." She gave me a meaningful look.

I hastened to say, "No, no, not company." Doorknob in hand, I moved back and gazed at Britney. "Was there anything else you wanted to tell me?"

In an irritated voice, she said, "Guess not. Except I have three boxes of your junk in the truck. I wanted to deliver all the stuff I found while I was packing."

I said, "Let me grab a coat, and I'll come down and cart things up."

"Three boxes?" Rebecca asked. "I'll get my jacket, too, and I can help carry one up."

By the time Rebecca came back, Britney was already halfway down the stairs on the way to the car. Rebecca shot me a quizzical look. "Later," I mouthed.

The spell I'd been captivated by a couple minutes earlier totally exploded the moment I realized that Britney continued to drive the truck I'd paid for. The sympathetic feelings were replaced with bitterness. She used the keyless opener to unlock the Toyota Tundra while she was still thirty feet away, stamped her way over to the truck, opened the extra-cab door, and stood aside, obviously not willing to help. I saw the expression on her face. She was royally pissed. I didn't understand why.

Rebecca gestured toward the back seat. "We take all these cartons?"

Britney nodded.

Rebecca grabbed the first box and dragged it out. Must have been heavy, but she lugged it off with energy.

I said, "None of this looks like camping equipment."

"I haven't gotten to the garage yet. You could get off your butt and pick the stuff up yourself, you know."

"All right. I'll get to that as soon as I have time." The other two boxes weren't as big. I leaned in to pull one toward me, but before I could pick it up, Britney moved closer. "You screwing her?"

"Who? You mean Rebecca?"

"No. The Queen of England—who do you think?"

"It's none of your business." I didn't have any intention of giving her even the tiniest bit of information.

She paused. "I never understood why you left, Sky. We had a good thing going."

"We did?"

"Of course," she said.

"But you went and ruined it."

She let out an angry breath. "You're the one who left the ruins. The house is going to be repo'd, and I'll probably have to sell this truck."

"You lost the house?"

"Not yet, but by early January. So you better get your shit from the garage sometime early in the new year before the bank shows up and locks me out."

She was losing the house? How the hell had she done that in less than a year? We hadn't accumulated a lot of equity, and the housing market was in the toilet, but still—she ought to have been able to keep up the payments.

I was too stunned to say another word. I stood there like a statue, feeling stupid and sick to my stomach.

"Yeah, right," she said. "Go ahead and judge me like you always have. You're more organized. You're the smart one. You make all the wise decisions while I'm a dummy."

"That's not true. I've never said that."

"Just take your stuff and leave me alone." She grabbed the steering wheel, pulled herself up and into the cab, and started the truck.

I hastened to get both boxes out and set them on the curb. As soon as I slammed the extra-cab's door, she gunned the engine. Without closing the driver's door, she hit the gas and squealed off. The door shut on its own.

I watched the truck speed away, getting smaller. The rear taillights lit up. The truck turned at the stop sign, and she was gone.

I stood next to the boxes feeling a terrible sense of loss coupled with a fatigue that made me bone-weary.

A warm hand grasped my wrist. "You okay?"

It took a second for me to focus. Rebecca stood peering at me, a concerned expression on her face.

I brushed hair out of my eyes. "I think so."

"She's the ex?"

"Uh-huh."

She bent and picked up the bigger of the boxes.

"Wait, I'll get that," I said.

"Don't worry. I've got it."

I picked up the other carton and followed Rebecca up the long set of stairs, each step sucking more of the life out of me.

We stacked the three boxes near the front door, and Rebecca looked at me sympathetically, then guided me over to my sofa. "We could both use a little hot tea, don't you think?"

"Oh, yeah." She headed to my kitchenette while I sank down onto the blue monstrosity, shivering. My apartment felt like an icebox, but it had to be emotional because I had the heat set for seventy degrees.

"I see you've got both decaf or caffeinated. Which do you prefer?" Rebecca asked.

"Fully leaded."

I took a deep breath and tried to do an assessment of my emotions. How much time had passed during Britney's visit—ten, twelve minutes? Not long, so why was I so wiped out?

Rebecca came over and sat next to me on the loveseat. "You doing all right?"

"To be honest, no. I'm embarrassed that I feel like this much of a wreck."

"You sound overwhelmed."

"Exactly."

"Is this the first time you've seen her since the breakup?"

"No, but it's been a few months now. I didn't expect her to show up."

The tea kettle whistled weakly. Rebecca rose and went to the stove to take it off the burner before it started shrieking. She brought me a hot mug. I cradled it in my hands, relishing the warmth. "Thank you. This is great."

Juggling her own tea, Rebecca sat on the loveseat and settled back, not looking at me. I was thankful for that. It was a comfort to have her with me, but I also felt sheepish. "You must think this is all a lot of drama."

"You think I'd judge you? Weren't you the one sticking up for me when Steve came by and had the full-on violent meltdown?"

I had to smile at that. At least Britney hadn't threatened anyone or poked her finger into my chest.

Rebecca and I talked for a long while, and eventually my stomach settled and I enjoyed three of the ginger cookies that she'd brought over. When she left a little while later, she gave me a nice squishy hug, and though I didn't feel back to normal, at least I was warm.

Chapter Ten

I RAN A LITTLE late for the next date, entering Elmer's Pancake House parking lot in a heavy rain on the Saturday before Christmas. Shortly after noon I hustled for the front door, water in my face and eyes. In the foyer, someone rose and said, "Skylar. I'd know you in an instant from your photo."

The elderly woman looked fuzzy and rippled. I swiped my sleeve across my brow to wipe my eyes. When my vision was clear, I still saw the same ripples in her face, which I realized were deep wrinkles. Oh, wow, I thought, my date sent her mother. I moved closer and sort of recognized Mary from her online photo, but the picture I'd seen must have been over twenty years old. Fooled again.

Suppressing a sigh, I followed her and the hostess into the dining area. Mary slid into a booth, and I took the opportunity to survey her physique. Plump was an understatement. If you looked up the word "cankles" in the dictionary, you'd find a photo of Mary's swollen ankles next to it. She reminded me of an elderly Cabbage Patch doll dressed in a pale blue button-up dress and white tennis shoes. I reflected on my prejudices. I ought to be more compassionate. It wasn't a sin to be heavy...but what *was* a sin was being a big liar online.

Was I wrong that I wanted one—just one!—of these Gaylore Girls to tell the truth about their physical condition and ability to be active? In my lifetime, I'd met plenty of stout or stocky or heavyset women who could still kick my butt on the Larch Mountain Hike or getting to Devil's Peak from Cool Creek, but Mary wasn't going to be one of them.

She ordered the special: Two eggs, toast, three slices of bacon, two sausages, and a stack of pancakes. To balance it all out, she asked for a diet coke.

Oh, boy. I wondered if it would be possible to hook her up with that woman from the diet center.

After a lot of small talk I determined that Mary was a nice enough woman, though seriously ethically challenged. She worked in the office at a nearby church assisting the minister. To get the job she said she'd studied up on various religions and told everyone she was a Presbyterian when, in fact, she was raised Catholic. "Steady jobs are so scarce," she said, laughing. "As far as I'm concerned, all these mainstream Christian sects are one and the same. I don't even believe in God."

We talked for close to an hour. Most of the conversation was made easier because of her knowledge of computers and technology. She was definitely a smart cookie. I thought perhaps she could be good friend material, but then she disputed the bill. She proceeded to totally ream the waitress, reducing the poor girl nearly to tears, then left a miserly tip for her part which I had to surreptitiously make up for.

Mary gave me her phone number, but I had no intention of calling her. She wasn't the kind of person I needed in my life. If she could be that rude to a perfectly sweet stranger, how would she be with people she knew? Besides, I wasn't in a place where I needed any new friends who might soon collapse from a stroke or heart attack.

I felt a sense of satisfaction that I was halfway to my goal. Four dates down, four to go, and then I'd meet Mitchell's challenge. When I hit the mark, I was going to gladly run screaming from the Girls Gaylore website. Or write a book, *Eight Dates and How They All Fizzled*. Or maybe I could join a monastery or convent or something like that. Did they have computers at the nunnery?

I drove from Elmer's to Mitchell's house and found him in a foul mood. He scowled as he opened the front door, and though he stood aside to let me in, I didn't think he wanted a visitor. He wore stretched-out gray sweat bottoms, a black long-sleeved sweatshirt, and mules on his feet.

"What's happening with you?" I asked.

"I'm sick and tired of being sick and tired. I want off these meds because I'm pretty sure that's what's making me feel like shit."

He looked pretty bad, too. His blond hair had grown out a bit and hung limp and greasy. His face was pale, and he'd clearly lost weight. I slipped out of my coat. He took it and tossed it over a wingback chair before making his way to an easy chair by the fire.

Mitchell's living room had been stripped of all the Thanksgiving décor, and nobody had put up any Christmas decorations. Very unusual. The room was dim and dusty, totally different from what was acceptable to the neat-freak and holiday hound I knew and loved.

"What does your doctor say?"

He shook his head slowly. "He wants me to sit around on my ass. Resting. Indefinitely. Last thing on the planet that I want to do."

"What *have* you been doing?"

"A big fat nothing. Reading. Sleeping. Zoning out in front of the TV. On the bright side, I finally had the chance to watch all five seasons of *Queer as Folk*. Yay, thumpa-thumpa."

I'd never watched *Queer as Folk,* so I had no idea what thumpa-thumpa meant, and I wasn't about to ask. Instead, I wanted to deal with business matters. "If you're bored, do you want me to bring you some of the recent paperwork to reconcile here at home at your leisure?"

"I'm way ahead of you. Philippe and I took a drive yesterday, and I stopped by the office to pick up everything."

"Well, aren't you sneaky."

"I feel like a big loser. You're doing all the work, and I'm sitting on my ass waiting for the damn doctor."

"When's your next appointment?"

"Monday. I'm telling you, though—if he doesn't clear me to get back to a normal life, the hell with him. There's no reason why I can't sit around at the office and get you back to your regular routine."

"I'm doing okay, Mitchell. Really." A big fat lie, but I didn't want to stress him. I could manage for quite a while without him and without a Life. I hadn't had a Life for months on end anyway—who needed one now?

"It's not okay with me," he said. "I need to make this all up to you. You've been carrying the business. You deserve a gargantuan chunk of the end-of-year profits. God knows we wouldn't have any revenues at all if it weren't for you working your ass off. I realize now that we may have made a big mistake in not taking out insurance against this kind of thing occurring. I'm sorry, Sky, but I never ever thought anything would happen to me."

We'd had the option of buying a few different kinds of disability insurance, but it was incredibly expensive, so we'd only purchased life insurance with accidental death and disability provisions. Mitchell's heart attack didn't fall into that category of "disability," even if it was an "accident" that he apparently had some congenital issues with his arteries.

I said, "The way I figure it, the amount of money we'd have spent on the insurance is way higher than any extra funds I might be due for my extra time hours. We're talking several thousand dollars higher, you know?"

"I guess that's true, but still, you deserve some compensation. I've been doing some figuring, and we're definitely well into the black this year."

"We are?"

"Hell, yeah. Look how much work you've done lately."

I'd definitely had quite a heavy load, that was for sure. But I hadn't kept track of the revenues all that work represented. I didn't consider myself much of a business mind, which was why Mitchell and I made a good team. He kept track of the details.

"Don't worry about it." I said. "We'll work it all out in the new year. Just don't stress."

"I know, I know. But I *will* make it up to you. In the meantime, I'm going to start coming in to the office every morning. I can't in good conscience do any of the upcoming installs until the doc clears me, but I do want to field the phone calls and accept drop-offs. That'll give you back your weekends."

"Are you sure that's a good idea?"

"It can't be any more stressful than sitting around the house. I cannot possibly stand it one minute longer." He ran his hand through his hair. "I need a salon appointment. And my nails need buffing. I'm a mess. I'm lucky Philippe hasn't dumped me."

"How is good ol' Philippe?"

"He's well. He's been a super trouper throughout this whole mess. He's a little younger than me, you know, so I'm lucky he's been so understanding."

Philippe wasn't just a "little younger." Mitchell was at least fifteen years his senior.

"You said something about installs?"

"Yes, the first day after Christmas." I must have had a dumb look on my face because he went on. "The Kelton Kandy Kompany?"

Of course I'd heard of Kelton Kandy. I'd eaten plenty of the Kelton products and loved their chocolates, peppermints, and caramel treats. But that was the extent of my knowledge.

Mitchell said, "We're outfitting the candy company's entire front office and also their supervisory offices back in the factory area. Surely you remember that?"

Surely I should, but surely I didn't.

"Sky! We talked about this weeks ago."

I had a vague memory—very vague. "Why in the hell would we do this on the freakin' day after Christmas?"

"Because that's when they give most of their staff annual leave, and we'll have run of the building without a bunch of front line workers in our way."

"I haven't seen any deliveries."

"The hardware was delivered to Kelton last week. We'll get software and other odds and ends by Monday. So you see, I do need to go into the office now and in the new year. No doubt about it. I hope I'm able to come with you to Kelton to handle the details."

"We'll see. I'm sure we can make it work." I was concerned he'd push himself too hard, but if things went wrong or I simply needed help, I did know some guys through Cahill's Computer Cave who could give me a hand. Too bad I wasn't out of overtime hell quite yet, but once this latest pile of repairs was done, I had a hunch we'd have some dead time—at least that's how it'd been historically.

Mitchell sat frowning near the fire. He made a dramatic gesture with his arm as though he was an orchestra conductor. One hand in the air, he said, "I'm not happy about this either."

"Stop worrying, man."

"I'm not talking about the job. I'm referring to this hellhole."

I looked around the room. "Then I think your main goal right now should be getting this living room into shape."

"I'd like that—if I had more energy."

"Why don't I go up in your attic and get the holiday boxes so you can direct me in setting up your decorations and trees."

Yes, plural trees. He usually put them up in the living room, the TV area, and the dining room. He had more boxes of holiday crap than I'd ever seen in my life.

He brightened at my suggestion, though he said, "You don't have to do that."

"Look, pal, I can't face another computer repair, and I'd like to do something fun."

"You may not be aware, but I'm rather picky."

Ha. I managed to keep a straight face.

He said, "I can't guarantee how much fun it'll be."

"Let's just do it, okay?"

He rose with more energy than I'd seen so far, so I figured it wouldn't be too bad.

FIVE HOURS LATER, BLEARY-EYED but well-fed, I drove away from Mitchell's house, satisfied that I'd managed to do something compassionate for my fellow man. Never mind all the nitpicking he'd done while I performed all the Santa Elf hard labor. His house was decorated, though, and all was right in his world.

Note To Self: One gay decorator and one lesbian decorator does not equal two decorators. Clearly I needed some major lessons in *feng shui* and interior design. I was lucky I got out of there without tinsel up my butt and ornaments hanging off my nose.

Back at The Miracle Motel, I passed an apartment on the lower floor. The door opened, and a scruffy-looking dude dressed in jeans and a hideous yellow sweater poked his head out. He looked like Shaggy from *Scooby Doo*.

"Who are you?" he asked.

"I live upstairs."

"Oh." He retracted his head and smacked the door shut, and that's when I smelled the faint odor of marijuana. Good times.

I hadn't stepped more than ten more feet when another door opened, this one across the courtyard. A chubby middle-aged guy stood backlit by dim light, one hand on the doorknob, the other holding a bottle of beer. He raised the bottle. "Cheers, dude."

"Uh, yeah. Happy Holidays."

"Got any good hooch?" His eyes were bloodshot, and he looked like he'd been drinking for a few days.

"Nope."

"I'm hoping for some good liquor later, so stop by if you hear the party revving up."

"Oh, great. Thanks."

He swayed and smiled, then stepped back awkwardly and let the door close but not before I caught sight of a whole lot of dark furniture behind him. A big brown couch and chair, a bunch of tables and ladderback chairs, a standing mirror, and more. I wondered if he'd crammed an entire household of stuff into the small apartment and shuddered to think of what the bedroom must look like. Not something I was curious enough about to show up for his holiday party, though.

I passed by and headed for the stairs. Just what I needed—some guys on the first floor whooping it up later tonight. I hoped they smoked or drank themselves into a stupor and chilled out in a big way instead.

Don't let anyone tell you that "Three's a Charm." That's bullshit.

The third guy I caught sight of when I got up to the walkway was Maya's utterly charm-free father. By the time I recognized him, he'd seen me, so I didn't feel like I could sneak back down the stairs and wait for him to leave. I dragged myself forward while something inside my chest felt tight.

"Oh, you," he said. "Good. You need to tell me where they are." Today he wore khakis and a polo shirt under an unzipped heavy-duty ski jacket.

"I can't help you."

"Can't or won't?"

"I've been gone all day. I have no idea where they are."

"I don't believe you."

"You're kidding, right? How would I know? Maybe they're out Christmas shopping. Or getting groceries." Maybe Rebecca was out looking for a new place so she could hide from this ass-wipe.

He reached inside his jacket and pulled out a piece of paper, which he thrust at me. I tried to ignore it as I unlocked my door.

"You need to take this," he said.

"No, thanks." I tried to squeeze into my apartment without opening the door much, but he came at me.

"This is a subpoena. You better pay attention."

He shoved it up against my chest, so I took it. Reluctantly. "I don't have anything to say. I'm serious. I can't help you."

"You will testify about all the ways she neglects my daughter. Doesn't feed her properly. Leaves her alone. No kid of mine is gonna be a latchkey kid."

I wanted to mention that perhaps if he paid some child support Rebecca could afford to sign the kid up for afterschool daycare and other activities, but I figured it'd make things worse for Rebecca. Instead, I said, "Do you think I just sit around all day watching my neighbor's comings and goings? I have a job, pal. I'm busy. I don't know what you think I'll testify to, but I haven't got anything to say that'll help your case."

He sneered and brought that index finger up again. "You bitches all stick up for each other."

I hated guys—and gals—who felt the need to use their fingers to poke and stab at others. Why hadn't anyone ever taught this man any manners? "I'm merely informing you that I'm not a witness or whatever you want me to be. Got to go."

I ducked into the apartment, whipped the door shut, and leaned back as my heart beat fast. I hoped Rebecca came home soon because she ought to know that Stupid Steve had been hanging around her front door.

I unfolded the crumpled paper. The heading read CIVIL SUBPOENA DUCES TECUM, and at the bottom where the judge was supposed to sign, someone had inked in *Judge Judy Sheindlin*.

Judge Judy? Seriously?

Using a black marker, someone had written in a case number and "Talarico v. Talarico." I almost laughed out loud when I read the text. "*IN THE NAME OF THE STATE OF OREGON: You are commanded to produce certified copies of the documents listed on annexed Addendum....*"

I turned the paper over. No addendum. Nothing "annexed," whatever that meant. And what the hell kind of certified copies of documents would I be providing anyway? I didn't have a single piece of paper about Maya or her mom.

The guy got this template somewhere on the Internet and was using it to intimidate people. What a piece of work. I hoped Rebecca wouldn't fall for the ploy. I wanted to throw the paper away, but I figured I ought to keep it just in case it became evidence of Steve's fraud. Because that's what sort of nonsense this was.

I went to the window, moved the curtain aside with one finger, and scanned the walkway for Steve, but he wasn't there anymore. Thank God. I hoped he'd left for good.

LATER THAT NIGHT REBECCA knocked on the door. "Can you pop over for a few minutes?" she asked as she leaned around her door frame into mine.

I wasn't doing anything but binge-watching the first season of *Orange is the New Black,* so I followed her into her apartment. The Christmas tree lights were not on, but even in the low light I could see a couple of new presents wrapped—badly—under the tree. Maya's work, no doubt.

"Maya already asleep?" I asked as I seated myself on her couch.

"I sure hope so. We've still got four days until Christmas, and she's been so wound up."

I remembered being a small kid and how full of expectation and excitement I'd been. I could only guess how crazed Maya must be. "Will she spend any time with her father?"

Rebecca went to the kitchenette and put the tea kettle on the stove. "I wish she wasn't, but of course she has to see her dad."

"Did Steve reach you earlier tonight?"

"He left half a dozen messages. I tried to call him back twice, but he didn't answer."

I told her about my encounter with him and described the fake subpoena. She closed her eyes and gripped the edge of the counter as she shook her head.

I said, "Do I take this subpoena seriously or what?"

"I wouldn't, not if he thinks we're going to LA to appear before Judge Judy to settle our differences."

I couldn't suppress the laughter. "What did you say he does for a living?"

"As little as possible. He's a bookkeeper at a taxi cab company. What's wrong with him? He didn't used to be this way."

"When did he change?"

"Good question. I don't know. Once Maya was a toddler, I guess."

By my calculation, that meant six or seven years. The honeymoon sure didn't last long.

"I never should have married him." She sighed and poured water into mugs. "I was young, and there was so much pressure not to have a kid out of wedlock. You'd think in this day and age, that kind of Victorian attitude wouldn't have affected me, but it did." She scooped up the mugs, brought mine over to me, and got comfortable at the other end of the couch.

I was growing to hate Steve Talarico and didn't want to talk about him anymore. If I were Rebecca, the thought of having to deal with him for the rest of my kid's childhood—and probably beyond—would make me feel homicidal. I didn't know how she could stand it. I'd be tempted to get some black market identity papers and go off into my own little witness protection program. Rebecca was clearly a better person than me.

I changed the subject. "I had another funny date today."

"An online matchup?"

"Yeah. Not the nicest person, though she was smart." I told her about meeting Mary, and she was as appalled about the woman's treatment of the waitress as I had been.

She said, "I hate it when people are mean to servers and cooks. I worked in a diner during high school. Between the rude jerks and the men who thought it was their right to pat me on the ass any time they wanted, I had enough of that. After my junior year I found a job working in an insurance office doing typing and filing, and I kept the job during my senior year. They let me work on the weekends and any days that we had off school. Much better situation, though I did miss the tips."

"I worked in fast food. No tips, but no butt-patting either."

"Where?"

"McDonald's one summer. Burger King the other. I knew pretty quick that wasn't going to be my chosen field. You work there long enough, you start feeling like you're breathing in airborne oil. Even after a shower I could smell the grease."

"Oh, yes, Eau de Fatty Slime."

"Exactly. I'm thankful every day that the worst odor I'm ever stuck with from computers is a little burnt dust. Give me technology any day."

"How's your business partner getting along?"

"He coming back to work this week."

"Isn't that awfully soon?"

"Yeah, he'll probably be fine. It doesn't have to be too stressful for him. Usually this time of year everything tails off to next to nothing, then the day after the new year begins, all hell breaks loose."

"So you may get some relief from the load you've been carrying?"

"It's already been happening. I think I'll only have one repair to work on."

Rebecca nodded, her expression serious. She pinned her dark eyes on me and hesitated. She seemed to want to tell me something, but the way she bit her lip and agonized, I wondered what it could be.

I blew on the tea and took a tentative sip. Minty lemon. She hadn't asked what I wanted to drink but apparently remembered what I liked. "What's on your mind?" I asked.

"I'm debating about whether I should bring this up or not."

"What?"

"Well...it's my problem...though it's possible you could help. But I want you to say no if it wouldn't work. Promise me you will."

"Okay."

"Maya's off school the next two weeks, and I work every day."

"Even Christmas?"

"I agreed with Pete that I'd stay here on call Christmas Day. Probably nothing much will happen, but I'm on duty, though I am allowed to spend the time here in the apartment. Maya will stay at her dad's parents' house from the day after Christmas until Sunday, but Monday and Tuesday are a problem because I need to hang out in the office."

"What about New Year's?"

"I'm on call during the Eve but I'm off for the actual holiday. I'll take Maya to her grandparents on New Year's Day and get her back on Sunday. Once I drop her off New Year's Day, I'm driving down to Roseburg to visit with my brother and his wife for a few days. The kids don't go back to school until Monday, the sixth, and Pete's going to cover the complex for a few days."

"Nice break for the kids anyway."

"It's one thing to have Maya hanging around in the office for a couple of hours after school, but day in and day out will be tough before Christmas and New Year's."

"So what're you going to do?"

She got that uncomfortable expression on her face again. "If I leave her in the apartment and Steve shows up, he'll throw a fit and probably use it against me in this spurious custody thing he's threatening. I'm wondering if maybe you would have a snack with her and check on her a couple of times a day. I'll make some treats, and your time commitment doesn't need to be very long so that your day isn't interrupted too badly."

"I can do better than that, Rebecca. Why don't you bring her over to my place Monday and Tuesday, and she can watch TV and surf the Internet here. That's all she'd be doing at home, right?"

"I can't expect that from you. I know you have work to do."

"Like I said, it's a lot slower now. I've got time to chill out, and I don't have a job out in the field again until the day after Christmas."

"I can pay you a little."

I waved that off. "Forget it. It's not a big deal."

"Sky, I can't help but feel rotten for asking this. I also feel so grateful for your willingness to help. I don't know where else to turn. I'll make it up to you."

The kid in question chose that moment to make an appearance. She stood in the bedroom doorway, squint-eyed and one hand rubbing her nose. "Mommy?"

Rebecca said, "You have a bad dream?"

Maya trudged over and settled on the middle of the sofa between us. Her pajamas were covered with goofy-looking yellow Minions from the *Despicable Me* movie. She said, "I keep hearing noises."

Rebecca rose and hastened over to the doorway. "I'm

not—oh." She disappeared into the bedroom.

Maya looked up at me. "Santa comes in three days."

"Not such good math. We have the rest of today and Sunday, Monday, and Tuesday to get through before Wednesdsay when Santa will have arrived. It's close to four days."

"Nuh-uh. Today is over."

"It's still Saturday."

"Not very much." She leaned to the side and snuggled up next to me with her head on my thigh.

Rebecca came back into the living room. "She's right. The downstairs neighbors are banging around. Not sure what they're doing, but I can see how it would wake Maya up."

I said, "She's not awake anymore." The kid was exhaling slowly and making little wheezing sounds.

"You can scoot her down the couch if she's in your way."

"She's okay." I set my mug on the side table and cautiously put a hand on the kid's back. I've never been an overly maternal person, but I felt a wave of tenderness for Maya. The apartment temperature was cool, but she felt surprisingly warm.

Rebecca sat on the sofa again. "If those dolts below get too rowdy, I'll go talk to them."

Was it Scooby Doo whose apartment was below my apartment? I thought maybe so. "Is that guy usually noisy? I haven't heard him before."

"He's new. Just moved in on the fifteenth, so who knows how loud he'll be. He's a salesman at that used car lot down by the freeway entrance."

"He's a bit of a stoner."

"As long as he keeps that inside, I don't care. I had the warning conversation with him that I have with all new tenants."

"Guess we'll wait and see."

"Have you talked to Norma lately?"

"I picked up some groceries for her a couple days ago."

"That was nice of you, Sky."

"She offered to pay me a ridiculous amount of money to get her some coffee and eggs and odds and ends. I told her she was crazy. She keeps an eye on things around here, and that's plenty enough for me. We're less likely to get burgled with her watching out the window."

"Especially with the shotgun." Rebecca smiled. "Pete ought to give her a cut in the rent for acting as security."

"No kidding."

"I'm not hearing any major noises now. Let's put Maya back in bed."

I felt reluctant to do that. There was something sweet about the little squirt cozying up with me, but she'd probably sleep better and stay warmer in her own bed. I slid out from under and hauled her up. She was lighter than I expected, considering I was lifting dead weight. And she was definitely dead to the world. Maya didn't stir as I followed Rebecca into the dimly lit room and lowered her into her bed. I backed up so Rebecca could cover her up and kiss her forehead.

I was struck for a moment by the memory of my own mother carrying me to my bed. I must have been about six or so, still in kindergarten. I was wrapped in a warm blanket, and she put me into snug, comfortable covers, kissed me on the forehead, and whispered she loved me. At the unexpected memory, my heart filled up, and for a brief moment, my eyes went all teary. I took a deep breath and composed myself before Rebecca noticed.

Back in the living room Rebecca said, "Thanks. Now even if they're noisy downstairs, she probably won't wake. She's always been a pretty good sleeper."

"I better go."

"Oh, no. Stay for a while. We can have a refill on our tea."

"Okay."

She snagged the mugs on the way by the couch, and I said, "I forgot—I wanted to talk to you about something anyway." I followed her to the kitchenette and sat on the other side of the bar on a stool while she filled the tea kettle. "You've noticed all the computer gear I have on the shelves in my front room, right?"

"Uh-huh." She ducked her head into the fridge and pulled out a couple of items.

"With all the repairs I do, I end up with tons of used parts. Actually, many of them are nearly new so they're still in great shape. I could probably build eight or ten computers—gee, I don't know, maybe twelve or fifteen—with all the parts I have."

Rebecca got out a cutting board and a knife. "Okay."

"I pulled together a bunch of those old cast-off parts and assembled a laptop for Maya for Christmas."

She stopped slicing and gazed at me, her face full of surprise. "Why? You're already letting her use that Netbook. And your Internet connection."

"The Netbook is limited. It's got very little memory, and it's slow."

"But she doesn't care. She's a kid."

"I know."

Rebecca didn't sound very happy about what I'd done, and I felt at a loss. "But she's smart. And curious, and right now is the time when she's open to learning and getting accustomed to how technology works in our lives. In ten years she'll be going to college, and the more resourceful she is, the better she'll do."

Rebecca stopped slicing and trained her eyes on the counter. She gripped the knife so tightly that I saw her fingers go white. When she raised her head and met my gaze, she was crying.

Stunned, I sat on the stool, not knowing what to say. I didn't understand what was wrong. The kettle started to hum. Before it shrieked, she turned, whipped it off the burner, and set it nearby on a metal trivet. She took a plate from the cupboard and put it on the breakfast bar in front of me. With deft hands, she arranged squares of cheddar cheese and some whiter cheese in a circle around the edge of the plate, then opened a box and poured crackers in the center ring.

"Have I offended you?" I asked.

Her back to me, she poured water in our mugs. When she turned around, her face was clear and any tears that might have fallen were gone. "Take your cup and the plate, will you?" She grabbed some napkins and her own mug, and I hastened to follow her back to the couch. We both got settled, and I awaited her response.

"You haven't offended me, Sky. I'm just so torn. And sad. And a little overwhelmed. I have to be honest and say it doesn't feel right to accept such a huge gift for my daughter. Then again, most of what I'm getting her for Christmas will be things she needs for school. Clothes. A new coat. Some boots and school supplies. I don't have the funds to afford many of the toys and exciting playthings she has on her Christmas list."

"I hope her dad comes through for her."

"Even if he does, that doesn't make me feel any better. He's got all the money in the world to beguile Maya with, and mean old mom has to buy her stuff she needs."

She sounded so bitter and defeated. I felt terrible for inciting those emotions. I didn't know what to do to make anything better. Whatever I said was likely to make it worse, so I kept my mouth shut.

Rebecca picked up two crackers and slid a slice of cheese between, then sat back and took a bite of the sandwich she'd made.

"What if I handed over the computer and *you* gave it to Maya?"

"Oh, no, that wouldn't be right."

"Wait a minute. Why not? I know you said money's tight, but what if you paid me for the parts that were worth anything?"

"I could never afford that, Sky."

"Um, I think you could." I smiled. "A couple of times a year, I go through and weed out the parts that I'm unlikely to need. We give them away to a recycle place or I get a flat fee from Cahill's Computer Cave to take them off our hands. I get fifteen or twenty bucks for a whole box of stuff, and trust me, I hardly used a whole box to put together Maya's unit. Fifteen dollars would be more than enough from you."

"But your labor. You must have spent hours."

I laughed. "It was fun to put it together and made me happy. It was kind of like a puzzle, too, and I enjoyed the challenge. It didn't take all that much time."

She looked doubtful, but I could see I was swaying her. "How about you give me fifteen bucks and make me some cookies or brownies. I like sweets, and I never make any holiday stuff. Your labor in the kitchen would cancel out my labor."

"Thirty bucks—and I'll make you cookies, brownies, and whatever kind of pie you want. And a cake, too."

"Unless you want me to weigh three hundred pounds by the new year, I'd be happy without the cake and pie."

"But the others?"

I stretched out a hand. "Deal."

She squeezed my hand and held it a couple of extra seconds. "Thank you. My child is lucky to have you for a next door neighbor. So am I," she said shyly. "Where do you go Christmas morning?"

"Nowhere. I've got a present to take to Mitchell that night. I'll go there for dinner."

"Do you want to come over here for breakfast and watch Maya open her gifts?"

"Sure. But you'll have to let me see her Christmas list because I'll still want to get her a little something."

"Her list is about ten pages long. I'm sure you'll find

something that'll do. Don't spend a lot, though. Please?"

I could only nod and grin. I helped myself to some cheese and crackers. The white cheese was Havarti. My favorite.

Chapter Eleven

MONDAY MORNING, ON THE heels of receiving the delivery of only one computer, the mail carrier knocked on the door. Not one but three packages. Yippee. I quickly discovered that one was for the guy in apartment 202 and handed it back, but the other two were for me. My Aunt Peggy, my mom's sister, sent me a flat present wrapped in cheerful Santa bear paper and a holiday card. I opened the card and read her kind words but decided to save opening the gift for Christmas morning.

The other item was from my father—or, more accurately, from his wife, Ingrid. Every year she sent me a blouse or a turtleneck or sweater. She had good taste in clothes and made her purchases from stores like Macy's and Nordstrom, but I was just a little too butch for cashmere or scalloped necklines.

Ingrid always included a gift receipt, and every year I returned the item and bought something else. Last year I remembered I'd gotten three flannel shirts in the exchange. In fact, I looked at the shirt I was wearing and chuckled when I realized I had one of them on.

I opened the cardboard box and pulled out the present. The gift label was addressed *To Skylar with love from Dad, Ingrid, Connor & William*. She had beautiful handwriting. She seemed like a nice person. But she wasn't my mother, and the gift wasn't really from my father at all. What had he done to facilitate the purchase and delivery of the present? Did he even know what she'd gotten and sent? He knew I was a lesbian and not particularly femmy. Why didn't he ever suggest a different style of clothing or some other outdoorsy item? He should know that much about me, but apparently he didn't communicate that to Ingrid.

Every year I sent the boys money or gift cards in a box that contained See's chocolates for my dad and stepmom, and that was it. Sort of empty, if you ask me, so every year I wondered why we bothered.

I slit the shiny, thick red-and-gold wrapping paper, opened the box, and shifted the tissue paper. The blouse inside was cobalt blue and gorgeous. I lifted it out. Long-sleeved, dense material, and such a deep beautiful color. But no way would I be able to get my shoulders in. As I held it in the air I realized it'd fit Rebecca. This amazing blue would highlight her dark hair and eyes. Did I dare give it to her? I wasn't much of a re-gifter...but this was too perfect not to share with her. I decided to take a chance that she'd like it. I would rewrap it later.

I checked the time. Rebecca had to open the motel office at ten, so I had about fifteen minutes before she came by with Maya. I hid the blouse and tidied up the living room. I'd seen Maya briefly the day before, and she'd been excited about spending the day with me. What the heck was I going to do with an eight-year-old kid? Rebecca told me to carry on with my regular day and Maya would occupy herself. "When in doubt," Rebecca had said, "there's always TV. I'll bring over a stack of DVDs she can watch if cartoons get boring."

They knocked on the door a couple minutes before ten. I opened it to find Maya grinning ear to ear and Rebecca shaking her head. The kid had a backpack on, the Netbook under one arm, and she lugged in a cloth grocery bag stuffed full of God knows what.

"Hi, Sky," she said, dropping the bag next to my blue couch. "I'm all ready for our day together." She nattered on about TV shows and DVD movies while Rebecca caught my eye.

"Don't worry," I mouthed to her.

"I'm not worried at all. I wrote down my cell and office numbers." She handed me a slip of paper and squeezed my forearm. "Call if you need something or have any questions. I can be right up here in moments."

"I'm running some errands after lunch."

"No problem. I'll give you one of Maya's booster seats to use in the car for the next couple of weeks. I've got a spare."

"Mom," Maya whined, "I don't need a booster."

Rebecca shook her head. "Yes, you do. The seatbelt won't fit right without it. Besides, Sky could get in trouble without it." She met my eyes. "She's got to weigh forty pounds and be over four feet tall before the belt fits right."

"How much does she weigh?" I asked.

Maya said, "I'm over forty pounds."

Rebecca laughed. "She's forty pounds carrying that Netbook and wearing rain boots, her backpack, and a heavy coat filled with a bunch of toys."

Maya had that stubborn look on her face, but she didn't protest.

The kid had spirit. She said, "You can go to work now, Mom. We'll be fine." In a rather comical way, the kid shuffled her mother toward the door.

Rebecca went through the doorway and leaned back in to say, "I'll take a break at half past twelve to make lunch."

"See you then, Mom."

As the kid pushed her mom out the door, Rebecca rolled her eyes. We both laughed a little before Maya shut the door. She turned to face me, and I expected her to brush her hands together as though she'd completed a tough task. Instead she said, "Mom says not to bug you and that I should offer to help whenever I can. Is there anything I can do to help?"

"Nope. I have this one computer to work on. Once that's done, we'll probably take it back to the shop and run some errands, but that'll be after your mom makes us lunch."

"Okay. What should I do?"

"Read? Watch TV? Surf the Net?"

"I have a project I'm working on for when school starts again. I'll watch some TV while I use the Netbook."

I got her set up with the TV in the other room and came back and booted up my main computer to check email. I had pages of new messages from the GirlsGaylore site. I couldn't understand why I was getting all these emails. Didn't these women have anything better to do?

I also had a message from Mitchell to notify me that he was in the office and all was well. Good to know. I'd repair the broken computer and after lunch I'd take it in to Mitchell and check on him.

But first, I systematically opened and skimmed the dating emails.

> Hi, Geekgrrl – Saw your profile and am interested. I see that you like to take risks, and if you are creative and crazy and like fun adventures, we might be right for each other. I don't have a couch on purpose because sitting on our butts doesn't appeal to me. My special someone needs to want to hike and rock climb and parasail and surf, then come home and ride a different kind of crest if you know what I mean. I'm cute enough but not looking for a stalker so hope to hear from you with reasons why I ought to give up my phone number. ~SandollarSal

Oh, brother. Something was very wrong with that woman's approach. Did she actually get people to respond to her? I thought I had removed the references to me being a risk-taker. Once I got rid of all these emails, I needed to go find that and delete it.

I went on to the next message.

> I am 34 years old and looking to get to know a woman and have a blast together. I am an outgoing but reflective person and enjoy all kinds of activities. My friends say I'm very outgoing but I'm also shy at first. I am very sociable and enjoy being around people. If you want to meet up or get to know me, just send me a message. ~ShyGal

So was she outgoing or not? The message was confusing. I looked at her profile, and she hadn't completed all of it, nor had she included a photo. I hit delete and went through another several badly written messes before I came upon this gem:

> Hi, how R U? You mentioned that U like tall, dark, sporty women, so thought I wd get in touch. I hv dark eyes, dark hair, and a deep tan U wd like. I lift @ a gym and my arms & legs are cut. I M pretty sporty, I play flag football & soccer. U said U like sports, wd U like to come to some of my matches and cheer me on?? ~SportsPro

Wow. No conceit in her family. She had it all. Out of curiosity I tracked down her profile to see what she looked like. SportsPro was definitely tall, a real mountain of a woman. Her head was close to shaved, and she had the kind of square jaw I've only seen in female professional wrestlers. She wore a proud smile, and she was right about her musculature, but I wouldn't have called her "cut." Her sleeveless shirt showed her enormous biceps, but she had size, not definition. I had a hunch that she juiced. No way did a woman develop the kind of muscles she had without healthy doses of steroids.

She was clearly way too butch for me, not to mention too self-absorbed, so I went back to the emails and cleared out another dozen. Then I came upon this one:

> Hi, Geekgrrl – My name is Denise, and I live in the Pearl District. Looks like we share a lot of interests, like

hiking and technology. It also appears that we have similar music and movie tastes. I like action films, dance music, and classic rock 'n' roll is the best! I noticed in your picture that Multnomah Falls was in the background. That's one of my favorite places to take friends when they come to town. Would you like to meet up there after the holidays? We could hike up and look around, then have a snack or coffee at the lodge upon returning. I actually haven't hiked all the way up to Wahkeena Falls for a very long time. Anyways, I hope to hear back from you because you sound and look interesting. Have a nice day! ~Denise

Would wonders never cease? Finally, someone who sounded normal. I checked out her profile and photo. She was a solid-looking woman with sandy blond hair and a nice smile. In the photo there were trees in the background, and she held a booklet against her chest. I enlarged the picture, and lo and behold—it was an Oregon State Hiking Guide dated from last summer. So this wasn't a twenty-year-old picture. It was current.

I wrote her back and asked when she wanted to schedule time to hike. As I sent off the reply, Maya came to the door.

"Sky?"

"Yeah?"

"I have to go to the bathroom."

"No problem. Go ahead."

The kid looked down, her face slightly pink. "I think I should go over to my house."

"Why?" Suddenly I "got" it. "Are you saying you need to poop? No problem. Come on." I rose and led her to the bathroom in my front room rather than the one back by my bedroom. "Just go, and when you're done there's some spray there on the edge of the sink."

"Mom says that stuff is bad for you. It's got error—error—"

"Aerosol?"

"Yeah, I guess."

"Then when you're done, you can open the little window if you feel you need to."

She still looked uncomfortable.

"Maya, everybody poops. It's totally normal. You don't need to be embarrassed about it around me. Go in and close the door, take your time, and make the biggest smell on the planet. I don't care. Okay?"

She nodded solemnly.

"There are some great hiking and outdoor magazines in the rack on the door that you can read."

"Okay." She went in and closed the door.

Less than ten minutes later, I heard the flush and she came out carrying a magazine and looking excited. "Sky! I've been here."

She rushed over and held up a magazine. I squinted and saw an article about Powell Butte Nature Park.

"Your class went there on a field trip?"

"No, me and mom went. It was very cool. Did you know it's a distinct volcano?"

"Extinct, you mean."

She frowned. "What's the difference?"

"Distinct means something is kind of like special or specific. Extinct means it's wiped out or gone. Maybe it was destroyed—or killed off."

"But the volcano is still there."

"The volcano part has died out, though. It'll never blow up and spew lava."

"Oh. Well, that's good. Lava is hot and icky and would wreck all the paths. Besides, there are a lot of aminals that would be hurt."

Did I hear that wrong? "Do you mean animals?"

"Yeah. Aminals. The aminals we saw were a bunch of squirrels and a rabbit and a raccoon. We looked for deer but Mom said they were probably hiding until it got darker. We looked for coyotes, too, but I never heard any howling."

"So you like nature hikes?"

"Of course. Who doesn't? Can I read this article?"

"Sure. You can read any of my magazines any time."

"Thanks, Sky."

She carefully rolled the pages back and carried it into the other room. When I glanced in the room a few minutes later, she was lying on the floor in front of the TV but all her attention was focused on the magazine in front of her.

WHEN REBECCA KNOCKED AT half past twelve, I was done repairing the computer Eddie had delivered and looking forward to lunch. I had no clue what Rebecca had in mind. We went next door, and Maya and I sat at the breakfast bar to watch Rebecca prepare our meal. She took the lid off a Crock-Pot.

"Do you like vegetable barley soup?" she asked me.

"Sure."

In no time, Maya and I had cups of soup in front of us, and Rebecca took instructions for making ham sandwiches. Maya liked hers with mayo and pickles and the crust cut off. I took mine with lettuce, tomato, and mustard. Rebecca used only mustard on her own, then stood at the end of the breakfast bar and ate her sandwich and soup.

"Mom, can we take Sky to Powell Butte?"

I looked up, surprised.

Rebecca said, "We could. It's pretty sloppy these days, but if we stuck to the paths it'd be all right. Are you two making plans?"

Since I hadn't heard a thing about this, I didn't reply, but Maya said, "I love that place. Sky has a magazine all about it. We should go back and look for more aminals."

I bit back a smile about her word usage. Had I mangled words like that when I was eight?

Rebecca said, "Maybe after the holidays we could make some time."

When we finished eating, Rebecca whipped around the tiny kitchen to put it in order then handed over a black plastic booster seat with a stained purple cloth cushion. My butt couldn't fit in that tiny thing, not if my life depended upon it. Maya carried herself tall, and her attitude was big, but her frame was quite tiny.

Our lunch had taken less than half an hour before we went back to my apartment. We had plenty of time to run errands, and I set out feeling happy to be outdoors where the sun was out and a cool, blustery breeze blew. The sun made all the difference in the world.

At the office, Mitchell welcomed us like long-lost visitors who were days late in arriving. He asked what had taken us so long, and I ignored his plaintive whine, asking instead what kind of customers he'd seen.

"Customers? Are you kidding? The only people coming in are asking for directions to other stores."

Our shop was located at one end of the mall, and the whole front was glass. With the counter running the length of the store, people did tend to think they could poke their heads in and ask for help as though Mitchell ran some sort of end-of-the-line customer service desk.

"So this is Maya, huh?" Mitchell looked her over. "Aren't you the sporty type," he said in his most disdainful queen voice. I shot him a hard look and he shrugged.

I hadn't paid any attention to what Maya wore, but now I noticed her black jeans, white sneakers, and an unzipped blue and gray ski jacket over a blue Superman t-shirt. Her dark hair was tousled. I suspected she hadn't actually brushed it today. She hadn't yet spoken to Mitchell but stood instead peering up at him with a quizzical look on her face while he frowned down at her.

They seemed to be having a stare-down.

"Yo, people!" I snapped my fingers. "Earth to Maya. Earth to Mitchell."

Mitchell said, "Shall we lock up and I'll take you out to lunch?"

"We already had lunch."

"That's a shame. I could have treated you at the Cadillac Café."

Right. First off, Maya wasn't likely to want vinaigrette or cilantro ranch salad dressings on a mélange of fancy greens that even I didn't want to eat. Besides, the Cadillac Café, though known for its amazing menu, was pretty spendy. Mitchell would never suggest such a restaurant if he thought we'd really eat there. The only times we'd gone were when we had a gigantic celebration to make memorable.

I said, "We have a little shopping to do here. If you want to come with us, you're welcome."

"Oh, no. I ought to stay here at the office. I've got a bunch of holiday phone calls to make to our best clients."

"How are you feeling?"

"Great."

His face had color and his blond hair was newly cut and expertly styled. His red tie was knotted just so, and his dark gray suit and white shirt were sleek and wrinkle-free. He made a great first impression for our company. I, on the other hand, was dressed much the same way as Maya. We both looked seriously sporty, and what was wrong with that?

"Any work for tomorrow?" I asked.

"Not so far."

"Maybe then I'll take the day off."

"You deserve it. Take off the rest of the week as well," Mitchell said. "Tell you what. If I get any computer repairs, we can roll them over into the new year unless someone makes a rush request. Nobody *really* expects service so close to Christmas, but if I get a rush job, I'll call. Otherwise," he made a queenly wave, "just go have fun."

"That's a plan I can get behind."

He arched an eyebrow. "Have you met anyone yet who you can get behind?"

I glanced at Maya. She was looking out into the mall and didn't seem to have picked up the double entendre. "Four duds so far. Got another one coming up."

"Another dud?"

"I hope not."

"That's the right attitude. Be positive." He leaned in. "You need a new squeeze for the coming year. Even if she's only a fuck buddy."

"Mitchell!" I glanced behind me. Had Maya heard? God, I hoped not. Not sure what her mother's take was on swearing and crude allusions, but I suspected she'd have a low tolerance. "We'll talk more on Christmas morning."

"Absolutely. Excellent plan."

I got Maya out of there as quickly as I could, and we struck out into the mall. I wondered how I could broach the subject of Mitchell's comment and whether she'd heard it, but she beat me to it.

"What's a fuck buddy?"

Oh, my God. How did I deal with this? I wanted to kill Mitchell. In an even voice, I asked, "What do you think?"

"I don't know."

"Do you know what the F word means?"

"It's a really bad word. A kid said it last year and had to go to the principal's office."

"Mitchell was very inappropriate. He shouldn't have used that language, and if I could have sent him to the principal's office for a spanking I would have."

She looked up at me, alarm on her face. "Kids don't get spanked at Mrs. Benson's office. I don't think they do. There's not supposed to be capital pun—pun—"

"Punishment?"

"I guess?"

"You mean corporal punishment, not capital punishment."

"What's the difference?"

"Corporal punishment is spanking. Capital punishment is where a person is put to death."

Maya stopped in front of the See's Candies shop and gave me the oddest look. "I don't understand. Put to death?"

"Killed."

"You mean, like, shot by a gun?"

"No, not exactly. Have you heard of a thing called the death penalty?" Solemnly she shook her head. "Let's say a guy goes out and kills some people."

"With a gun?"

"Or a knife or a bomb or maybe he burns down a house on purpose, and people die. The police find him and arrest him and then he has a trial. Do you know what a trial is?"

"Not exactly. Doesn't a judge do something?"

"Yes. Lawyers who are called prosecutors bring all the proof into a place called the court, and they show that the bad guy did do a crime and is responsible for the killings. The bad guy gets to have his own lawyer and try to show that he didn't do it, but if he did, he can either go to prison for life or else the judge can decide that he should be put to death because what he did was so evil that it can't be forgiven."

"I didn't know about this."

"That's because our state hasn't been using capital punishment, but there are some states that do. Our governor decided it wasn't quite right, so for now, killers in Oregon go to jail until they die."

"But if you kill someone, it's only fair if you get killed back."

Very astute of her. "Sometimes mistakes are made. What if we think he's the bad guy but we find out later he isn't guilty after all and a mistake got made? What if they've done capital punishment and he's put to death, but later on they find the real killer."

"Does that happen?"

"It has. Sometimes."

"Oh. But if you're sure the guy did it, he should die, shouldn't he?"

"Maybe. What do you think?"

She was thinking so hard that I almost expected smoke to start coming out of her ears. Suddenly she blinked. "Um, where are we going, Sky?"

The change in topics took me by surprise. "Why? You have something in mind?"

"Can we go to a toy store—just to look, I mean?"

I figured she'd done all the deep thinking she could for the moment, and to be honest, not going back to the fuck buddy topic was fine with me. "Good idea. I've got some kids I want to buy Christmas presents for. Will you help me pick them out?"

"Sure. Is it boys or girls?"

"Three girls around your age, so I figure if you like the gift, they will."

We hiked through the mall, and I led her into Kids' Toy Bonanza. She was obviously no stranger to toy stores. She asked me a bunch of questions, and we eventually settled on Diary of a Wimpy Kid's Cheese Touch Game, a LeapFrog LeapPad, and a gigantic set of art supplies including 24 different kinds of paper, coloring books, stickers, crayons and colored pencils, stencils, and the largest assortment of felt pens I'd ever seen. We headed to the checkout counter and found long lines. I'd thought going before rush hour would mean fewer crowds, but so much for that idea.

Maya was very excited about our purchases and yammered excitedly. "The Pet Pal on the LeapPad is very cool, Sky."

"What exactly is a Pet Pal?"

"You get to have your own puppy and walk her around. You answer questions and read and learn stuff so you can earn money to buy special treats. They also have a Fetch-and-Fling competition."

"Ah, I see."

"My friend Moses has this kind of LeapFrog. I've played with it. You can make your own cartoons and songs. It's really cool."

We put the purchases on the conveyor belt and I shelled out close to a hundred bucks, more than I'd expected, but I was satisfied with the purchases. "You going to help me carry this stuff?" I asked.

"Sure. I'll carry the LeapFrog."

Of course she would. I suppressed a smile at her proprietary attitude toward the gift. Next stop the post office, then to the grocery store. In the meantime, she could drool on the toy all she wanted, but the plastic wrapping wasn't coming off. Not until Christmas morning, for sure.

BACK AT THE MIRACLE Motel, Maya helped me put away groceries, and we wrapped the three presents. There were a lot of looks of longing and much sighing over the gifts, but she was a good sport and didn't whine. When it came time to label them, I had her write Chrissy, Andy, and Sammy on the tags, and then she shuffled off to watch TV.

I booted up the computer. Denise The Hiker had replied to my email and agreed to a hike the first Saturday after Christmas. It occurred to me that I better go through the boxes stacked up in the other room and find my hiking boots.

I sat back in my chair. I'd lived at The Miracle Motel for seven weeks, and already I felt better. Nothing much had happened, but something had changed in me. I still thought about Britney, and my anger toward her did reignite at times, but I could actually imagine a day coming when I no longer felt such deep grief and rage. The betrayal, though...well, I wasn't so sure the bad feelings about that would leave so quickly.

Chapter Twelve

CHRISTMAS MORNING DAWNED GRAY and rainy, matching my mood. I tried to fall back asleep, but by seven a.m. I knew sleep wasn't happening. I got out of bed, dressed, set the coffee perking, and put on a coat with a big hood.

Outside, I walked a few blocks in the cold drizzle, hands in my coat pockets. Nothing was open until I came to the convenience store, which was all lit up and shiny looking, as if elves had visited in the night and installed 500-watt lightbulbs. Gaily wrapped packages sat in the front window. Somebody had gone to town wrapping them in blue and green and gold foil with great gobs of frizzy ribbon. I stepped inside, through glass doors decorated with red bows bigger than my head. There had to be ten fluorescent light fixtures, and all of them had plastic blow-up figurines hanging from them. Three different Santas, Rudolph, a snowman, a couple of angels, a Snoopy dog, and Mrs. Claus swayed ever so slightly in garish excess. Back near the beer cooler, I saw what looked like a ten-legged spider hanging from the ceiling, a red bow around its neck. Perhaps it was leftover from Halloween, the ghost of another holiday past.

A middle-aged clerk popped up from out of nowhere behind the counter and hovered near the cash register. "Good morning." He smiled, his teeth very white against deep brown skin. He was of Middle-Eastern descent and spoke with a thick accent. His golden name tag was emblazoned with inch-tall letters: WALIY.

"'Morning," I mumbled.

"May assistance be given to you for any purchases? We have every forgotten thing needed for that special Christmas meal."

"No, thanks," I said before he could launch into a list of what was available. As far as I was concerned, he was way too perky for this early in the day. "I just want a newspaper." I took one from the stack near the door and set it on the counter so he could ring it up.

After he took my money and carefully counted out change, he raised his index finger in the air. "Late, very late we are open today. Remember this if it's found that something is required for making your holiday a perfection."

As if to prove his point, somebody pushed through the glass doors. A heavy-set man dressed in jeans and a rain-spattered sweatshirt hustled in followed by a pack of small children all talking and whining.

"Hey, dude," the man said, "thank God you're open. Can you believe the wife's out of butter?" He ran his hands through thinning red hair and drops of water flew through the air.

"We are stocked for you, sir," Waliy said. With a majestic sweep of his arm, he gestured toward the first cold case along the wall. "We are carrying two brands for your convenience."

As the man hoofed it over to the fridge, the children sorted themselves out, and I saw that there were four boys, all younger than Maya. Two of them had runny noses, and the other two looked like they'd been crying. None of them wore any headgear, and their red hair was wet and mussed, as if they'd never been introduced to a hairbrush. Standing shoulder to shoulder, shivering in the candy row, they stared hungrily at all the packs of gum and M&Ms and Skittles and Nerds. I was surprised at their restraint.

I picked up my newspaper and turned to go.

"Daddy…" one of the boys whined.

The man slammed the freezer door and crossed the floor to toss two pounds of butter and a sheaf of dollars on the counter, then went to loom over his progeny. "We had this discussion. No candy. Mikey, find the cough drops. That's the closest thing to candy that any of you little rats are gonna get today."

"Thanks for the paper," I said. "Happy Holidays."

Waliy paused with the cash drawer open and gave a proud head bow. "My pleasure to provide for you and yours."

I hastened out the door into dark gloom, tucking the newspaper under my coat. My eyes needed a full minute to adjust to the dimness. Perhaps next time I visited that store I'd have to wear sunglasses.

The rain had let up, so I took the long route back home. As I walked I hoped Waliy had a Christian staff member available to cover for him on his own high holy days. He was certainly in good spirits, and I guess I would be, too, if I was the only store open for miles around. I bet he'd sell a lot of butter today.

But I couldn't seem to force myself into good spirits. I felt bluer than blue. The Christmas season had been an empty time for me for most of my adulthood. From the moment my mom had died, nothing had ever been the same, even when I'd been with a partner.

Christmas Eves I had spent with Britney's giant clan at her parents' six-bedroom place in Salem. Christmas Days happened at Britney's house – that is, *my* old house – when a pack of lesbians started arriving mid-morning for a jam-packed day of celebration. Nothing Britney loved more than a crowd. Lots of people would come and go all day, and there'd be piles of good food, a variety of tasty wines, and an hysterical, funny, white elephant gift-giving game. All the activity helped me to pass the time. If it wasn't raining too badly, the butches would put together a mini-bonfire in the fire circle out back, and we'd have the Ceremony of Letting Go where everyone wrote their pet peeves, worries, fears, and hatreds on sheets of paper, then shared whatever they wanted to about their issues before throwing the pages into the fire.

Would I be damned for all time if I simply wrote RITA on one page and BRITNEY on another and tossed them into an inferno? I'm sure no one would care if I started a bonfire in the cement planters in the courtyard below. Too bad it was starting to rain again.

The more I thought about Christmas Past, the more I wanted to have a lobotomy to gouge out the part of my brain that still had memories of it. And I couldn't drive around town listening to Adele songs anymore while mourning the loss of my old life.

I desperately needed to take my mind off all the negativity. I wanted to do something productive, something pleasant. As soon as I got back to the apartment, I drank a cup of hot coffee to warm up, ate some toast, and opened the present from Aunt Peggy. The package felt like a book, and it was, a hardcover by comedian Carol Leifer called *When You Lie About Your Age, the Terrorists Win: Reflections on Looking in the Mirror*. Carol Leifer had come out as lesbian a few years back, so it was smart of Aunt Peggy to send me this book. She knew I liked humor, and she was cool about me being gay, so the book was a thoughtful gift.

I set it aside and got under one of the tables to dig out a box containing bows and ribbon and paper to wrap up the shirt for Rebecca and re-label the three gifts for Maya. I'd also bought some oil paint for Norma. I'd been so lethargic lately that I hadn't figured out when I could swing by Norma's to give her the gift and chat a bit. Oh, well. I'd walk over sometime later in the day, maybe leave her a note if she wasn't home.

When I finished the wrapping, I surveyed the brightly colored gifts with satisfaction. Maybe the goal of my Christmas Present and Future ought to be to make other people happy so I could bask in the vicarious glow. I was especially looking forward to seeing Maya open her gifts.

I took a shower and put on jeans and a green Henley shirt. In stocking feet, I sat down on the couch in front of the TV with the Leifer book, which turned out to be hilarious right away. Then I'm not sure what happened, but I don't remember a single thing until I heard knocking at the front door. I rose, groggy and confused, and peeked through the curtains. Maya stood there, shivering with either excitement or cold, maybe both.

I opened the door, and she said, "Sky, we're ready for you to come over."

The clock over the computer desk showed it as 9:03 so I was late. "Lucky you came over, Maya. I took a catnap and lost track of time."

Maya grabbed my hand. "Come on."

"Wait, wait. I have to bring some stuff. Hang on."

I collected the gifts and put them in a paper bag with handles. I took a last glance around, wondering what I was forgetting. I realized I should have picked up some food items to take over, maybe a bottle of wine or a gift for the hostess, but until now, it hadn't occurred to me. Damn! I was seriously out of sorts.

I grabbed my keys, locked the door behind me, and followed Maya into their apartment. I set down the bag and gazed around the apartment in disbelief. Only four days had passed since I'd been inside their living room. Since then there'd been an explosion of decorating. Every few feet of wall sported a white paper plate that had been colored with various Christmas scenes and hung up by using a hole punch at the top and stringing ribbon through. The closest one, behind the front door, dangled from a red ribbon. The picture was apparently the jaundiced version of Frosty the Snowman. The three snow balls that made up his body were colored bright yellow. He wore a black top hat and a blue scarf. The cigar that emerged from his carrot-colored lips was the size of a small baseball bat. Odd art, but she was eight—what did I expect?

The primary standout in the room was a homemade paper chain looped along all four walls, over doorways, and around the Christmas tree. Made with strips of red, green, yellow, and white construction paper, it had to be over a hundred feet long. "Wow," I said. "It's so long. You must have spent hours on it."

"I did," she said proudly. "Every time I added more, I thought I was done, but it took me, like, a month to finish."

"Seriously? A month?"

She paused and considered. "Maybe half a month."

"That's quite the project. I made one of those when I was a kid, but it took forever for the glue to dry."

Maya squinched up her nose. "Why use glue? The stapler is way, way faster."

I didn't want her to think I grew up in the Dark Ages, but I don't recall having a stapler when I was a kid. "I think you did a great job. You were very patient to make so many links for the chain."

Rebecca said, "Yes, she was, wasn't she." Her eyes met mine, and she gave me a quirk of a smile. "She's been quite the art decorator."

"Look at this, Sky!" Maya presented me with a round plastic tray that held a stack of three boxes wrapped in colorful Christmas paper. A 5-by-5-inch square sat on top, a rectangular one in the middle, and an even larger rectangle on the bottom. The stack was held in place by a complicated netting of badly tied red Christmas ribbon with a pine cone glued to the top next to a green and white bow.

Maya said, "This is for you."

Behind the kid, her mother fought back a grin as I accepted the gift. The creation was light, not more than ten or twelve ounces.

"Thank you, Maya. Did you make this?"

"Yes. I made it special for you." Her face was alight with joy, as if she were giving me the keys to a brand new Maserati.

"It's quite...impressive. You must have worked awful hard on it."

"I did. You use it as a decoration. It's made from Kleenex boxes."

"Ahhh, I see. Very clever of you. And...and a good use of recycling."

Maya beamed up at me. I couldn't meet Rebecca's gaze, but out of the corner of my eye I could tell she was laughing so hard that she was nearly crying. Kids made the damndest things for art projects. I wondered where I'd put this mini-monstrosity, and would I have to get it out next year at Christmastime?

Maya took it from me and tossed it next to the front door. "You can take it home later. Right now, Mom says I'm supposed to keep you company while she makes our eggs."

"Will the eggs be decorated?"

"No, silly," Maya said.

From behind the breakfast bar, Rebecca said, "I could add some green food coloring if you simply must have color."

"Like *Green Eggs and Ham*," Maya said.

I smiled. Her glee was contagious. "Not necessary at all. I'll stick with the regular color. Thanks for the thought, Rebecca." I gave her a meaningful look, and she turned away to choke back laughter.

Maya took my hand and led me to the Christmas tree, apparently to "introduce" me to the gifts underneath. She pointed to a stack of oddly wrapped shapes. "Those are for Mommy. That one's for Daddy." The gift was expertly wrapped and about a foot square. "These are mine over here, and these are for you."

I got the chance to see a jumble of little things wrapped in red and topped with miniature blue bows before she pulled me toward the doorway to the other room.

"Look up," she said.

"What?"

She pointed at the top of the doorway frame where a bundle of crumpled strips of green construction paper and red ribbon were taped. "If sports guys get bad feet, what do astronauts get?"

I gestured to Rebecca for help, but she was laughing too hard to be of any use.

Maya said proudly, "Mistletoe. Good joke, huh?"

"You bet. Did you make the mistletoe yourself?"

"Yep."

"You've got quite the artistic eye."

"Yep. Wanna see what Santa gave me?"

"Sure. You already opened the Santa presents?"

"Uh-huh." She skidded onto her knees next to the couch to grab at a pile of clothing. She caressed a two-toned purple and lavender jacket with white zippers for the pockets and front. "Don't you love purple?"

"I sure do."

With excitement she showed me a pair of new tennis shoes, pants, and a couple of shirts.

"Santa has good taste," I said.

"Probably the elves, actually. I don't think Santa knows much about fashion since he wears the same thing all the time."

She said that with such certainty and knowing that I suspected Rebecca would be laughing again. I glanced toward the kitchen, and she looked like she was splitting a gut. She recovered enough to say, "Maya, could you and Skylar set the table?"

The kid was up on her feet so fast that she went by like a blur.

She grabbed a folded-up card table leaning against the wall near the breakfast bar.

"Careful," Rebecca said.

"I know, I know." Maya methodically unfolded the legs, and we turned it right-side-up.

A tablecloth and stack of dishes and silverware sat on the bar counter. Maya unfurled the cloth and fussed with it until she had it straight all around the table. We put the plates and silver down along with napkins, salt and pepper, and Tabasco sauce.

"The folding chairs are in the back closet," Rebecca said.

"I'll get 'em," Maya said.

She lugged all three chairs out one by one. I would have helped her but I felt uncomfortable about going into their bedroom. Besides, it gave me a couple of brief moments to talk to Rebecca when Maya left the room.

"She's crazy excited," I said.

"That's putting it lightly."

"Thank you for letting me share in your Christmas morning."

"Maya is delighted. We're both delighted." She handed a covered serving bowl across the bar. "Will you set that on the table?"

"Sure."

By the time the table was set, I was feeling quite hungry. We ate scrambled eggs, bacon, and coffeecake with peppermint sprinkles on top. Everything tasted wonderful, and I complimented Rebecca on it. Maya finished quickly and excused herself to go kneel by the tree. As far as I could tell, she seemed to be praying over the presents. I was reminded of being a child and doing something similar. For a brief moment, I remembered the sound of my mom's laughter. A giant hole opened up in the middle of my chest, and I thought I might start crying.

Rebecca reached over and touched my forearm. "You okay?"

"Yeah, oh yeah. Just...just a moment of old nostalgia."

"Thinking about your parents?"

"My mom, in particular."

"Sounds bittersweet."

"Definitely. It's fun to see Maya's excitement but also a little disconcerting. I keep having flashbacks to being a little kid."

"Exactly. There's nothing like having a child to run a person back through all the issues of their own childhood. Believe it or not, it's been healing for me."

"How so?"

"The older I've gotten, the more I've forgotten about a lot of my youth. Raising Maya has brought many memories back, lots of old issues that I hadn't considered but that still have an effect on me. I've been forced to reconsider a lot of stuff, and in the process, there's healing. I'm forgiving myself for stuff that happened, understanding other people's mistakes, and remembering some things positively that were anything but that."

"I mostly try not to give any of it a lot of thought. Who wants to sit around weeping all the time?"

Rebecca nodded. "When you have a kindergartner come home and talk about big kids being mean to her, about bullies on the playground or cranky teachers, you can't help but think about it. I was reminded of my own experiences. The helplessness. The unfairness. The fury."

"I'm glad Maya has a supportive parent to be there for her. That's one good thing."

"I had some older brothers who stuck up for me. Maya has no one."

"What did you do to stick up for her?"

"Went to see the principal, who was sympathetic but short staffed. So I organized other parents to help on the playground. Having one teacher serve as recess monitor was ridiculous. It made a huge difference for all the kids to get some parents there to help."

"I bet it did."

"Have you ever wanted to have children? Did Britney?"

"Britney was too self-absorbed, and how could she compete with a child? As for me, to be honest, kids seem like an awful lot of work. A big financial consideration, too. So no, I haven't ever considered it." The thought of having children, even just one child, was too much for me. "Being responsible 24/7 for the life of another human being is not something I would want to take on."

"I thought that, too, but as it turns out, there are a lot of unexpected rewards. I like how having a kid helps to heal the issues left from your own childhood. All that unresolved crap still floating around in your memory—well, it gets worked through again as your own child goes through it. Weird how that works."

"Seems like a lot of heartache and expense, and I'd be worried I'd screw up a kid."

"Of course you wouldn't. You'd be a perfectly fine parent."

"I didn't have such a great childhood myself, so why would I want to subject some poor little child to my issues?"

Rebecca laughed. "I saw a Facebook graphic the other day that said: The first fifty years of childhood are the hardest."

Took a moment for that to register. "Oh, that's funny. But I hate to think I have almost two more decades before that passes."

"No kidding."

A plaintive little voice came from across the room. "Mom? When can we open presents?"

Rebecca set her napkin on the table and rose. "Skylar and I will clear the table, then we can start. Will you put the chairs back?"

Maya scrambled to her feet, folded up the first chair, and scurried off with it. Rebecca and I both smiled, but I kept my thoughts to myself. She had a lot to face to raise a child by herself, and I didn't envy her.

She put away the leftovers, left the dishes in the sink, and soon enough she and I were both on the couch, with Maya playing Elf Delivery. The kid was so excited—practically manic. She crawled around under the tree examining every package, periodically rising to stack up presents on the coffee table in front of her mother or me. She made us scoot over so she could put her own packages on the end of the couch.

She'd nearly pawed over everything under the tree when I remembered the paper bag I'd brought. "Maya, there are a few other gifts in that bag." I pointed toward the door, and Maya scooted over on hands and knees to pull them out.

"For me. For me. For Norma." Maya looked up.

"I should have left that at my place. I'll take it to her another time."

"We made her something for Christmas, too." Maya shook my present to Norma. "It's heavy."

Rebecca said, "Remember how we're not supposed to poke and pry."

Maya got that pissy look on her face for a fleeting second, but it passed. "All right, Mom." She put Norma's package of paints back in the paper bag. "Here's another present for me and...one for you." She distributed them and sat cross-legged on the floor at her mom's feet near her stack of gifts. "I think we're all set. If you want, we could have a race to see who could open all theirs first."

Rebecca chuckled. "Nice try. We're going to do this the slooow, polite way. In fact, let's have Skylar open a present first. She's our guest, right?"

"Okay." The voice was resigned, but as I unwrapped a square

package she perked up. As soon as I lifted the lid on the box, she burst out with excitement. "We made those last night! They're fresh and good." She crawled over and leaned against my legs.

The piles of chocolate chip cookies in the box smelled wonderful. I picked one up and took a bite. "These are totally drool worthy. Yum."

"That's the first installment," Rebecca leaned into me and winked. "You know there'll be more to come."

"Thank you." I offered the box and they each selected one. I took another bite. The cookie was slightly crusty on the outside and soft and chewy inside with big hunks of delicious chocolate. "This is really good."

Maya stuffed the other half of the cookie in her mouth and chewed like crazy. Once she managed to swallow, she said, "Mom, you go next. Open this one."

"How polite of you. Thank you for using such good manners and letting me go before you." She accepted a flat, dilapidated present, obviously wrapped by Maya, so there was some extra time involved to extricate the gift from about forty pieces. Inside was a hand-drawn picture of an Indian brave decorated with felt pen.

"Nice use of color," Rebecca said. "Very attractive art, Maya."

"I took Minco and outlined him on the page then drew what he looks like and colored it in."

"I remember Minco," I said. "Last time I saw him he'd fallen to his death from the balcony."

"Minco can never die," Maya said. She leaped to her feet and sped from the room. I didn't get a chance to make a comment to Rebecca before she was back. "See. Alive and well."

"Good to know. He's definitely a lot heartier than you or me. If either of us fell off the balcony, that might be it for us in this life. Look behind you there. See that red package with the gold ribbon? Maybe you might want to check that one out next?"

"Sure." She ripped it open in two quick swipes, putting both her mother and me to shame for our slow progress in unwrapping. Then again, the packages I'd assembled used three or four strips of tape, and who could compete with thirty or forty pieces of tape?

"Whoa..." Maya said. She stared at the LeapPad with surprise written all over her face. She turned to stare at me. "You tricked me!"

I laughed.

"What about the other kids, uh, Sam and umm...you know. What about them?"

"They don't actually exist."

Her eyes went wide. She set down the LeapPad and fished out the other two presents I'd brought, looking first at them, then me. "So..."

"Kid," I said, "you're too smart for your own good."

Rebecca elbowed me. "I'm not sure I follow."

Maya said, "She took me shopping for some other kids, and I helped her pick these out."

"Oh, so you chose your own Christmas presents and didn't even know it?"

"Yeah, I guess."

"She did trick you then. Well, let's have Sky open another gift."

We made our way through more homemade creations a lá Maya. I thought the Stack o' Kleenex Boxes gift was the most hilarious things she could have made, but the next one rivaled it. I opened a six-inch-square tongue depressor house glued to a piece of cardboard and festooned with enough glitter to make a six-pack of soda cans. I hate glitter. It gets all over everything, and for months you find little bits of it on your lips, in your hair, on your tongue. As far as I'm concerned, glitter is the Chlamydia of the craft world. I set that gift aside as politely as I could, and when my turn rolled around again, I opened a weighty box that contained a gel-filled wrist rest for the computer. "Hey, this is cool."

"We picked the purple one," Maya said. "I hoped it'd be your favorite."

"Definitely. Totally my favorite."

Maya grinned and shook with glee, like a little dog waiting for a puppy treat.

That made me laugh. "This is a great gift. I'll use it every day. Thank you. And I'll put this glittery house up on the shelf so I can easily see it."

Rebecca saved my gift for last. When she opened it, her eyes went wide. "This is lovely." She held it up against her, and the cobalt blue looked even better than I'd thought it would. She was stunning in such bright blue. I examined her face and realized how attractive she was with that happy expression on her face.

"Mom, everybody got new clothes but Sky. We should have bought her that t-shirt we looked at."

I said, "I think the cookies more than make up for not getting clothes."

"Can I open the LeapPad and start playing with it?"

I glanced at Rebecca. "It's okay with me if your mom is all right with it, but I think you still have a few things to open."

Rebecca opened her mouth to speak, but before a word came out, someone banged on the door. "Who could that be?"

"You expecting anyone?" I asked.

"Not a soul." She rose and went to peep out the curtains. "Oh." Her shoulders sank as though she'd deflated.

Another round of banging on the door and a man's voice shouted, "Open up. I know you're in there."

Rebecca unlocked the door. As she swung it open, I read reluctance all over her.

"Hello, Steve," she said in a resigned voice. "Why are you here?"

"Because it's Christmas. Ho, ho, ho. Let me in." He pushed past her, smiling wide, a stack of packages in his hands. "Merry Chri—" His gaze landed on me and he choked back his greeting. "What the hell?" He noticed Maya. "What have you got there?" His voice rose. "Goddammit, what is that? Is that a LeapPad?"

Maya's mouth was open, but she was dumbstruck. She cast a brief look at the gift in her hand, which she hadn't yet had a chance to take out of the plastic, then tipped her head back to stare up at her father.

I rose, heart beating fast.

"Steve," Rebecca said. "Maya is coming to your parent's house later this afternoon. That's supposed to be your time. You're not supposed to be here now."

He bent a little and dumped the gifts in front of the tree. If anything was glass, I'm not sure it would survive the drop. "What? A man can't have some private time with his wife and little girl?"

Rebecca winced at the word "wife," but she didn't rise to the bait. "That wasn't the plan. I'm bringing Maya over in a few hours, which is what your mother mediated on your behalf. You agreed to that."

"But I'm here now."

"We have other things going on at the moment."

"I can see that." He looked me up and down and shot me a scathing scowl. "At least I dressed up." He wore dress slacks, a white shirt, and a tie with little figures of Santa Claus dancing.

"I'll stop by another time," I said.

"No, that's all right. Please stay," Rebecca said. She turned to Steve. "This is inappropriate."

"No, this is bullshit," he said. "She's right. She can come back another time." He bent and took the LeapPad out of Maya's hands. "Did you buy this for her?" he asked me.

"Yes."

He handed it over. "Thank you, but go ahead and take it with you."

Rebecca's face was red now, her outrage finally coming to the surface. "You are so out of line. Get out, Steve."

"Not gonna happen, and I'm sorry, but you can't expect me to spend our family time with this complete stranger."

My face burned now, as much as Rebecca's did, but I hastened to the door.

"Wait!" Maya called out. "She's my guest, Daddy. You can't be so mean—"

"Shut up," he said through gritted teeth. He elbowed past Rebecca, who still stood near the front door. He whipped the door open wide, letting in a chill breeze.

Rebecca gave me an apologetic look. "So sorry, Sky. I'll catch up with you as soon as I can."

I scooped up the bag by the front door that contained the gift for Norma, dropped the LeapPad in, and stepped out into the brisk air. "I'll touch base with you later, Rebecca."

"Wait!" Maya shouted. She launched up from her seated position and came at me like a miniature missile. Her head hit me in the mid-section. Lucky I tightened my abs in time or that would have hurt.

She hugged me tightly. "Thank you for the presents, Sky. Thank you." She tipped her head back, and I saw she had tears in her eyes.

"I'll catch up with you very soon, kiddo."

Her father reached out, grabbed Maya's collar, and plucked her away. "Goodbye," he said. The door closed.

As I keyed my lock, Rebecca's voice came through clearly. "You are behaving like a complete asshole. I will not have you in my space. You can..."

I didn't want to hear anymore. I went into my own place and sat on the loveseat. The blood was still rushing in my head, and the surging adrenaline caused an unpleasant feeling. I rose and paced, worried a little about Rebecca and Maya. I hated leaving them, but it wasn't my place to fight Rebecca's battles.

AFTER A WHILE, I calmed down enough to move around the apartment and put things in place. I'd left out the wrapping materials, so I stowed them back in their box. I dealt with the few dishes in the sink and wiped down counters. In the bedroom, I dumped a basket of clean laundry onto the bed, folded it, and put it away.

Once things were tidy, I picked up Norma's present, donned a jacket, and went around the walkway to her apartment. She was home and delighted to receive the gift of the paint. We talked for the better part of an hour, and when I went to my car to head to Mitchell's house, it was close to noon. I'd be about three hours early, but I knew Mitchell wouldn't mind. He'd have plenty of work for me to do to help get ready for the party.

Chapter Thirteen

I WASN'T SORRY WHEN Christmas Day was over, but the day after Christmas always seemed a little bleak, too. At least Mitchell and I had an excellent paying job to do, though drinking too much wine at his house the night before hadn't put me in a good mood. As I walked through the Kelton Kandy warehouse, my head ached—as if my skull wasn't quite big enough to contain my pulsing brain. I wasn't ever too bright at seven a.m. anyway and wanted to curse out Mitchell for scheduling the job at the butt crack of dawn. Things could have been worse, though. I got a look at a sign-out board that listed all employee's names and shifts. The early crew worked from four a.m. to 12:30. The late crew started at noon and went until 8:30 at night. Bleck. I was thankful to be able to schedule my own hours—most of the time, anyway.

The woman I was following was some kind of sexy. A lithe blonde in tight black skinny jeans, she wore a purple muscle t-shirt and black boots. Her long hair was tied back in a pert ponytail. I guessed she was a little older than me—maybe mid-to-late thirties. Her name was Nina Kelton, and she was the granddaughter of Karl Kelton, the patriarch of the company. I'd met the beefy, silver-haired Karl upstairs in a wood-paneled room with a 12-foot-wide window that overlooked the candy production floor below. Karl sat behind the biggest walnut desk I'd ever seen and told me with pride that there'd be no computers littering his office. He would continue to keep his records on paper, the only safe way to avoid frequent computer crashes and compromised data that he heard happened to most businesses. He nodded toward a bank of eight four-drawer file cabinets and said, "I've got it all, fifty years' worth, right there if we ever need it. If it weren't for my pigheaded sons and granddaughter, we wouldn't be upgrading technology now, but they've talked me into it."

All I could do was smile politely and bite my tongue. What I wanted to say was that all his files would make some great tinder if there was ever a fire. And what about roof leakage? Mitchell and I had done an all-new install at a bed-and-linen company earlier in the year. The roof cracked open from a windstorm, and heavy rain had poured in. They not only lost seventy thousand dollars in mattresses and bedding, but the computers and all the paperwork in their office was destroyed. Same thing could happen to Karl Kelton's office. I suppressed a sigh. Another Luddite. I got tired of this kind of shortsightedness. Hadn't he read any recent business magazines? *Forbes*, anyone? Even the *Wall Street Journal?* He had his head buried in the sand all the way up to his ass. The difference between him and the mattress company was that every night the mattress manager backed up their computer documents offsite, and that had made all the difference in the world. All Mitchell and I had to do was outfit them with new hardware and software, and they restored their records and were back in business.

After we left Nina's grandfather's office, in a low voice she said, "Grandpa recently handed the reins over to my dad and uncle and me. He still thinks he's in charge. We're humoring him."

"He's in great shape. How old is he?"

"Eighty-eight."

"Wow, he's in better than great shape."

"He says, 'One piece of Kelton candy a day keeps the doctor away.'"

I laughed. "I guess that's better than the hundred-year-old woman I read about who attributed her long life to eating a teaspoon of petroleum jelly every morning."

Nina threw her head back and let out a hearty guffaw. Still grinning, she looked me over with her blue eyes, and she seemed to be seeing me not as a fatigued contractor in a tool belt but as a fellow lesbian in a tool belt.

"Let me carry that toolbox," she said, almost purring. "It looks heavy."

Something had happened, like a snootful of pheromones wafted my way and left me standing with a dopey smile on my face. I let her take the toolbox and enjoyed seeing the way her biceps tightened and bulged. She turned and sauntered off, making the toolbox look light as a lunchbox. She was one of those tall, lean women who were deceptively muscular. You didn't see those muscles until she used them, and then the ripples and cut were sexy as hell.

I followed, watching the way her legs and ass moved in those black jeans. Whew, it had gotten quite warm down on the factory floor.

Opposite Grandpa Karl's office Nina led me to another set of metal stairs and we went up to an office identical to Karl's—only this one had a bank of two computers and two printers on the far wall instead of the file cabinets.

Karl's giant desk was absent. In its place four cubicles formed a square, and each little cubicle held a computer, all of which were five or six years old.

I said, "Mitchell, my business partner, probably already asked this, but are you donating these computers or what?"

"Actually," Nina said, "we decided yesterday that we want to clean 'em up and let our employees give them to their kids. Can you make sure they all work properly and have sufficient memory?"

"Sure. No problem."

"I know that'll cost extra. We didn't include that in the initial work bid. Maybe we could pay you separately to come in and do the work after hours?" She arched an eyebrow and gave me the kind of Mona Lisa smirk that set my heart beating faster. Nina Kelton was flirting with me. Wow, I didn't know what to make of it.

"I'd be happy to, uh..." I ran out of moisture in my mouth and couldn't finish the sentence.

Nina put a hand on my forearm and squeezed.

Definitely flirting.

Big mouth Mitchell and a middle-aged version of Karl Kelton chose that moment to hit the top of the stairs and barge into the office. Damn my partner and his bad timing. Despite the fact that he was blah-blah-ing with Nina's uncle, Mitchell's keen eyes swept the room, landed on Nina, and then met my gaze. When Zeke Kelton looked away to point at the computer and printers, Mitchell stuck the tip of his tongue out, slooowly licked his lips, and eyed me with the kind of lascivious stare that made me want to smack him. After a quick glimpse at Nina I was relieved that she hadn't caught Mitchell's "subtle" message. I'd be having a few words with him later.

The next twenty minutes we spent going over the installation plan, and once Mitchell and I were on the same page, he headed off to the front office while I began work in the office with the cubicles. We had some wiring to do, wi-fi to install, computers and printers to uncrate and set up. Enough to keep me plenty busy, though I had a hard time concentrating every time Nina came around.

At noon I was crawling under a desk bundling some wiring when I saw those boots and the lower part of Nina's long black-clad legs. I ducked my head out and peered up. She met my gaze with a sexy little half-smile. Holy crap, Batman. This woman was hot.

"Will you let me take you out to lunch?" she asked.

"Sure. I ought to check in with Mitchell."

"Don't bother. My uncle and grandfather hauled him off. I told them we girls would stick together and they could go enjoy their man talk."

"Alrighty then. I'll catch up with you in the parking lot." I went to the women's room, took off my tool belt, and cleaned up as best as I could. The streak of dirt on my t-shirt wasn't going away, but I was otherwise moderately clean. I finger-combed my hair and tightened up my regular belt, and that was the best I could do. I left the tool belt on the bathroom counter and went in search of my coat.

Outside, Nina stood in the gray afternoon light next to a black Hummer the size of my apartment living room. I'd never had the opportunity to ride in one, but I can't say it was all that comfortable. The thing was like a tank. Portland isn't known for wide streets or large intersections, but Nina drove expertly. Being up so high was kind of cool. I could see far off past the cars ahead of us, unlike my Honda which gave zero visibility with even the smallest truck ahead. She said the Hummer was two years old, but I noticed it still had that new car smell. She kept it immaculately clean.

She spared me any embarrassment about my apparel by zooming over to Weidler to Bellagio's Pizza, and we each ordered a mini-pie. I had vegetarian with broccoli, black olives, and sun-dried tomatoes. She ordered Canadian bacon and pineapple and offered me a beer. No way do I drink alcohol on the job, though a little hair of the dog would have taken away the mild headache I still had. But my professional ethics didn't allow me to drink when I was going to be working back at her shop in the afternoon. She ordered a Miller Lite, and we settled in at one of the comfortable booths next to a window where we could look out at the gray day.

"Have you always worked at Kelton?" I asked.

"Pretty much."

"What do you do—office stuff?"

"Oh, no," she said, surprise in her voice. "I train on the floor and supervise everybody, including the team leads."

"You like to get your hands into the production work?"

"I do. But I'm interested in being a CEO or CFO. I'm taking the organizational behavior concentration at Marylhurst University."

"I'm not familiar with that at all. It's a BA program?"

"No, I have a business degree from Linfield. This is a

post-graduate course in leadership and human resources management."

"That'll come in handy at Kelton, huh?"

She reached across the table and squeezed my forearm. For the second time today, blood rushed to my neck and face, and I got a little over-warm.

"Don't tell my dad or my uncle," she said, "but staying at Kelton isn't my goal. I'd like to get some experience somewhere else—you know, someplace where you don't go home at the end of the day smelling like you were dipped in caramel." She let go of my arm with what I can only describe as a leer on her face.

I said, "Oh, I don't know—I happen to like the smell of caramel."

"You do, do you?" She licked her lips and there was no mistaking the heat in her expression.

Between her and Mitchell, I guess it was a gay and lesbian lip-licking day all around.

"You doing anything tonight?" she asked.

"Nope."

"Feel like grabbing a drink?"

"Sure."

We worked out details then got into her Hummer and went back to the office. Parts of me were tingling that hadn't tingled for quite some time, and for a while I had some trouble focusing on uncrating the computers, but before too long I got back into the flow of things. When Mitchell came up to the office at the end of the day, I was surprised how fast the time had flown by.

I returned gear to my toolbox and tucked it under a desk. The building was secure, and I wasn't going to carry it out when I had to be back Friday morning at seven a.m.

Mitchell followed me to the parking lot, gabbing about the next day's tasks, then instead of getting into his car, he got in mine.

"We're in private," he said. "Finally. Methinks you had all the fun at lunch. I was stuck with the geezer and the do-gooder. You, on the other hand, you've got a hot one on your hands there, girl."

"Oh, please." I wanted to be more convincing, but my face was burning, and he didn't miss that, especially with the streetlight shining into the car.

"That Kelton girl is hot stuff. Chase her down, Sky, and don't let her go."

"Enough about that. You've got some other things to answer for."

"Like what?"

"You're out of control, dude."

"Whatever could you mean?" he said innocently.

"For starters, you're lucky Nina's uncle didn't notice that little tongue trick and kick the shit out of you. You're lucky that I don't kick the shit out of you."

He made that tsk-tsk sound, so I smacked him on the shoulder with a tight fist.

"Hey! You can't abuse a poor man who's recovering from a heart attack."

"You didn't actually have a heart attack. Besides, you'd have to *have* a heart for it to get attacked. And I'd like to attack you in a big way if you ever say anything suggestive or off-color in front of Maya Talarico again."

"What? Your little friend? She couldn't have heard me."

"She did! She heard you loud and clear, and you should be ashamed of yourself. She asked me questions as soon as we left the office. I still haven't figured out how to inform her mother about your crassness. I keep hoping Maya will forget, but I can't count on it."

"Oh, shit."

"Yeah, that's right. Listen..." I took a deep breath. "I love you, man, but you have to be more respectful when we're around other people, including these Keltons. Can you lighten up a little?"

"Yeah, yeah, yeah." He popped the door open and the overhead light came on. "Tell the kid I apologize."

"For crapsake, I can't do that without bringing up the topic again, and I'm not doing that."

"I get it. Well, she's an odd little girl. Very weird. She stared at me like I was a butterfly pinned on a display."

"We all know you're a flaming exotic bird, not a butterfly."

"Who's the 'we all'?"

"You know what I mean. And there's nothing wrong with Maya. She's a good kid."

"Future lesbian is what I see."

"Mitchell," I said in my most threatening voice, "you will keep such thoughts to yourself any time you're around that child. She's had enough trauma and dislocation in her life, and she doesn't need more from you."

He put one foot out the door and looked back at me with a smile on his face. "Don't get too close to the little shrimp.

You're not her mother. You'll get your heart broken."

"Oh, shut up."

"Just sayin'. When the mother figures out what kind of influence you are on her very easily influenced daughter, you'll be out the door."

I saw red then and didn't dare say another word on the topic. All I could choke out was, "Get out, Mitchell. I'll see you tomorrow."

He gave me a big, shit-eating grin. "Have a splendorific time tonight with Miss Kelton. Don't do anything I wouldn't do."

I put the car in reverse and he hastened to get out. "Jesus, you could be a little more patient."

He slammed the door and I didn't wait for him to back away. I hit the gas, shot out of the parking spot, and drove away. I had less than two hours to get ready to meet Nina, and I needed to stop by the gym and burn off some frustration first.

I MET NINA AT eight p.m. down at Jones Bar in Old Town. The place was pulsing with 80s and 90s dance music, and it was dress-up night. I'd worn oxford shoes, shiny silver slacks, a dark blue shirt, and a white tie. The rain had slowed down, so I didn't bother with a regular jacket over my white sports blazer and hoped that I didn't get drenched later. At the last minute, I'd put a compact umbrella into my blazer pocket that folded up and squeezed down into a six-inch long, inch-wide tube. I regretted bringing it when I found Nina at the bar. She leaned in, gave me a full-body hug and a kiss on the cheek—which I didn't regret—and purred into my ear, "Is that something interesting in your pocket, or are you just glad to see me?"

Oh, my God. I hoped the flashing lights in the bar prevented her from seeing how embarrassed I was. It'd been a day of me being off-balance, and I suspected the rest of the night wasn't going to be much different.

She gave a wave to the bartender. "What's your pleasure?" she asked me. A half-smile quirked at the corners of her mouth.

"Vodka Seven with a twist of lime."

"Same for me," she told the bartender and shifted so her back was to the bar and her elbows leaned against the black counter. Her outfit, all black, was almost lost against the dark surface. Shoes, leggings, a short skirt, and long-sleeved blouse served only to highlight fair skin and her white-blond hair which she'd taken from the earlier ponytail and given so much volume that it formed a mane. How did women do that with their hair? She looked like a giant jungle-cat with hungry eyes. I glanced around. Both men and women openly admired her, and I'll admit it—I felt a swell of pride to be the one out with her tonight.

Our drinks arrived and I took a big swig of mine. Nina was much more ladylike and sipped. The music was loud enough that we had to huddle up to hear one another, and I can't say I was unhappy about it. She smelled delicious, like flowers and citrus and something else deep and sensual that I couldn't identify.

A rare slow song started. I asked her if she wanted to dance, and she nodded. After downing the last of my drink, I squared my shoulders and said a little prayer that I wouldn't embarrass myself. I was a terrible fast dancer, but I could hold my own cozied up to someone.

She came away from the bar and straightened up. Was she wearing twelve-inch heels or what? Holy crap, she was tall. I looked down at her shoes. Indeed, her pumps had spikes that must have been four inches long. How did women walk in those things?

She took my hand and strode confidently forward without a single wobble. We wormed our way into the middle of the many couples where it was darkest on the dance floor. The strobe light swirled above, and I felt like glitter bouncing around in a blackened snow globe.

Nina put her hands on my shoulders as I gripped her waist. She met my gaze, gave me a little smile, and we moved with the music.

I didn't recognize the song playing, but a sultry, throbbing beat pulsed up through the floor and swirled all around me. With the alcohol giving me a little buzz, I felt breathless and light on my feet. Slow dancing has always come from my heart, and I closed my eyes for a moment and breathed deeply, letting my body feel the thrum of sound. When I opened my eyes, Nina stepped closer and pressed her body against mine. We melded together perfectly. Time seemed suspended, and I lost myself in the flow of our movements.

Far too soon the slow cadence was overlaid with a quick beat, and the DJ segued into a new song. This one I recognized as "Bad Romance" by Lady Gaga, with all its words of love and want, drama and revenge. Nina and I stepped apart, and I did the best I could to sway and keep the beat, but the words gave me a momentary flashback to Britney, to the wounding I still felt. If I could have shook myself I would have because here I was with this sexy, intelligent woman, and why was I wasting my time thinking of my old, nonexistent relationship? But I had to admit to myself, that for a few seconds, I felt an overwhelming sense of loss. Damn dancing. Always made me feel so vulnerable in so many ways.

I pulled myself together just as Nina moved in closer surprising me with a knee between my legs. Hands slid down to the back of my pants and cupped my ass, and suddenly we were doing the nasty on the dance floor in front of God and everybody.

Screw Britney. I threw myself into the dance and tried not to feel self-conscious. A couple of times we stopped long enough to order fresh drinks, then hit the floor again.

I had no idea how much time passed, but at one point we paused to catch our breath, and Nina said, "How about we go up to my place? I don't live too far away."

"Okay."

She suggested we go in her Hummer, and that seemed like a good idea to me since the alcohol had gone to my head and she didn't seem affected at all.

We drove out of downtown and up to Vista Drive. She wound around a few streets until we came to a modern-looking five-story building tucked into the hillside. The ground floor was mostly devoted to a spacious carport with four parking slots. We got out of the Hummer and walked to a security door that, once opened, led to an elevator flanked by a couple of other doors.

Nina pointed to one door. "I've got an office down here next to the laundry room, and beyond the laundry I made sure there was plenty of storage space for the tenants."

"You own this place?"

"I designed it myself."

"Cool."

We got on the elevator and went up to the top floor. I took stock of my energy level while she unlocked her door. I still felt seriously buzzed from the booze. I'd lost count of how many glasses I'd drunk.

"Come on in," she said.

We entered a foyer with a hallway to the right that was shrouded in darkness, and I couldn't see where that led. To the left, Nina flipped a switch and illuminated a living room area furnished with three leather sofas and the most gigantic big-screen TV I'd ever seen. Deep inside the TV room I saw a table covered with trophies and framed pictures, and above it, a collage of photos on the wall. I couldn't make out who the photos were of or what kind of trophies they were. Nina set her keys on a side table, slipped out of her jacket, and tossed it over the back of a couch. "Care for a drink?" she asked.

"I'm feeling pretty well tanked up right now, thanks."

She stepped closer to me and touched her fingers to my chin. With a smile, she leaned in and pressed her lips to mine. She tasted of something citrus. Her tongue teased mine, and she deepened the kiss. I reached for her, pulled her close, and returned the kiss.

As though we were dancing, she took a step, and I went with her. We sashayed across the room and through a doorway. Next thing I knew, the back of my knees hit something soft, and I stumbled onto a bed.

Nina straddled my hips, her elbows on either side of my head. She ducked down to kiss me again, and all that hair, tumbling down, caressed the sides of my face. Her shirt had shifted up, and I slid my hands along bare skin. She shivered and straightened up to slowly unbutton her shirt revealing a black lacy bra that just barely contained her breasts.

"Nice," I whispered.

"So you like that?"

"Uh-huh." I cupped her breasts and she leaned forward, breathing deeply. I ran my hands down her sides to her hips. She rocked her hips as if she were a cowgirl riding me. I pulled at her shirt, and it slipped down her arms. With nimble fingers, Nina freed the front clasp of her bra, releasing her breasts. I tucked my fingers under the straps and massaged the front of her tight shoulders, then helped the bra off her arms. She sat above me, eyes closed, as I moved my hands back to her breasts. My head swirled, partly from excitement, but also from all the alcohol. I was aroused and my heart beat in my chest like a tom-tom, but I was in no great hurry to do anything but enjoy touching this woman.

Nina had other ideas. Her eyes snapped open, and she grabbed my tie. She held it in her fist and forced my head up from the bed so she could deliver a blistering kiss. When she finally broke it off, she asked, "Is this what you wanted?"

I didn't bother to answer. I grabbed her shoulders, twisted her to the side, and put her flat on her back. I had one foot on the floor and the other knee on the bed between the V of her legs. She still had hold of my tie and pulled my face close to hers. Her tongue was hot in my mouth. When I pulled away, she slid her hands down to her skirt. I heard a bzzzz sound as she worked the zipper on the side.

"That's a great invention."

"A side zipper? Yes, it's very handy."

"But leotards—not so much." I stroked her thighs, feeling the texture of the leotards smooth against her skin. "Even handier that you didn't bother with underwear."

She shot me a sexy grin. "Let's get you out of that shirt and tie."

Her hands were deft, and next thing I knew, I was shivering from the cool air on my torso and from her hot hands fingering my nipples. I closed my eyes and took in gulps of air. She chose that moment to flip me over on the bed and hold my arms down while she writhed above me. That girl obviously liked to ride 'em, cowboy. Somehow, she wriggled out of her leotards, and I opened my eyes to see her buck naked above me.

She unbuckled my belt and pulled it from the loops. "I could use this on you, if you like. Or you could spank me a little."

I wasn't up for pain, and she must have thought the same. She tossed the belt aside and unzipped my pants to get her hands inside the waistband and reach behind to cup my ass. Her mouth was hot on my neck, nipping, biting, licking. We were both panting. I rolled her over and managed to get my pants off before falling upon her like a starved lover. We kissed, our hands exploring, by turns gentle and then rough.

She forced me on my back, and I fought against that. I managed to reverse positions and held her down. She pulled me in for a hard kiss and rebelled against being on the bottom. And it was like that the whole time—both of us fighting for dominance, her on top for a while, kissing, scratching, caressing, then me turning the tables.

Nina seemed insatiable. I came twice, but she kept begging for more, and I lost track of how many times she climaxed. As the alcohol haze wore off, I began to think more clearly and worried that I didn't have the stamina she required, but with a loud cry, she had one more orgasm and slumped onto her side, finally spent.

I AWAKENED SOME TIME later. Nina lay sprawled next to me, her mouth open and wheezy sounds coming out. It was still dark out, but I had no idea of the time. My head felt muzzy and my thoughts were muddled. Pale light from a streetlight streamed in through a gap in the curtains, and I saw some of my clothes strewn on the carpet next to the bed. Where was my watch? I didn't remember taking it off.

I rolled out of bed noting that I still had one sock on. Where was the other?

I bumbled around looking for all the parts of my outfit. Found my watch on the floor and saw that it was 2:44. Took me the longest time to find that one stocking, which turned up all the way over by the doorway. How the hell it ended up there was beyond me.

I found my belt and threaded it through the loops of my pants. Around the side of the bed, I bent to pick up my tie and tucked it into my pants pocket. When I straightened up my low back and shoulders were sore. I felt scratched and bruised and so fatigued.

Nina lay quietly, with one arm, a shoulder and breast exposed. Sleeping, she appeared innocent and childlike. I pulled up the sheet to cover her and arranged the blanket. She didn't budge. I leaned down and kissed her cheek, and she didn't stir. With my jacket over my arm, I made my way out of the room.

The low light in the living room drew my eye to the trophy display. As I slipped my jacket on, I stepped between sofas and made my way over to the table. What I saw there took my breath away. The biggest framed photo on the wall was of a handsome dark-haired woman in a tan military uniform with a black beret. She was in all the photos, including some with Nina. Was the woman Navy? Air Force? I would recognize Army dress blues or BDUs because one of my high school pals had joined up, but I wasn't sure about this particular uniform.

I picked up one of the standing framed photos. Nina's arms were around the dark-haired woman who wore what looked like a rugby outfit. Nina looked up at her with adoration all over her face. Nina was tall, but the other woman had her by three or four inches.

The awards were all for rugby accomplishments. Other than a couple of cheesy-looking shiny silver versions from a decade back, the trophies were bronze and gold. The most impressive showed a female rugby player in action beside an oversized silver rugby ball. The athlete was sculpted beautifully. If you overlooked the ponytail, she looked a great deal like the woman in all the photographs—especially the muscular arms and legs. The largest trophy was antique gold with a rugby ball on fan-style columns stacked on a patterned base complete with a gold engraving plate that read, Most Valuable Player: Victoria Andrews.

Who was this woman? Why would Nina have a shrine to her? I realized the significance of the word shrine. I hoped it wasn't a shrine.

I stepped back and made my way to the front door, head pounding. I felt a little sick to my stomach and the feeling only intensified as I stood waiting for the elevator and realized I didn't have my car.

How stupid was I to end up stranded? I might have to call a cab.

I took the elevator down and walked out to the street to get my bearings. Where was I? I meandered down the street to a hill. I heard traffic a couple of blocks away and walked north toward the sound. By the time I reached Burnside Street, I determined it was twenty blocks to First and Couch Street. Then I remembered I'd parked up the way from Jones Bar on Davis Street. Was it at Fourth? Fifth?

Good God. I chastised myself again for my lack of reasonable planning. Booze plus sexual arousal obviously equaled idiocy. I could call a cab, but somehow I felt I deserved a cold wake-up walk. At least it wasn't raining.

As soon as that thought came to mind, a light drizzle misted around me. It figured. I grimaced and pulled my sport jacket tighter. I was well on the way to being nicely drenched when I remembered I had a mini-umbrella in my pocket. Duh. I got it out and put it up thinking it was like locking up the barn after the horse has been stolen.

I stayed on Burnside as I trudged along. Cars came by occasionally, so I felt a little less unsafe. After all, three in the morning wasn't the wisest time to be out and about, and when I got down closer to Old Town and Chinatown, there'd be a lot of vagrants and unsavory characters wandering around.

I reviewed the evening, which started out filled with excitement, moved into feeling a lot of pleasure, and ended with a cold, wet walk in shoes that were now pinching at the toes.

I'd never been a one-night stand kind of gal. I'd certainly never in my life met someone at seven a.m. and slept with her in the same day. I did remember one girl from Rex Putnam High School who I played basketball against my senior year. Lea and I ran into one another at a shopping mall after the season was over. She arranged to meet up with me a couple of times, and third time was a charm. I had my very first sexual encounter four days after the first "date." We fumbled around in her twin bed at her parent's house, and wowee, was that ever an eye-opener. All doubt about my sexual orientation was swept away.

But I guess you could call it a one-night stand because when I talked to Lea on the phone the next day, she hemmed and hawed and talked about some guy, and it was soon clear she'd been experimenting and didn't want anyone to find out, especially her boyfriend.

I promised confidentiality and never spoke of her again. I remember feeling such disappointment, though. I was young, a little smitten, and I'd had such high hopes for being with Lea. What the hell did I know back then? I was so idealistic and hopeful. And now? I had a sinking feeling—and an upset stomach—when I thought about relationships.

But what about sex? How did I feel about going out and catting around? I'd had a good time with Nina, but something didn't feel quite right. I realized that I wanted it to mean something, and I had the distinct impression that she was only playing with me. I wanted something more serious. Of course how did you figure out if you were compatible and wanted something ongoing with a woman unless you spent quite a lot of time with her? What was I thinking in sleeping with her on the first date? I had to be a little nuts. I wasn't thinking at all.

I cut over to Couch Street and found my car, relieved that it was where I left it and that it started right up. Shivering, I cranked up the heat, but it didn't get warm until I was near home.

SLEEPING FOR LESS THAN two hours didn't do a thing for me. I woke up bleary-eyed, and the right side of my head ached like someone was beating on it with a stick. What would it be like when the left side pain chimed in?

After a warm shower, I downed three aspirins and as much water as I could stomach. I pocketed the whole aspirin bottle.

When I got to the job site, Mitchell was already there.

"My God, doll," he said, "you look like the ass end of a dead donkey."

"Yeah, thanks for that vote of support."

He sidled over and spoke quietly into my ear. "I hope you got a little to make it all worth your while?"

Rather than answer him, I said, "Thank you for not bellowing that comment out for all to hear."

He raised his hands, palms up. "Who would hear? Other than half-deaf Granddad, we're the only people here. Let's get going. It would be nice to get the job done today. I don't expect it, but if we move fast enough, it's always a possibility."

I wasn't making any promises about speed. Every time I bent down, my head hurt. I was carrying myself as though I had a basket of eggs balanced on my head.

I gave it up at ten and went to the employee break room to heat water for some black tea. I hoped maybe the caffeine would cut the pounding in my head. They had oversized cups that held at least twenty ounces of fluid, so I made a triple teabag drink and carried it around with me when I resumed working.

At noon, Mitchell and I left for lunch. He wanted to go out for sushi, and I told him he was completely insane. The thought of eating raw fish made me want to hurl. We eventually went to a soup and sandwich place, and I ate some vegetable stew and drank a lot more tea. By the time we got back to the office, the intense head pain let up some, and I had the garden-variety headache. I figured I could power through that.

In mid-afternoon, I crawled out from under a desk after stringing the very last bit of wire, and Nina stood leaning against the doorway. I scrambled to my feet.

"Hey," she said in a raspy voice.

"Hi. Did you get some sleep?"

"Perhaps more than you did. When did you go?"

"Middle of the night."

"I would've driven you home, Skylar. Or back to your car, I mean."

"No biggie. It's all good." I noticed how embarrassed I was feeling, and it was hard for me to meet her eyes. This didn't bode well.

"Thanks for going out with me last night." She came into the room and sat on one of the other desks.

"Sure, it was fun." I felt like an idiot and had no clue what to say. But all of a sudden, one thing did strike me as important. "I saw the rugby trophies and all the photos in your TV room. Who is Victoria?"

"Vic? Oh. Well, Vic is my wife."

"A wife." I didn't ask it as a question but as a flat statement. "Huh. You have a wife. You're still married?"

"She's stationed in Iraq right now. Won't be back until summer."

At least she was alive. At some level, I realized I'd had a fear that the shrine was for a soldier who hadn't made it back. But if Vic Andrews was alive and kicking, what was Nina doing with me?

She must have read my mind.

"Don't worry, Sky. Vic and I have an agreement. No harm, no foul."

A flash of anger hit me and my face flamed with instant heat. No harm? No foul? I thought it was pretty damn foul that a woman would flirt, hit on me, take me home, jump my bones...and *then* tell me she was married. Why would anyone want to sleep with a married woman? I suppose plenty of people did, but how dare she not tell me in advance? I had the right to know what I was getting into. Still, who seeks out married women anyway? Not me.

Seeking or not, what a stupid question. Stupid was the operative word all around. And naïve, foolish, and unwise. Give me a Thesaurus. I could beat myself up with words for the rest of the day.

Nina said, "Vic has her own fuck buddy back in the Green Zone. She doesn't care if I have one, too."

"So, um, last night was just for fun." Even as I said it, the devil on my shoulder was screaming, "Stupid, stupid, stupid!"

"It was fun, wasn't it?" Her expression was uncertain, as if she wanted my approval. I was hard-pressed to give it to her. "You had a good time?" she asked.

Time to be straight-up even if it was hard. "I should have talked with you further before falling into bed. I don't sleep with people when they're involved with someone else."

Her face took on a haughty look, and she rose, arms folded over her chest. "That's old-fashioned."

"That's me. An old-fashioned kind of gal."

"I was going to ask you to go away for the weekend. I have a condo on the ocean with a stunning view of Cannon Beach."

Tempting as that was, I felt I had some standards to uphold, and in order to get the mocking devil off my shoulder, I needed to stay strong. "You're very kind, Nina. I appreciate the offer, really, I do, but that won't work for me." I watched her closely to see what kind of person she was. Would she turn into a raving bitch? Or accept my refusal with grace?

"Sorry to hear that. I had hopes that we could get to know one another well."

It crossed my mind that we already knew each other waaaay too well—physically at least—and getting to know her any more was a dangerous road. The road to hell was paved with fucked-up decisions, and I didn't intend to compound the situation.

Chapter Fourteen

I AWAKENED SATURDAY MORNING still feeling a little thickheaded, but the intense headache was gone. I was grateful because I had a date to meet Denise the Hiker at the Multnomah Falls parking lot at ten.

I opened the front window drapes and was greeted with a gray, bleak-looking day. At least it wasn't raining. Intermittent rain had fallen over the last twenty-four hours, and I hoped it stayed that way.

While I collected items for my daypack, I thought about the events of the previous two days. I didn't want to label and judge myself and my behavior as stupid, but that little devil still sat on my shoulder mocking me. At some level, though, I felt distinct disappointment that I was trying to ignore. Nina and I had hit it off. I'd liked her immensely. She was a hot lover, and I felt better than competent at bringing her pleasure. Then to find out that any relationship we had would be temporary...well, that sucked. Even if her wife returned and was okay with some sort of polyamorous relationship, I sure as hell wasn't. Britney had tried to force me down that road, and look how that turned out.

To paraphrase the old song, when I fall in love again, it will be forever. I wasn't interested in something just for kicks and giggles.

I guess it was good to know where I stood, to have it verified by experience. I had to admit that sometimes Mitchell's insistence that I go out and sleep around for fun seemed a little attractive. But would it be? I read a book when I was younger, *The Front Runner*, and the main character, Billy Sive, always said he only slept with people he loved. Maybe when I was a lot younger and still thought I loved everyone I could have played around without much thought. I'm older and wiser now, and that's not what I want.

In a perfect world, I'd never have to see Nina Kelton again. Unfortunately, Mitchell and I didn't quite finish the install so we'd have to return to the company on Monday. The thought of it made me want to run screaming.

I wondered how things were going for Rebecca. Maya was

probably still at her grandparents' house and spending time with her nitwit father. I hadn't seen Rebecca around The Miracle Motel the last couple of days, not that I'd been home all that much. When I'd walked past the office the day before, the lights had been on, but only Pete sat in there staring blankly at a computer screen. I wanted to make a point to touch base with Rebecca. I hadn't gotten to see her give Maya the computer I'd built which made me want to pop Steve's car tires. Or put sugar in his gas tank or a potato in his tailpipe.

Funny how I thought of all these devious methods of revenge, but I was a big chicken. I'd never do any of it. I guess my fantasy life was pretty pathetic if this was what it had come to.

I turned my attention to prepping for the hike. I considered bringing my CamelBak water hydration reservoir, but hell, we were only going up to the Falls. I put a couple of regular water bottles in my pack along with the first-aid kit, compass, a lightweight roll-up raincoat, waterproof matches, lip balm, TP, a pair of thermal gloves, a couple of energy bars, and a small towel. I wore hiking boots, jeans, and a long-sleeved thermal shirt. I put on a wool baseball cap, a Patagonia vest, and tucked my GPS and cell phone into the vest pocket. I didn't have much fear about hiking around the Falls. I'd be on one of Oregon's most popular sites, so if we sprained an ankle or got sick, not more than fifteen minutes would pass before some other group of hikers would come trudging along and find us.

As I drove east on I-84, I felt blue and distracted. I sincerely hoped that hiking would give me some energy, maybe even a little excitement.

The parking lot was half-full, but a string of cars followed me in. With the weather lightening up, I expected by noon the place would be rockin' busy.

I put on my daypack and headed toward the lodge. A wiry-looking woman with short blonde curly hair stood waiting. I recognized her from the photo on the GirlsGaylore website. She wore boots, brown hiking pants, and a flannel shirt under a lightweight down jacket. No way was she going to get cold.

"Hey, Denise," I said as I approached.

"Skylar?"

"That's me." I held out a hand and she shook it. Her hand was chilled and seemed large compared to her frame. I was quite a bit taller. We looked each other over, and in a moment, without a word passing between us, I thought, "This Denise will be like a brother to me."

A recognition passed over her expression, too, and she gave a nod. "Ready to tackle the trail?"

"Definitely."

Denise scooted to the lodge wall and picked up her own daypack, shouldered it, and said, "Lead on."

I made my way along the well-traveled path. The ground cover around the trail looked soaked through, but we didn't have any problem as long as we stayed in the dry middle. We were silent as we warmed up on the paved switchback trail up to the stone bridge. It took me a while to get into the rhythm of the uphill movement. I hadn't done anything more than walk occasionally since Halloween, so I was short of breath before we'd traveled a quarter-mile. I glanced back at Denise who was also huffing and puffing.

I stepped to the side of the footpath onto a wide flat rock with room for both of us. Denise stood next to me, shoulder to shoulder.

"I haven't been out hiking for a while," I said, and we both chuckled.

"Me neither, obviously. But I'm glad to be getting back into it. Thanks for coming out today."

I caught my breath in less than a minute and counted myself lucky. "We can stop periodically, and I know I need to tank up on water. If you don't mind, let's just take it easy."

"Yeah. Good plan," she said. "You ready?"

"Absolutely." This time Denise took off first and I followed. I stayed close enough that we could chat, and we talked about all the stuff we packed when we went out for a day hike versus a longer, overnight trip. It was interesting to discover that she had the same kind of thorough, well-thought-out plan as I did. I suspected that if we opened up our daypacks, we'd have matching gear.

The Falls are split into two sections, and we came upon the lower segment quickly. Most tourists went that distance, took a lot of photos, and didn't travel any farther on to the upper falls. We passed a dozen groups of visitors cheerfully snapping away and we kept going.

To gain the nearly 700 feet of elevation and reach the top of Multnomah Falls, we had to travel way over a mile. The hike took us almost an hour, but I felt a real sense of accomplishment when we arrived. The dual plumes of the waterfall plunged into a mossy grotto below. So much mist wafted up that we couldn't see anything more than maybe fifty feet down, and the noisy, churning stream and the power of the chute of water were a joy to see. This was nature at its best. I glanced at Denise. She stood grinning with the same look on her face that I probably had on mine.

I drank half a bottle of water as we silently observed the grandeur of the Falls. I'd come here once with my father and mother when I was in grade school. Before they stopped getting along, we often went camping and enjoyed outings to places like Multnomah Falls. Back then, the waterfall looked a little different. When I was in my early teens, a 400-ton boulder broke free and splashed into the upper cascade pool. To my eye, the middle of the waterfall looked lumpier and thinner. I couldn't remember what the pool looked like, but if erosion caused such huge chunks to separate from the cliff periodically, I didn't want to spend much time down below. I had to admit that it was cool to be seeing the bird's-eye view.

Denise put away her water bottle. "Do you want to take the Larch Mountain Trail or the loop to Wahkeena Falls?"

"I'd like to see more waterfalls."

"Yeah," she said, "I agree."

We set off. Noon hadn't yet arrived, and the weather was great for hiking. The sky was partially overcast, but the sun might poke through if we were patient. We came to the path that led to Weisendanger Falls. I didn't recall ever seeing that waterfall, and Denise was willing to hike off the main path and up the rocky trail. We went half a mile and passed the small Dutchman Falls and several rapids. I stopped at the destination and admired water plunging fifty feet. The tumbling water was more petite than Multnomah Falls, but nearly as mesmerizing. We stood companionably, resting for a while, without saying a word. After a while, Denise shuffled back, and I was ready to go, so without a word, we headed toward the Larch Mountain Trail.

We skipped Ecola Falls and after steady progress reached the path that split off the mountain trail and took the loop toward Wahkeena Springs. I kept an even, medium pace, not rushing, and Denise and I both stayed with the rhythm, sometimes able to walk side by side, but most often single file. Occasionally we talked about other hikes we liked, time at the Pacific coast, and camping trips we'd taken. We'd been to a lot of the same sites over the years, even at overlapping times. I was a little surprised we hadn't ever run into each other.

We meandered along the Wahkeena Trail, encountering a couple of hiking duos. I thought there'd be more people out and about, but we mostly had the paths to ourselves. After a while, Denise paused and pointed to the sign marking the descent to Fairy Falls. "Wanna hike down?"

I laughed. "I've always loved the name. Let's do it."

Fairy Falls was nothing like Multnomah Falls in scope or size and was smaller than Weisendanger. The water only dropped about twenty feet, but the way it fanned out and burbled over stair-like boulders at multiple levels was quite lovely. We sat on a bench and each pulled energy bars from our packs.

"Hey," I said, "I see we're both fans of the Power Bar brand." I had chocolate, and hers was peanut butter. "You have a hydration pack?"

"CamelBak. Didn't bring it today."

"Didn't bring mine either. Too much trouble for such a short hike. What camping gear do you find yourself recommending the most?"

"I'm real fond of a lot of North Face products. I've got a great tent."

"I just read an article about some new tents they make."

"In *Outside* magazine?"

"Yeah," I said. "Exactly."

"I read that, too. I love *Outside*."

"So do I. What other sports do you like?"

"Boogie boarding, kayaking, canoeing, lots of water sports. I love to dive."

"SCUBA or snorkel?"

"Both. How about you?"

"I've enjoyed all of that but haven't had the opportunity to go too often in the last couple of years." Actually, that damn Britney was afraid of the water. I'd hardly been able to do any fun water outings at all because of her. "Do you play any gym sports?" I asked. "Basketball, volleyball, handball?"

"Some. Used to a lot more back in high school and college though."

"Do you mountain bike much?"

"Love it," Denise said.

"Me, too. I don't currently have my bike, but I need to go get it from where it's stored." I still had to get a bunch of stuff out of the garage, and as Britney suggested when I last saw her, I'd better make some time to reclaim all of it soon. I hoped none of her light-fingered friends had carted off the bike and my camping gear and various other odds and ends.

The thought of Britney and her failure to keep up the house payments made me angry. Lucky my name was never on the home, but still, I'd put a lot of time and energy into the yard and repairs and painting inside. I'd treated the place with great care, and damn Britney for her irresponsibility. I closed my eyes and vowed to kick her right out of my mind.

I opened my eyes. "What kind of car do you drive?"

Denise gave me a puzzled look. "A Honda CRV."

"What do you do for a job?"

"I run a tutoring business to teach people—especially seniors—how to use computers."

"That's cool. Do you do a lot of the coaching or administer it all?"

"Nowadays, it's mostly the latter. I started out solo ten years ago, but now I have four staff. I never expected to get so much business, but computer usage and people with problems have exploded exponentially and we're still getting customers despite the fact that the economy isn't so good."

"How interesting. We both have computer interests, and we have a lot in common with things we like and how our lives are set up. We even have the same kind of car."

"Recipe for good friends," Denise said.

I met her gaze. We were both nodding. "Yeah." We were definitely going to be "brothers." I didn't feel a single spark toward her. We were too similar. But so far I liked her a lot.

She rose and folded the plastic around the last couple of bites of her bar and stowed it in her pack. "Shall we carry on?"

"You want to go back up and around the long way to Bridal Veil?"

"Not so much."

"Me neither. How about we hike to Wahkeena Falls, check that out, then make our way down toward the lodge?"

"Works for me," she said.

We hiked down the hill and continued on the lower trail. My legs were pleasantly fatigued, but stepping down the incline made me feel my quad muscles in a big way. This was the point where I wished I had a staff or some poles. "Denise, you ever use a hiking staff?"

"Oh, yeah. I went on a week-long seventy-mile trek in the Wallowa Mountains two years ago and used a pair of terrific hiking poles. They were a lifesaver. You have any?"

I shook my head.

"Get some. They make a huge difference. I considered bringing mine today but didn't. I should have. We're hitting some good downward slants at times, and it's wearing."

We soldiered on, now much more cautious because we were both tiring. We stopped when we finally came to Wahkeena Falls. After seeing all the previous falls with their sheer drops, these were different. Instead of "falling," they tumbled down the hill, cascading and flowing in chutes that looked sculpted. Denise shrugged out of her pack and pulled out a camera. I hadn't thought to bring one.

"A selfie?" she asked. "If we can get a decent one, I'll email it to you."

We put our backs to the water and she held up the camera. The shots were off-center the first three times, but the fourth shot looked great. We took turns taking pictures of each other alone, then moved on, eventually crossing the stone bridge below Wahkeena Falls and heading back toward the lodge.

"I'm starving," I said. "You feel up to having an expensive burger or sandwich at the lodge?"

She smiled. "I would. Good idea. And yeah, last time I was there, I think I spent twenty bucks."

We hit level ground and walked on the trail in the woods that paralleled the Interstate next to the two-lane Old Columbia River Highway. I preferred it to I-84. The highway is more romantic than an interstate, not to mention beautiful.

We dropped our packs off in our cars, strolled into the lodge and actually got a table without much of a wait. I ordered a hot turkey sandwich, and Denise got a hamburger. Our meals arrived hot and tasty, and we both dove in like we hadn't eaten for days. Food always tastes better after a nice hike.

I got halfway through my meal and was able to slow down enough to talk. "Thanks for meeting up, Denise. I've been out of the flow of hiking, and this reminds me of how much I enjoy it."

"I've always loved the waterfall." She smiled. "It's a joy to be up there. I go often during the year."

"Have you found many women on the website to go hiking with?"

Denise rolled her eyes. "Surely you jest. They all say they love to hike. What they must mean is they don't mind wandering slowly through department stores. I was thrilled to see that you'd actually hiked in the past, though there was no way for me to know if you put up a picture that was ten years old like so many of these women do. A shocking number of them are liars, and the scary thing is that a lot of them seem to actually believe they like hiking."

"Right. Isn't it strange?"

"If you ask me, Internet dating is the Theater of the Bizarre and Disappointing with a side order of big fat lies."

I almost spit a bite of my sandwich across the table. "That's hilarious."

"But true. And really, not so funny after you've been at it a while. I went on a date with a woman before Christmas who said she loved hiking and canoeing. No kidding—she weighed at least three hundred and fifty pounds. She could hardly walk. I guess she must have liked *watching* hiking and canoeing because no way I could have got her into a canoe without a block and tackle. Trust me, I'm trying not to be judgmental, but I don't have the patience for that sort of deception."

"Wow," I said, as much surprised by her vehemence as by the fact that I was having similar issues with dishonesty, though on a much smaller scale.

Denise said, "I hope that I don't end up as aged and decrepit as women like her have been. Despite her profile, this gal is not interested in any of the stuff I am, and of course she's not fit *at all*. In fact, I suspect she's in worse shape than she appears. She's also never had a long-term relationship with anyone, and I can see why. She's so intellectual and 'clever' that she must wear people out. She was smart, but she was also more than aware of that and very ready to share instances of her superior intellect. Man, dealing with that kind of subtle arrogance wore me out. I keep wanting to ask why so many women around my age seem like such old crones who have given up on being active at all."

"No kidding," I said. "I haven't had too many dates off the site yet, but I'm having similar experiences with the women contacting me."

"Just for once I'd like to see a real, true description from some of these gals who lie. Something like 'forty-year-old sedentary office worker with good sense of humor who loves to eat, chat, and sit around watching TV, seeking same.' Is that too much to ask? All those people ought to pair up and leave the sporty ones for us. I tell you, Skylar, I've gotten to the point now where I'm measuring a good 'date' by whether I feel somewhat energized afterwards. Or at least neutral. Too many of these twits are sucking the life out of me."

I scooped up the last bit of turkey and gravy and savored the final bite. "How many dates have you had now?"

"Hmmm...I've lost count. Maybe forty?"

"Holy crap! Forty? I've had six, and I'm ready to call it quits."

"You've got to pace yourself. I've been at this for most of the last year." She pushed her plate away and took a long drink from her water glass, then raised it and caught the waiter's eye. We were quiet while the server refilled our glasses.

When he left, I said, "What happened to the old days when we used to meet women at the gym or on sports teams or at work?"

"I know, I know. I'm having a hell of a time. Where are all the femmes and sporty gals and the soft butches? Why the hell do the same batches of lyin' bitches keep turning up? For crapsake, for a while I had a photo of me in a tuxedo in one of the pix I put up on my profile, but I took it down because it seemed to attract the totally wrong crew. Why can't I find someone who's a Sandra Bullock type. You know, healthy, active, and game to try some athletic stuff. I may be forty now, but I'm not looking for overweight, under-exercised, creaky ancient gals who appear to be pushing eighty."

I snorted with laughter. Denise was really getting warmed up now.

"Not that I have anything against the wisdom and loveliness of older women, but it's my general preference to date someone who could go hiking without a ventilator. Or rafting without water wings. Or workout at the gym with me. Or—sheesh—could I find someone who's actually able to HEAR."

I burst out laughing. "You didn't happen to date a woman named Barbara who had recently quit—"

"Smoking. Oh, my God, yes! She quit smoking but still looked like warmed-over death. She's one of the worst liars I ran into. Depressed. Angry. In terrible health. And yet she billed herself as a big hiker. I could hardly get away from her. She was one seriously clingy woman."

"Sounds very frustrating for you, but I'm glad I'm not the only one. How did you get away from Barbara?"

"I told her I had to go because I needed to feed the dog and let her out."

"Do you have a dog?"

"No, but she didn't need to know that."

Denise was so droll that I couldn't help but snicker. "I'll keep that excuse in mind."

"I have a pack of them."

"Yeah? Like what?"

"The best ones are that I can't go out for a drink because I suddenly remembered I'm on call tonight. Or I say I have a meeting with a big-time presentation in the morning so have to get home to bed early. One time I went out for dinner with this woman who wanted me to hear her tale of woe about her last seventeen girlfriends. Total turn-off. I pulled out my phone and said it was on vibrate, then told this woman that my child's babysitter was sick and I needed to go home. Now."

I pulled my phone from my pocket. "Oh, geez, Denise. I just got a text that my dog has a presentation in the morning and my babysitter is on call so I have to go home."

For the briefest second she blanched, then laughed out loud. "Hey, you gotta be careful with some of these women. They can be real messed up. I started requesting that dates meet me for a walk or a hike. That weeds out a lot of the wannabes. One time this thirty-ish punkster showed up in a diaphanous blouse, short skirt with no underwear, and those weird shoes with the ropy-looking soles—on the heels, you know?"

"How'd you know she had no underwear on?"

"Didn't I mention that her little black skirt was short? The fabric whipped up and I saw her privates waving there in the wind."

I couldn't stop laughing. Privates waving in the wind? Ha ha. "Hope you took a selfie with her."

"Not a chance. Let me tell you, she picked a trail out by Fanno Creek, and as she tottered along, all she could talk about was her sex appeal. I couldn't wait to escape. She was so self-absorbed that I didn't take her seriously. To get away, I gave her the first smart-ass comment that came to mind, something about helping my sister hang curtains. Wouldn't you know it—she woke right up and told me that's what she did for a living, and she got all excited." Denise pitched her voice in the falsetto range. "She said 'I'll put up your sister's curtains. Let me do it. I will. I will. Please?' Oh, brother."

"So how did you finally manage to escape?"

"I had to say it wasn't working between her and me. I wished her good luck and literally ran to the car. It's not like she could keep up in those goddamn freaky shoes. Since then, I learned to set up a call from a coworker who gives me a call twenty minutes or so into the date. If I don't answer, Paula knows all is well. Unfortunately, I usually do have to pick up the phone."

"I didn't see you talking on the phone twenty minutes into our hike."

"That's right. You didn't."

"Dating is a shitload of work," I said. "Why bother?"

Her face went solemn and she let out a sigh. "I made a promise to my partner before she died." She raised a hand. "Don't worry. You don't have to make up an excuse to leave. It's been almost five years, and I've done my grief work so I won't be dumping a load of whiny emotions in your lap. She got pancreatic cancer. She was only 44. I was barely 36 at the time."

"I'm sorry that happened. Sounds like a terrible thing."

"It was. And it happened so damn fast. One minute she was fine and we were hiking and camping and wind-sailing. Next minute she was so sick. As Carol was dying, she made me promise I wouldn't go all turtle and hibernate. She wanted me to get over her and go out and find someone else to love. I couldn't consider that for a long time. But in the last year, I've been lonely, and I've felt ready to find someone new, so I undertook this like it was a project that Carol set up for me. Every so often I look to the heavens and wonder if she's laughing her ass off up there. I mean, couldn't she guide someone decent my way?"

"You're due, Denise. Somebody's out there waiting. Don't give up."

"From your lips to God's ears." She wiped her mouth with a napkin. "So, shall we hike again in a couple of weeks?"

"Hell, yeah."

She rose and held out a hand. "Glad to meet you, Skylar. I think we're going to be great friends."

Chapter Fifteen

THE DAY AFTER THE hike, my legs were tight and achy and so were my shoulders, which had never fully recovered from the physicality of the sex with Nina Kelton. At least the scratches on my chest and neck had faded. Thinking about her made me shake my head at how dumb I could be sometimes. Nina was not the kind of woman I could ever make happy. If you looked up High Maintenance in the dictionary, there'd be a picture of her next to the entry.

I sat in the living room on the blue loveseat for a while and read a book, but it was hard to stay focused. I kept thinking about how Monday afternoon I had to go back to Kelton Kandy Company, and I wasn't looking forward to it at all. The hike at Multnomah Falls had made me forget all about the Monday job, but now it weighed heavy on my mind.

I liked Denise, and I was fairly certain that we'd be friends, but there was definitely no romantic connection there. At least she seemed normal compared to the others I'd spent time with.

I set the book down on the cushion and rose. I'd stashed three big boxes of stuff under one of my work tables. I pulled the first one out and lifted the flap. Nope. I shoved it back and dragged the second one out. Bingo. Several framed pictures stood on end separated by bubble wrap. I rooted through until I found the one I was looking for and carefully lifted it out.

The gold frame had a dent and a couple of ugly surface scratches but had otherwise survived the move intact. The impressionist-style painting was awash with color—blues, silver, and white in the night sky. Lampposts topped with white balls of light. The trees lining the walking path were spattered orange, red, gold, maroon, with an occasional edging of green. Two small figures, pressed close to one another, stood on the path surrounded by all that color. Their heads weren't close enough that they could be kissing, but they stood so near that they must be holding hands while pausing to absorb all the light and color swirling around them in the evening sky.

I'd always loved the painting. Almost a decade earlier I'd seen it tacked up on a wooden board at Saturday Market alongside half a dozen other colorful paintings. This was the one that spoke to me. Despite Britney making fun of my choice, I bought it from the poor starving artist for fifty bucks. I spent three times that having it double-matted and framed.

The painting made my heart ache. Something about it touched me in a way that was difficult to explain...except to say that this was the feeling of love I had sought and never found. Something in bloom, lovely and shared with someone special, full of color and light even during dark times.

I wondered if Norma was home. Without any further thought, I grabbed a dish towel off the breakfast bar, laid it over the painting, and carried it outside as I cut around the walkway to Norma's apartment.

She answered the door with the chain lock on, but when she saw it was me, she opened right up.

"Why, Skylar, what are you up to? Come in, come in."

"I wanted to show you this painting and get your opinion of it." I whipped the towel off. "I thought I might be able to get some gold paint from you that would touch up the dings here on the frame." I showed her the scratches, and she nodded the whole time, then took the painting out of my hands and stood it on an empty easel.

"Where'd you get this?" she asked. I explained its provenance, and she said, "You got a terrific deal. This is fine work. Are you well-versed in aspects of painting and art?"

"I have to admit, I'm not. I never studied art beyond a calligraphy class in high school and don't understand the lingo. I know what I like but not exactly why. I love this because it's so full of color."

"Yes, the artist used color masterfully. Look at how he depicted the play of light and shadows, and yet the color is still so vibrant, even though it's clear this couple is walking at night. The content is asymmetrical."

I squinted at the painting and said I didn't understand what she meant.

"In the olden days," she said, smiling, "a long, long time before I was ever born, artists balanced their paintings along a central axis. There'd be a bowl of fruit in the center, for instance, and other elements, like the table it sat on and the little geegaws on the wall behind it would be given equal weight within the scope of the painting's content. Take the Mona Lisa for instance. She sits on an imaginary line in the middle of a piece. She's painted in the center and her head and hands are equidistant—or symmetrically located—and that's how da Vinci created a balance that's somehow pleasing to the eye."

"Okay. But this one isn't quite like that, right?"

"Good eye. With your painting, both sides and the top and bottom of the central axis are not identical, but somehow it all seems to have a balanced visual weight. Don't you *feel* the balance between the parts of the composition, the sky, the building in the background, the trees, the ground, and the tiny people?"

"I guess I do, though I would have been hard-pressed to describe it that way."

"It's a dynamite piece, Sky, and dynamic as well. These rough irregular strokes are masterful. The surface texture is uneven, and yet it all seems seamlessly smooth and connected. Very nice work. You're right that the frame needs a little touch-up."

"Do you have some gold paint I could use to fix that?"

"I can take care of that for you. I'll have to mix up something so it matches. I can also fill these dents in the frame. Leave it with me for a few days, and I'll fix it right up."

"That'd be great. I can pay you for the paint."

"What? Are you nuts? You gave me paints for Christmas."

"But not gold."

She laughed. "Don't be silly. Besides, you get my groceries so often that I owe you. I ought to be painting something special for you."

"No need for that. And I don't mind picking up extra items at the store for you. I'm already going there, so it's no big deal. But I'm kind of excited to hang this in my apartment once you have a chance to correct those scratches. It's been a long time since I've seen it on a regular basis."

Norma patted my arm and gave me a big grin. "You know, they say that real art doesn't match your couch, but there's enough of that loveseat blue in this painting that it actually would look fine hung in your living room over the loveseat."

"My thoughts exactly."

I stayed and chatted with Norma for another fifteen minutes then headed back over to my apartment. As I came around the walkway, Rebecca and Maya hit the stairs and headed up. Rebecca carried a duffel bag. Maya, wearing a purple backpack that seemed half as big as her, scurried up the stairs ahead of her mom and caught sight of me as I reached my apartment door.

"Sky," she shrieked. Next thing I knew, forty pounds of midget energy—plus ten pounds of backpack—hit me in the thighs.

"Glad to see me, huh?"

"It's been forrr-ever!" she said.

"It's actually only been fourrrr days."

"Seems like weeks." She inched back a little but still kept a hand on my hip as she gazed up at me with a big grin on her face. "What have you been doing?"

Rebecca arrived at that moment. "Maya, what have I told you about invading people's personal space?"

Clearly reluctant, the kid dropped her hand and stepped away six inches. She got an expression on her face that anybody could read in an instant, the patented "pissy" look of displeasure I'd come to know and love.

Rebecca dropped the suitcase next to her and inserted her key in the door. "How's everything been going, Sky?"

"No complaints."

Maya recovered from pissy status and said, "I got a bike from Grandma and Grandpa."

"Wow. That's very cool. What color?"

Rebecca pushed open the door, and Maya bolted through. The door smacked against the wall, and Rebecca looked at me with exasperation. "She's killin' me."

A bike tire emerged from their apartment. "See, Sky. It's purple."

"Maya. Watch out." Rebecca steadied the bicycle.

The kid was very excited. And not quite correct with the color description. The bike was more accurately lavender...with a dark purple seat, a lavender basket, and pink and lavender tassels hanging from the ends of the handle bars. I wanted to ask her if it came with a Barbie and her Dreamhouse.

"What a nice bicycle," I said. "Once I get my mountain bike, you'll have to come riding with me."

She gasped, her mouth open. "When are you getting your bike? Soon? I hope it's soon. Tell me it's soon."

Uh-oh. Probably not a good idea to have mentioned that. I was in no hurry to go over to Britney's place, and now the kid was probably going to ask me every day, every day, every damn day until I retrieved it.

"My mom's getting a new bike, too. My dad sold her old one."

"Maya, please don't go around telling everyone our private information. Take the bike inside."

Wearing the pissy expression she was so good at, Maya backed up and took her bike inside.

Rebecca said, "Sorry if she seems a little out of control. She's was at her grandparents' house until noon today. She's still wound up. Takes me a day or two to get her back to her semi-calm and respectful self after she's been with them being spoiled to death."

"Seems pretty normal to me but a little more energetic than usual."

Maya reappeared in the doorway. "I might be a bike racer when I grow up. Either on a bicycle or maybe a motorcycle. My mom and me have that in common because we have the same pants."

Rebecca said, "What?"

"You said, Mom. Remember? We have the same pants, so I'm gonna be as good at racing as you were. You can buy me some just like yours."

Rebecca burst into giggles. "Genes, Maya. We have the same genes."

Maya frowned. "That's what I said." She looked back and forth between us.

Rebecca's eyes met mine, and the bit of merriment we shared caused Maya to go pink with anger. She could tell we were having a moment of glee at her expense, but she didn't understand why.

"What?" she said, with a stomp of her foot. "What are you laughing at?"

"I'll explain inside," her mother said. "I'll be there in a minute. Please take your duffel to your room and start unpacking."

Maya snatched up the bag and stomped off in a huff.

Rebecca said, "I'm very sorry about what happened Christmas Day."

"Yeah. It was kind of a shame." I realized I still felt disappointed. "How long did it take you to pry him out of your living room?"

"Over an hour. I eventually let him take Maya to his parents' place, which saved me the drive but deprived me of that extra bit of afternoon with her. And with you." She grasped my forearm. "I'm really sorry about that."

"It's not your fault. You can't control him."

"That's for sure. I put your cookies in the freezer, and we'll revisit the Christmas gifts. Maya doesn't know this, but she still had a couple of gifts under the tree. With Steve there, I tucked them away and thought I'd save them for New Year's Eve. Do you have plans Tuesday night?"

"No." Mitchell always had a big bash, but I'd already decided I wasn't in the right frame of mind. Other than calling my father that afternoon to wish him a Happy New Year and to chat about the holidays, I had made no plans.

"Would you consider coming over to ring in the new year? That is, if nothing else comes up that you'd rather do."

"That sounds okay. What time?"

"Let's make it after dinner, say seven-ish? We could watch a movie together. Maya got the entire Harry Potter collection from my parents. Have you seen all those?"

"I saw the first couple but it was ages ago. I'd watch the first one again."

"Okay. Not sure Maya will manage to make it until midnight. We usually keep an eye on the celebrations on TV until the ball drops. In the past, they've played and replayed the New York countdown, and she's never realized that it was only nine or ten p.m. when we rang in the new year. But this year she's gotten good at reading the clock, so there's no pulling the wool over her eyes."

"Rebecca Talarico, I'm shocked. Do you mean to tell me you've been lying to your child?"

She threw her head back and laughed. "Not lying. Merely terminological inexactitude. That's what Churchill called it."

"I'm shocked and appalled at your callous disregard of truth."

"Sometimes a parent has to go to extremes to preserve her mental health."

"I see." I gazed at her merry eyes and thought that she didn't go to near the extremes that I'd have to. Maya could be a handful, and Rebecca was a saint to put up with it.

"So you'll come over?"

"Sure. What should I bring? I could make some snacks."

"I'll be making the snacks. I owe you that much."

"I have to bring something."

"Do you like wine?"

"I do."

"Maybe bring a decent merlot? I've found it goes well with movie popcorn."

"You got it. Anything else?"

"Just you."

She flashed a warm smile and ducked into her apartment. I went into my own place and thought about how nice Rebecca was. She could be a real taskmaster with Maya, but her kid was going to turn out fine because it was clear how much Rebecca cared about her. The two of them were in a tough transition, and I felt for them.

I fixed myself a grilled cheese sandwich and tomato soup for lunch and made short work of that. As I cleaned up the pan and dishes, I felt out of sorts. I had nowhere to be and nothing to do and no one to call. Once more bitterness seeped into my thoughts. Things felt bleak in this chunk of time after a sad Christmas and before the new year, which I could only hope would be full of a lot more celebration than mourning.

I picked up my book and carried it into the other room. Stretching out on the couch, head on a pillow, I read for a while, but the mystery didn't keep my attention and I fell asleep.

A COUPLE HOURS LATER, I awakened with the book on my chest and a low back screaming for relief. I rose and stretched. My back was definitely stiff. I got my coat and went outside for a walk.

A fine mist hung in the air, and rain threatened. Totally matched my mood. I walked up to 20th and headed south for a long walk to a coffeeshop I'd always liked. When I got there, it was closed. Figured. Today was just one of those days.

Stretching my legs and moving felt good, so I carried on toward Burnside and walked along for several blocks until I found an open coffeeshop. Parts of the Sunday newspaper were stacked on one of the tables so I took my coat off and put it on a chair there. The bakery case was still half full of croissants and cookies and cute little round pies. I debated getting one, then decided to spare myself the extra calories and ordered a black Americano coffee. To make up for my avoidance of pastry excess, I loaded it up with sugar and real cream and sat at the table to page through the paper. Local news, sports, entertainment, travel, business—all of it was boring. I was surprised at how many sections of the paper had articles about marijuana. Washington state, a five-minute drive away, had legalized pot last year, and it was in the news, in an article about athletes using it medically, and all over the business section regarding growers opening up medical marijuana businesses.

Nothing interested me, not even the comics. I took the last swig of my coffee and noticed that it was getting dark outside. The afternoon had blown away without me accomplishing much of anything.

I stepped out of the coffeeshop. The rain had stopped. I was five blocks from my ex's house and way over a mile from my apartment. I could go get my bike and ride it home. I struck out for Britney's and arrived to find her driveway empty. She hadn't taken back my key yet, so I went to the door at the side of the garage, let myself in, and turned on the light.

Full boxes labeled "kitchen" and "basement junk" and "summer clothes" were stacked against the wall near the entrance to the house. She'd obviously been packing. There must have been forty flattened boxes, the kind you buy and tape together, lying in piles in the middle of the floor. I saw a handheld tape dispenser on the floor next to an assembled box that was empty.

My bike hung upside down from two hooks screwed into the garage ceiling. I wrestled it to the floor, glad to see that the tires were still inflated. I'd be able to ride it, no problem. I put down the kickstand and went to the shelves on the wall opposite the entrance. Britney had crammed more junk than I thought possible in every little cranny, and there was an awful lot of oddball stuff. A stack of kitchen pans, plastic butter tubs full of used nails and metal items, old paint gear, rolls of very ugly wallpaper that should be thrown out immediately. I stuck my hand behind a row of boxes and located my camping gear shoved back against the wall. I found the tent, sleeping bags, a utility bag with cooking gear, the Coleman stove, folded tarps, and a ground cloth with poles, rope, and stakes wrapped up in it. After a bit of digging, I also discovered the two Rubbermaid plastic tubs that contained the rest of the necessary gear. Clearly she hadn't touched it since I'd last put it away, so that was good to see. I'd have to come over and get it all soon.

I heard a noise and stood back from the shelf, and that's when all hell broke loose. Two shouting figures came in the side door, one standing tall, the other squatting low. They pointed guns at me. I stood, mouth open, unable to process what I was seeing.

Through the pulse beating in my ears, I finally realized they were telling me to get on the ground.

My knees hit the floor. I put my hands behind my head and felt like my heart was going to burst. "Wait," I said. "I'm not an intruder."

"Shut up," one cop said as he pushed me to the cold cement and grabbed my hand. Something cold snapped around my wrist. He jerked my arm down.

"Ow! You're hurting me."

"I said to shut it." He had his knee in my back and twisted my other arm to click shut the second cuff. "Now you can talk," he said.

I lay face down, my hands cuffed tightly behind me. No way was I going to be able to get up without help. I tried to turn my head, but that hurt. I couldn't roll over to face them, so I rested my forehead against the stained floor and said, "I have keys. I used to live here. I'm getting my stuff."

"That's not what the owner says."

"Britney Alton. She's the owner. When she comes home she'll tell you I used to live here."

A different voice, lower and more dangerous sounding, said, "Who do you think called us about the break-in?"

"Britney!" I shouted. "Britney, come tell the cops there's been a mistake."

"Quit the hollering," the first cop said. The two of them loomed over me. They bent and grabbed me under my arms. I flew up through the air and had trouble getting my feet under me.

"Steady," the deep-voiced cop said. He was black, six inches taller than his partner, and quite young. The other cop was probably in his mid-forties with a silver crew cut. Deep Voice patted me down, poking and prodding everywhere.

"Guys," I said, "look in my right pocket. I have keys to the garage. This is my stuff here." I made a motion toward the shelves with my head. "Open that big blue tub. I can tell you everything that's in it because it's mine. I'm not stealing. I was just here to get my bike."

"Yeah, yeah, yeah," Crew cut said. "Good story. You can fill us in on the way to the station."

"You can't arrest me. I haven't done anything wrong. Britney! It's Skylar. Get out here!"

They hauled me out the side door and around to where their squad car sat at an angle at the end of the driveway, blue and red lights flashing. They got the back door open, and Deep Voice put a hot hand on my head as he shoved me in. I barely had room for my legs and knees behind the driver's seat. It smelled like disinfectant and something rank in the back. Somebody had thrown up in here in the recent past, and the smell hadn't quite worn off.

I shuddered. This was a nightmare.

The flashing of the lights alternately made the tan house look bluish, then pink. I watched the cops go to the front door and knock. Someone answered. What the hell? She was home? I should have knocked. I wouldn't make that mistake again. Though I couldn't see her all that well, I knew from the shape in the doorway that it was Britney. I breathed a sigh of relief. The mistake would be corrected now.

Crew Cut was doing a lot of nodding, and then he gave a wave and wheeled toward me. Deep Voice followed. They opened the cruiser doors simultaneously as though on cue and slid in.

"Thank God she was home," I said. "Her truck's not here, so I thought she wasn't home."

Crew Cut started the car.

"Wait a minute," I said. "You're letting me out now. Right?"

Deep Voice said, "She says she doesn't know you."

"She does. She knows exactly who I am, and she had to have heard me hollering. She knows me perfectly well. Go get her and bring her out here."

"Settle down, ma'am," Crew Cut said. "You can call your attorney from the station."

"But—but—you can't...you can't." I stopped. Protesting would only make it worse because they could. They would. And they did.

Crew Cut turned off the roof rack lights and backed out. As he whizzed past the house, I saw Britney standing in the window, the curtain pulled open. Was she grinning? I hoped I was imagining it, but in the brief view as the patrol car sped away, I'm pretty sure I saw her laughing.

First a sick feeling hit my stomach, and then a cold fury made me want to scream. I bit my top lip to keep from saying anything further. What was the point of arguing? The home owner gave me up without a single thought, and what reason would the police have not to believe her?

I closed my eyes and took a deep breath, then another and another. The closest police station was across the river in downtown Portland, but that's not the direction they headed. I quickly recognized we were on Washington heading east. When we crossed over I-205, I knew we were way to hell and gone away from where I lived.

Sooner than I expected we pulled up to the police station and I was hustled in and stuffed into a caged holding cell.

"Wait a minute," I shouted. "Take these cuffs off. Hey! You can't leave me cuffed."

They ignored me.

"Shit." My hands were going to sleep, and my neck and shoulders ached. When they'd whipped me up onto my feet in the garage, it was like they'd tried to dislocate my arms. My muscles were feeling worse by the minute. How long would I be here? That was a scary thought. On a Sunday there wasn't any chance I'd reach a lawyer to get me out. Would I have to spend the night in this dirty little shithole?

At least I was in the cage by myself. Bubba the Prison Matron was nowhere in sight. Not even a Lady of the Night to converse with. The bench along the wall was eight inches deep. I tried to sit but because of my hands behind my back, I had to lean forward too much, so I stood back up and paced.

Deep Voice came back a couple of minutes later, opened the cage, and unlocked the cuffs. "Step this way, Miss."

I rubbed my sore wrists. Just that little bit of time and pressure, and I could see I'd have a ring of bruises around my wrists.

He took me to a table and said, "Empty your pockets."

I did what he said, but then a brilliant idea occurred to me. As I took out my wallet, I flipped it open so it showed my driver's license through the clear plastic. "Officer," I said, "what address did you arrest me at?"

He looked at me blankly. I pointed to my wallet. "You see my driver's license there? If I'm a liar and a thief, why would my license show the address you just arrested me at?"

"What?" He picked up my wallet and looked at it.

I had never gone to the DMV and changed my address. Just hadn't gotten around to it. I'd updated the post office so the mail got forwarded, but I wasn't in any hurry to stand in line at the DMV.

"Huh," the cop said. "That certainly is the address." His dark eyes squinted at me before he looked away and let out a sigh. "All I can say is you must have done something major to piss that woman off."

I put my hands on my head and grabbed hanks of my hair. He believed me. Thank you, God. All I could do was close my eyes and breathe for a moment. When I opened my eyes and dropped my hands, he was gazing at me like I was a lunatic.

"Look," I said, "I used to live with her, and I left because—doesn't matter. We broke up earlier this year. It's over. I'm still getting my stuff out of there little by little. I honestly didn't know she was home."

"We're going to have to verify this situation. Sorry, but it's back to the cage for a short while. I won't cuff you, though, if you promise to behave. I'll be back shortly."

How could I possibly misbehave in an empty room with an eight-inch-wide bench that ran along one wall? I wanted to make a smart-ass comment but restrained myself. No use antagonizing him when it sounded like I might avoid being booked and spending the night somewhere in this hellhole.

"Shortly" is a relative term. I sat there for well over an hour before Deep Voice came back, keys jingling, to let me out. The clock on the wall showed that it was 9:41. This ordeal had lasted more than three hours.

He swung open the door to the cage. "You're free to go now, Ms. Cassidy."

I was instantly furious. "Where is she? Did you bring her back with you?"

"Who?"

"Britney Alton."

"Uh, what do you mean?"

"Where is she?"

"I'd guess she's still back at her home."

"Why didn't you bring *her* in and book her for making a false police report?"

"Ma'am, we didn't have any cause to arrest her."

I controlled my tone and my anger with great difficulty. Through gritted teeth I said, "Please tell me why you so cavalierly dragged my ass down here, but now that you verified that she lied to you, there aren't any repercussions?"

"She said it was an honest mistake, that she didn't recognize you."

"You know that's a big lie, right? C'mon, Officer. You talk to people all night and day. You know she was lying."

He shuffled his long legs and looked uncomfortable. "Well, ma'am, I couldn't say. We did question her thoroughly. It's not for me to say if she was lying or not, but to be honest, we did tell her you might have cause to file a civil suit against her. You'd have to consult an attorney because I can't give you legal advice. That's your call. You can see the sergeant at the desk to get your belongings and call a cab. I've got to go now. Thank you for your cooperation."

Cooperation? Oh, my God. I thought of my ex laughing in the window. Britney, Britney, Britney, how many ways do I hate you?

REBECCA DROPPED OFF MAYA at ten Monday morning, and Maya scampered into the apartment with glee. Rebecca took one look at me, though, and asked if I was okay.

"I must look pretty bad?"

"You look tired, like you've been up all night."

I told her what had happened the night before.

"My God, she actually stood by and let the cops haul you off?"

"Yup."

"That's—that's unbelievable. You must be so angry."

"So furious I could hardly sleep."

Maya grabbed my hand and looked up at me with worry etched into her face. I wasn't sure how much she'd heard.

"Do you have to go to jail?" she asked.

"No. It was all a big mistake."

"So you didn't do anything wrong?"

"No, not at all."

"Why was Britney so mean then?"

I sighed and met Rebecca's eyes. She gave me a shrug as if to say I could tell her whatever I wanted.

"After lunch, I have to go by a job site and finish off some installing. Do you mind if Maya comes along?"

Maya let out a tiny squeal. "I could be your helper."

Rebecca said, "You do whatever Sky says, and don't get in the way."

"I won't get in the way, Mom."

"Okay, fine. Gotta run, Skylar. I'll see you at half past twelve for lunch."

I shut the door, hoping Maya could be diverted, but no such luck. She was one hundred percent focused on the details of my arrest and asked about Britney again. I sat on the loveseat, and she cozied up next to me.

"Maya, it's important that you understand that sometimes people get mad at each other, and they aren't very nice."

"Britney was mad so she was mean?"

"Something like that."

"But she called the police on you. What did you do wrong?"

"Nothing, it was all a big mistake. Sometimes grown-ups do stupid things."

"Like my dad, you mean?"

"Um, well..."

"He's being a real dummy lately. Mommy called him an asshole." She looked up at me with a smirk on her face. "Don't tell her I said that bad word, but Dad did some asshole things."

"He didn't hit anyone, did he?"

"No. He acts like he might. He scares me."

"Could you possibly tell him that he's scaring you and ask politely if he would speak more softly?"

"He would probably yell at me more. He used to be nicer. Mommy keeps telling me to remember when he was nice. I try, but his meanness is so big that the niceness is easy to forget."

"He did bring you some nice Christmas presents, right?"

"Yeah."

"He must care about you, kiddo. He's just not very mature about his feelings."

She reached for my hand and gripped it in both of hers. "If you had a little girl, would you yell at her all the time?"

"Not all the time. Maybe sometimes. Depends on what she did. Remember when you crawled over the railing to my balcony? That was yell-worthy."

"You and Mommy are just the same. Why can't you trust me?" Her face pinked up, and she spoke forcefully. "I'm a little monkey. I never fall. I'm the best girl on the playground monkey bars. Nobody believes me, so I guess I don't ever get to go out to the balcony anymore, so you can be not worried."

"You promised your mom not to open that door again?"

"Yep. I keep my promises."

"Well, that's good to hear. You know what that's called?"

"What?"

"Integrity. When you keep your promises it means you have integrity."

"And that's a good thing?"

"Yes, very much so." I extricated my hand and rose. "I want to show I have integrity, so I have to work on some computer repairs."

"Did that big guy bring a whole bunch of them?"

"Eddie. Yes, he brought four. The slow season of the holidays is over. Everyone's computer has a problem. I'll probably have more tomorrow, and next week will go gangbusters."

She peered at me, puzzlement written all over her face. "What do gangs have to do with it?"

"You are such a literal child."

Chapter Sixteen

MONDAY AND TUESDAY PASSED in a swirl of work. The trip over to Kelton Kandy turned out to be fine. I didn't see hide nor hair of Nina, and Maya turned out to be a good helper. She learned the names of my tools in a heartbeat and was more helpful than I ever expected. I was surprised that she didn't get bored. She asked questions incessantly, but that made the hours pass more quickly.

During the rest of the time when we were back at The Miracle Motel, I tried to take breaks to talk with Maya, but I had a lot of work. She spent much of both days glued to the TV watching cartoons. I hoped her brain wouldn't turn to mush any faster than mine seemed to be. I was able to get through Monday's four repairs, but the next day's work proved an impossible dream. Eddie delivered nine computers on Tuesday, two of which were brand new Christmas presents upon which Santa clearly hadn't installed virus or malware protection. Didn't people know that when you went to an online whorehouse without "protection," computers contracted Cyber Space Transmitted Diseases? Cyber STDs could totally screw up an operating system.

No way could I diagnose and fix nine computers in one day, though I tried. When Eddie came for the afternoon pickup, I only had five ready. Looked like I wasn't going to run out of work any time soon. I didn't have anything going on New Year's Day, so maybe I'd get caught up then.

Rebecca had been harried at lunchtime. Some of the tenants were making preparations for parties, and she was worried about noise and rowdiness. I'd personally seen the paunchy alcoholic man in 214 limp by with a case of Maker's Mark bourbon. He was followed by a staggering old guy carrying two twelve-packs of beer. A beer truck pulled up shortly before Rebecca came up for lunch and delivered a pony keg downstairs across the way from my apartment. I couldn't remember if that size of a keg was seven or eight gallons, but how many people could the guy fit in his apartment to drink that much beer? I sure hoped he wasn't planning on drinking it all himself.

Rebecca had gone around to the different units to discuss the party policy for The Miracle Motel, and she'd had a couple of arguments, including with Mr. Pony Keg. I was glad we were on the end of the complex and that pot-smoking guy below was generally pretty mellow. Maybe we wouldn't have to call the police like Rebecca said she had the year before.

At six, Rebecca came by and scooped up Maya, and I promised to come over in an hour or so or whenever they were ready. I went back to work and lost myself in taking apart an HP computer that I hoped needed a new motherboard and not a new hard drive. People usually became incensed to find out that their hard drive had fried and they could no longer get data off of it. No matter how often we included an ADVICE FOR THE HEALTH OF YOUR COMPUTER sheet with our repair invoices, customers still did not backup their precious documents and images. How frustrating. Talk about screaming into the abyss. I guess the only good thing was that due to people's laziness and ignorance, I'd apparently never be out of a job.

I heard a firecracker go off outside, and with a start, I noticed that it was seven p.m. Uh-oh. The midget would be over to roust me any time. I went to the other room to find a clean shirt. I'd been cycling through a lot of the same t-shirts and polos lately. Where were my long-sleeved shirts? I rooted through a box containing a jumble of clothes and came up with a dark green blouse—a little too femmy for my tastes. Must have been Britney's. Fat chance that I'd return it now. Maybe I could use it to dress up a dummy and hang her in effigy. For a moment I visualized that with a little too much vengeance, then I got hold of my feelings and tried to put her out of my mind.

A little deeper in the box I discovered a black shirt with two button-down breast pockets. I'd always liked that one, and the color certainly matched my attitude.

I sniffed it. Laundry soap was all I smelled, but I was going to have to do a quick ironing job. Rebecca always looked so put together. I would hate to admit to her that most of my dress clothes were languishing in a big cardboard box. Unless I did something quick, she'd definitely see that this shirt was a wrinkled mess. The iron was in a box in the living room. I paused to look around my bedroom/TV room area. I'd been here all this time, and I hadn't done a single thing to make the place look livable.

Except for the couch.

I wasn't a complete failure with decorating after all. Nothing says fancy living like a great big giant neon blue couch.

As I moved into the front room, I heard a voice outside and thought Rebecca had called out to me. I started to the door but stopped when I caught the sound of a different, bossy tone.

"You've got a lot of nerve." Britney said in her most haughty voice.

Jesus, help me. What was she doing here?

Rebecca made a choking sound. "You think *I* have a lot of nerve? You've got to be kidding me. You should be spanked."

"Oh, yeah. And you'd be the one to do it."

I leaned against the wall next to the door frame and was grateful I hadn't pulled the door open. I was so filled with fury that I wanted to punch my ex. I twisted the shirt in my hands like it was her neck and knew I needed to get a grip on myself.

Rebecca said, "*Somebody* ought to kick your ass."

"Where is she?" Britney asked.

"You don't get to know that. You don't get to know jack-shit about her anymore. You should be ashamed—"

"Get off your high horse. Just butt out and tell me where she is."

"She's out."

"What are you doing at her door then?"

"None of your business."

"Does she know you're here?"

Rebecca let out a sigh. "Why have you shown up? You need one last chance to ruin her year?"

"I guess that's none of your business."

"Go away then."

"I have every right to wait here for her."

"You have no rights at all. This is private property." Rebecca laughed. She sounded strangely menacing. "How would you like me to do the same thing to you that you did to her? You're probably not aware that I'm the manager here. If I say get out, then you have to. I'd be oh-so-happy to call the police and have them toss you in the pokey like you did to Skylar."

"That was—a—a mistake."

"Yeah, right. She told me how you stood there laughing and did nothing while the cops arrested her. Mistake, my ass. You go home and pack up all her stuff and bring it back, and then I'll think about letting you hang around waiting for her."

"You can't make me do that."

"What are you—twelve? I can't make you do anything, but you could make a good faith effort to show her that you're sorry. If you are."

There was silence for several beats.

"You're not sorry, then. I see."

"It's not like that," Britney protested. "I wanted to touch base with her, this nearly being a new year and all."

"Look, I don't know your history with Skylar, but getting her arrested says to me that you don't care about her half as much as you're pretending. So get the hell out of here unless you have a major peace offering. Like her bike and camping gear and anything else you're holding onto in your godforsaken garage."

"You have no say," Britney whined.

I could tell Britney was at the end of her patience and about to relent and leave, but she was giving it one last irritating try.

Rebecca came back smoothly, her voice assured. "Oh, but I can. With great pleasure. There's an awful lot you don't know about me. Like the fact that I have a black belt in Tae Kwon Do."

Alarmed, I went to the curtain and peeked out. Rebecca was advancing toward Britney, who stood near the rail. Britney's eyes went wide. She backed away without taking her eyes off Rebecca. Before I could move to open the door, she wheeled around and skittered toward the stairs like a giant navy blue cockroach.

Rebecca knocked, then crossed her arms and turned to watch Britney's rapid departure. When I opened up, she faced me with a smirky grin on her face.

She stepped into the living room. "Well, hello, Skylar. I've just had the most invigorating conversation."

"I heard. Let me guess—you've never done Tae Kwon Do in your life."

"Of course I have. I would never lie about that. But I only attained green belt status. She didn't need to know that. She also doesn't need to know that I quit practicing after I graduated from high school."

"About the same time you stopped racing motorcycles and bikes?"

"No, I did that up until I got pregnant."

"I see." She was full of surprises.

"Lucky your little Britney is a chickenshit."

"She's not mine, believe me."

"I'm glad she didn't rush me. I'm pretty sure I could take her, but I'd be rusty today if I had to do combat."

"So you could break a brick barehanded or take my head off with one chop?"

"Not really. Karate focuses more on use of the hand. Tae Kwon Do is almost all kicking techniques. Lots of fun when you're eleven or twelve and being manhandled by your brothers and all the boys in your class."

"I see. You must have gotten good at ironing your karate outfit."

"You mean my *do bok?* Tae Kwon Do is Korean in origin, and we wore a V-neck style *do bok*. The Japanese wear a *gi*. You want me to iron that for you?" She whipped the shirt out of my hands. "This is definitely a mess. I'm a great ironer. Where's your ironing board?"

I know I blushed. "Um—I usually use a towel on a table."

"I suppose you go outside and find a flat rock to heat, too."

"No, no, no. I have an iron." I crawled under one of the long tables and pulled out two clunky boxes and opened the flaps of the first one. Not there. Everything you look for is always in the last place it could possibly be—if it was there at all. I shoved that box back under and opened the other. "Here it is. Oh, look. Here's my Xena chakram. I'll have to give that to Maya." I took it out of the box, handed the iron up to her, and came out from under the table.

She tucked her hair behind her ear and checked it out. "Not bad. The steam works?"

"Of course it does."

"All right. Get me a towel and direct me to your ironing surface."

I set her up at the breakfast bar and leaned on the stool to watch. She filled the iron with water and plugged it in.

"Where's Maya?" I asked.

"Visiting over at Norma's."

"That's nice of Maya," I said.

"Oh, please, it's nice of Norma. My kid is a lot to handle sometimes, and she's in high gear today. She'll be on a roll for hours."

"Because?"

"You're coming over, why else? We're both happy about that." She ducked her head down and focused on ironing between buttons.

"Did you give her the computer yet?"

"No. I wanted you to be there."

"Cool. That's great. Have you let Maya take Tae Kwon Do?"

"Are you insane? She already calls herself The Monkey Master and can run faster than I can. I'm afraid if she learned any skills she'd use them at school and get kicked out."

"I'm pretty sure she uses her mouth for protection a lot of the time."

"Probably. She may be small but she's scrappy. Did you ever have the opportunity to take martial arts classes in school?"

"No, I never did."

She paused and tipped the iron up. Her face took on a far-off expression. "A Korean master came to my middle school to teach for a quarter, and I loved him. He was so kind."

"Like Mr. Miyagi in *The Karate Kid?*"

"Much thinner." Rebecca smiled. "He was a very small, quiet, patient man. His kindness got me through a very difficult time. I learned a lot from him, and when the quarter was over, I found a *dojang* to join to learn more. Kept me sane all through high school."

"Please tell me Steve didn't take classes with you?"

"Hell, no. He's too undisciplined. That's why I'm not afraid of him physically. He knows I could literally kick his ass."

"I guess Britney knows that now, too." I couldn't hold back the laughter. "While you're doing the hard work of ironing, you want me to cut around to Norma's and collect Maya?"

"Yes, please. You can bring Norma, too, if she wants to watch the movie. She said she didn't have anything going on today. I told her I'd take her out for dinner sometime soon if she watched Maya for a couple of hours this afternoon. She's a saint, and she's good at keeping Maya calm."

I went around the walkway and over to Norma's door. The curtain was shut, and I couldn't see any light peeking out. I waited perhaps half a minute for my knock to be answered. Norma opened up and stood grinning in the darkened doorway. Behind her, Maya sat Indian-style on the floor. A ring of smooth, flat rocks about the size of pieces of bread formed a large circle around her, and I thought of Rebecca's comment about using a flat rock to iron. Norma had clearly been sitting inside the circle facing Maya. In between them was a cookie sheet on which sat a variety of different sized burning candles that shed the only light in the room.

"Hi, Sky," Maya said. "Wanna join our medication circle?"

"Meditation?"

Maya shrugged. "Whatever. We're focusing our energy for the good of the Universe."

"Looks interesting, but I can't join in now. Your mom sent

me over to get you. It's movie time. Norma, do you want to see the first Harry Potter movie?"

"Thank you for offering, but I'll stay in tonight," Norma said. "I'm going to put on the headset to listen to Mozart and drown out any firecrackers that go off. I want to start my new year feeling peace and harmony."

"Sounds like a good plan. I think you deserve it. Thanks for looking after the kid."

"It's my pleasure. She has an amazing heart chakra. I'll have to teach her some yoga before too long. She's nimble and strong and would be very good at it."

Maya said, "Monkeys are nimble."

Norma turned to smile at her. "Yes, they are."

I said, "Listen, little monkey, how about you and Norma close out the circle and then meet your mom and me over at your apartment in five minutes? She has a surprise for you."

"Okay."

Norma gave me a knowing nod. As she closed the door, I heard her say, "Whoa-up there, little lady. I have a special candle extinguisher..."

INSIDE THE TALARICO APARTMENT, nothing much had changed since Christmas except the wrapping paper had been removed. The tree was still up, and Maya's over-exuberant decorations still adorned the place. Maya's new bike leaned against the wall near the front door. Rebecca had placed a couple of carpet squares under the wheels, but the tires didn't look like they'd ever been ridden on.

I set a bottle of merlot on the breakfast bar. Rebecca opened it and offered me a glass, which I accepted. We sat on the couch, but before we'd begun any serious conversation, Maya came blasting into the apartment, full of excited joy. Even though Maya sometimes reminded me of being a child, I didn't recall ever being that wild and free. Sometimes I had a hard time remembering I'd ever been a child.

Rebecca's assessment of her child's endurance was right on. She expended an amazing amount of energy upon opening the laptop. I'd never actually thought about what swooning looked like, but that's how I'd explain what the kid did once she saw what Rebecca had for her. She couldn't stop hugging her mother with intermittent pauses to do a strange monkey dance that made me snort with humor. She put the computer on the coffee table and turned it on. I helped her pick out a desktop photo and a screensaver from the dozens I'd downloaded ahead of time. Of course she picked Xena Warrior Princess for both. I handed over the chakram and she swooned again. There was so much joy in the room that Rebecca hugged me, then Maya knocked me back to the couch and gave me a full body attack hug.

We watched *Harry Potter and the Sorcerer's Stone,* which I'd forgotten was over two-and-a-half-hours long. I'd also forgotten how young and innocent the three main characters were. Now they were all grown-ups.

It was half past ten when we switched over to the TV to see the replay of the pre-ball-drop scenes in Times Square. Within minutes, Maya was flagging. One minute she'd been cackling and asking questions, then, like a switch had been pulled, she went silent and sat yawning on the couch between Rebecca and me. She fell asleep in the middle of an all-star musical rendition of Ella Fitzgerald's "What Are You Doing New Year's Eve."

Rebecca opened another bottle of wine and sat telling me funny stories about New Years Past. I wished I had some amusing stories to share, but I realized ever since my mom died, I'd been a sad sack over the holidays. That had to change. That's all there was to it. This year would be the start of a new attitude for me.

I roused Maya thirty seconds before the ball dropped. Heavy-lidded, she watched and mumbled, "This is the best new year ever." She closed her eyes and conked out.

Over the top of the kid's dark head, I met Rebecca's eyes and smiled. "I see what you mean about how handy it is that we can watch the Times Square celebration more than once. Three hours of time difference is a great invention. Maya has no clue that it's not midnight yet."

"Exactly." She reached down and untied Maya's shoes and slipped them off. "I'll put her to bed."

"I can do that." She was half in my lap anyway, so I scooped her up and carried her to the twin bed in the other room. Rebecca pulled the covers back, and I set Maya down and backed away to lean against the doorway. After unzipping her jeans and pulling them off, Rebecca covered Maya up and kissed her forehead. The kid was dead to the world and didn't stir in the slightest.

Though it was only a couple of minutes after eleven, I felt tired, too. We could see in the new year, maybe have a bit more wine, and then I planned to hit the hay. Rebecca came toward me and touched my arm. Next thing I knew, she'd put her other hand behind my neck and pulled my face toward hers. Our lips met, gently at first, then she was cupping my face and kissing me with all her might.

Whoa. Rebecca was kissing me. Kissing me? I broke it off and backed up a step. For a second I couldn't catch my breath.

"What's the matter?" she asked shyly.

"Um, well, I...

"I couldn't help myself. You were under the mistletoe."

I looked up, then I glanced across the room at Maya in confusion. "You've got a kid."

Rebecca's expression went from shy and sweet to tempest-tossed. Even in the low light, I could see how red her face got, and now I saw where Maya's "pissy" face came from. "Oh, that's right. I should have known. You've never wanted anything to do with kids."

"Wait, I—"

"I think you'd better go." She looked like she was going to cry.

"Rebecca, you've misunderstood—"

"I sure have. It must be the wine. Please go."

She pushed past me and opened the front door. A draft of cold air blew in along with the smell of some dank substance—probably marijuana—burning.

I shivered and opened my mouth to speak, but she raised an index finger. "Don't worry," she said, "I'll drop the cookies by before I leave in the morning."

"Leave? Where are you going?"

"Maya will be with her grandparents, and I'm heading to see my brother in Roseburg."

I had forgotten all about that. "I'd like to talk about what—"

"I know, I know. I've made a fool of myself. Please don't rub it in. We'll talk next week. Good night."

I stepped outside just as a string of firecrackers went off out on the street. Rebecca's door closed behind me so quickly I literally felt off-balance. Another round of mini-explosions rocked the night. Some kids hooted with laughter, and I heard the sound of distant footfalls as someone ran away.

Down in the courtyard, Mr. Pony Keg had his door open. A lot of cigarette smokers stood around in his apartment and outside the doorway laughing and talking. A radio played, but it wasn't all that noisy. The whole complex hummed with sound, but wasn't too loud.

I heard quiet laughter from below and someone gunned a car engine in the distance. Otherwise, the noise level was acceptable.

The night air was cold and stinky from the fireworks and ganja. My head hurt. My heart hurt. I went into my apartment and stretched out on the couch in the TV area. My head spun a little.

Rebecca had kissed me. Straight, married, competent mother Rebecca. What the hell. Was she actually a lesbian? Or was she checking out the grass on the other side?

What did that matter now? I'd just blown it all big-time. Me and my moronic mouth. She'd taken my words wrong, though. My response had nothing to do with Maya and everything to do with the sense of confusion I'd felt from the unexpected advance. Could I think of Rebecca as a lover? I realized I'd spent the entire time of our friendship accommodating the fact that she was straight. I'd stifled my emotions and never once allowed myself the luxury of feeling one iota of attraction to her.

Chapter Seventeen

NOT SO BRIGHT AND early the next day, I awoke from a night of troubled sleep. I'd slept for a while on the blue couch, but it was still new enough that it smelled faintly of chemicals. Nonstop firecrackers went off until about one a.m. After that, the periodic isolated mini-explosions kept waking me with a start. You'd think by two a.m. the little bastards would be tired, but no such luck. I moved to the bed, not bothering to change out of my clothes.

At ten a.m. Eddie knocked on the door. I staggered out to the other room in a half-daze and accepted delivery of six computers. I felt like I hadn't slept at all. Eddie didn't seem to notice.

In the new light of day, I hoped Rebecca would feel less upset. She'd drunk a lot of wine the night before. Maybe this morning she'd be able to talk about what had happened.

I took a shower and dressed carefully in clean black jeans, a tee shirt, and hoodie. I opened the door to my apartment. The air outside was damp and still smelled a little like rotten eggs from all the firecrackers. I took a step and nearly stumbled over a cardboard carton. I bent down and unfolded the flaps. Inside was a box that I recognized as the one containing the chocolate chip cookies Rebecca and Maya had given me on Christmas Day. I lifted it and looked underneath. No note, nothing else in the box. Now I remembered what Rebecca had said the night before about their plans. No use knocking on their door. They were gone, the kid to her grandparents' house and Rebecca to see her brother.

I picked up the carton and took it inside to the breakfast bar. The interior box was cold, and the cookies inside were still half-frozen. I wondered if I'd just missed them leaving. I lifted out a cookie and took a bite. When I went to swallow, it stuck in my throat, and I had to force it down. I didn't try to eat the other half.

All right, so Rebecca was gone and whatever rapport we had was broken. I had to accept that, but it left a bitter taste in my mouth—or at least the cookie had left a bitter taste.

My phone rang. For a brief second, I hoped it might be Rebecca, but no, it was Mitchell.

"Happy New Year," I said.

"Why so listless? Why so glum?"

"Oh, shut up."

"Did someone dip a little too much into the wassail bowl?"

"Not at all. Why? Did you?"

"We made our way through quite a number of punch bowls. Alas, you were not on the premises to provide your patented spiced elixir, and we all had to settle for whatever Philippe was able to whip up. Did you have a hot date and get lucky? Don't tell me you saw that Kelton woman again?"

"Oh, no. That was a one-time thing and won't be happening again."

"That's too bad, doll. She was positively hot."

"Yes, and positively partnered."

"No," he said, his voice fake-appalled. "What a slut to step out with you while some other woman pined at home."

"It wasn't quite like that. Her woman is pining from overseas, if she's pining at all. But you know me, Mitchell. I'm not into threesomes. Or twosomes with a third. Or being a third and watching the twosome."

"Yes, sweetheart. You've made all that abundantly clear. So how did you spend the final day of the year? You *must* have gotten laid. Please tell me you did because if not, how could you have possibly missed the social event of the year at my house?"

I wanted to confide in him—in someone anyway—but the repercussions of having blabbermouth Mitchell privy to my New Year's awkwardness was far too risky. I'd probably never hear the end of it.

"I hung out with Rebecca and the kid and hit the hay early. I haven't felt all that great the last couple of days, so I stayed in."

"What a shame. I've got tons of leftover prime rib and mashed potatoes and about two dozen dibs and dabs of side dishes and desserts. Needless to say, every damn fool brought liquor and wine, so we have scads of alcohol lying around waiting to be consumed. The dining room alone has at least a dozen half-full bottles just waiting to be finished off. You want Stoli or Smirnoff or Absolut or Grey Goose? There's enough vodka here to pickle a pig." He let out an excited gasp. "Here's a bottle almost full of Chateau Clinet Pomerol."

"English, please."

"You Philistine. It's a Cabernet Sauvignon. I believe you'd like this one."

I never could recall any particular types of wine. Mitchell poured me glasses of reds and whites at meals and explained details about how my palate should experience them, and none of it sunk in. Basically, all my palate could communicate was, "Yum, good," or "Too much tannin," or "Yuck, this tastes like sour gym socks."

He waxed eloquent, and I could imagine him standing in his dining room, clutching at the bottle and sniffing away at the lip as though it were nectar of the gods.

"This one has the aroma of black cherry, roasted plums, and..." He took a deep breath that I heard clearly over the phone line. "Oh, my, how glorious. It's licorice! Plus the slightest hint of coffee. I'll bet you'd enjoy this."

Before I could venture a response, he sucked in a breath and said, "Oh. My. Gawd!"

"What?"

"Some fool left a 1992 Bryant Family Cab. It hasn't even been opened! Oh, my lord. What a find. This is truly knock-your-socks-off wine, Sky. You need to get in the car and come here directly and we'll start sipping. It'll have everything—intense blackberry, spicy pepper, and a stunning hint of oak. It's absolutely delicious. Philippe and I had some of this on our anniversary. It was so intense that it went right to my head and overpowered the food. All we wanted to do was drink more and—well, I won't go into details, but it was the best aphrodisiac I've ever drunk."

"And you want me to come over and share the bottle with you?"

"Not for the aphrodisiac properties, silly girl."

"Where is Philippe anyway?"

"He's crashed. He cooked at the restaurant until after midnight, then came here and partied until three a.m. The poor boy will be conked out for simply hours."

"I see what you have in mind. A little wine, a few snacks, and then four hours of me cleaning up the signs of New Year's revelry there at your place."

"Possibly. But you'll never have a cabernet like this, I guarantee. You know how much this bottle of wine is worth?"

Hell if I knew. I made an exorbitant guess. "Fifty bucks?"

"Try five or six times that."

"Three hundred bucks for one lousy bottle of wine?"

"Glad to know you can still do math."

"I could buy a whole new stereo system for my car for that. Or a new bike or kayak. Or sixty or seventy cups of Caffè Macchiato."

"But you wouldn't have the experience of being transported by this amazing wine created by this prestigious winery."

"Wonder what dummy brought that over and left it?"

"Probably one of Kevin and Oliver's friends. They brought along a Hollywood producer who's in town. He's working on the next Colin Firth project. Let me tell you, that fellow loved wine. We must have talked about our favorite reds for twenty minutes."

"Right." I'd had enough talk about wine and wanted to get Mitchell off the topic. "So when will you have your casting call?"

"Excuse me?" he said.

"You met this producer. Surely you're going down to Hollywood to try out his casting couch."

Mitchell laughed softly into the receiver. It wasn't often that I was able to tease him so that he missed the point. "The producer met up with Trey. Remember Trey Newton from the Thanksgiving party?"

"The Nordstrom shoe magnate?"

"The very one. Good memory, Miss Smartypants. The producer looked absolutely smitten with Trey, and next thing I knew, they were hightailing it out to the car and never came back."

"No wonder the wine got left behind."

"Exactly. And all to my benefit. He gets the boy, I get the wine."

"What a treat." In my mind's eye, I now saw him hugging the bottle to his chest as though the cabernet was his long-lost lover.

"What about you, sweet'ums. When's your next date? You can't afford to get out of practice. Have you considered going to a speed dating meeting? A lot of gals I know are finding true love there."

I'd heard of speed dating but never done it. The thought of spending five or six minutes trying to convey the depth of my personality to some stranger who was attempting the same feat was alarming. Considering doing it repeated times throughout an evening made me want to barf.

Mitchell said, "Don't give up, Skylar. There's someone out there for you. You just have to get off your fanny and find her. It's a new year and time for important resolutions. Promise me you'll see at least four women this month—one per week—and I'll share any bottle of booze I've got here. And believe me, I've got a lot."

No way was I making that kind of commitment. Instead, I got Mitchell off the phone by promising to come over later in the afternoon to help finish cleanup and eat leftovers. Until then, I wanted to moon around the apartment and think about my life and where it was headed. Or, actually, where it didn't seem to be going at all. I'd had—what?—six dates? Not a one of them was productive—though I might have at least found a good hiking buddy in Denise. But I was no closer to romance than I'd been all those weeks back when Mitchell signed me up for that stupid site. And now a beautiful woman I never expected could harbor romantic feelings blindsided me, and I totally blew it. Was I a waste of air or what?

I went to my computer and signed in with the GirlsGaylore site and was shocked to find 78 messages, some of them written on Christmas Day. What was wrong with people? Even I wasn't on my computer on Christmas.

> Hi, Geekgrrl,
> I'm a bit geeky myself. Absolutely love Battlefield 2142, Diablo, and the StarCraft Series, but my favorite of all time is Assassin's Creed. One time I played for 33 hours straight. Wanna be a pirate with me?
> Blackbeard's Sister

I knew that all of those were video games, and I'd played a few online games before, but the thought of obsessing for 33 hours over a game was not a turn-on.

I read half a dozen suggestive messages (and one outright nasty proposition involving rope, a blindfold, and bodily fluids), then came to this one:

> I really really like your profile and you sound like someone I ought to meet and I can see you any time in the evening when I have release time so if you write back to me we can set up a time and talk about some hiking and biking.
> Happy Z.

Release time? From what? Jail? Junior High? At least that writer was economical. She'd wasted no periods in her one long sentence.

I skipped through another half dozen messages and came upon this one:

> DO NOT READ THIS!!
> You opened this after I told you not to! I see you can't follow directions either, Geekgrrl. That's okay, I just wanted you to notice my message. I'm sure you're getting hundreds of them. Your profile is excellent and did catch my eye, and it wasn't only because your picture was a good one. I see you're interested in a lot of the same things as I am. I like action movies, the outdoors, technology, good coffee, and Mexican food. Would you like to meet up at one of my favorite coffee shops? I'm around after work Thursday or Friday in the late afternoon.
> Call me Franny because it's the name my parents gave me, and here's wishing you have a great day.
> Franny

I clicked over to her profile and looked through the details. Her description sounded normal and the photo of a 30-ish woman showed her to be fit-looking.

I wrote her back to say I'd be willing to meet and asked where, then moved on through the next messages. When I finally got to the bottom, two more messages had come in. 79 was from some freak who wanted to know if she (or was it a he, disguised?) could meet me and talk about the best positions for sacred sex.

But #80 was a response from Franny again:

> DO NOT READ THIS!!
> You're still not following my directions, so I'll just give you the address to a coffee shop called The Stopgap and you can figure it out on your own. <g> Shall we say tomorrow (Friday) at 5PM?
> Franny

I wrote back to confirm and shut down my computer. Somehow time had barreled by, and it was now after three and I was hungry. Mitchell loved chocolate chip cookies so I packed up a dozen and headed for his house.

I MET FRANNY ON Friday over at The Stopgap in the Hawthorne District. I came in the back door and noticed two women. One was a redhead, and since the other one was a brunette, I figured

I'd spotted Franny. Her profile had described her as a thin brunette, and the photos she'd posted of a dark-haired, smiling woman were obviously current. Check One in her favor. I saw no evidence of an oxygen machine nor was she abusing the hired help, so that was Check Two in her favor. She already had a cup of coffee on the table where she sat leafing through a magazine. Before I intro'd myself, I ordered a cappuccino in a to-go cup and studied Franny from the distance while the barista rang me up. Seeing her in person, I estimated she was closer to forty, and she was either a speed-reader or was only looking at the magazine's pictures.

The Stopgap staff was fast and friendly, and the cappuccino was on the counter in a jiffy. After stuffing my change in the tip jar, I took a deep breath and a sip of the hot beverage, burning my tongue. How dumb of me. This shop never served anything merely warm. The food was hot and spicy, and the coffee was a raging inferno. I should have remembered that. I got a spoon and shuffled over to her table. "You must be Franny."

She gazed up at me with a big smile, her teeth white and even. "Why, I must be Franny, so you must be Skylar." She pronounced my name Ska-luh. She had quite the Southern accent and used a lot of teeth action to chew her way through those few words.

"Nice to meet you." I slid into the chair opposite and set my cup of molten lava on the table.

"I declare that the pleasure is all mine."

She wore a lot of makeup that made her eyes look sort of freaky. Like a ring-tailed lemur, but not the cute kind of lemur in that Disney movie, *Madagascar*. More like the Corpse Bride from the Tim Burton movie of the same name. All that makeup only served to give her a devious look, but I decided to look past it.

She kept smiling maniacally, her lemur eyes glowing a strange orangey-brown. "So good to faah-nally have a lil sit-down with you."

"Yes, it is. How long have you lived here in Portland?" I took the lid off my to-go cup and stirred the contents.

"Going on three years."

"Where were you raised?" I asked.

"I was raised up at the Holy Tears of Jesus Christ Baptist Tent Revival back when I was eleven." She grinned. "I 'spect that my born-again status isn't what you're referring to, though. I grew up in Meridian, Alabama. Just a hop, skip, and a jump from Intercourse." She cackled. "Which is not that far from Moundsville." She hee-hawed loudly at that.

"I see."

"What's yo' last name? Mine's Utliss. Rhymes with cutlass."

More like witless, I thought as she let out a honking braying noise that someone needed to tell her was not a style of laughing conducive to romance. She'd probably scare all the donkeys and asses in the barnyard. I didn't want to tell her my last name, so instead, I asked if she'd ever actually wielded a cutlass.

"What? Wield?" She spoke the word wield as though she'd never heard of it. "My daddy had a Cutlass. We drove in it all the time."

I vaguely remembered Cutlasses. "Wasn't that a Plymouth—or wait. Maybe an Oldsmobile?"

She shrugged. "It was close to lime green, kind of a pukey shade of chewed-up broccoli, and the plasticky seats made my legs break out in big ol' hives. I spent a lot of time riding on a gunnysack. That's all I remembuh."

"I take it you're not still driving it then."

"Definitely not, hon. I got me a Subaru Outback out back." She let out a hoot. "Get it? I parked in the back lot. So I got me an Outback out back."

I GOT OUT BACK and away from her as soon as I could. Took me a while, though. Ms. Franny Utliss Who Rhymed With Cutlass was one hell of a speed-gabber. With all the snorting and hooting and heehawing, I could hardly get a word in edgewise. Luckily, Mitchell called me twenty minutes into the date, as arranged, and I managed to make a marginally awkward exit using the excuse of being on call.

I put my still scorching-hot cappuccino in the cup-holder in the car, careful not to spill it on myself. I peeled out of The Stopgap lot and came to a hurried stop at the intersection. Traffic was going to be a bitch, I could see that. I took a deep breath and willed myself to be patient. After all, I'd dodged another bullet.

Where was Candid Camera or some YouTube chronicler when you needed them? The best thing that could happen to Franny was that she'd see a nice, long version of her shtick and the expression of pain and anguish on the other person's face, and then maybe she'd cool her jets.

Then again, maybe not. Perhaps she would need someone to actually confront her. Was there such a thing as a Boring Person Intervention? I'd met quite a few people over the years who were so self-absorbed they never had a clue how much they irritated the rest of the population. Why didn't anyone intervene? Yeah, right. God knows I was too chickenshit to do it. Probably everyone was. All we wanted to do was escape.

So how did she function in the world with her bossy, loud, and bizarre personality? I never found out what she did for a living. Where could she work that allowed her to avoid having someone whack her upside the head with a Shut-Up Stick? The only place that came to mind was that wretched pizza place for kids called Chuck E. Cheese. She'd fit in nicely in that environment. She certainly had the noise level down pat.

For her sake—and the sake of all the other introverts (and many extroverts) out in the world—I hoped she'd find her perfect match soon. But who would it be? Who could put up with all that crazy energy and nonstop blah-blah-honk-snort?

Was there anything about me that was off-putting to others? Perhaps I had something wrong with me that I wasn't aware of. I know I don't bray like a donkey, but I wondered if my laugh was irritating? Did I come off as a know-it-all? Did I seem unkind or self-absorbed or like a crappy listener? I hoped not, but maybe...

As I drove down 20th, tears came to my eyes. I was failing miserably at this whole freakin' dating business. I'd been through an Unlucky Seven, and the time and energy I'd devoted seemed far out of balance with the internal resources I'd wasted. Once upon a time, wasn't it fun to get to know people? What was wrong now? Maybe I needed to join a local women's group and meet people face-to-face. I'd heard from Mitchell that Equity Foundation was looking for volunteers for an upcoming social event. And I'd read that the Portland Lesbian Choir was accepting new members. I wasn't a great singer, but I could contribute adequately in a chorus. Maybe there'd be some nice single woman there who didn't have more hang-ups than I did?

Perhaps all this failure was the Universe's way of telling me that I was better off alone. God knows I hadn't had any luck in love, and managing the drama had always eluded me. Maybe I wasn't just unlucky—I was unsuitable.

Seven dates was enough. Mitchell could take his stupid dating plan and shove it. Unlucky Seven...I was done.

I cut over to Broadway and took the long way around to my apartment. All was quiet at The Miracle Motel. Not a single door was open, and the place looked deserted. I saw no signs of life other than

Pete sitting like a lump in the office, an elbow on the desk and his open palm holding up his head. Not sure if he counted as a sign of life. Rebecca deserved a better boss than that sad pathetic man.

I dragged my ass up the stairs. Over the jingle of my keys I thought I heard hissing. Across the way, Norma had her head poked out her door. She gestured me to come over. I pocketed my key ring and went around the walkway.

"Happy New Year," she said. As I came closer her face took on an expression of concern. "What's the matter, child? You having a bad year already?"

"I guess you could say that."

"Come in and have a cup of tea. Or maybe you'd like something stronger?"

I was fed up with alcohol. I didn't want to drink again for a long while. "Tea would be great, thanks."

Inside her apartment the first thing I saw was my painting on an easel. I touched the edge of the gold frame. "Wow, Norma, it looks like brand new. Thank you."

"You're welcome." She bustled around in her little kitchenette while I settled into a chair. "Hardly took any time at all to repair, and it turned out well. It'll hold up fine so long as you don't drop or bump it too hard."

"Aye, aye, Cap'n." I peered up at the paintings on the wall. A framed black and white portrait, at least three feet high and two feet wide, sat between two wildly colorful landscapes. The drawing was of a handsome woman in a leather jacket, her chin held high and an amused expression on her face. Arms crossed in front of her, she leaned back against a motorcycle seat. I wasn't sure how Norma had done it, but I got the impression of dust and road grit, as though the woman had ridden a long distance.

"Norma, I don't recall seeing this art last time I was here."

She wiped her hands on a towel and came to stand by my chair. "I put them up last night. I did the two oils recently, but the one in the middle I drew many years ago."

"Is it Helaine?'

"Yup. Haven't been able to look at it until now. Too painful." The kettle started to make that preparatory hissing sound before whistling. She went to the mini-stove and grabbed it off the burner.

"You said you were with Helaine for a number of years."

She paused, tea kettle in hand. "I was."

"How did you meet her?"

"Well, that was a funny story. Unexpected, but lucky." She dumped a couple of tea bags into the mugs, poured hot water over them, and set the kettle down. "She'd been a barrel racer in her younger days, and we went to a rodeo reunion in eastern Oregon and ended up sitting next to one another during the festivities."

"You performed in a rodeo?"

"Sometimes. I went to the Pendleton Round-up every September starting when I was a small child and kept on going as often as I could when I grew up. You ever been?"

"No."

She brought me the cup of tea and sank down into the chair opposite me holding her own mug. "My parents and aunts and uncles made saddles and leather chaps and boots for sale. We kids loved to go every year to Pendleton and watch all the action. I did a little barrel racing in the teen division for three years, but when I was sixteen, I got bucked off my horse and broke my leg. It was a couple weeks before the rodeo, and that was it for my parents. They refused to let me ride anymore. They'd always been a little squeamish."

"Were you good at it?"

"Fair to middling. I've still got some blue ribbons tucked away somewhere. I thought I could've kept improving and been a force to reckon with."

"That's too bad. Specially if you loved it."

"I was a wild and crazy hot-blooded lesbian in training. Of course I loved it. But long before I was born, a gal named Bonnie McCarroll competed in the Cowgirl Bronco Riding. Unfortunately she fell or got dragged or something and ended up dying. I don't know how often I cursed that damn woman. Her death marked the end of the Cowgirl Bucking Contest and a bunch of other stuff that sounded like fun. All we got to do was barrel race. Seemed like her tragedy was another way to focus on the men and leave the women out. Anyway, after all these years, the place where I broke my leg aches any time it's rainy and cold, so I'm often reminded of that time, especially lately."

"What about Helaine?"

"I've got pictures of her from the Sixties winning barrel races. Wish I'd known her then. She was seven years older than me, so we never happened upon one another back in the day. Wish we had. I think we'd've been compatible even then."

"Did she ride long into adulthood?"

"Into her twenties, I seem to recall. But then she got into

motorcycles, and that was a lot more fun."

"To race?"

Norma got a mischievous look on her face. "No, to pack up a few things in the saddlebags and take your girl out into the sticks, set up a tent, and make love under the stars."

"Why, Norma, you wild thing."

With a demure expression on her face, she blew on her tea, and took a tentative sip. "Forgot to ask if you wanted sugar."

The citrusy, spicy tea didn't need sweetening. "It's good. Thanks."

"How are you and Rebecca doing?"

I was taken aback by the question. "What do you mean?"

Norma's dark eyes were merry. "Surely you can see she's nuts about you?"

Surely I *hadn't* seen that. I didn't know how to answer, so I asked, "What do you mean?"

She made a tsk-tsk sound. "I think you've been a little too lost in your own head trip, but it's been clear to me that she's interested in you. And that kid of hers—well, let's just say, when she was over here with me doing what she calls The Magic Circle, all she could talk about was you."

I thought I could give new meaning to the word dumbfounded—if only I could speak. I took a sip of tea and composed myself.

"Don't you return the feelings, Sky?"

"Hell if I know. I like them both a lot. I had no clue Rebecca had the slightest interest in me until New Year's night, and I guess I completely screwed it all up."

"How? What happened?"

My face burned, but what was the use of keeping it all inside? I described how dumb I'd been, leaving out none of the details.

Norma listened, occasionally nodding. When I finished my embarrassing, dense-headed tale, she said, "So you haven't had a chance to talk to her about any of this?"

"No. Not sure when I will. Or if I will."

"I think it'll all be okay. Your response must've caught her by surprise. When she has some time to calm down and think, you can bet she'll touch base with you again."

I hoped so and told Norma that. I wasn't holding my breath though.

WHEN I RETURNED TO my apartment, I took the time to hang up the painting, which looked great above the couch—so long as you ignored the ugly tan walls and the orange shag carpet.

Next up, it was time to finalize my desertion of that horrible GirlsGaylore website. I booted up the computer and went to the site. Five messages had arrived today. I considered deleting the entire profile and all the messages, sight unseen, but my curiosity got the best of me and I clicked on the Inbox.

The first was from someone nearly illiterate. Delete. Number two was from a smart-ass. Delete. Then another illiterate one and a smutty come-on. Delete, delete, delete... Last was Franny Utliss's DO NOT READ THIS!! heading.

> You still aren't following directions. I enjoyed talking with you at the cafe. Will you come with me to see the new Captain America movie Saturday night? It's on all over town. Let me know.

Would she bray through the movie? No one could pay me enough money to go out with her. I hit delete which took me to the Inbox, and BLIP. Another message came through, this one titled MISTLETOE IS HIGHLY OVERRATED...

I opened it.

> ...but friendship could be forever. If you're interested in a friendly meet-up with no strings attached, meet me at Old Town Pizza on MLK Blvd Saturday night at 6PM. I'll treat.
> R

Was this a coincidence or was it really Rebecca writing? My heart beat fast, and I hoped like hell it really was Rebecca. I clicked on the profile link which took me to a bare-bones page containing the absolute minimum of data. No pictures, and the details she'd included were sketchy. Guess I had to assume it was her. At least I knew what Rebecca looked like.

Chapter Eighteen

I WAS NERVOUS ALL day Saturday. I worked on computer repairs but had a hard time focusing. I took a nap at one point and awakened feeling more centered.

I made a peanut butter and jam sandwich around two p.m. and stood at the breakfast bar to eat it and drink milk. My cell phone rang, and the ringtone surprised me. I hadn't heard "No One Mourns the Wicked" for a very long time.

"Britney, what do you want?"

"And hello to you, too."

"Why are you calling?"

"I have some things of yours I want to return."

"So you can have me arrested again?"

"Dammit, I suppose you're never going to forgive me for that."

"I'm not sure that you deserve forgiveness."

"Look, I'm trying to make up for it now. I found some correspondence from your mom, and I know you'll want that."

I'd forgotten all about the stash of cards and letters from my mom. Of course I wanted those items. "I'll come over soon and get the stuff."

"Actually, I'm calling you from out front."

"Out front? Here?"

"Yeah, at this totally misnamed Miracle Motel. If you come down and help me, we can bring the stuff up. Or maybe a miracle will happen and it will levitate up the stairs all by itself."

I clicked the phone's OFF button, grabbed my hoodie, and headed down the stairs. I know it was cynical, but I wondered if there was some trick up her sleeve. Had Britney packed up all the garage items and actually brought them to me? That wasn't like her.

But I walked around the office and out toward the street, and sure enough, the truck sat idling with her in the driver's seat.

She turned off the engine and hopped out. "I thought for a moment there you weren't coming."

She pulled a tarp off the pickup bed, and I'll be damned if it wasn't loaded with boxes, the tent, and my bike. "What's gotten into you, Brit?"

Tarp in hand, she turned to face me. "You scared the crap out of me when you let yourself into the garage. When I called the police I thought I was being robbed. Your car wasn't in the driveway, Sky. How was I supposed to know it was you?"

"And then?"

She put her hands in jeans pockets and had the decency to look embarrassed. "Then I fucked up."

"You heard me shouting and you ignored it."

"Yeah. About that. I was angry at you. What I did was wrong, but at that moment in time, I felt like you deserved a little punishment. You left me in the lurch."

"I—I"—a cough sputtered out of me—"I left *you* in the lurch? What the hell? You went off and found yourself a brand new fuck buddy and left me in the dirt."

She closed her eyes, wincing. "It wasn't supposed to be that way. I didn't mean for you to leave. That's not what I wanted." She opened her eyes and gazed at me intently. "Really. Truly. I didn't want to hurt you at all. But we had no passion anymore, no nothing. Neither of us was happy. Come on and admit it. But I did still love you."

The use of past tense didn't escape me. She didn't love me anymore, but at one time perhaps she had.

"The house is in foreclosure," she said. "I managed to salvage the truck. I moved in with Dad, and I have to get the house cleared out, like yesterday. I have to give them all the keys by Monday or they'll send out the sheriff."

"I'm sorry you're going through that."

"Thanks. I can finally admit now that it's all my fault. And Rita's. She was never a cheap date. I've never run through so much money in my life."

That was more information than I wanted to know. Though I did have a bit of sympathy for Britney, I didn't harbor enough good feelings to spend any time showering her with empathy and support. I leaned into the truck bed and lifted my bike out. "Thanks for bringing this. And for anything you brought from my mom."

"Oh, right." She opened the truck door and pulled out a brown grocery bag. "Here's all the letters and a bunch of the more fragile items you'll want."

We made multiple trips back and forth before the truck bed was empty and the computer shelves in my living room were blocked by piles of stuff that I currently had nowhere to put. I wasn't sure what was in most of the boxes she'd brought. I needed to look through everything and determine what could go to Goodwill and temporarily stack up the remainders next to the couch. I was focused on planning for some level of order when Britney spoke up.

"So, did you have a good Christmas?" She stood in the doorway, halfway in, halfway out, letting the warmth of my apartment be sucked right out the open door. I gazed at her face, her kind eyes, and square jaw. She was an attractive woman, still young and desirable. But I had no desire for her at all, not as a friend, and definitely not as a lover. I let out a long breath and felt a strange weariness come over me. All my anger and rage burned out right then and there. It's not that I felt nothing. I just didn't feel enough of anything to want to have any sort of relationship with her at all.

"Did you hear me?" she asked. "Earth to Skylar." She snapped her fingers. "You've got that space cadet look on your face."

"I know. Sorry." I took a step toward her and gripped the edge of the door. "Thank you for bringing all of this. I appreciate it. If I should happen to find any items that are yours, I'll get them back to you, okay?"

"Sure, thanks," she said, discomfort showing in the way she fidgeted. "So is that it?"

"Yes. I think that's it."

She gave me an imploring look. For a moment I wondered if she expected a hug or perhaps wanted to impart some final words of wisdom, but then she stepped back. "I'll see you around, Sky."

WHAT A STRANGE AFTERNOON it turned out to be. I opened boxes and hauled items out to examine and sort them, all the while feeling like something in my head had been extracted—a battery or a power generator—and replaced with condensed fog. A shift had happened, and I was hard-pressed to understand it or explain it to myself.

I couldn't focus on computer work, so I opened the cartons of stuff and surveyed the wreckage. At least a third of the items stacked in the boxes were survival gear or camping equipment. Probably another third was clothing that was either out of style or would no longer fit. Why had I kept these dated pants and shirts and sweaters? Instant donation for almost all of it. I filled two garbage bags and set them by the front door.

The rest of the stuff consisted of mementos from another time: a photo album of my babyhood, lovingly assembled by my mom; a wood jewelry box full of earrings and tangled necklaces; my high school yearbook; cards and letters I wrote my mom during the brief time I was in college; a stack of older CDs; a photo album from my parents' early relationship up until I was about four years old.

I opened the album and thumbed through the pages. I'd rarely looked at the collection of pictures after my mom died. I couldn't remember taking the album out in recent years. Some of the shots were quite good. In particular there was a 5x7 of Mom and me where we both looked happy and healthy. I was about fourteen, and my hair had been cut short for the first time ever. I remembered how free and light my head had felt.

I closed the album, a lump in my throat. If Norma could finally hang up a portrait of Helaine, I could do the same. I resolved to choose a dozen or so of the pictures and make a collage. At long last, it was time to get my mother out of storage and enjoy looking at her cheerful face.

Two other boxes contained mementos from my days with Britney: letters, a Portland Timbers baseball-style cap, an envelope of photos, Christmas decorations, some useless knickknacks, and a velvet ring box. Inside, my grandmother's wedding ring was tucked into the decorative seam. I'd forgotten that I'd given the ring to Britney. When had she stopped wearing it? I was stunned that she'd returned it. I mean, that's what you're supposed to do when a relationship is over, but Grandma's ring was a sweet little diamond set in 14-karat gold and probably worth a couple thousand dollars. I'd have to rethink my opinion of Britney if she had the class to give it back to me instead of pawning it to pay her bills.

I combined the mementos into one box and took a few minutes to break down the empty cartons for recycling. I stacked up the full boxes and realized I was procrastinating. The sun had gone down, and it was after five. I had less than an hour to get to Old Town Pizza.

I took a quick shower and dried off, then stood shivering while trying to decide what to wear. The restaurant was very casual, so I put on a pair of nice black jeans and a long-sleeved white shirt under a V-necked green sweater. I slipped into some light hikers that gave me another inch in height. For some crazy reason, I felt that I needed to be taller, maybe more powerful. At the moment I wasn't feeling all that sturdy or confident.

I picked up my gray hoodie and opened the front door. The wind whistled in. January cold had finally hit Portland with a vengeance. I smacked the door shut and tossed the hoodie on the couch. It took me a while, but I tracked down a ski jacket and a pair of leather driving gloves that would keep me toasty warm.

All the way to the pizza joint I pondered what to say to Rebecca and came up with absolutely nothing smart or amusing or in any way clever. Who was I kidding? I wasn't smooth or witty. All I could do was be sincere and honest. At least I had those two qualities to work with. Then I reminded myself that at least I didn't bray or honk or snort—nor would I abuse the wait-staff, so maybe I wasn't so bad off after all.

From Old Town's back lot, I stepped inside the rear door and looked around the cozy dimness of the restaurant. I was fifteen minutes early, so I figured Rebecca wouldn't have arrived yet. The server who greeted me was a young woman with several facial piercings and hair dyed bright pink. "Welcome. Are you meeting someone tonight?"

"Yes. It's probably under Talarico, party of two?"

"Aha." She pointed toward the stairwell that led up to another level. "She's in the booth under the stairs."

Rebecca sat on the side where the stairs were lowest. The other side had a colorful stained glass window up above. Old Town Pizza had a lot of funny, rustic, and odd things on display. Outside the booth was an old-fashioned crank telephone.

I moved toward the table. "Impressive," I said when Rebecca caught sight of me. "You snagged the cool booth. I don't believe I've ever managed that."

Rebecca grinned. "That's what you get when you arrive extra early."

I slid in across from her. Miss Pink Hair threw a couple of drink coasters on the table and took our order, Coke for me, lemon tea for Rebecca.

When the waitress left, I met Rebecca's gaze. She didn't seem nervous at all, but suddenly my stomach was doing flips and calisthenics and the tango. "How are you?" I managed to squeak out.

"Feeling nicely rested."

"Where's the midget?"

"She's still with her father and grandparents. I'll pick her up on the way home."

"I'll bet she's missed you."

"You know it. I've talked to her on the phone morning, noon, and nighttime, and she's now at the point where she can't wait to come home."

"How did it go at your brother's house?"

"Very enjoyable. I had time to think. I thought a lot about you." Her dark eyes sparkled in the low light, and I was aware as never before that Rebecca Talarico was a beautiful woman. "I thought a lot about our friendship."

I nodded, with what I hoped was encouragement because I was too nervous to speak.

"I'm sorry about New Year's Eve. I was rash. I should have spoken to you about my feelings instead of laying a big lip-lock on you."

I swallowed and choked out, "You surprised me."

"I got that."

"Sometimes, um," I paused, "sometimes I'm not very fast at processing things. I'm sorry for what I said, but you didn't give me time to explain what I meant."

"Sky, no need to apologize. I'm the one at fault here, not you."

"Wait a minute. Please. I want you to understand what I was trying to say. It's important to me that you hear this."

She nodded and gave me her full attention. That was something I very much liked about her. Ever since we'd had that first cup of tea, she'd been a very good listener.

"You have a kid. You're getting out of a marriage. You seemed like you were living the straight life. I've never let myself think of you as anything but a soon-to-be-divorced heterosexual mom. So you surprised the hell out of me. I needed time to reset, to get with the new program."

"I know that now. I'd sort of been flirting with you, not so much in words, I guess, but by sitting near you and touching you and—well, obviously I wasn't direct enough."

"Or I was just too dense to notice. I must admit I haven't been my best self lately."

"You've been through a lot."

"And so have you."

"Yes, we have. The end of the year was rough. I'm glad it's a new year. We can still be friends, right? I haven't ruined anything?"

She had this heartbreaking look on her face, like if I said anything discouraging right now she might cry. I held my hand out across the table palm up. She glanced at it, confused, as if she couldn't decide whether I was wanting to shake or hold her hand.

"Rebecca, we will always be friends." I threaded my fingers through hers.

"So you don't think I'll be stuck as an untouchable gay divorcée with a kid who no one will want to date?"

"If you filled out your profile more completely at the GirlsGaylore site, I suspect many women would be in hot pursuit of you." Some of them would honk and bray with delight.

Her face turned red. "After all you've said about the online dating game, I'm not sure I'd be up for that."

"Trust me. It's hellish."

She squeezed my hand, then pulled hers away as the waitress swung by and dropped off our drinks.

Rebecca continued to blush. "I have a confession to make. By the time you got to Denise the Hiker, I was rooting against your success. I probably jinxed your dating plans. I—I'm sorry, Sky. I should have been more supportive."

I started to laugh, and I couldn't stop. She stared at me for a few seconds, then she laughed as well. I managed to choke out, "Tamra, the Dominatrix, should have been my first clue that dating wasn't in the cards for me."

"She certainly was a handful. Then you saw that woman at the Dragon the Lion pub."

"Barbara, the grieving diet center worker. She'd be no competition for you. Then it was Linda, the emaciated exercise addict. She was nice, but still, no comparison to you."

Rebecca said, "Then you went to Elmer's."

"Oh, yeah. Mary, Mary, Quite Contrary."

"At least I don't have cankles."

"No, you have great legs."

Rebecca blushed, and so did I. How did that fall out of my mouth? Some filter that I usually paid attention to had completely disappeared.

She said, "Then you had that one-night stand."

I froze. How did she know about that? I hadn't mentioned one word. I must have looked like the proverbial deer in the headlights because Rebecca hastened to say, "I saw you come back at about four a.m. You were drunk, I think. I could see that when you let yourself in the apartment."

"You could just tell?"

She got a funny look on her face and shrugged. "I think the best word to describe your condition was disheveled."

"Oh, disheveled. Hmm, good word. What were you doing up so late?"

"Couldn't sleep. I was drinking some tea and looking out the front window."

"Guess I'm busted then."

"I was surprised you didn't notice me."

"Yeah, I was kind of out of it. I met the woman through work. The crazy candy company owner turned out to be a lot like Britney."

"She looked like her?"

"No, she wasn't the monogamous type."

"Ah, I see. So you had five dates? Or Six?"

"Seven. You already mentioned Denise the Hiker. She was number six, and she's going to be a good pal. You'll like her. And then I went on one more date just yesterday."

"Oh?" The worried expectation on her face was priceless. I launched into the story of Franny Utliss Rhymes With Cutlass, and pretty soon she was laughing so hard, I thought she'd fall out of the booth. I finished my tale by saying, "I'm calling them the Unlucky Seven."

"But didn't Mitchell challenge you to eight dates in eight weeks?"

"Aye, lassie, that he did, but before I left the apartment tonight, I deleted my profile at GirlsGaylore, and I don't care if I never do an online date ever again. Besides, I do believe I'm going to count tonight as the last date ever. So I *have* met Mitchell's challenge."

I slid out of the booth and sat beside Rebecca, angling my body so I faced her. I think she was holding her breath, but she met my gaze. "Could I have a re-do on that New Year's kiss, even without the mistletoe?" I was amazed that the request came out sounding confident because I was shaking inside.

She put her hand on my shoulder and leaned in, tilting her head, and I pressed my lips to hers. Closing my eyes, I savored the softness, the rightness. She tasted like sweet lemons. I cupped her face in my hands, and she deepened the kiss.

Behind us someone cleared their throat. I heard it, but I wasn't in any hurry to break off this marvelous experience.

"Sorry, gals."

I recognized Ms. Pink Hair's voice and reluctantly pulled away from Rebecca. I swiveled on the booth bench. "I bet you need to get our order."

"As long as it's for food and not a room." She winked and I could see she was amused and not being judgmental.

Rebecca leaned over my shoulder and said softly in my ear, "How about we get your favorite pizza?"

"Sure," I said, surprised that she knew I had a favorite. Then I remembered we had gone out with Maya and Norma a few weeks back. She must have taken note.

Rebecca said, "Give us a small pizza with Rosemary chicken and tomatoes, and we'll split a Caprese salad."

"You want the salad now?" the server asked.

"Sure," Rebecca said.

"Got it."

She whirled off and left me peeking at Rebecca out of the corner of my eye. "So," I said, "shall I return to my side of the booth or stay next to you?"

She took my hand and cozied up to me. "I like you right here."

"This is going to sound strange, but I have to ask. Where'd you learn to kiss like that?"

Rebecca tipped her head, embarrassed, but in a sweet way. "Definitely not from Steve. Time to confess some more details. I had two relationships with women in college. I was on the rebound from a bad breakup when I met Steve. I don't know what I was thinking."

"Say no more. Unless you want to, that is."

She sighed. "I don't regret Maya. I never will. But I've wasted a lot of time because of this stupid marriage. I never loved him. He doesn't know how to love me—or anyone, I guess. I've been ready to move on for a long time, and when I met you…"

I didn't say anything for a moment. "What does moving on look like to you?"

"I want to be done with this never-ending bunch of bullshit about the custody so the divorce will be finalized. It's a foregone conclusion that he can't take Maya. Even his mother admitted that to me. She's doing all the work, not Steve, when Maya comes to visit."

"Why does she let him get away with that?"

"They all do. He's spoiled rotten. He's lucky he can find matching socks most days unless his mother has done the laundry. He's in no shape to raise a child. Besides, he doesn't have the time or energy for her. He just wants to get back at me."

"He wasn't an only child, was he?"

"No. He's the youngest of six. Everybody pampered and babied him, and they still do."

"Aren't you a youngest child, too?"

"I had three older brothers, but as the only girl, I got some responsibilities dumped on me. Housekeeping, hostess, cooking. All those gender-related roles. Meanwhile, Steve's older brothers and sisters let him be the clown and constantly rewarded him for screwing up. He had zero life skills by the time he hit college. He didn't know how to load the dishwasher when we got married. By the time I was eight months pregnant, I could hardly bend, much less load and unload the dishes, so I forced him to learn. Pretty ridiculous, huh?"

"Look at the bright side. If you get pregnant now, there's no dishwasher to worry about."

"Very funny." She said it with a smile on her face, so I knew I hadn't offended her. "When you came to The Miracle Motel last fall, you were moving on, too. It seems like we both have a whole new world opening up. Do you feel ready for that?"

"I guess I do. I know I'm letting go of the past so I can move on. I had a surprise visit from Britney earlier today, and the—as you called it—never-ending bunch of bullshit from an ex seems to have drawn to a close."

"You sound okay about that."

"I am." I told her about the whole experience and ended by saying, "There's this little feeling of emptiness I'm still aware of, but the acute pain I felt before is gone."

"Kind of like scar tissue?"

"Huh. Maybe that's it." Something to ponder later. For now I wanted to focus on Rebecca and what we had to offer one another. "What else do you see happening as you move on?"

"To be honest, it doesn't include living at The Miracle Motel anywhere near as long as Norma has. I literally want to move on, as in move out to somewhere larger than two postage stamp-sized rooms."

That made me laugh. "How could you leave behind that lovely shag carpet?"

"Well, there is that. At least mine doesn't look like a pumpkin threw up on it."

"Touché. Regardless of the carpeting, you need more room. Some people do well in small spaces. Obviously Norma has. Maybe you could, but not Maya."

"No, my kid deserves more, and a better environment would be nice."

"Winos and transients coming and going at The Miracle Motel aren't a good influence. Besides, your kid deserves a giant backyard and a safe place to ride her bike and a tree house she can dangle Minco the Wonder Warrior from."

"Exactly. I'll get us there. I just hope it happens before she becomes a teenager."

"She's going to be a handful as a teenager. You know that, right?"

"She's a handful at eight."

"She sure is. Can I go with you to pick her up after we eat?"

"Really?" Rebecca said. "You want to?" She took my hand and squeezed it.

"I do."

IS THERE ANYTHING MORE touching than having a child be so happy to see you that she squeals with delight?

We stepped into the Talarico's foyer, and I did feel sort of bad that Maya ran to me before her mother. She grabbed me around the waist and tried to lift me off the ground. "Hey," I said, "no judo moves."

"Sky, Sky, you're here." She leaned back and stared up at me. One of her hands found my front pants pocket and gripped it. "I've missed you. It's been days and days. We still have your Christmas presents."

I thought of the "creations" Maya had made, now with considerably more fondness. I was going to have to display them after all. Somehow, it didn't seem to matter as long as Maya came over to visit them periodically. With her mother.

I realized that Rebecca was watching my interaction with her kid with great interest. Our eyes met, and with a grin, she squatted down. Maya let go of my pocket to throw herself into her mother's arms.

In the living room doorway a middle-aged woman stood taking everything in. She met my eyes.

"Hi," I said. "I'm Skylar Cassidy, Maya and Rebecca's neighbor."

She came forward, holding out a hand that proved to be quite strong when we shook. "We know all about you, Sky." That took me aback. She let go of my hand and continued, "Maya has many complimentary things to say about you."

"That's good to know." She didn't tell me her name, which I thought odd. She was perhaps in her late fifties and looked sporty in jeans, tennis shoes, and a pale pink sweatshirt with a bunch of kitty cats on it. I saw a resemblance to Steve, though where he presented himself with an anxious energy, she was the opposite. Fatigue was etched in her face.

Rebecca said, "Thank you for having her here, Evelyn."

"It was our pleasure. Maya was the perfect guest."

"I was, Mom. I set the table before every meal, and Grandma only had to remind me once. I also learned how to run the dishwasher here. It's a little different from our old one."

She was way ahead of her father, I thought.

After a few more pleasantries, Rebecca managed to get Maya's stuff corralled, and we said our goodbyes. All three of us were loaded down when we got to the car. Juggling a full paper sack and a suitcase, Rebecca managed to pop open the trunk. I placed a couple of bags of toys in there, and Maya added her backpack and two stuffed animals. She hustled into the backseat and got situated in her booster chair.

Rebecca closed the trunk. "Thanks for being so kind to Maya."

"That's not hard. She's great. She's a very lovable child."

As Rebecca headed to the driver's seat I realized that I could love Maya. In fact, I was already attached and cared about her more each day. And I could love Rebecca, too. I was well on the way to saying something about it, as if love were on the tip of my tongue.

I got in the passenger's seat and listened to Maya babble about how much fun she'd had at Grandma and Grandpa's house and that she'd hosted a sleepover for the three kids next door ages six, eight, and nine. Four grade-schoolers? Sounded like a recipe for disaster to me. If Evelyn Talarico had raised six kids, it was probably no big deal to her. Then again, no wonder she looked so tired.

In the dim light of the car, I watched Rebecca out of the corner of my eye as she drove us back to Old Town Pizza to get my car. Competent. Loving. Kind. Committed. Sexy. She was all of those things and more—and mine for the asking. I put my hand on her shoulder at the same time that Maya said, "Sky, we should have a sleepover tonight! You could come over to our house and we would watch TV and eat popcorn and stay up late and then crash in sleeping bags and get up tomorrow and have breakfast together."

"What a great idea," Rebecca said as she gave me an evil leer.

"Can we do it, Mom? Can we?"

Rebecca pulled up behind my car, and we both got out. "How about it?" she asked.

"How about what?"

"You can't turn down my child and break her heart."

I moved closer to Rebecca and tipped her chin up so I could see her expression in the streetlight. I can only describe it as devilish. She had a smirk on her face a mile wide.

"Let me get clarification here. You're asking me to spend the night? Or to come over and watch TV?"

"Yes. I'm asking you to come over and stay as long as you want to. Maybe spend the night if you feel like it. I want to be clear that after Maya goes to sleep there may be the opportunity for some dishevelment, though we'll have to be quiet."

I laughed.

She put the flat of her hand on my chest. "If you're stopping at eight dates, then don't you think you ought to make this one extra special?"

"Uh-huh." I bent to kiss her. This date should definitely be extra special. And extra long—like years. Decades. Long enough to build a life with Rebecca, a house, a home, a partnership that lasted. Long enough to see Maya graduate from college and find meaningful work and someone to love, maybe even pop out some grandkids. Long enough for Rebecca and me to watch our hair go gray and our faces develop laugh wrinkles. Could it be possible?

All of it was possible. Hope soared in my heart and I kissed her again.

The End

About The Author

Lori L. Lake lives in Portland, Oregon, and is the author of eleven published novels (so far), two books of short stories, and editor of two anthologies. Lori has received numerous awards for her writing, and in 2007 she was blessed with the Ann Bannon Award for the novel "Snow Moon Rising." The bestowing of the award by Ann Bannon herself was one of the greatest thrills of her professional life. When she's not writing, Lori's at the local cinema with her sweetheart, teaching writing craft, admiring her nieces' sport and thespian events, or curled up in a chair reading. She's currently at work on the third book in The Public Eye Series and a writing book called *Sparking Creativity*. She loves to hear from readers and can be contacted at: Lori@LoriLLake.com or through her website: www.LoriLLake.com.

Other Romances by Lori L. Lake

Like Lovers Do

Kennie McClain moved from upstate New York to Portland to escape bad memories. In her off hours, she rehabs apartments and nurses a broken heart.

Lily Gordon, a nationally-acclaimed painter, lives in the penthouse where Kennie works. She's beautiful and accomplished – and haunted after her lover ditches her.

Sparks fly when Kennie and Lily finally connect . . . but then in one shattering moment, Lily betrays her, and Kennie's world comes crashing down, leaving her untrusting and in deep emotional pain. Can Kennie ever rise above these losses and risk her heart again?

Different Dress

Three women set off on a cross-country music tour. Jaime Esperanza is the assistant production manager in charge of both stage and stars. The headliner, Lacey Leigh Jaxon, is a fast-living, heavy drinking prima donna with intimacy problems. She's had a brief relationship with Jaime, then dumped her for a series of new band mates. Lacey still comes back to Jaime in between conquests, and Jaime hasn't gotten her entirely out of her heart.

Lacey Leigh steamrolls yet another opening act and, in desperation, the tour manager brings on board a folksinger from Minnesota named Kip Galvin, who wrote one of Lacey's biggest songs. Kip has true talent, she loves people and they respond to her, and she has a pleasant stage presence. A friendship springs up between Jaime and Kip—but what about Lacey Leigh?

It's a honky-tonk, bluesy, pop, country EXPLOSION of emotion as these three women duke it out. Who will win Jaime's heart and soul?

Ricochet in Time

Dani Corbett has only been with her new girlfriend a short while, but after a vicious hate crime, Meg is dead and Dani is left physically injured and emotionally scarred. Since her injury prevents Dani from fleeing on her motorcycle, which is her normal response to a crisis, she must find a way to deal with her grief and rage. But as one door has closed for Dani, another opens when Grace Beaumont, who works as a physical therapist at the hospital where Dani is treated, befriends her and helps her to heal. With Grace's friendship and the help of Grace's aunts, Estelline and Ruth, Dani must get through the ordeal of bringing Meg's killer to justice.

Ricochet In Time is the story of one lonely woman's fight for justice – and her struggle to resolve the troubles of her past and find a place in a world where she belongs.

Other Novels by Lori L. Lake

The Gun Series – Romance/Adventure/Mystery

Gun Shy – Book One

While on patrol, Minnesota police officer Dez Reilly saves two women from a brutal attack. One of them, Jaylynn Savage, is immediately attracted to the taciturn cop—so much so that she joins the St. Paul Police Academy. As fate would have it, Dez is eventually assigned as Jaylynn's Field Training Officer. Having been burned in the past by getting romantically involved with another cop, Dez has a steadfast rule she has abided by for nine years: Cops are off limits. But as Jaylynn and Dez get to know one another, a strong friendship forms. Will Dez break her cardinal rule and take a chance on love with Jaylynn, or will she remain forever gun shy?

Under The Gun – Book Two

Under the Gun is the sequel to the bestselling novel, *Gun Shy*, continuing the story of St. Paul Police Officers Dez Reilly and Jaylynn Savage. Picking up just a couple weeks after *Gun Shy* ended, the sequel finds the two officers adjusting to their relationship, but things start to go downhill when they get dispatched to a double homicide—Jaylynn's first murder scene. Dez is supportive and protective toward Jay, and things seem to be going all right until Dez's nemesis reports their personal relationship, and their commanding officer restricts them from riding together on patrol. This sets off a chain of events that result in Jaylynn getting wounded, Dez being suspended, and both of them having to face the possibility of life without the other. They face struggles—separately and together—that they must work through while truly feeling "under the gun."

Have Gun We'll Travel – Book Three

Dez Reilly and Jaylynn Savage have settled into a comfortable working and living arrangement. Their house is in good shape, their relationship is wonderful, and their jobs—while busy—are fulfilling. But everyone needs a break once in a while, so when they take off on a camping trip to northern Minnesota with good friends Crystal and Shayna, they expect nothing more than long hikes, romantic wood fires, and plenty of down time. Instead, they find themselves caught in the whirlwind created when two escaped convicts, law enforcement, and desperate Russian mobsters clash north of the privately-run, medium-security Kendall Correctional Center. Set in the woodland area in Minnesota near Superior National Forest, this adventure/suspense novel features Jaylynn taken hostage by the escapees and needing to do all she can to protect herself while Dez figures out how to catch up with and disarm the convicts, short-circuit the Russians, and use the law enforcement resources in such a way that nothing happens to Jaylynn. It's a race to the finish as author Lori L. Lake uproots Dez and Jaylynn from the romance genre to bring them center stage in her first suspense thriller.

Jump The Gun – Book Four

Dez Reilly is a patrol sergeant with the Saint Paul Police who is trying to decide which direction to go with her career: To SWAT? Or to Investigations? Or does she continue with the patrol supervision she is heartily tired of?

Jaylynn Savage cheerfully patrols the city's skyways and is happy with her work and with Dez, who is the love of her life. But when a colleague is murdered on duty, Dez and Jaylynn are both stunned. Before they can even process the loss, a witness is killed, Dez is targeted by a dangerous man, and nobody she loves is safe. Can Dez protect those she loves and also stop a nameless, face-less murderer?

Lori L. Lake's fourth novel in The Gun Series is full of twists and surprises. Don't miss this one if you enjoy a suspenseful and entertaining mystery/thriller.

The Public Eye Mystery Series

Buyer's Remorse – Book One

Leona "Leo" Reese is a 33-year-old police patrol sergeant with over ten years of law enforcement experience. After she fails her biyearly shooting qualification due to a vision problem, Leo is temporarily assigned to the investigations division of the state's Department of Human Services. She's shell-shocked by her vision impairment and frustrated to be reassigned to another department, even temporarily. On her first day on the new job, she's saddled with a case where a woman at an independent living facility for elders has been murdered by an apparent burglar. But all is not as it seems, and it will take all her smarts to outwit a dangerous criminal. Will she uncover the murderer before other people are robbed and killed?

A Very Public Eye – Book Two

Greed? Hatred? Retaliation? Or a Cover-up?

Winter has not yet set in, but young Eddie Bolton will never see another snowfall in his hometown of Duluth, Minnesota. Someone has diabolically killed him in what should have been a secure juvenile detox ward at the Benton Dowling Center. Leona Reese, a state investigator of fraud and licensing infractions, has been out of commission for three weeks due to surgery. On her first day back on the job, she is faced with the aftermath of the 17-yearold's death and is shocked by the brutality. Working with the local police, Leona discovers far too many people with motives for the killing, but precious little evidence. As she uncovers long-buried secrets, someone else is murdered, and now Leona realizes that she, too, is in danger. In the midst of her own emotional turmoil, is Leona strong enough and smart enough to confront and catch a clever and ruthless murderer?

Historical Novels

Snow Moon Rising

Mischka Gallo, a proud Roma woman, knows horses, dancing, and travel. Every day since her birth, she and her extended family have been on the road in their vardo wagons meandering mostly through Poland and Germany. She learned early to ignore the taunts and insults of all those who call her people "Gypsies" and do not understand their close-knit society and way of life. Pauline "Pippi" Stanek has lived a settled life in a small German town along the eastern border of Poland and Germany. In her mid-teens, she meets Mischka and her family through her brother, Emil Stanek, a World War I soldier who went AWOL and was adopted by Mischka's troupe. Mischka and Pippi become fast friends, and they keep in touch over the years. But then, the Second World War heats up, and all of Europe is in turmoil. Men are conscripted into the Axis or the Allied armies, "undesirables" are turned over to slave labor camps, and with every day that passes, the danger for Mischka, Emil, and their families increases. The Nazi forces will not stop until they've rounded up and destroyed every Gypsy, Jew, dissident, and homosexual.

On the run and separated from her family, Mischka can hardly comprehend the obstacles that face her. When she is captured, she must use all her wits just to stay alive. Can Mischka survive through the hell of the war in Europe and find her family?

Collections

Shimmer & Other Stories

In these tales of hope and loss, lovers and found family, Lori L. Lake has once more given us an amazing slice of life. A frightened woman stumbles through her daily existence, unsure of her place in the world, until she comes into possession of a magic coat... Tee has a problem with her temper, and now that she's being tested again, will she fail to curb it again? Kaye Brock has recently been released from prison and doesn't have a single friend—until Mrs. Gildecott comes along...

These women and many others, unsettled and adrift and often disillusioned, can't quite understand how they arrived at their present situations. But whether rejected, afraid to commit, or just misunderstood, even the most hard-bitten are not without some hope in the power of love.

Lori L. Lake's talent shines like never before in this collection of glittering tales. Sharply rendered, the tone of these stories reflects their title: silver and gray, shimmery and wintry, yet also filled with the shiny hope of summer. These are stories that bear rereading.

The Milk of Human Kindness:
Lesbian Authors Write about Mothers & Daughters

This remarkable anthology contains stories, essays, and memoirs by some of the brightest stars in the lesbian writing world: Katherine V. Forrest, Lee Lynch, Radclyffe, Karin Kallmaker, Cameron Abbott, Ellen Hart, Lori L. Lake, Caro Clarke, J.M. Redmann, Jennifer Fulton, Gabrielle Goldsby, Lois Hart, Carrie Carr, SX Meagher, Jean Stewart, Cate Swannell, Therese Szymanski, Kelly Zarembski, Georgia Beers, Talaran, Julia Watts, and Meghan Brunner.

Stepping Out: Short Stories

In these fourteen short stories, Lori L. Lake captures how change and loss influence the course of lives: a mother and daughter have an age-old fight; a frightened woman attempts to deal with an abusive lover; a father tries to understand his lesbian daughter's retreat from him; an athlete who misses her chance—or does she?

Lovingly crafted, the collection has been described as a series of mini-novels where themes of alienation and loss, particularly for characters who are gay or lesbian, are woven throughout. Lake is right on about the anguish and confusion of characters caught in the middle of circumstances, usually of someone else's making. Still, each character steps out with hope and determination.

In the words of Jean Stewart: "Beyond the mechanics of good storytelling, a sturdy vulnerability surfaces in every one of these short stories. Lori Lake must possess, simply as part of her inherent nature, a loving heart. It gleams out from these stories, even the sad ones, like a lamp in a lighthouse—maybe far away sometimes, maybe just a passing, slanting flash in the dark—but there to be seen all the same. It makes for a bittersweet journey."

Romance For Life

A collection of 25 love stories from your favorite lesbian authors including: Robin Alexander, Lynn Ames, Bridget Bufford, Carrie Carr, Caro Clarke, Stella Duffy, Nann Dunne, Jane Fletcher, Vada Foster, Verda Foster, Jennifer Fulton, Gabrielle Goldsby, Melissa Good, Lois C. Hart, Ellen Hawley, Karin Kallmaker, Lori L. Lake, Lee Lynch, Marianne K. Martin, Val McDermid, Radclyffe, Elizabeth Sims, Jean Stewart, Ida Swearingen, and Jane Vollbrecht, with Foreword by Kathy L. Smith.